About the author

Sharon Booth writes uplifting women's fiction — love, laughter, and happy ever after. Happy endings are guaranteed for her main characters, though she likes to make them work for it.

Sharon is a member of the Society of Authors and the Romantic Novelists' Association, and an Authorpreneur member of the Alliance of Independent Authors.

She loves Doctor Who, adores Cary Grant movies, and admits to being shamefully prone to crushes on fictional heroes.

Sharon grew up in the East Riding of Yorkshire, and the Yorkshire coast and countryside feature strongly in her novels. Her stories are set in pretty villages and quirky market towns, by the sea or in the countryside, and feature lots of humour, romance, and friendship.

If you love stories with gorgeous, *kind* heroes, and heroines who have far more important things on their minds than buying shoes, you will love her books.

I0587883

Books by Sharon Booth

There Must Be an Angel
A Kiss from a Rose
Once Upon a Long Ago
The Whole of the Moon

Summer Secrets at Wildflower Farm
Summer Wedding at Wildflower Farm

Resisting Mr Rochester
Saving Mr Scrooge

Baxter's Christmas Wish
The Other Side of Christmas
Christmas with Cary

New Doctor at Chestnut House
Christmas at the Country Practice
Fresh Starts at Folly Farm
A Merry Bramblewick Christmas
Summer at the Country Practice
Christmas at Cuckoo Nest Cottage

Belle, Book and Christmas Candle
My Favourite Witch
To Catch a Witch

Summer Wedding
at
Wildflower Farm

Sharon Booth

Green Ginger
Publishing

Published in 2021 by:
Green Ginger Publishing
Yorkshire, England

Copyright © 2018 Sharon Booth.

Cover design by Berni Stevens. www.bernistevenscoverdesign.com

The moral rights of the author have been asserted.
All rights reserved. No part of this publication may be reproduced, stored in
any retrieval system, or transmitted in any form, or by any means electronic,
mechanical, photocopying, recording or otherwise, without the prior written
permission of the publishers.

This book is a work of fiction. Names, characters, businesses, organisations,
places and events other than those clearly in the public domain, are either
the product of the author's imagination or are used fictitiously. Any
resemblances to actual persons, living or dead, is entirely coincidental.

ISBN: 978-1-8384242-1-3

"No matter what anyone does or says
I must be emerald and keep my colour"
~ *Marcus Aurelius*

Chapter 1

'Libby, can you just pass George another spoon please, love, and put that one in the sink? There's a good lass.'

Eliot surveyed his four-year-old son and wondered how any child could make so much mess eating a simple bowl of porridge. Most of it seemed to be on the table or smeared around George's mouth. He nodded his thanks as his eldest daughter handed her brother a clean spoon, then gave an impatient sigh as the phone continued to ring against his ear.

Where is she? Why isn't she answering?

'What time's Auntie Beth coming?' Ophelia, his youngest daughter, licked a splodge of jam from the back of her hand then reached for another slice of toast. 'You ought to get a shifty on, you know. If you're late, Mum'll throttle you.'

Was she really only ten? Eliot often thought she had the mind of a forty-year-old. Mind you, she wasn't wrong about him needing to hurry up. He glanced at his watch. He'd better start getting ready.

'Should be any time now,' he informed Ophelia, then brightened as the phone was finally answered. His heart leapt, and he found he was smiling. 'Hello? Thank God. I thought you were never going to pick up. I — oh, hell! Hang on a minute.'

He rushed over to the table and just managed to prevent George from catapulting a spoonful of porridge into an unsuspecting Libby's face. 'Right, me lad, I think that's quite enough from you. You can do without breakfast now, and if

7

you're still hungry it serves you right.'

George folded his arms and pouted. 'I want some toast.'

'*I want never gets.*' Eliot blinked, wondering when he'd turned into his mother. It had been one of her most-used sayings.

'Do you want me to clean him up, Dad?' Libby offered.

'If you don't mind, love. I won't be a minute. Just going to have a word with your mum.'

Clutching the phone in his hand, he rushed out of the kitchen and into the boot room, where he closed the door behind him and leaned against it with an exhausted sigh, deliberately ignoring the piles of washing on top of the dryer, the puddle of water that Tuppence, the aged border collie must have caused by knocking over her bowl, and the bundle of coats that lay on the floor because the children always hung too many on the hooks and, inevitably, some always slipped off.

'Right. I'm back. God, I've missed you so much. I can't wait to see you again.'

He shuffled, the phone hot against his ear. He wasn't a natural flirt, and he was useless at romantic stuff, but the fact was he'd missed Eden, and he worried sometimes that she'd like him to be more open about how he felt.

Feeling a bit stupid, he murmured, 'Bed were empty without you. Kept imagining you beside me, and what I'd be doing to you if you were here. Are you wearing that sexy lilac satin nightie? The one with the tie strings up the side?'

'Actually,' came the reply, 'I'm wearing a pair of tartan pyjama bottoms and a t-shirt that says *If you're feeling down, I can feel you up.* But hey, after that little speech, I'm willing to wear anything you like.'

Bloody hell! Horrified, Eliot almost dropped the phone. 'Who's that?'

The sound of laughter reached his ears, and heat seared his cheeks. He felt even more stupid than if Eden had heard his pathetic attempts at flirting. He knew he didn't do seduction for a reason. Basically, he was rubbish at it.

'Sorry, mate. I should have told you, but truthfully, you had me at hello.'

8

Eliot swallowed. 'Is that Cain?'

'You've guessed it. But you can call me Cainey, now we're so well acquainted.'

'Oh, shut up. Where's Eden? What are you doing with her phone?'

'She's in the next room with the rest of the coven. It's like bleeding *Loose Women* here, with all the cackling and gossip going on. It's all face masks, hairspray, and push up bras. I feel threatened, mate, I'll be honest, and you ain't helped, wanting me to wear some sexy nightie. Where are you, anyway? Nearly here? I could use some male company. I can feel me testosterone draining away as we speak.'

Cain Carmichael, seventies rock god turned respectable country gent. He wasn't fooling Eliot. Cain wore almost as much makeup and hairspray as any woman, and more than Eden who rarely wore any.

'Er, not exactly. I'm still at home.'

'You're kidding me, right? How long's it going to take you to drive down here?'

'About five hours, if the traffic's okay,' Eliot admitted, crossing his fingers that during his long drive from Skimmerdale in the Yorkshire Dales down to the Cotswolds, he wouldn't encounter any unexpected delays.

'You do know the wedding's at four?' Cain demanded. 'Cutting it a bit fine, aren't you?'

'Not really. Besides, what could I do? Weather's bin bad. It's freezing here, and we've still got snow. Sheep needed feeding, and Beth's not here yet to mind the bairns.'

'I suppose so.' Cain heaved a big sigh. 'Well, you'd better be here before the service starts, that's all. And I hope you'll make yourself presentable. No wax jackets or wellies, please. It's not snowing here, remember.'

Eliot scowled. 'I have a tuxedo, as requested on the invitation. Eden took it with her. I'll be at the hotel by three at the latest, no problem.'

'Hmm, if you say so. Now, do you want me to get your fiancée, or have I turned you with my talk of tartan trousers?'

'If you could get Eden, that would be grand.' Eliot moved away from the door as the handle rattled behind him.

Ophelia peered round.

'What is it, love?'

'Auntie Beth's here. Didn't you hear her at the door?'

'No, sorry, I was a bit, er, preoccupied. I'll be with you all in a jiffy.'

'Righty-oh. Can I speak to Mum?'

'She's not on the phone yet, love. I'll tell her you send your love.'

Ophelia nodded, seeming satisfied, and Eliot closed the door after her.

'Eliot?' The sound of Eden's voice flooded his body with warmth, and he leaned back, feeling all his tension slipping away. 'How's it going? Are you missing me?'

'Hell, you have no idea.' He wanted to say so much more, but he didn't know how. 'I—it's not the same here without you. I hate it.'

Bloody hell, couldn't he do better than that?

'I hate it, too. I'm counting the hours. I love you.'

Her reply soothed his frazzled nerves. 'I love you, an' all.'

'I can't wait to see you. Are you setting off soon?'

'Aye. Beth's just arrived, so I'll sort meself and the bairns out, then I'll be on me way. I'll be there in time to get a shower and get changed, don't worry.'

'I'm not worried,' she replied, and he could hear the smile in her voice. 'I know you'll be here. Take care, okay?'

'I will. Kids send their love.'

'Give them all kisses from me.' He heard someone calling her name, and his spirits sank when she said, 'I've got to go. Apparently, I have to have my nails done. Honey thinks they're a disgrace, now I'm a farmer's wife or as good as.'

'Happen she's right. Can't say I've noticed your nails, but you do your fair share of grafting round here, and I don't suppose it's good for your hands.'

She laughed. 'As if I care. I'll see you soon, my love. Love you.'

'Love you, too.' Bloody hell, he'd forgotten what he'd meant to say to her! 'Eden—'

The phone went dead, and he left the room, replacing the receiver on its base in the hallway. Bugger! He'd not wished her a happy Valentine's Day. Well, no matter. He'd wish her it in person soon enough.

Right, time to get organised. He had to give Beth instructions, put his overnight bag in the Land Rover, and get himself off to the Cotswolds hotel, where the grand wedding of Cain's daughter, Honey Carmichael, and Theodore Scotman was taking place. He couldn't say he was looking forward to it. It was being paid for by *All the Goss* Magazine, and there would be lots of posh people and celebrities there.

He only hoped that none of Honey's mother's relatives would be present. Since they were also relatives of his late wife, Jemima, it would be awkward, to say the least, particularly as they'd thoroughly disapproved of him, and had practically cut Jemima off from the family, as a punishment for marrying a lowly sheep farmer. Oh, well, if they were there, he'd deal with it. Things had moved on since Jemima's death. He had Eden in his life now. With her beside him, he could cope with anything.

****

Beth laughed as Ophelia and Liberty launched themselves at her, taking no notice of her wet coat. 'All right, all right. You'll knock me over in a minute. Goodness, you get taller every time I see you.'

She cast a sideways glance at George and forced a smile. 'And you, too, young man. Getting to be a big boy, aren't you?'

George beamed at her, and she felt the familiar pang of guilt. It wasn't his fault, any of it. She couldn't hold him responsible for the actions of his parents. Yet, every time she looked at him, she could see James. It was becoming more obvious who his real father was as time passed, and he was a constant reminder of her husband's betrayal.

How could Eliot stand it, she wondered. He clearly loved George as much as he did his own two daughters and didn't seem to harbour any resentment. Maybe because he'd moved on. His late wife Jemima's affair with James didn't hurt him any more, now that he had Eden in his life, whereas she was still with James — still struggling to forgive and forget. Perhaps that was the difference.

'Sorry Beth. I didn't hear you arrive.' Eliot strode into the kitchen, and her eyes widened.

'Aren't you ready? Good grief, I thought you'd be standing by the car, ready to go.'

'Eh? Oh, you mean this?' He glanced down at his jeans and boots and shrugged. 'I'm good to go. Need to get my bag in't Land Rover, then I'm done.'

She raised an eyebrow. 'Don't you think you should shower and change first?'

He frowned. 'I have. Not half an hour ago.'

She shook her head. 'You mean, you deliberately changed into those clothes for the journey? I assumed you'd been working in them. Haven't you got anything a little smarter?'

He reddened. 'Does it matter? I'm only driving, and I'm getting changed into me wedding suit at the hotel.'

Beth shrugged. 'Fine. I mean, it's up to you. It's just that you haven't seen Eden for two days, and I would have thought you'd have wanted to make a better impression on her than that.'

'Dad's useless with clothes,' Ophelia said. 'He's done well, putting on a clean shirt.'

Eliot glared at them. 'Thanks a lot. If it matters that much, I'll get changed again.'

'I would, if I were you,' Beth confirmed. As he turned, she murmured in his ear, 'I'm sure Eden would appreciate the effort. And have a shave for goodness' sake.'

He scowled. 'I can do that at the hotel. Besides,' he tilted his chin, 'Eden's quite fond of my *designer stubble*.'

She saw the gleam in his eyes and felt a moment's envy. Had she and James ever been that much in love? It was hard to remember. She blinked and gave Eliot a shove. 'Go on, get on with it. You're up against the clock, aren't you?'

He left the kitchen and she turned to the children.

'Right,' she said, unbuttoning her coat, 'time to get this place —

and you lot — cleared up, don't you think?'

By the time Eliot returned, the kitchen was gleaming. She glanced up, noting his smart black trousers and navy-blue shirt. His hair was still a tangle of black curls, but that was rather attractive. He wasn't one to faff around with mousse or gel. And she had to admit, the *designer stubble* didn't detract from the overall effect. Eliot Harland was a good-looking man, no doubt about it.

'That's better.' Beth smiled. 'Cup of tea on the worktop for you. The children are all cleaned up and I've got them settled in the living room, watching television. I'll take them out this afternoon.'

He'd been about to take a sip of tea, but hesitated. 'Where are you taking them?'

'Probably the playground in Ravensbridge.' She saw the fleeting fear in his eyes and moved to reassure him. 'Don't worry. I'm not going anywhere near Thwaite Park.'

She knew he didn't want his children around James. Especially George. That had been the unspoken deal when he'd allowed her back into their lives. Once, Beth had been Jemima's best friend, but after the affair had been revealed, and Jemima had died, she'd chosen to stay with James. It had taken a long time for Eliot to trust her with his family again. Despite her assurances that James had no interest in George, he wasn't prepared to take the risk, and she wasn't prepared to gamble on losing the Harlands' friendship again.

'Sorry, Beth,' he mumbled. 'I know you wouldn't do anything behind my back. Didn't mean to insult you. Cheer up, eh?'

She shook her head. 'Don't worry, I understand. It's not that. I have a feeling things are going to take a downward turn at the house. Even worse than they already are.'

She felt disloyal saying the words, but had an inkling that Eliot already knew she was still struggling with her marriage, despite James's best efforts to make it up to her. He wasn't a stupid man, and he knew her. He would be aware that, although she'd been whisked away on a cruise, and taken to New York for the last two Christmases, as well as being showered with gifts and attention, the damage hadn't been repaired. The fact that she still wasn't pregnant wasn't helping, nor was James's refusal to discuss other options. Now she had more problems to contend with.

'It's Deborah and David,' she burst out. 'They're coming home.'

He looked blank for a moment, then his face cleared. 'James's parents?'

'Yes.' She pulled a face. 'They've decided they've had enough of living in London and they're coming back to Thwaite Park.'

'And you're not happy about it?'

'Neither of us are happy about it.'

'So, can't he refuse? Tell them to find somewhere else to stay?'

'If only.' She sank down into a chair and put her head in her hands. 'Truth is, they own Thwaite Park. We're the ones staying there by grace.'

'Bloody hell. I thought—' He shook his head. 'You're stuck with them then? How long are they staying?'

She wrinkled her nose. 'Permanently. At least, that's the impression they've given us. It seems David's sick of the city. He claims he's seen enough shows and visited as many art galleries and museums as he can stand. He's ready to return to the life of a country gent. They'll be arriving in a few days and then, well, that's my life pretty much in the dustbin.'

'Are they that bad? Daft question. They're *his* parents.' He bit his lip. 'Sorry. I shouldn't have said that.'

She didn't rebuke him. 'David's awful. An obnoxious, rude, money-mad boor. And she's so disapproving, so brittle. She thinks I'm not good enough for her precious son. And, of course, I've failed to provide them with a grandchild. Let's face it, I'm sunk.'

'I'm sorry, Beth.'

She nodded at the clock on the wall behind him. 'You'd better get going. You've a long drive ahead of you.'

'Bloody hell, you're right.' He put down the cup, shrugged on his leather jacket, and carried his bag into the living room to bid farewell to the children. They all clung to him, telling him they loved him, begging him to give cuddles to their *mum* and making

14

him promise to ring them as soon as he arrived. Beth watched, feeling the usual sadness that she would probably never know what it was to be so loved by a child.

It had stopped snowing at least, but it was still bitterly cold as she followed him out to where the Land Rover was parked in the yard. Shivering, she nodded patiently as he reminded her, for the second time, that his occasional farmhand, Adey, would be around later to give the sheep a second feed. She knew he was hyped up, not just about the wedding. The vet was coming in two days to scan the ewes and he would soon know how many lambs were due in the spring. As cruel as it seemed to her, she knew that lambs were money in the bank to the Harlands, and cash was in short supply at Wildflower Farm. It mattered.

As Eliot climbed into the driver's seat and started the engine, she tapped on the window. 'Enjoy yourself,' she told him. 'And be polite. I can't wait to see the photos in *All the Goss*.'

He pulled a face as she laughed. She was aware that a celebrity wedding was the last place he wanted to be. In fact, it was his idea of hell. But he was doing it for Eden. As the car left the farmyard, she realised, rather wistfully, that she couldn't imagine James being so unselfish for her sake. Then again, she had to ask herself the question, would *she* be willing to make any sacrifices for *him*? The sad truth was, she was no longer sure she would.

Chapter 2

Chessingborough House was a sixteenth century manor, tastefully converted into a beautiful country hotel. Standing in almost twenty acres of grounds, its honey-coloured stone and mullioned windows made it the perfect setting for a celebrity wedding. The fact that it had forty guest bedrooms, a spa, and a Michelin star restaurant, had ensured it had hosted its fair share of them.

Even so, as Emerald Carmichael entered through the impressive front door, glancing around her at the ancient panelling on the walls, and noting the deep pile carpet that was so soft beneath her feet she felt as if she were walking on cushions, she thought that, really, Honey could have shown more imagination.

Then again, she conceded, what more could she expect from Daddy's spoilt little princess? It was clichéd and predictable, just like her half-sister. And to sell the whole event to a tacky magazine! Honey was a media whore, with no taste and no self-respect.

Now, if Emerald was in charge of organising this wedding, she would have done things very differently. Of course, she was relieved she *hadn't* been asked to plan the wedding, or to be a bridesmaid, or to be involved in any way whatsoever with the wedding. Honey was very lucky that she'd agreed to attend at all. It had been a last-minute decision, taken merely to shut her mother up.

'You can't be the only one of Cain's children not attending! Even Jed and Scarlet are coming back from America to be there. And I'll bet my last penny that Marcus goes. Marcus! I won't have it, Emerald. You belong there far more than that boy does.'

Marcus was a sore point with her mother, Cassandra, as Cain had still been married to her when his fling with a pub waitress called Sandy had resulted in Marcus's birth. That had caused the end of that marriage, and Cassandra had never forgiven Sandy, nor Marcus come to that.

Emerald thought Cassandra had asked for it. She was a very whiny woman, who always saw the worst in people. Emerald could see why Cain had looked elsewhere for some fun. She had long suspected that her mother wouldn't have minded half so much if he hadn't gone looking for it in a Steak 'n' Bake pub. According to the company website, you could get a three-course meal in those places for less than a tenner, which said it all, as far as Cassandra was concerned.

The reception hall was a hive of activity, and Emerald hovered uncertainly, car keys clutched in her hand. A long queue snaked towards the desk, and a harassed looking receptionist was battling to deal with the clamouring guests. Emerald began to panic. If she wasn't shown to her room within the next few minutes, her chakras were in danger of becoming unaligned, and she wasn't having that. Not when it had taken her the best part of a week to get them sorted. It was all the stress of having to attend this damn event. She wasn't the celebrity type. She was a simple girl at heart, after all, and all the superficial trappings of fame didn't suit her in the slightest.

'Can I 'elp you with that bag?'

Upon hearing the broad northern accent, Emerald glanced round, her eyes widening as she caught sight of a tall, dark-haired man, smiling kindly at a woman who was struggling with a valise. Good grief, the lady was positively ancient, and if she was so frail she couldn't manage a small bag like that, she really shouldn't be out on her own. She didn't seem to be the slightest bit grateful, either. She shook her head and clutched the bag to her drooping bosom quite defensively.

'Certainly not! I'm perfectly capable, thank you,' she said, in a cut-glass accent, eyeing the man with suspicion.

He shrugged but left her to it and strolled towards the reception, carrying someone's overnight bag. Emerald felt some relief. At least she could get the car sorted, even if she would have to wait a bit longer for a room.

'Excuse me? My keys.' Emerald held out the car keys and waited for him to take them. 'There are three bags in the boot. It's the cobalt blue coupé outside. Please, be careful.'

He stared at her, and she found herself staring back. It was hard not to gape at him to be truthful. He was an extremely attractive man. Those black-brown eyes were quite mesmerising, and those raven curls... She swallowed. Good heavens, what was she thinking? She'd be trawling for men in a Steak 'n' Bake at this rate. Her mother would be appalled.

'My keys,' she repeated, rattling them in his face.

'Happen they are. Are you telling me that for a reason, or do you allus mither on about nowt?'

Emerald gaped at him. She wasn't sure what he'd just said, but she had a feeling he hadn't been entirely complimentary. 'Can you park my car, or not?'

His eyebrows knitted together. 'Why would I want to park your car? It's taken me best part of ten minutes to park me own. Flaming place is heaving. Didn't you pass your test or summat?'

'Well! How bloody rude!' He'd hit a nerve there. It had taken her eight attempts to pass her driving test, and parking wasn't her strong point.

Despite her indignation, she had to admit he looked rather handsome as he scrutinised her, a stern expression on his face. She had a funny feeling he could be quite firm with her, if he chose. It wasn't an altogether unpleasant thought.

'I'm so sorry to keep you waiting.' The receptionist, wearing an apologetic expression, finally dealt with the last guest in the queue before her, and turned to them, forcing her to look away from the porter, or car parking attendant, or whatever the hell he was. 'It's quite busy here, I'm afraid, what with our grand event. You're here for the wedding, I presume? Double room was it?' he enquired, smiling at the dark-haired man beside her.

Emerald blushed. It would be rather interesting to share a room with this northerner for a short while and find out exactly how firm he could be. The fact that the receptionist didn't recognise her, though, rankled. And anyway, why hadn't he recognised the porter? Probably temporary staff, hired for the wedding, she supposed.

'I'm not with *her*!' The man in question sounded quite put out, and Emerald's temper flared. She should be the one who was offended, after all.

'Of course he's not. He works here!' she snapped.

'I don't bloody work here,' he protested. 'What the hell gave you that idea?'

She was about to say, *your accent*, but thought better of it. She didn't want to be accused of racism, of all things. 'Then why did you try to take that old woman's bag?' she demanded.

The receptionist eyed him, a definite trace of suspicion in his face. 'You tried to take someone's bag?'

'I bloody didn't. I asked her if she wanted a hand, that's all. I were being polite. Not that she were having any of it. I shouldn't have bothered.'

'A likely story,' Emerald said, still smarting from his vehement rebuffal.

'I'm not so sure,' admitted the receptionist. 'Was she small, wearing a blue hat and carrying a paisley valise?'

The man nodded.

'Positively ancient,' added Emerald, 'and with an alarmingly droopy bosom. Practically swept the carpet as she walked.'

The receptionist sighed. 'Yes, I know the person you mean. She wouldn't thank you for trying to help. And she won't part with that bag. Takes it everywhere. Goodness knows what she's got in there.'

'Who is she?' It sounded to Emerald as if the ungrateful old woman was carrying around a fortune.

'I couldn't possibly say.' The receptionist gave her a smug grin. 'Anyway, back to business. I apologise for the delay. What name is it?'

Humiliation made Emerald snap, particularly when she spotted a huge board saying *Wedding of Theodore Scotman and Honey Carmichael*. No doubt the receptionist knew damn well who Honey was.

'Emerald Carmichael, sister of the bride. And before you do anything else, you can get someone to park my car, and collect my luggage. Honestly, this is supposed to be a five-star hotel. It's a disgrace, and I shall make that point very forcefully in my review.'

'I'm sorry, Miss Carmichael. I'll rectify the situation, immediately. Ah, Robert!' The receptionist smiled in evident relief as a man in a smart black suit appeared at the desk. 'This lady's car needs parking, and her bags need to be retrieved.'

'Straight away, miss. Car keys?'

Emerald handed them over with some reluctance. He looked awfully young. She supposed they *had* checked that he'd got a valid licence?

'It's the cobalt blue coupé just outside,' she told him.

Nodding, he backed away from her. She took a few steps towards him. 'Be careful, it's quite new, and there's not a mark on it.' *It's not mine*, she thought, *and I can't lose the deposit from the car rental firm.*

He gave her a reassuring smile, turned and headed towards the door. Emerald half followed him, then thought better of it.

'I shall be checking it over!' she called, as he ran down the steps. Turning back to the desk, she felt an odd pang of regret as she noticed that the dark-haired man had already been attended to and was striding towards the stairs. Evidently, he saw no need of lifts. No wonder he looked so fit, she mused. His thighs, straining against those dark trousers, were quite muscular. She'd bet he looked even better without the trousers on. She gave a little shake of her head as the receptionist handed her a key card.

'The Coleridge Suite, Miss Carmichael. I'll have your bags sent up to you. If you wait a moment, I'll get someone to show you the way.'

'No need. I'll take her.'

Emerald's heart thudded as a scrawny arm was draped over her shoulders, and she peered up into a pair of watery blue eyes, rimmed with black kohl.

'Very good, Mr Carmichael.' The receptionist practically bowed.

'Emerald, me darling. Great to see you. It's been ages.' Cain sounded as sincere as a dodgy timeshare salesman. Emerald's eyes narrowed as he forced a smile. No change there then.

'Hello, Daddy.'

'Let's go upstairs and you can get yourself ready, then I'll take you to see Honey. She can't wait to see you.'

Emerald scowled as Cain began to lead her towards the lift. The truth was, it was hard to say who would be least pleased to see her — her father or her sister. It was too close to call.

****

'Room service.'

Eden's heart leapt in recognition at the sound of his voice. She would know it anywhere, no matter how much he was trying to disguise it. She threw open the door, laughing. 'You're here!'

'I'm here.' Eliot didn't even bother to shut the door behind him. He hurled his overnight bag across the room and pulled her to him. His kiss told her how much he'd missed her, and she melted against him for a moment, allowing herself to surrender to the inevitable chemistry between them. Then she remembered and forced herself to back away.

He looked hurt. 'What's up?'

'This.' She waved a hand, indicating her bridesmaid dress, immaculate makeup, and coiffured hair. 'If I mess this up, Honey will kill me. And it would be very easy to mess this up, trust me. I mean, look at you! God, I'll bet I already have a rash from your stubble, haven't I?'

Eliot looked her up and down, and she saw the expression in his face change.

'What is it?' she asked, suddenly nervous.

'You look, er...'

'Beautiful? Luscious? Exquisite?'

'Different.'

'Oh, well, thanks for that. I feel irresistible now.'

He pushed the door shut and leaned against it, surveying her. 'I don't mean that in a bad way. I mean, you always look gorgeous, no matter what. But, well...'

'Well, what?'

'Oh, come on, Eden,' he burst out. 'What the hell have they done to you?'

She giggled. 'I know. I don't look like me, do I? And my hair, for God's sake!'

'It's a bit — structured.'

'With half a can of hairspray on it, it should be. So, don't you like me looking so elegant?'

His lips curved into a knowing smile. 'I prefer you a bit more natural.'

'I'll bet you do.' They stared at each other, desire sparking between them.

Eden swallowed. 'You'd better start getting ready. The shower's through there, and your suit's hanging in the wardrobe. I'll have to get back to Honey's suite. She's a bag of nerves.'

'Aren't you going to wait until I've changed?' he asked, his voice husky.

She shook her head. 'No chance. The minute I see you in that tuxedo, I'm going to want to pounce on you. You know it and I know it, and I can't mess this outfit or my hair up.'

He sighed, and her lips twitched. 'Mind you...'

He shot her a hopeful look. 'What?'

'Once I've done my official duties, there's going to be no reason that we can't sneak back up here and spend a bit of time away from the party. I mean, I can soon brush my hair and reapply my makeup. You know — *afterwards*,' she teased. 'Once the photos are done, who'll care?' She saw the gleam in his eyes and grinned. 'Deal?'

'I'll hold you to it,' he promised.

'You'd better.' She kissed him. 'Now, have you done your homework?'

He groaned. 'No, I bloody haven't. You weren't serious, were you?'

22

'If you know who's who and what's what, it will make things much easier for you,' she assured him. 'Where's that card I gave you?'

Eliot shrugged. 'Left it at home.'

She grinned. 'Thought you might. Lucky I have a copy here, isn't it?' She hurried over to the bedside cabinet and pulled a piece of paper from the drawer.

Eliot scowled.as she handed it to him. 'How's anyone supposed to keep track of this bloody lot?' he demanded, seeing the long list of names and complicated family relationships in the Carmichael family.

'Exactly,' she said. 'Which is why you need to revise. Go on, read it, 'cos I'll be testing you in a minute.'

'Bloody hell, you're strict. Now I know how our Ophelia felt the other night when you made her do her maths revision instead of watching a film. I told her off for whingeing an' all, poor kid.' He shook his head, surveying the paper gloomily. 'Why do I need to know all Cain's wives? Surely they won't all be here?'

'No, but all his children will be, and you don't want to give them the wrong mothers, do you?'

'I won't be speaking to any of them anyway!'

'Yes, you will. What if they approach you? Wouldn't you feel better knowing who you were talking to?'

She could see on his face that he didn't give a monkey's who he was talking to and had little intention of making conversation at all, but she persisted in her belief that forewarned was forearmed.

'Ready?' she said at last.

'As I'll ever be,' he muttered.

'So, Cain Carmichael has been married three times. Who are his wives?'

'Katherine of Aragon, Anne Boleyn and Jane Seymour.'

'Eliot! Be serious.'

He rolled his eyes. 'Lowri, Cassandra and Freya.'

'Oh, well done!'

'Throw me a bloody fish, why don't you? Feel like a performing seal.'

She laughed. 'You are grumpy! Now, who is the mother of his

one illegitimate child?'

She saw him squinting at the paper in his hand and bit her lip in amusement.

'Er, Sandy.'

'Correct. Now, name all five of his children.'

'Really?' Eliot groaned. 'Do I have to?'

'There'll be a bonus in it for you,' she said, giving him a meaningful look.

'That's not fair,' he protested. 'All right, all right. Well, Honey for starters, obviously. And then there's them twins, whose names I can't remember. And Emerald. And — and Marcus?'

'Yes, but the twins are the eldest. They're Lowri's children and have lived in America for years. Jed and Scarlet. Scarlet's an actress, married to an actor called Luke, and Jed's a musician. Then there's Emerald, who is Cassandra's daughter, Marcus who is Sandy's daughter, and Honey is the youngest. You know Freya, her mother, of course.'

They exchanged uncomfortable glances. Freya was, after all, related to Jemima.

'Anyway,' she continued, 'do you know who's the best man?'

'No idea and couldn't care less.'

She sighed. 'Right. I'll reel this off once only, so listen. Honey is marrying Theodore — Teddy — Scotman. Teddy's father is Rex Scotman who used to be a star in the seventies and is Cain's big rival. Seriously, there's no love lost there so whatever you do, don't sing one's praises to the other.'

He gave her a withering look. 'Am I likely to?'

She had to admit he wasn't. 'Marcus and Jed are ushers. The best man is one of Teddy's university friends.' She looked stricken. 'Gosh, I can't remember his name!'

'You failed then,' Eliot told her. 'Happen test is over.'

She folded her arms. 'Anyone would think you weren't interested.'

'I know,' he mused. 'Funny that.'

'All right,' she said, winking at him, 'we'll leave it there. I have to go anyway.'

'Really?'

'I'll see you downstairs,' she promised. 'The Barrett Browning Room, four o'clock. Make sure you're there at least ten minutes early. Don't worry, you won't be able to miss it, and there'll be plenty of people and notices to guide you.'

He nodded, looking unsure.

Her heart melted. She knew this wasn't his type of thing at all, and she appreciated him making the effort for her. 'It will be fine. Promise. I love you. Happy Valentine's Day, sweetheart.'

'Happy Valentine's Day, my love. See you down there then.'

They stared at each other for a moment, then he cleared his throat.

'You'd better go,' he said gruffly, 'or I won't be responsible for my actions, posh frock or no bloody posh frock.'

She laughed and left the room, closing the door behind her.

Honey was in the Wordsworth Suite on the next floor and, as Eden walked in, the overpowering smell of hairspray, perfume and makeup hit her. Four women getting ready in its confined space had left their mark in the atmosphere.

A little boy in velvet knickerbockers and a ruffled shirt was sitting on the carpet, watching cartoons on the fifty-inch television.

'Okay, Justin?'

He nodded and smiled at her, and she patted him on the head, thinking how remarkable it was that such a sweet, quiet child could be Cain's grandson and Honey's nephew.

Scarlet, Honey's oldest sister, was sitting on the bed, reapplying her lip gloss for what must have been the hundredth time. She was a television star in America — that is, she appeared in some soap opera there which, in her own mind at least, put her on a par with Jennifer Aniston. The fact that no one in Britain appeared to have heard of her was neither here nor there.

She'd been positively gushing towards Honey all day, which had annoyed the already nervous bride-to-be, and baffled Eden. It was, after all, the first time that the two half-sisters had met in person, and there was such a thing as over-familiarity. But then again, Scarlet had been brought up in America, and didn't have that English reserve.

'How's she doing?' Eden asked, knowing that Honey had been on the verge of hysteria when she'd last seen her, around half an hour previously.

'I think she's calmed down a bit,' Scarlet drawled, surveying her reflection in the mirror. She pouted, applied more lip gloss, then put down the mirror and scanned Eden. 'Your hair's kinda mussed up. What have you been up to?'

'Oh, hell.' Eden patted the back of her head, remembering the way Eliot's hand had cupped it as he kissed her. 'Well, it will have to do. I'm not letting them apply any more hairspray.'

'I don't blame you. If anyone tries to light a cigarette within ten feet of any of us, we're history.'

Scarlet smiled, and Eden thought that, although she was a bit full-on, she was nice enough. At least she'd always made the effort to keep in touch with her half-sister, which was more than Honey had ever done. 'Anyway, by the time her mom's through with her, I doubt she'll notice your hair.'

'What do you mean?' Alarm bells rang in Eden's head. Freya wasn't exactly a doting mother. What was she up to?

'I think she's trying to persuade her to take a pill. You know, calm her down. She's already given her a glass of wine. They disappeared into the bathroom ten minutes ago, and Freya was clutching the bottle. I think it's a big mistake, but apparently, we Americans don't understand anything.'

'You're kidding!'

Eden charged into the bathroom, not even bothering to knock, and was somewhat taken aback to discover Freya and Honey perched on the edge of the bath, each with a glass of white wine in their hand. Alarmingly, Freya was waving a box of pills under Honey's nose and urging her to take one.

'It will put those nerves at bay, ensure you look calm and poised. Remember those dreadful wedding photos of Marion Lerwick's daughter? My God, she looked appalling. Like a bewildered beaver — all teeth and tears. That was down to nerves. Usually, she looks almost passable. You don't want people saying such things about you, do you? And you're going to be in a magazine, for goodness' sake. Those glossies are terribly unforgiving.'

26

Eden snatched the box of pills out of her hand and gasped when she saw what they were. 'Are you insane?'

'I beg your pardon!' Freya looked staggered that Eden had dared to speak to her in such a fashion. After all, it wasn't that long ago that she'd worked for Cain, and Freya still considered her staff. Well, those days were over, and as Honey's chief bridesmaid it was her job to look out for her. Freya could lump it.

'If she takes one of those, she'll be so zonked out that she won't even be able to say her vows, never mind pose for photos.'

'I'll have you know that I take eight of those, every single day, for my back problems, and they don't have any effect on me,' Freya insisted.

Probably drowned out by the effects of the alcohol, thought Eden. It was a wonder Freya's liver hadn't packed up years ago.

Out loud she said, 'But you're used to them. Honey's not, and they could knock her out entirely. How would you feel if you were responsible for the wedding being cancelled?'

'Oh, nonsense,' snapped Freya, snatching her medication back.

'I'm not risking it.' Honey finally seemed to have found her voice. 'And I'm not having any more of this stuff, either,' she added, pouring her wine down the sink. 'I'll smell like an old lush at this rate.' She gave her mother a pointed stare, then turned to Eden. 'Where the hell have you been? I've been frantic without you.'

'Sorry. Eliot's arrived. I needed to settle him in, show him where everything was.'

'That's what staff are for,' said Honey. She clutched her stomach. 'Oh, God. My guts are churning. I feel sick. What time is it?'

'Half past three,' Freya said, glancing at her watch. 'Well, if you're not going to take my advice, I see no reason to hang around. I'll be downstairs in the Barrett Browning Room.'

Honey's eyes widened. 'You're not leaving me?'

'Your father will be here in a minute,' said Freya. 'I hardly want to be here when he arrives. Besides, there's nothing more I can do for you, and you have your half-sister, and — her.' She gave Eden a curl of the lip, then left the bathroom.

Honey gave Eden a beseeching look. 'Do I look all right?'

'Perched on the edge of a bath with an empty wine glass in your hand? Not really. Good job the photographers have gone.'

'Not gone. Circling. Like sharks. They'll be in the Barrett Browning Room, no doubt. Oh, why in God's name did I sell this wedding to them? Teddy was right. It's made it all so tacky.'

She looked so stricken that Eden felt quite sorry for her. She held out her hand and pulled Honey to her feet. 'You look beautiful, and Teddy's going to be so proud of you. And you'll be glad you sold the wedding when the magazine comes out and you can look back on your big day in glorious technicolour. You're going to be so busy today that it will all be a haze, but you'll have a great record of it all in print, and all the people who love you and Teddy, but couldn't come to the wedding, will be able to share in it after all.'

Honey smiled. 'Thank you, Eden. What would I do without you?'

'You have Teddy now. You're going to be fine.'

Eden knew Teddy adored Honey, and that the two of them were going to be happy. He'd transformed Honey from a spoilt, selfish brat into someone much nicer, and far more likeable. Eden wanted them both to enjoy their big day, which was why she didn't feel bad for lying about the magazine deal. She couldn't think of anything worse than turning your wedding day into a media circus, but then, she wasn't the daughter of a rock star and a top model. She was the daughter of a retired bus driver and a cleaner. There was a big difference. Thank God.

As they heard the muffled sound of a knock on the door in the next room, Honey smoothed down her dress and flicked back her freshly curled hair. 'That will be Dad, no doubt. God, I hope he's made himself presentable. He's not happy about wearing a tux, and you know what an attention seeker he is. The slightest sniff of a camera and he's got to be the star of the show. Well, if he's in leopard skin leggings, I'll kill him with my own bare hands. Still, at least he hasn't got those awful teardrop tattoos on his face, like Rex. Poor Teddy's mortified. Fathers are such a bloody embarrassment.'

Maybe so, thought Eden, *but between them they've given you and Teddy the kind of lifestyle the rest of us can only dream about.* And Honey wouldn't have had the option of a grand wedding paid for by a magazine if her dad had been someone ordinary. It was Cain and Rex who were the celebrities, not their children.

Honey opened the bathroom door, and she and Eden stepped back into the bedroom, to see Cain standing there, looking almost normal in a tuxedo, and not even half the amount of eye makeup he sometimes wore. Eden's glance fell on a young woman standing beside him. She was undeniably attractive, with a cloud of wavy, blonde hair, large blue eyes, and a curvy figure that was showed off to perfection by the long, white dress she was wearing.

'Hello, Honey,' she drawled, her smile strictly limited to her gloss-free mouth. 'Don't you look, er, pretty.'

'Is this some kind of joke?' demanded Honey, who looked as if she were about to explode. 'Emerald, you total fucking bitch.'

Eden sighed. Maybe she should run downstairs and beg some opiates from Freya, after all.

Chapter 3

'All right, girls. Let's calm it down, shall we?' Cain held up his hands in what he probably knew, already, was a vain attempt at keeping the peace. Eden could see the nervous expression in his eyes, and she didn't blame him. All three of his daughters together for the first time, and at least two of them, from what she could see, headstrong and fiery. This was going to be interesting, although whatever showdown was about to happen, they'd better make it quick. The wedding was due to start in less than fifteen minutes.

She wondered if Eliot had found the Barrett Browning Room all right. She couldn't help imagining him in his tuxedo. *Concentrate, Eden*, she thought. *You're Honey's bridesmaid. You don't need any distractions.*

'Nice to see you, too,' said Emerald, putting down her clutch bag and peering round the room. 'What a delightful turn of phrase from a blushing bride. Such a shame the journalists didn't catch it.'

'You always were a cow,' Honey informed her.

Justin stood up, looking a bit worried, and Eden put a reassuring arm around him.

'Can you two tone it down a bit?' she asked, nodding meaningfully at the little boy.

'I'm quite sure I don't need to tone down anything,' said Emerald.

'How about that ghostly look, for a start?' Honey snapped. 'Pale and interesting is so out of fashion. Buy some fake tan, for Christ's sake.'

Emerald shrugged. 'I've been living on the Scottish coast all winter. I'm only just thawing out. A few days ago, I was pale blue.'

"Well, why don't you piss off back there then? You'll be costing the Scottish Tourist Board a fortune, now their monster's missing.'

'Come on,' pleaded Cain. 'No need for all this. You haven't seen each other in ages. Can't you kiss and make up?'

'Kiss and make up!' Honey glared at him. 'You *have* seen what she's wearing?'

Cain looked puzzled. He turned to Emerald and ran his eyes over her. As Eden watched, she realised the penny had finally dropped.

'Oh.' He sighed. 'What did you wanna go and do that for, Emerald? Wear a long white dress when it's Honey's wedding day?'

'It's the bride's prerogative to wear white,' Honey said bitterly. 'Everyone knows that. She's trying to upstage me.'

'For goodness' sake, how was I supposed to know you'd wear white?' said Emerald, sitting down on the bed beside Scarlet. 'Funnily enough, it never occurred to me. Most brides wear ivory or cream these days. You know — so they don't look like hypocrites.'

'Ooh, cheap shot,' murmured Scarlet.

Emerald glanced at her. 'Scarlet, isn't it?'

'You remember me? Hey, well done. I mean, it's been, like ... How long has it been now?'

'Twenty-two years, three months and five days.'

They all gaped at her.

'How the hell do you know that?' demanded Cain, sounding awestruck.

'Because, Daddy dearest, Scarlet and Jed left for America on my fifth birthday. I remember distinctly, because Lowri brought them to see Mother and me before she left, and they bought me a doll for my birthday. I didn't even realise they were leaving. I saw Lowri and Mother talking and then I was told to give them a goodbye hug. Later, while I was waiting for you to come to my house to watch me blow out the candles on my cake, you were at the airport, having a screaming row with their mother about access rights and threatening her with the best lawyers in London. I saw the whole thing — as did most of the population of Britain — when I watched the news that evening before I went to bed. And I still hadn't blown out my candles. Funnily enough, with you not bothering to turn up, and then realising my brother and sister were leaving the country for good, I didn't much feel like cake any more.'

Eden's heart melted. Poor Emerald.

Scarlet put her arm around Emerald's shoulders. 'Aw, that's so sad. I'm sorry, sweetie. We should have kept in touch more. Things were kinda awkward with Dad an' all for a while, and then you and your mom moved to France and... Well, you know how it is.'

'We were only in France for a year that time.' Emerald's tone was icy. 'But yes, I know how it is. Yet you contacted Honey, even though she wasn't even born when you left?'

Scarlet looked awkward. 'Well, you and your mom moved around quite a lot, didn't you? And when we finally got back in touch with Dad, Honey was living with him. Well, for half the year, anyway. Though, we never met until yesterday. Funny, huh?'

'Hilarious,' Emerald agreed. 'Yet, for some mysterious reason, she still chose *you* to be her bridesmaid.'

Scarlet clamped her mouth shut. Eden wondered if she'd ever be able to open it again, given the amount of sticky gloss she'd been plastering on it.

'Is Jed here, too?' asked Emerald, a hopeful tone entering her voice.

'He's probably in the Barrett Browning Room, as we speak,' said Cain. 'The blokes stayed over at another hotel last night, but they'll no doubt be on duty by now.'

'On duty?'

Cain swallowed. 'Well, er, Jed's an usher.'

32

'I see.'

Eden could see, too. Emerald was hurt, and desperately trying not to show it.

'Look, I think this is a discussion for another time,' she said firmly. 'The wedding's due to start in a few minutes, and we need to head downstairs.'

'And you are?' Emerald raised one neatly shaped eyebrow.

'Eden. Honey's friend.'

'Friend? Honey has friends? Staggering. And Little Lord Fauntleroy here is your son?' She looked enquiringly at Justin, who stared up at her with worried eyes.

Cain cleared his throat. 'Er, no. This is my grandson. Your nephew. Justin, say hello to your Auntie Emerald.'

Poor Justin looked terrified but obeyed. 'Hello, Auntie Emerald.'

'He's your son?' Emerald looked at Scarlet, who shook her head.

'Nope. He's our brother's kid. You know. Marcus.'

'Marcus!' Emerald glared at Honey. 'So, Marcus's brat is your pageboy, but I'm not even worthy of being a bridesmaid?'

'Oh, give it a rest,' Honey said. 'I didn't imagine for one moment that you'd turn up. Thought you'd be off somewhere, polishing your crystals and sniffing incense.'

'You want to watch it, mocking other people's beliefs,' said Emerald darkly. 'Karma can be a bitch.'

'I'm sure she didn't mean to be rude,' Cain interjected.

'Yes, she did. She's taking the piss. I can read it in her aura.'

'Oh, for God's sake.' Honey rolled her eyes.

'There you go again,' Emerald snapped. 'I have to warn you, your aura's gone a distinctly funny colour. It's clashing terribly with those drab bridesmaid dresses. I must say, I'd have chosen something in a warmer colour. Far more flattering to the complexion. I can't believe you've put them in grey.'

'They're not bloody grey, they're blue haze,' Honey corrected her. 'And I may not be blessed with the gift of reading auras, but I'll bet you a pound to a penny that yours is green. Oh, and while we're at it, I may as well tell you right now that Marcus is an usher, too, so stick that in your bong and suck it.'

33

Emerald swallowed, seeming at a loss for words. Eden couldn't help feeling sorry for her.

Honey evidently felt no such pity. 'Now, unless you've changed your mind about attending, bugger off and find something to wear that's less bridal. Dad, are you ready? Right. Come on. I've a gorgeous man waiting to marry me.'

'Thank God for that.' Cain held out his arm to her, and she hooked her own through it. 'Half the bleeding Tory party are at this wedding, not to mention directors of most of the charities I've donated to. I'll never get me knighthood if you two start brawling. This wedding's got to be a success, right?'

'Well, of course,' Honey said. 'Funnily enough, Teddy and I were hoping it would go well, too. Eden, can you pass me my flowers please?'

Eden obliged, quite touched when Justin reached for her hand again as soon as she'd done as Honey asked.

'He looks anaemic,' Emerald observed. 'I don't know how he's going to live this humiliation down. When his school friends see the pictures of him in that get-up, he'll be a laughing-stock.'

'Okay, that's enough,' Eden held up her hand. 'If you and Honey want to row, go ahead, but leave Justin out of it. He's a little boy, who's done nothing to you, so shut up.'

'I beg your pardon!'

'You heard. I won't have it. You're making him nervous, and he's supposed to be enjoying today. Now, if you're coming to this wedding, zip it, or push off.'

'Have you heard the way this person spoke to me?' Emerald demanded, as Cain opened the door.

'I have, and she's got a point. Leave me grandson alone, Emerald. I don't want to fall out with you, but keep your trap shut now, okay?'

Eden watched as a look of rage crossed Emerald's face, and she didn't miss the poisonous look that Honey's sister gave her. She'd made an enemy there. Well, she couldn't worry about it now. She squeezed Justin's hand and gave him a reassuring smile. Time to face the cameras. The show was about to commence.

****

Jed directed a bewildered-looking man into a chair on the bride's side of the room, then hurried to the front to take his own seat. Beside him, Marcus cast a nervous glance at his cell phone.

'I think you'd better turn that off, don't you?' Jed said, not without sympathy. His half-brother's wife, Janette, was due to go into labour any day, and Marcus had made it crystal clear that he absolutely couldn't miss the birth of his second child. He'd almost backed out of attending the event and had only agreed because Janette had insisted that he take his rightful place at his sister's wedding and didn't want Justin to miss out on being a pageboy.

'That's Janette all over,' he'd told Jed, Cain, Luke, Teddy and Rex, many times during the *stag night,* as the British called it, at the Chimneys Hotel. 'So unselfish and thoughtful.'

He'd sung his wife's praises the entire evening and had filled them in on every stage of the pregnancy, which would have been kind of sweet another time. Right then, though, it was the last thing Jed had wanted to hear, and the rest of the party had looked bored to tears.

It had been the quietest, most restrained bachelor party Jed had ever been on, and Lord knows, he'd been on plenty. He still had a hangover from his brother-in-law's raucous night, and that was nearly a year and a half ago. If Scarlet knew the half of what he and her husband had got up to, she might never have married Luke at all. He grinned to himself. Nothing illegal or immoral, of course — he wouldn't stand by and let anyone make a fool of his sister — but great fun, all the same. He'd expected even worse shenanigans — or better, depending on your point of view — at Teddy's bachelor party, considering the wild reputation of both their fathers. Cain and Rex, however, were apparently paragons of virtue these days, with respectable lives and well-to-do friends. Who'd have thought it?

Marcus dutifully switched off the phone and shoved it in his jacket pocket. Jed ran a hand through his fair hair and adjusted his bow tie, though he knew perfectly well it didn't need adjusting. He cast a nervous glance at the photographers, standing to his left, waiting. He hated these celebrity weddings. Scarlet's had been the same. What was wrong with a private, family event? If he ever got married, he'd make damn sure no journalist got anywhere near. Not that he was likely to get married. Especially not now.

He got to his feet as music began to blare out of the speakers. Opposite him, he watched Teddy rise, trembling. Beside him, his best man — some friend from university who'd only arrived that morning, leaving Teddy in a real panic that he wouldn't turn up on time — frantically patted his jacket pocket, as if checking for the rings, then nodded at the groom. Jed grinned and turned to watch the bride's entrance.

His jaw dropped as a young, blonde woman strolled down the aisle alone. She was wearing a simple, white floor-length dress that had none of the sophistication he'd expect at a glamorous event like this, but it suited her, somehow. She wore little makeup, but her face was so pretty she didn't need it. Something stirred in his mind, and he frowned. *Is that Emerald?*

What the hell was she doing, walking down the aisle to the wedding music? And wearing a white dress that could easily be mistaken for a wedding gown. A camera flashed, and Jed's eyes scanned the back of the room. Where was Honey? He took a deep breath as she appeared at the door, arm in arm with their father. Her face was hardly that of a contented bride. She looked furious, and Cain's face was like thunder. Uh-oh. Emerald had obviously put the cat amongst the pigeons, and no wonder. He shot a look at Scarlet, who was walking behind Honey. She gave a little shrug of the shoulders and pulled a face, and he vowed to collar her after the ceremony and find out what the hell was going on.

Emerald pushed her way into a seat near the front, just as Honey reached her. Jed thought, for a moment, that Honey was going to lunge after their sister and throttle her, but luckily, her eyes fell on Teddy, and she seemed to decide that getting married was the main priority. Jed heaved a sigh of relief as, beside him, Marcus whispered, 'Doesn't Justin look *adorable*! Wait until

36

Janette sees the pictures. Oh, I wish she could have been here.'

Jed bit his lip. Yeah, Justin looked cute as a button. He felt the familiar churning in his stomach and tried to concentrate, as the music ended.

'Dad looks almost normal,' Marcus was clearly surprised by the fact. Had he expected their father to walk down the aisle in his platform boots and leather pants? Maybe, a few years ago, he might have. His mom would never believe it when he told her that Cain was now a country gent, mixing with politicians and the cream of British high society. He could hardly believe it himself.

Jed watched as Honey and Teddy turned to each other to begin making their vows. He saw Honey's face transform as she gazed at the man who, in a few minutes, would be her husband. She loved him and, having spoken to Teddy for a good long time the previous night, he knew the feeling was mutual.

They were lucky to have found each other so young, he thought. How old was Honey now? Maybe twenty-three, twenty-four? And Teddy wasn't much older. Yet here *he* was, in his mid-thirties and right back at square one as far as his love life went. In fact, he was further back than that. Minus numbers for him, given what had happened these last few months. Life was a bitch sometimes, no doubt about it. And he still hadn't broken his other news to his father. Now, that was something he wasn't looking forward to.

He decided that, press or no press, he was going to have quite a few shots of alcohol that evening. If he couldn't live up to Cain's past glories, he could, at the very least, live up to his past excesses — at least for one night.

****

Emerald was the first to take her seat in the reception room. She felt she needed a stiff drink after witnessing that sickly sweet display and had bypassed the official line-up to grab a glass of wine from the waitress at the end of the queue. Honey and Teddy had apparently written their own vows, and they'd overdosed on the sugar. Emerald found it hard to believe that they were as smitten with each other as they pretended to be. She suspected there was another reason for their weird behaviour. Maybe it was something to do with Rex and his boring charity work. Or Cain's endless quest to achieve a knighthood. They were all in it together, and this over-the-top wedding, paid for by that tacky magazine, was serving some darker purpose. She had no intention of exchanging air kisses and gushing how happy she was for them. She'd leave that to the more gullible guests.

'Emerald?' She paused in lifting the glass of wine to her lips and eyed the tall, fair-haired man with dimples in his cheeks, as he slipped into a seat beside her. She would know those warm blue eyes anywhere.

'Jed!'

'You remember me! Wow, it's been a while. It's so good to see you.'

Her own eyes widened in surprise as she was pulled into a warm embrace. She'd always liked Jed, she remembered. He'd been kind to her, not like most boys of that age who, to be honest, were generally bullies and stupid beyond words.

'It's good to see you, too,' she admitted. 'You're looking well.'

Though, as he pulled away from her, she thought he wasn't looking as well as she'd supposed. He had dark shadows under his eyes, and there was something else. She wasn't sure what it was, but she had a funny feeling he'd not had an easy time of it lately, and the thought stirred an unfamiliar feeling of compassion in her.

'How are you?' he asked. 'You look great. And how's your mom doing?'

No one ever asked her about her mother. Despite Emerald's own uneasy relationship with her, she was touched that Jed had bothered.

'She's fine. Currently living in Scotland. She's gone very tartan.'

Hadn't she just! Cassandra, a historical novelist, moved around a lot, choosing to stay in the location of the book she was writing at the time. She always thoroughly embraced the atmosphere of the place she was in. Every time they stayed in France, she became rather revolutionary and refused to speak English. It didn't bother Emerald much anymore, but as a little girl it had proved rather difficult, given that her childish grasp of French had been minimal.

In Cornwall, Cassandra had rented a hovel on the cliff top and dragged Emerald out to view abandoned tin mines every day.

Emerald didn't even want to remember their six months in Ireland. Suffice it to say, she'd never eaten mashed potatoes or cabbage since. 'And how's *your* mother?'

'Doing great. On husband number four, and it looks like he's a keeper. Been eight years, which is a record. Anyway, she's happy enough for now. I'm glad you made it here. I feel bad we didn't keep in touch. We must make sure we don't let that happen again. Right?'

Emerald found herself nodding. It was good to see him again. When she was four years old, Jed and Scarlet had been the cool big brother and sister. They must have been around twelve when Lowri had taken them away, she realised. It had hurt like hell at the time. Scarlet had always been okay with her, but Jed had been a real friend. She hadn't got to see him every week because Lowri and Cain were bitter enemies after their divorce, and then, when Cain split from her own mother, Cassandra had frequently dragged Emerald off to far-flung places as she began her writing career.

But Lowri and Cassandra had got on well, and they'd made the effort to ensure their children kept in touch, which was more than Cain ever had — at least, until their return to America, when it had all gone to pot and Lowri had ceased contact.

She remembered sobbing in her bedroom when she realised Jed and Scarlet wouldn't be visiting again. She'd felt so alone, and Cain was absorbed with his new girlfriend, Sandy — the only one of his children's mothers he'd never married. Marcus had become his new priority.

She remembered the night of her fifth birthday. She'd watched him on the news, threatening Lowri with all sorts for taking his eldest children away, and she'd realised how much he cared about them. Then, she'd heard her mother speaking to him on the phone, demanding to know why he wasn't at the house, visiting their child on her birthday.

'Fine,' she'd heard her snap. 'Stay with your brat if you must. I'm sure the fact that poor little Marcus has a temperature is far more important than your little girl's birthday. Screw you!'

It had occurred to her, for the first time, that she probably wasn't as important to her father as his other children. She'd always hated birthday cake after that.

'So, are you here alone?' Jed glanced around, as if he'd find a man standing in the room wearing a badge proclaiming *Property of Emerald Carmichael* on it.

'Yes. All alone. I prefer it that way. What about you? Are you here with a partner?'

She saw a bleakness in his eyes. 'Nope. Like you, I prefer it that way.'

Liar, she thought. *So, who's broken your heart, Jed?* She felt quite outraged on his behalf. He was a good person. The only decent person in her family. How dare some bitch hurt him?

'Hey,' he said, noticing the place card in front of her, 'how come you're at this table, anyway? You should be nearer the front, with the rest of us.'

Emerald watched as Honey, Teddy, Teddy's best man, his father and stepmother, Cain, Freya, Scarlet, Eden, Marcus, and the little prince in knickerbockers, took their seats at the top table. Twelve people would be sitting there, once Jed took his place. She was well and truly out in the cold. She shrugged. 'I'm fine back here.'

'But it's not right.' Jed looked concerned. 'And how come you're not a bridesmaid?'

'Let's just say, Honey and I never really got on,' said Emerald wryly.

'Look, Scarlet's husband Luke's at the front table. I'll try to get you moved next to him.'

'Really, don't bother. Not on my account. Besides, most of Freya's relatives are sitting up there. I certainly don't want to be swamped by those people — oh!'

She broke off, recognising the old lady with the paisley valise,

40

who was now knocking back a glass of wine. She was wearing a pillbox hat with a veil, and what looked like a dead fox hung around her shoulders. Emerald shuddered. So, the old bat was related to Honey? Why didn't that surprise her? No way did she want to be anywhere near her.

'But I don't like to see you so far back on your own. Honestly, I don't...' Jed's voice trailed off and he shrugged. 'Okay, if you're sure. But look, when this meal and the speeches are over, we'll have a proper catch up, right?'

'Sounds good,' she said, realising she was smiling for the first time in ages. Really smiling, not forcing her mouth into position and trying to look as if she meant it. 'Speak to you later.'

He nodded and headed off to the top table, and Emerald took another sip of wine and tried not to feel abandoned. As the other chairs at her table began to fill up, she fought to suppress the mixture of dread and irritation. She just hoped nobody tried to make conversation with her. She wasn't in the mood.

She heard a scraping as the chair beside hers was pulled out, and glanced up, hoping she wasn't going to be lumbered with one of her father's common relatives. Not that he'd invited many. They didn't fit in with his new, pillar of society image, after all. Her heart leapt, and she found herself smiling for the second time, as she looked up into a pair of dark eyes, which were showing confusion and quite a lot of embarrassment. As she watched, she saw recognition dawn in them.

'We meet again. Seems I'm sitting next to you,' he said gruffly, sitting down and tugging at his shirt collar, as if he were being strangled by it.

'It seems you are.' So, the porter who wasn't a porter was to be her companion for the time being. Maybe it wasn't going to be such an ordeal, after all.

Chapter 4

Eliot felt as if the wedding was dragging on forever. He didn't belong here, and he didn't want to be among all these strangers. He lifted a spoon and prodded suspiciously at his crème brûlée, not sure he fancied trying it. He'd already ploughed his way through four courses. How much did these people eat? And how come they were all so bloody thin? He longed to be at home with the bairns. He wondered what they were doing at that moment. Were they having their tea? Had Beth coped all right?

He felt his stomach tighten at the thought that James Fuller might visit the farm in his absence. Would he really let his wife stay at Wildflower Farm all night without him? He couldn't imagine it, and the idea that his loathed nemesis might dare to enter his home made his skin crawl. He swallowed. Surely, even Fuller wouldn't be stupid enough to risk it? His girls would tell him if he did, and by God he'd make him pay.

He tried to calm down. He was being ridiculous. Beth wouldn't allow it. She wouldn't do that to him.

He glanced across at Eden, sitting calmly at the top table. She looked different, and not like his Eden at all. She looked like that other Eden. The one he'd first met when she'd arrived in Yorkshire, almost eighteen months ago, all blonde highlights, designer clothes and cutting comments. That hadn't been the real Eden, of course. She hadn't even been using her real name.

The real Eden was the woman who wore jeans and baggy jumpers, pulled her fair hair into a ponytail, and rolled up her sleeves to clean out the hen house, deliver lambs, feed the hens. She was the woman who baked cakes and cooked hearty meals for them all, who drove to the supermarket and loaded up the car with the weekly shopping.

The one who occasionally donned a dress and heels to attend meetings at the bank with him, as they tried to sort out their finances, or attended parents' night and took a keen interest in the children's education.

She was the one who'd sat round the kitchen table with him, her brow furrowed, as they listened to the architect's plans for the bunk barn business they'd set their hearts on. The one who laughed and joked with, and made strong cups of tea for, the builders who were converting the barns so that business could take shape.

The one who took his children to school every morning, picked them up every afternoon, and loved them as if they were her own.

The one who gave him so much love that he was full to the brim, and so happy that he had to remind himself that it was allowed, and nothing bad would happen to spoil things.

'I don't blame you. It's dismal, isn't it?'

'What?' He blinked, realising someone was talking to him. His heart sank. That snooty piece he'd met in reception. Trust him to get landed with her again. Telling him to park her bloody car for her!

'The meal. I can see you're not enjoying it. Awful food isn't it? Do you know, this place has a Michelin star?'

'Oh, right. I don't have much truck with them sort of things,' he admitted. 'Truth is, I've never eaten in such a posh place before.'

Her eyes lit up. 'Me neither! And probably never will again.'

Really? Well, that surprised him. Maybe she wasn't as bad as he'd thought. 'I'm waiting for it to be over,' he confessed. 'How long do these bloody things go on for?'

She grinned, and the upward curve of her mouth and twinkle in her eyes transformed her face. He realised she wasn't that old, either. Probably around Eden's age. She may be snooty, but at least she wasn't plastered in makeup and hairspray. He couldn't be doing with all that artificial stuff.

'Too long,' she said. 'Isn't it boring? Weddings are awful. I wish I'd never come.'

'Why did you then?' It wasn't an unreasonable question, he thought. He certainly wouldn't have gone anywhere near the place if Eden wasn't a bridesmaid. She'd asked him to go quite hesitantly, knowing it wasn't his thing, but how could he refuse? He'd been filled with dread at the thought, but he couldn't let her down.

She sighed. 'Duty. You know how it is.'

'Oh, aye,' he agreed. 'Duty's a right bugger sometimes.'

'Emerald.' She held out her hand, and he shook it, surprised. 'Eliot.'

'Pleased to meet you, Eliot. I'm terribly sorry I was so rude to you earlier. I should never have spoken to you like that. I'm afraid I was quite stressed. I've been dreading this day.'

'Well, I suppose... Me an' all, to be truthful.'

She leaned forward and whispered in his ear, 'Do you recognise that old bat on the front table? The one with the dead fox on her shoulders?'

He glanced across at the woman in question and his eyes narrowed. 'Oh, I recognise her, all right. Fancy her being at the wedding.'

'Judging by where she's sitting, I assume she's one of Freya's relatives. Ghastly people.'

'You're not wrong there,' he said with feeling.

She looked at him, surprised. 'You know them? Gosh, you're not related to her, too, are you?'

'I used to be. Sort of. By marriage, at least. Freya was my late wife's cousin, or summat like that.'

'Your *late* wife?' She stared at him a moment, then patted him on the arm. 'Well, I expect she was entirely different to Freya. You'd never have married her otherwise. I'm sorry for your loss.'

He didn't reply. There wasn't a lot he could say without getting into a whole conversation about all the reasons he should never have married Jemima, and he didn't want to talk about it. It was bad enough having to be in the same room as some of his ex-in-laws. He wondered how many of them realised who he was? Not many, if any at all, he supposed, since they'd refused to have anything to do with him. It shouldn't have surprised him that the old lady who'd spurned his help was one of *that* family, a fact he pointed out to Emerald, feeling he should make some effort at conversation, since she was being so friendly. 'Last time I offer to help anyone here out,' he added.

'I don't believe you,' she said. 'You strike me as the sort who'll always offer to help if you can. You're the gallant type.'

She peered up at him, looking quite coy. He wasn't sure how to answer that.

'Not really,' he managed in the end.

'You're far too modest. So, Eliot, if you're not a hotel employee, what do you do?'

'I'm a farmer.'

His eyes widened as she put her hand on his arm and squeezed it.

'Are you really? That's amazing'

Was it? He couldn't see why. And what was she looking at him like that for? All doe-eyed and weird? How much had she had to drink? He realised that her expression had changed, her face hardening.

'Oh hell. Bloody Freya's coming over and she's bringing the brat with her. She's done it on purpose.'

Eliot raised an eyebrow. 'What do you mean? Done what on purpose?'

'Long story. Suffice it to say, Freya thinks she's found another way to make me squirm. She always finds a person's weakness. Well, I won't give her the satisfaction.'

'I need — er, will you excuse me a moment?'

Ignoring her look of disappointment, he stood and made his way out of the room towards the toilets. There was no way he was going to sit there while Freya lorded it over him. He'd only met her once before, but that was enough, and besides, he didn't want to be reminded of the time she'd turned up at Wildflower Farm. It was a painful memory. He'd been shocked and devastated, but even so, he'd been horrible to Eden. It still made him sweat when he thought about how cruel he'd been. He was bloody lucky she'd understood his reasons and forgiven him.

Washing his hands in the luxurious gentlemen's toilets a few minutes later, he surveyed himself in the mirror and pulled a face. He was hot, and he felt stifled with the dratted bow tie on. He ran his finger around his collar again and a fair-haired man, roughly his own age, who was washing his hands at the next basin, grinned at him.

'Feel like you're being throttled?'

It was an American accent, and Eliot found it a lot friendlier than the posh accents everyone at his table had been speaking with.

He relaxed a little and nodded. 'Aye, you could say that.'

They both dried their hands and the man said, 'Maybe we could risk unbuttoning our collars now? I mean, the formal bit's done with, right? The service and the meal.'

'I wish,' said Eliot gloomily. 'We've got all those bloody speeches to listen to now. No doubt that will go on forever and a day. Then more photos, and the cake and then dancing. I mean. Dancing!'

'Guess you're not one for socialising.' The man's blue eyes twinkled with amusement.

'Depends who it's with,' Eliot admitted. 'I'm feeling a bit like a fish out of water, to be truthful.'

'Me, too. My family seems to have a fondness for courting fame. I'd love to attend one of their weddings and find no journalists present. What a treat that would be.'

'Your family?' Eliot studied him. 'You're related to Teddy? Or Honey?'

'Honey's my kid sister,' he said. 'Sorry, I haven't introduced myself.' He held out his hand. 'Jed Carmichael.'

'Ah, right. One of them twins. Eliot Harland.'

'Hi, Eliot. Good to meet you. So, how come you're here? Who blackmailed you into attending?'

He grinned, and Eliot laughed, liking him, despite him being a Carmichael.

'My fiancée's a friend of Honey's.' It felt good to call Eden his fiancée, but he wished he could have said wife. How much longer would it be?

'Great. So, you're obviously familiar with our weird family set-up.'

'Had to take a test, would you believe?' Eliot tutted. 'Eden used to work for Cain, otherwise I wouldn't be anywhere near this place. I'm not one for all this celebrity lark, you see, but Eden's Honey's bridesmaid. Well, one of them. She's the fair-haired one.'

'Yeah, I figured. The one with the reddish hair is my sister, Scarlet.'

'Oh, your twin.' Eliot felt quite pleased with himself for remembering. 'Complicated, your family tree, isn't it?'

'Sure is, and who knows how many more illegitimate kids will crawl out of the woodwork?' He winked. 'My brother's also an usher, and my other sister's at some table somewhere. She and Honey aren't real close. Poor Emerald.'

'Emerald?'

'Yeah. You know her?'

'She's sitting next to me at my table.'

Jed shook his head. 'I don't know who organised the seating plan at this wedding. You're the bridesmaid's fiancée, and Emerald's the bride's sister. I think you should both be at the front table, never mind a load of Freya's relatives who Honey hasn't seen for years. Look, do you mind if I ask you a favour?'

Eliot looked at him in surprise. He barely knew him, and he was asking for favours? 'I suppose so. Depends what it is, mind.'

Jed nodded. 'Sure. It's nothing major. Only, Emerald's here on her own, and she's not had an easy time of it. Between you and me, I think she's kind of been pushed out by Dad and Honey, and she tries to pretend everything's fine and she's not bothered, but I can see she is. Would you keep her company? You know, be nice to her, make sure she's not on her own? Until the speeches are over, and we can all move about freely. I'll come over and talk with her then, and you can go off to be with your fiancée. Deal?'

Eliot shrugged. 'Don't see why not. She's friendly enough.'

'Great. By the way, I like your fiancée. I saw the way she took my nephew under her wing and looked out for him during the service. She's been making him laugh during the meal, too. I'm impressed.'

Eliot beamed with pride. 'She's great with kids. I've got three, and she's amazing with them. They've started to call her Mum these past few months. We didn't ask them to,' he added, 'and they'll always know who their mummy was, but—'

'You're divorced?'

Eliot shook his head. Bloody hell, how had he got into this conversation again? 'Widowed.'

'I'm sorry.'

'Yeah. Thanks.' He felt a hypocrite and changed the subject. 'So, do you reckon we can risk taking these bow ties off then?'

'Maybe not yet. I wouldn't worry, In an hour or so, everyone will be drunk as skunks and half undressed, if past experience is anything to go by.'

'Bloody hell.' He'd be long gone before that happened.

Jed clapped him on the shoulder. 'Come on then, Eliot. Back into the fray. And thanks again for taking care of Emerald. I appreciate it.'

Eliot nodded. Glancing at his watch, he wondered how much longer this would go on for. All he wanted to do was take Eden back to their room, take off that posh dress, and mess up that structured hair. He couldn't wait. Sadly, it seemed he would have to.

****

Emerald was fuming. Freya had been as patronising as expected, rubbing it in that both Marcus and his child had a seat at the top table while she, Cain's *legitimate* child, was relegated to the back of the room.

Freya disliked Emerald because Cain had been caught up in a battle with Cassandra over maintenance payments for Emerald while Freya had been married to him, which she insisted had quite taken the shine off their entire marriage. Never mind his well-publicised affairs and penchant for drugs and alcohol. Emerald was the cause of their divorce, clearly.

Well, everything was her fault, wasn't it? She'd always been aware that her mother felt that if she hadn't been saddled with a child, Cain might not have looked elsewhere. Cassandra was blameless.

With Sandy more-or-less bringing up Marcus alone, Lowri dragging Scarlet and Jed to America, and Cassandra moving Emerald from place to place in a desperate attempt to forget her husband's betrayal and carve a new career for herself, Honey had become their father's main focus in life. His little princess. No one else came close. It was all right for the others. They'd got stepfathers, settled homes, real lives, whereas it seemed to her that she'd not had the chance to be a child. She wasn't Cassandra's daughter. She was luggage.

Freya might still be gloating if the little prince hadn't whined to go to the toilet. At least she had one thing to thank him for.

She tapped her fingers on the table, as an uncomfortable feeling of guilt attacked her. Wasn't she being as unfair to the child as everyone had been to her? It wasn't his fault, after all, that Cain Carmichael had been a rake, any more than it had been hers. Nor, and she hated to admit it, was it Marcus's fault. He hadn't asked to be born into this chaotic family, any more than she had. If truth be told, the blame for all this mess lay at her father's feet. It should be him that felt guilty, but look at him, sitting there at the top table as if butter wouldn't melt.

She glared as she saw him lean over and kiss Honey on the cheek. What a slimeball he was. And he was all over that rude bridesmaid, too. Emerald gaped as he went over to her, put his arm around her and hugged her to him. Honey said something, and they all laughed. How very cosy.

'She's gone then?'

The northern tones made her jump, but not in an unpleasant way. She turned, glad of the distraction, and smiled as Eliot returned to his seat. 'Yes, she has. Not before making me feel like shit, though, but it's only what I'd expected.'

'Don't take any notice of her. You're worth ten of her.'

Emerald felt a bubbling warmth surge through her. His brown eyes were sparkling with a hint of mischief, and his very sensuous lips were smiling at her. He looked terribly sexy. Those dark curls were begging her to run her fingers through them. She realised she was staring at him and tried her best to look away, but he was mesmerising. All right, he had a broad northern accent and probably spent his days milking cows and ploughing fields or something but look at him! She was willing to overlook that thick accent and his obvious lack of social graces. She was willing to overlook anything. He was like Heathcliff without all that weird, cloying jealousy and the psychopathic tendencies.

'Oh, God, here we go,' he muttered, and she blinked, realising the toastmaster was introducing her father and he was about to start his speech.

'This should be fun,' she murmured, picking up the bottle of wine that was on the table and refilling her glass. As she went to top up Eliot's glass, though, he shook his head.

'Not for me, thanks. I've had enough.'

'Enough? You've only had a couple!'

'Aye, well, I need to keep a clear head.' There was something about the way he said it that made her think he was being mischievous again. Like, maybe he wanted to stay sober for a specific reason, and a specific person. She felt an immediate thrill and took a gulp of wine. Maybe this dratted wedding was worth attending, after all.

As her father droned on and on about how Teddy and Honey had first met — as if anyone cared — Emerald was all too aware of Eliot's presence beside her. When would he make his move? Or should she be the one to seduce him? She guessed he was quite old-fashioned and would want to be the one who approached her. That was fine by her. She hoped he'd hurry up and get on with it.

'So, she had Eden over a barrel,' she heard Cain say. What had *she* got to do with anything? She saw her father glance affectionately at Eden, and her stomach knotted with jealousy. Why was he so obsessed with that bloody bridesmaid? Probably shagging her.

'He's going on a bit, isn't he?' she whispered, turning back to Eliot. Surprised to see him listening intently to the speech, she thought he was too well-mannered for his own good, and not at all as she'd thought he was when she first saw him. She felt quite hot with shame when she thought how she'd spoken to him at the reception. What must he have thought of her? It said quite a lot that he didn't harbour a grudge.

'I'm a lucky man,' Cain continued. 'I've got five children of me own, and then Eden arrived on the scene an' all.'

'God, will he ever shut up?' muttered Emerald. What was this? A wedding, or a convention of the Eden Fan Club? He'd be saying she was like a daughter to him next, and that would be the final straw.

'I couldn't be prouder of my kids,' Cain said, beaming widely at his captive audience.

Wonders will never cease, Emerald thought.

'My eldest son is a songwriter and lead guitarist in a great band. They've had two hit albums already, and I know that's just the start.'

Yeah, dream on.

'My eldest daughter is a television star in the States, and I reckon she'll be in the movies before you can say Angelina Jolie.'

Selling popcorn, maybe.

'My youngest son has a very responsible position in the financial sector.'

He works in a sodding bank!

'As for Eden, well she's been like a daughter to me, and she's a brilliant step-mum to three lovely kids and is starting a new business venture of her own.'

My God, he's said it! Like a daughter to him! Look at her, pretending to be embarrassed. Like hell she's embarrassed. She's lapping this up!

'And now, my baby girl has gone and got married to a man with a heart of gold, and together they're doing great work for a brilliant charity in Africa.'

She visited for five days! She's hardly Bob bloody Geldof.

'So, I'd like to raise a toast...'

Emerald froze. *What about me?*

As everyone stood to toast the happy couple, she felt her heart thumping out a protest. He'd forgotten her. His middle daughter hadn't warranted so much as a mention. Jed was looking at her with sympathy written all over his face, and even Scarlet was eyeing her awkwardly. Honey, of course, wasn't remotely concerned. She was exchanging smug grins with Eden. Bloody Eden! She'd warranted a mention. She'd taken Emerald's place in her own father's speech. Why was everyone so besotted with her?

Emerald found herself loathing someone even more than she loathed Honey and Marcus. She had to get out of there. She felt sick and the last thing she wanted was to give anyone the satisfaction of seeing how angry and upset she was. Sod Eliot's masculine pride. She would have to make the first move, after all. She thought going to bed with him might be the only thing that would soothe her wounded soul. There was no harm in trying anyway.

As she turned to speak to him her world stood still. He was looking across at the top table, and there was no disguising the expression of love in his eyes. She turned back and saw Eden returning the look. They were together? That was why he hadn't been drinking. That was what he'd meant. And she'd thought...

As everyone sat down again, and a camera began to flash, Emerald grabbed her clutch bag. Without even offering a word of explanation, she headed out of the room and rushed to the toilets, where she locked herself in a cubicle and leaned against the wall, her throat tight as she fought off tears.

She was a fool. When would she ever learn? No one ever chose her. She was always at the back of the queue, and she had no idea why. She wasn't a bad looking woman, was she? And she was a decent person. At least, she thought she was. Her spiritual tutor, Dove, always reassured her that she had a beautiful aura, and she'd been spiritually cleansed so many times there couldn't possibly be an ounce of bad karma left. So why did no one ever want her? Why did her father prefer Scarlet and Honey to her? Why did he claim to see Eden as his daughter? And how could

Eliot possibly be attracted to someone like Eden Robinson, anyway?

Was it, she wondered, always going to be like this? Feeling like the odd one out? Like *The Little Matchgirl*, peering through the window at all those happy families, while she shivered in the cold outside?

No matter how well she talked the talk, she knew she didn't fit in with the rest of the Carmichaels. Her dress was a sale buy from a discount store. Her hair was only wavy because she usually wore it in plaits. No hair stylist for her. She didn't so much as possess any curling tongs. Even her car was hired.

The truth was, unlike her rich rock star father and affluent siblings, Emerald was broke. Not that Cain would ever believe that, even if she could bring herself to tell him, which she never would. He did, after all, pay her a very generous allowance. How was he supposed to know that she gave it all to her mother?

Cassandra may have immersed herself in the role of bestselling author, but the plain fact was, she barely made any money at all from her books. Her settlement from Cain had been frittered away on research trips to far-flung destinations. Flying first class in aeroplanes, travelling in luxury from airport to rented home, then living in squalor in some cheap hut or croft or yurt.

Emerald had little formal schooling, trying her best to fit in at whatever establishment her mother shoved her into — always supposing they planned to stay more than a couple of months. If their stay was shorter, she never made it as far as school, instead spending her days reading whatever book she'd managed to smuggle into her luggage and cooking and cleaning for her mother.

It was when they'd spent six months in the outskirts of Paris that Emerald had made her first real friend — a free spirit called Dove, who ran a spiritual retreat, Le Colombier, in Provence but was currently visiting her father, who was unwell. She'd seemed to recognise Emerald's loneliness and urged her to study techniques for self-healing and spiritual fulfilment.

Emerald had really taken it to heart and had kept in touch with Dove as best she could after Dove returned to her retreat, and

Cassandra whisked Emerald off to their next location.

Dove had invited her to stay at Le Colombier many times, but Emerald couldn't afford to travel back to France. It had seemed like an impossible dream, until something happened that meant the matter was taken out of her hands, and she was sent to Provence by her frightened mother and handed over into the loving care of Dove and her staff.

Emerald didn't like to remember that time too much. A nervous breakdown, her mother called it. The doctor said she was suffering from severe stress and needed somewhere to recuperate. He suggested counselling, and Emerald had remembered Dove and asked her mother if it would be possible for her to have the air fares.

It was a measure of how worried her mother was that she had handed back a lump sum from Emerald's allowance, and when Dove emailed her and told her there would be no charge for her to stay at the retreat, the matter was settled.

Emerald had found the weeks she spent at Le Colombier so soothing and so wonderful, she wished she could stay there forever. It wasn't so much the crystal therapies, or the chanting, or the aura reading, or the aligning of chakras that helped. It was being accepted by Dove and her friends. It was feeling that she mattered, that her opinion counted for something. For the first time in her life, Emerald didn't feel invisible. She'd been heartbroken to have to leave and head back to reality.

'Why do you stay with your mother?' Dove had demanded, knowing how unhappy Emerald felt. 'You're in your twenties now. You're not a little girl any more. You could use your allowance from your father to go anywhere, do anything. If your mother can't manage without your income, then she'll just have to get a job.'

Emerald had insisted that she couldn't do that to Cassandra, refusing to acknowledge the deeper truth, even to herself. She could, after all, have given her mother the allowance and headed off somewhere else to make her own way in the world, but the truth was, without Cain's money to back her up, she was afraid that she would have no way of supporting herself. She wasn't educated. She didn't understand how to relate to people. She felt worthless.

Her mother may be a whiny, irresponsible sort of woman, but she did care for Emerald in her own way, and at least she was safe. They may have had nothing else, but they had each other. Emerald was too afraid to step outside and discover that real life was even worse. She had little faith in other people. Worse, she had little faith in herself.

She pressed her palms to her eyes and willed back the tears. She didn't cry. She hadn't cried for years and she wasn't going to start now. None of this was her fault. It was all down to her appalling parents.

She straightened and unlocked the cubicle, then walked over to the mirror and surveyed herself critically. It was time she claimed her life back, time she got what she deserved, and she deserved a hell of a lot more than she'd had so far. She would start with Cain. He'd got away with paying her minimal attention all these years. Well, he was going to pay in other ways. She was staking her claim in the Carmichael clan. Things were about to change. She'd make damn sure of it.

Chapter 5

The door closed behind them and they seemed to let out a sigh of relief at the same time. For a moment they looked at each other, then one of them — Eden wasn't entirely sure which — moved, and they were in each other's arms at last.

He feathered her neck with gentle kisses, and she stroked his hair, closing her eyes as she breathed in the spicy citrus smell of his aftershave. Without a word, he shrugged off his jacket and threw it on the chair, then, his hands gentle on her shoulders and his mouth covering hers, he moved forward, taking her with him. She stopped after a few steps, the back of her legs pressing against the bed, and he lowered her gently onto it, still kissing her.

She could feel the hardness of his body pressing down on her, and her breathing quickened. He pulled back a little and she saw the desire in his eyes and moved to kiss him again.

'Your dress,' he murmured.

'Sod the dress.' How could he think about things like that when they had far better things to occupy their minds? 'You promised me my Valentine's Day present and I want it now.'

'You'll only regret it, and I don't want to worry about tearing it, do I?'

She felt a ripple of excitement at his words. 'You can tear it off if you want to.'

'Don't tempt me,' he said, his mouth curving in a wry smile. 'I might not be able to resist if you don't take it off now.'

'You'll have to unzip me,' she said.

He gave her a knowing look, and sat up, pulling her into a sitting position. Inch by inch, he lowered the zip, tracing its path with little kisses down her back.

'Oh, God.' Eden wondered how much more she could stand. Struggling to her feet, she dropped the expensive, designer vintage dress to the floor, and kicked it out of the way. Breathlessly she gazed at Eliot, smoulderingly sexy in black trousers, white shirt, and bow tie which dangled, unfastened, under his collar. She started to remove her basque, but Eliot held out his hand.

'Leave it.' His voice was husky, and she realised he was staring at the expensive lingerie that Honey had bought for her bridesmaids with undisguised lust. She watched his expression as he took in her stockings, and a spark of mischief flared in her. So, the stockings were doing it for him. Well, who'd have thought he'd be so predictable?

She climbed back on the bed and sat with her back against the headboard. As he reached out for her, she took hold of the ends of his bow tie and pulled him towards her. He gave a small sigh as she kissed him lightly.

'So, you like the stockings, do you?' she whispered.

He nodded, and she kissed him again. She could taste wine on his lips. 'And you like the basque?'

'I love the basque,' he admitted, and she pulled his bow tie from under his collar and threw it on the floor.

'Have you missed me?'

'You've no idea how much.'

She was unbuttoning his shirt now and heard his sharp intake of breath as she slid her hand against his chest. His heart pounded beneath her fingers and she began to unfasten his trousers as he practically ripped off his shirt and threw it across the room.

'Is there anything you *don't* like about me?' she breathed into his ear as she slid down the bed, taking him with her.

'Nothing,' he murmured, his lips against hers. 'Absolutely nothing. You're perfect.'

'That's not quite true,' she teased. 'My hair. It's — what was it you called it? — too structured. I think maybe it's time you messed it up a little. Don't you?'

He didn't answer her, but he didn't have to. He was already obeying her orders. Eliot always said he was hers to command.

****

'We'd better hurry. The last thing we need is a search party.' Eden didn't sound as if she wanted to hurry at all.

Eliot gazed at the ceiling and sighed. He could stay in bed all night. He wasn't in the mood to go back downstairs and join the party again. The only company he wanted was lying right beside him, flushed, breathless, and with her hair well and truly messed up. He turned over onto his side and reached out a hand, caressing her face.

'I know you do,' she whispered, as he stared into her eyes.

'I never said owt,' he said, startled.

'But you were thinking it,' she said, smiling. 'And I felt it.'

'Did you?' It mattered to him, and he took her hand and kissed it. 'Do you really know?'

'Of course I do. You have to stop worrying about stuff like that.'

'I'm not great with words,' he said. 'But that doesn't mean I don't feel it. I'd die without you, Eden.'

She laughed. 'No, you wouldn't.'

'Well, maybe not,' he conceded. 'But I reckon I'd want to. I just wish...'

'What? What do you wish?'

'I wish I could give you more.'

She propped herself up on one elbow, her face stern. 'What more could I want, for goodness' sake? I have you, and Libby and Ophelia and George. I have a gorgeous home, and we're about to start a new business which will bring in more income.'

'Aye, and more work for you,' he pointed out.

She stroked his hair. 'You're all damp,' she said, pushing back a tendril from his forehead.

58

'Well, I've worked very hard.'

'You always work hard,' she told him. 'And not only in the bedroom. Seriously, Eliot, you never stop from dawn until dusk on that farm. You do everything you can to keep it going, and all I want to do is help.'

'You already help,' he protested.

'I mean help you make more money, so you can ease off a little and stop worrying. The bunk barn and the cream teas were my idea, remember? It's not hard graft like you do every single day, and it won't kill me.'

'I want you to have nice things,' he muttered. 'Like Honey and Emerald.'

'Emerald? You met Emerald?'

'Aye. I was sitting next to her at the wedding do.'

'God, I'm sorry. What a dismal fate. I never noticed her.'

'Seems most people don't,' he said ruefully, thinking of Jed's words earlier and the shocking omission in Cain's speech. 'Anyway, I want—'

'— Me to have nice things. You've said. What's your definition of nice things? As far as I'm concerned, I have everything I could possibly want or need. Well, apart from one thing.'

'What's that?'

'A wedding ring. We've been engaged for months now. Don't you think it's time we made it official, or is there some doubt in your mind?'

'Don't be daft!' He pulled her to him and held her close, noticing over her shoulder the painting on the wall opposite the bed. What the hell was that about? A few splodges of colour in a posh frame. George did better at nursery. Modern art, he supposed. 'I've got no doubts at all.'

'It's okay if you have,' she assured him. 'I mean, I know you love me, but marriage is a different thing altogether, and after what happened before—'

'You're not like her,' he interrupted. 'And it won't be the same. I want to be married to you, my love, believe me. It's the same old story. Money.'

'It doesn't cost much to get married at a registry office. All we need is the licence and a ring. We could nip into town, get married and be back home in an hour.'

He stared at her, horrified. 'That's not a wedding. We put more thought than that into the weekly shopping list! Bloody hell, you deserve better than that.'

'A registry office is fine,' she said.

'No, it's not! You should have a proper do, with a party and a nice dress.'

She grinned. 'I suppose I could always recycle my bridesmaid dress.'

'No chance. Although,' he added with a gleam in his eye, 'I hope you'll wear that basque and stockings again.'

'Only if you promise not to ravish me before I get the ring on my finger,' she said.

'Can't promise that.' He cupped her face in his hands and she stared down at him, her expression changing. He felt the alteration in their mood and knew where it was going. With a heavy heart he let her go. 'Come on, we said we'd get back to this bloody wedding, and if we don't go now, we'll never do it.'

'You're right,' she said, sighing. 'Good job one of us is so responsible.'

'It's a curse sometimes,' he said, sliding off the bed and hunting around for his trousers. 'God, where is everything? My clothes seem to have disappeared.'

'Jacket's hanging off the chair, bow tie's at the side of the bed, shirt's by the door and trousers are draped over the bedside table. Scattered, yes, but hardly invisible.' She pulled on her dress and went round to his side of the bed so he could fasten the zip. He did so with a great deal more speed and self-control than he'd shown when unfastening it. She stepped into her shoes and rushed over to the mirror, pulling a face as she saw the state of her hair.

'God, you really did mess it up, didn't you?' she said admiringly.

'I aim to please.'

Ten minutes later, they entered the reception room, hand in hand, and were pounced on by Cain. 'Where the hell have you been? You missed the cutting of the cake, and the photographers were looking for you, Eden.'

'Haven't they taken enough pictures yet?' she pleaded. 'I seem to have done nothing all day but pose for the cameras. I don't know how Honey can stand it. She's barely had a moment to herself.'

'The curse of the celebrity wedding,' he acknowledged. 'Mind you, it's saved me a fortune. Can't deny it.'

'How kind of Honey to be so considerate then,' said a voice behind Eliot, and he turned, smiling as he saw Emerald and Jed.

'Hey, Eliot,' said Jed. 'Are you going to formally introduce me to your wife?'

'She's not his wife,' snapped Emerald.

'Oh, sure, I mean fiancée.' Jed held out his hand to Eden.

'Eden, this is Jed Carmichael,' said Eliot. 'Jed, this is my fiancée, Eden.'

Jed kissed the back of Eden's hand and Eliot tried not to feel offended. They were a funny lot, Americans. Very friendly. Jed didn't mean anything by it.

'Pleased to meet you, Eden. I've been hearing loads about you from Honey and Dad.'

'Really? Well, thanks, I think. Nice to meet you, too. I've heard a lot about you over the years.'

'I'll bet.' Jed glanced at Emerald, who looked distinctly cool. 'Emerald, have you met Eden?'

'Oh, yes. We've met,' Emerald confirmed. She glanced over at Eliot and fixed her big blue eyes on him. 'And I've certainly met Eliot, haven't I? You're a very lucky lady, Eden. He's an absolute gentleman. Quite a charmer.'

'Is he? I mean, yes he is.' Eden looked a bit bewildered, but not as bewildered as Eliot felt. A charmer? He'd never been called that before. Was she taking the mickey, or what?

'So, when are you two getting married?' Jed asked. 'Or has today put you off weddings for good?'

Eliot shuffled uncomfortably. It was a sore subject, and not one he wished to discuss in front of this bunch of people who'd probably never known what it was to be skint. God, he wished he could win the lottery. He didn't need or want a fortune. Just enough to give Eden the wedding of her dreams. Shame he didn't have enough money to buy a ticket. He raised his eyes to hers as she said, 'Oh, we'll get around to it soon enough. Don't worry about that. Can't wait.'

'Weddings are so expensive, though, aren't they?' said Emerald, with unnerving perception. 'Unless, of course, you manage to con some stupid magazine into paying for it. Then there's the honeymoon.' She smiled. 'Where do you have in mind for *your* honeymoon?'

Eliot squirmed. The rate things were going, they'd be lucky to manage a wet weekend in Filey. 'Well, er, we haven't really—'

'Wherever it is, you don't have to worry about it,' boomed Cain. 'In fact, you don't have to worry about anything. I was going to tell you tomorrow before you left, but since you've brought the subject up, I may as well tell you now.'

'Tell us what?' Eden looked puzzled, and Eliot held his breath, wondering what Cain was up to.

'Your wedding! It's on me, every penny of it. No, I won't hear any arguments,' he added, holding up his hands as they started to protest. 'Listen, I meant every word I said in that speech, Eden. You're family. It's a father's duty to pay for his daughter's wedding and I missed out every time. Scarlet's stepfather paid for her do. *All the Goss* paid for Honey's. And as for Emerald—' he cast a dismissive glance in her direction, 'well, there's no one on the horizon for her anyway, so I don't think I'll have to worry about that for a good while.'

Emerald was apparently too shocked to reply, judging by the look on her face, and Eliot felt a rush of indignation for her.

'I reckon you should save your money for your own daughter, Cain,' he said. 'Happen there's someone out there who'll sweep her off her feet before you know it. She's a right bonny lass, and someone will see it soon enough.'

He was rewarded for his efforts in gallantry with a stunned look from Eden and a grateful smile from Emerald.

'Besides,' he continued, as Jed clapped him on the back in evident approval, 'you said yourself that it's supposed to be the bride's dad who pays for the wedding. If me and Eden need any help, I'm sure her dad will want to be the one to provide it.'

Not that he'd ever ask. Hell would freeze over before he went cap in hand to anyone to pay for his own wedding.

'Well, that's as may be,' conceded Cain, 'but come on, we all know Eden's dad ain't got that kind of dosh. No offence, darls. And you want her to have a great day, don't you? I mean, you want the best for her, right? I won't interfere if that's what you're thinking. I want her to have the wedding of her dreams 'cos I happen to think she deserves it. That's all. But sorry if I've wound you up, mate, or overstepped the mark.'

Eliot's heart sank. What could he say to that, really? Cain was right. Eden's father was a smashing bloke, and the two of them got on well, but he was no better off financially than Eliot himself. In fact, he was probably worse off. And Eden did deserve a dream wedding. He'd said so himself. How could he deny her that? Besides, he had his own idea of how their wedding should be, and he didn't have a cat in hell's chance of funding it.

He took a deep breath. 'That's good of you, Cain. Thank you.'

Cain looked delighted. 'So, you agree?'

Eliot felt sick. 'Aye. I agree.'

He couldn't look at Eden, hoping she wouldn't feel he'd let her down in any way. He knew he should be able to pay for it himself, but the fact was, he would never be able to afford to buy her a beautiful wedding gown or pay for a proper party. If they waited for him to save up, they'd be getting married from a nursing home.

Cain clapped him on the shoulder, then hugged Eden, who was looking dumbfounded. Emerald watched them, her eyes narrowed, and Eliot murmured to her, 'Try not to take it to heart. You'll show him, one day.'

Emerald nodded. 'You're so right. I'll show them all.'

As Cain turned back to her, she tapped him on the arm. 'Now that you've got that sorted, Daddy, I'd rather like a word with you. You see, I have something quite important that I need to discuss.'

'Can't it wait until tomorrow?' he pleaded. 'This is a special day, after all.'

Eliot didn't hear her reply. He was too busy listening to Jed telling Eden all about America, and how it was such a beautiful country and the perfect destination for a honeymoon. His heart seemed to sink into his shoes. He'd really gone and done it now. He was back in the clutches of the Carmichaels yet again, and it was all his own fault.

Chapter 6

About an hour later, Eliot managed to get Eden on her own for all of five minutes.

'Can we talk?'

He didn't want to upset her, and he certainly didn't want to postpone their wedding for any longer than was strictly necessary, but the more he thought about it, the more he worried exactly what sort of glamorous event Cain had in mind for them.

Of course, he wanted Eden to have a wedding she could be proud of, but what if Cain took it to extremes? What if he decided their wedding would be every bit as expensive and grand as Honey's own? Eliot didn't think he could stand it. Suddenly, a quick trip to the registry office and a wet weekend in Filey wasn't sounding so bad.

'Of course. What is it?' She leaned towards him, her eyes bright from all the glasses of wine and champagne she'd consumed, her cheeks flushed, her lips parted in a teasing invitation. 'I'm all yours.'

'Aye, I should hope so.' He wondered how to broach the subject. 'Thing is—'

'Not long now,' she whispered in his ear. 'Then you can take me upstairs and we can start practising for our wedding night.'

Eliot swallowed. 'Aye, that'd be—'

'Not that you need any practice.' She undid the bow tie that he'd not long since managed to do up again and feathered his lips with kisses. 'You know exactly what you're doing, don't you?'

He caught hold of her hands and tried to concentrate on the matter in hand, although, God knows, it was a difficult task. He was half-tempted to drag her up the stairs right there and then, but he had to keep a clear head. It didn't look as if *she* had.

'I'm a bit worried, my love. About what Cain said.'

She frowned. 'Cain?'

'About the wedding,' he said patiently. 'I think it's grand of him to offer to pay for it, 'course I do, but I want to know what it's going to cost us.'

'Nothing! He said—'

'I mean, in terms of handing over control. Whose wedding is this really going to be?'

'Ours, silly.' She giggled. 'Nothing too posh, don't worry. A fabulous country house, peacocks on the lawn, ice sculptures, Jamie Oliver doing the catering, and Michael Bublé serenading us as we sign the register.'

Eliot's face must have shown his horror because she let out a peal of laughter. 'I'm joking!'

'Oh, right.' He forced himself to smile. 'Well, if you're happy about it.'

For the first time her expression showed doubt. 'Aren't you? Really? I thought—'

'Eden, there you are. Sorry, chick, but we've got work to do.' Cain caught hold of her hand and nodded towards the kitchen. 'Got to go in there.'

'The kitchen?' Eliot frowned. 'What for?'

Teddy grinned. 'The journalists want to get a picture of the wedding party thanking the staff. You know, compliments to the chef and all that jazz.'

'Like a flaming royal line-up,' Cain muttered. '*And what do you do?*' He squeaked, in a terrible impersonation of the Queen, holding out his hand to shake that of an imaginary waitress or pot-washer. '*How absolutely fascinating. Thank you so much for all your hard work.*'

He shook his head. 'Come on, let's get it over with.'

He clapped Eliot on the shoulder. 'You wanna thank your lucky stars that you're not part of this group. I tell you, there's no such thing as a free lunch and that's a fact. Always a price to pay.'

Which was very much what Eliot was afraid of.

Eden was scrutinising him. 'Are you okay? We can talk when I get back.'

He forced a smile. 'It's fine. No worries. You do what you have to do.'

She hesitated, but Cain grabbed hold of her arm and steered her towards the kitchen door before she could even begin to protest.

Eliot sighed and headed to the bar. He could use a drink. He decided, though, to stick to lemonade. One of them, he thought wryly, should be sober, and Eden had evidently had his share of alcohol as well as her own. Besides, he didn't want drink to impair his senses.

He smiled to himself, worries about the wedding banished for the night. He'd think about all that stuff later. Fact was, they were in a hotel, with a posh room and an enormous bed, and no kids to listen out for or worry about. Him and Eden, with a whole night ahead of them.

He carried his drink over to the table, noting that Emerald had left the room. She must have had enough of her father's behaviour and called it a night. He couldn't blame her for that. He felt highly indignant on her behalf when he thought about Cain missing her out of the speech like that. He couldn't, for the life of him, imagine a time when such things happened between himself and either of his own daughters. He adored Libby and Ophelia and the thought of pushing one of them out of his life like that — it was unthinkable.

Then again, he realised, with a sudden lurch of his stomach, who could say they would feel the same? If they ever found out the truth about what had happened between himself and their mother, the truth about the day she died, the truth about George...

He gulped down some lemonade and tried not to think about the future. Eden was always telling him he worried too much and happen she were right. There was time enough for all that in years to come. Right now, there was only tonight.

He glanced over at the kitchen door, tutting in impatience.

They'd been ages. He tried to imagine the scenario as the poor buggers in the kitchen lined up to have their hands shook by Cain, Rex, and their families. How galling to be so patronised by two blokes in their sixties, with embarrassing hairdos and kohl-rimmed eyes. As if the staff hadn't had enough to put up with today!

At least Eden would know what to say, and she'd probably be genuinely interested. She'd been to catering college herself, and she'd worked in a variety of kitchens before landing up in The Red Lion, where she'd bumped into Honey one fateful night and changed the entire course of her life.

He shook his head, marvelling at how one thing led to another. If Eden hadn't taken that awful job at the pub, she would never have gone to work for Cain, never been forced to go to Skimmerdale by the scheming Honey, never have met him. It didn't bear thinking about.

He drained the last of his lemonade and put the glass down, his fingers drumming the table. This was taking forever. He longed for bed and he wanted to get there before he got tired.

The kitchen door swung open and the journalists strode out, followed by Honey, Teddy, and their wedding party. He craned his neck, searching for Eden. She was hurrying, head down. Cain said something to her, but she didn't respond. Instead, Eliot saw her lift her head and scan the room for him.

He waved, and she caught sight of him and rushed over to the table.

'Are you all right, my love? You look pale.' He put his arm around her, concerned.

'I'm fine. I think it was the heat in the kitchen, combined with all the wine I've had. I'm all hot and bothered.' She didn't look hot. In fact, he could have sworn he'd seen her shiver as she reached his side.

'Shall we go to bed?' he said, taking her hand.

'Yes please,' she murmured. 'Let's get out of here.'

****

The morning brought grey skies and the promise of rain.

'I hate British weather,' said Scarlet, shivering and pulling her jacket tighter around her body, as she stood on the driveway of Chessingborough House, waiting for her taxi.

'We're used to sunshine and warmth, that's the trouble. We've been spoilt,' Luke said, hugging her close and smiling. 'Soon be back home, baby.'

'Can't wait,' she admitted. She glanced at Jed. 'Are you sure you won't come back with us? I know what you said, but we don't belong here. Not any more. Your life's back in the States. Can't you reconsider? For me.'

Jed shook his head. 'I'm sorry, Scarlet, but no. You know how I feel, and besides, I've already told Dad I'll be staying with him for a while.'

'Did you tell him why?'

When he pulled a face, she sucked in her cheeks. 'Good luck with that,' she said at last. 'You know what he's like. He won't be happy.'

'It's my life, not his,' Jed said. 'Anyway, here's your cab. You've got everything?'

'Everything except my brother,' she said. 'I'll miss you.'

'I'll miss you, too.' He pulled her into a warm embrace, and she kissed his cheek, tears brimming in her eyes. 'Take care of her, Luke, okay?'

'No worries on that score,' his brother-in-law promised, as they shook hands.

They loaded their bags into the trunk and climbed into the back seat of the cab. Jed smiled and nodded as they waved. He raised his hand in return, and the car swept down the drive. He turned and went back into the hotel to pack. It was done. Now he had to explain everything to his father. But he rather thought he'd wait until he was at the old man's home. He didn't want to get landed with a huge bill when Cain started throwing things.

****

'For God's sake, Emerald, the ink ain't even dry on the marriage

69

licence yet,' snapped Cain. 'Can't I have me breakfast in peace before you start on at me again?'

'No. You said we'd talk tomorrow. Well, it's tomorrow now, and I want to talk.'

'Talk about what? What are you after?'

'Who says I'm after anything?'

'When a woman tells me we need to talk, she's *always* after sumfink, and it's never cheap. So, if it's all the same to you, I'd rather let me bacon and eggs digest first. I ain't brought me Gaviscon with me. Big mistake.'

Emerald tutted. 'Bet you'd talk if it were Honey asking.' *Not to mention that bitch, Eden.*

'Not this again.' He shook his head. 'You've got to get over your obsession about Honey. She's your baby sister. Why can't you be nice to her for once? What's she ever done to you?'

'Let's not pull on that string,' she said. She sat at the table opposite him and watched in disgust as he shovelled half a sausage into his mouth. No wonder he drank antacid by the bucketful. 'I take it the happy couple got off all right?'

'Oh, yeah,' he said, and she winced. She hated it when people talked with their mouths full. He was so vulgar. She couldn't imagine what her mother had ever seen in him. 'They should be arriving at the airport about now.'

'Hmm. How lovely for them. So, if—' she broke off at a tap on the door.

Jed peered round. 'Am I okay to come in? Hi, Emerald!' He smiled at her, and she relaxed a little. A friendly face at last. 'Hey, Dad. I'm packed and ready to leave when you are.'

'Great.' Cain mopped up the last bit of egg, sausage and mushroom on his plate and gulped them down. Emerald watched in horrified fascination as a stream of yolk dripped down his chin. There was no doubt in her mind that her father had an overactive Svadhishana. His second chakra was clearly spinning out of control, leading to gluttony and addiction. Given his drug-addicted, sex-addicted past she shouldn't be surprised. He'd clearly replaced his previous addictions with a dependency on food. It was quite sad really.

'You're going back to his place?' she queried. 'Are you staying long?'

'Well, I...' Jed shrugged, looking awkward. 'I'm not sure what my plans are yet.'

'Be good to have you. Reckon you've earned a rest before your next tour starts.' Cain dabbed his chin with a napkin, leaned back in his chair, and patted his stomach in satisfaction. 'Great breakfast that. Sure you don't want any?'

'I don't think so,' she said, her lip curling. 'I had orange juice and a lightly boiled egg. That's enough for me.' She felt no need to mention the bowl of cornflakes, three rounds of toast and marmalade, and two pain au chocolats she'd also consumed. She wouldn't want anyone to think *her* second chakra was overactive. At least she paused for breath between mouthfuls of food.

'You don't eat much, do you?' he mused. 'Funny you ain't as skinny as a whippet, but you're quite meaty, ain't you?'

Meaty! She'd been called curvy, womanly and shapely before, but meaty! Bloody hell, that was all she needed to hear. Just because Honey looked like a praying mantis.

She scowled. 'Right, now you've finished stuffing your face, can we have that talk at last?'

He groaned. 'Not now. I'm proper bloated. Later, okay?'

'When later? You'll be going home soon. I'm not going to drop this, you know. I need to get something sorted.'

'Hey, Emerald, why don't you come back to Dad's house with me? I'm gonna be staying there a while, and Dad's got plenty of spare rooms. It would be great if we stayed there together. Right, Dad?'

Jed looked appealingly at his father, who stared back like a rabbit looking down the barrel of a gun.

Emerald waited, knowing full well that her father felt trapped. She could make it easy for him. Tell him she wasn't going back to the house, that she was going home instead. But where was her home, anyway? She didn't want to go back to the grotty coastal croft her mother had rented. It might as well have been in Alaska it was so remote and cold. And she wasn't going to let her father get away with his mistreatment of her any longer.

At least his house was comfortable and warm, and had all mod cons, with hot water, and toilets that were guaranteed to flush. Besides, Jed would be there, and it would be nice to see more of him. The car hire firm was a national one. She could drop her hire car off at a depot round here, rather than back in Scotland. Sod it, she thought. Why not?

She smiled at Jed then turned her gaze on her beleaguered father. 'What a fantastic idea. I'll go and pack right now. Meet you in reception in half an hour!'

As she headed out of his room, she heard a distinct groan behind her. Somehow, she just knew it wasn't down to Cain overindulging on the bacon and eggs.

****

Eliot felt like blasting the car horn. It was taking forever for Eden to say goodbye to everyone. He couldn't imagine why. He'd given them all a brief nod, grabbed the bags and practically run to the Land Rover. She seemed to be hugging and kissing everyone.

He frowned as Jed wrapped his arms around her and pulled her into a hug. Okay, he was a nice bloke, but he barely knew Eden. He was a bit — over-familiar.

Emerald didn't look so friendly, that was for sure. She had her arms folded, and even Eliot, who was no expert in body language, could tell she was giving Eden back-off signals. Not that Eden would want a hug from Emerald, anyway. She didn't seem to like her much, which was odd. He felt sorry for her. She seemed to be the black sheep of the Carmichael family, poor bugger.

Jed was chatting to Eden now. Clearly, he was telling her something amusing, because she threw back her head and laughed, as did Cain. Emerald glanced over to the car and gave him a sympathetic look, and he managed a smile because she was on the outside, like him. She gave him a small wave, and, awkwardly, he waved back. She continued to watch him, and he began to feel hot and a bit embarrassed. He turned his head, staring straight ahead, and prayed Eden would hurry up.

Finally, the passenger door opened, and she climbed in.

'About bloody time,' he growled, noting with relief that the Carmichaels had turned and headed back into the hotel. 'Thought you were never coming.'

She laughed, dropped her handbag onto the back seat, then fastened her seatbelt. 'Don't be so grumpy.'

He started the engine and, at last, they were leaving Chessingborough House behind.

'What was so funny?' he asked, cursing himself as soon as the words left his lips. Evidently, Jed had thoroughly entertained her. He'd like to know how.

'Sorry?' She was rummaging in the glove compartment, looking for a CD, and pulled an old movie soundtrack out before glancing across at him.

'Jed. Must've said summat hilarious, judging by the way you laughed.'

She raised an eyebrow. 'Yes, he did, actually. He was telling me about Lady Penrose and her gift for Honey and Teddy.'

'Huh?'

'You'll be interested in this. Remember that old lady you told me about? The one who was carrying that valise and wouldn't let you help her with it?'

He nodded. 'Aye. What about her?'

'Turns out she's Honey's maternal great aunt, and she was carrying her wedding present to the happy couple in that valise. She gave it to them last night while we were, er, busy, and Honey's horrified.'

'What was it?' He couldn't deny his curiosity was piqued. It had to be something pretty valuable, given the way the old woman guarded the bag. Probably some hideous but priceless vase, or something.

'Montague.'

'What's a Montague?' He was baffled, but his bewilderment turned to irritation when she burst out laughing again. 'Have I said summat funny?'

'No, no. But Montague is — was — her cat. A pure white

73

Persian. She had him stuffed, and she wanted to pass him onto Honey and Teddy to care for to make sure he still had a home after she's gone. Can you imagine Honey's face!'

'Oh, right. Yeah, side-splitting.'

She gave him a sideways glance. 'What's up with you? You seem narked, for some reason.'

'Must be my turn.'

He hadn't meant to sound so snappy but, truthfully, he was confused and — if he was being really honest with himself — worried. Something had gone wrong between him and Eden last night, and he didn't understand what.

Maybe it was his fault, he mused. Maybe he expected too much, took things for granted. Yet, she'd seemed as keen as him to make the most of their night together away from the children; at one point, she'd practically been pulling him by the hand towards the stairs and it was him who'd had to remind her that she was still required at the party. Yet, when they'd finally been able to say goodnight and had slipped away to their room, she'd been tense and not in the mood for making love. He'd stared at her, amazed, as she told him she wasn't feeling up to it and needed to sleep as it had been a long day.

Of course, she *had* had a long day, and she'd had quite a few glasses of wine, too. He'd offered to get her some paracetamol from the car, but she'd denied having a headache. Said she was tired. She'd got into bed and then, the real killer, she'd turned her back on him.

Eden never turned her back on him in bed, ever. Even if they'd been arguing, bed was always the place they put things right. Whichever one of them was in the wrong, it was all put behind them when they climbed between those sheets. He admitted, he was always the last to give in, being a moody bugger when all was said and done and having far too much pride for his own good, but she'd changed him a lot. He could guarantee that, no matter what had gone on during the day, she would reach for him in bed and he would — grudgingly sometimes, admittedly — wrap his arms around her in response. The tension would ebb away from them both within seconds. They always found their way back to each other. Always.

Yet last night, she'd seemed further away from him than she'd ever been, and he had no idea what he'd done.

'What do you mean by that?' she said.

'Nowt. Forget it.' At least, he thought grumpily, Jed could bring a smile to her face, even if he couldn't.

'Is this about last night?' She folded her arms, staring out of the window. 'I'm sorry. I was out of sorts. Forgive me?'

'There's nowt to forgive,' he said, meaning it. She'd done nothing wrong. It wasn't her fault that he was paranoid, and how was she to know that the overwhelming feeling of rejection he'd experienced, lying there, staring at her back, had kept him awake for hours? It had brought back bitter memories of his marriage to Jemima, but that had nothing to do with Eden. 'Ignore me. I'm being daft.'

She turned back to him. 'Are you sure? Because you can say, you know.'

He stared hard at the road ahead, feeling stupid. How could he explain to her? How to tell her that being around people like the Carmichaels made him feel awkward, self-conscious and inferior? How to make her understand that, with Cain now paying for their wedding, he felt as if he'd let her down. That he wasn't good enough for her. And with Jed making such easy conversation with her and making her laugh, it reminded him that he was useless at explaining himself to her.

How long before she tired of him? When would the endless round of working on the farm and caring for children stop being enough for her? What if she needed more than he could ever give her? What if... He swallowed. What if Daisy was right? Was he making the same mistake all over again?

Something had gone wrong last night, he could feel it. Something had happened. He'd lain awake, wracking his brains to figure out what. The only thing he could put it down to was when he'd tried to broach the subject of the wedding with her. Things had been fine between them before that, so she must have been upset with him, worried that he was backing out of the deal. There was nothing else he could think of. He'd done everything he could, over breakfast, to assure her that he was looking forward to the wedding and that he was grateful to Cain for offering to pay. She could have whatever she wanted now, and Eliot was glad of it. He'd been so keen to reassure her he'd almost convinced himself.

'Eliot?' She squeezed his leg, and he gave her an apologetic smile.

'Just tired. Hoping them scans give us good news tomorrow. And looking forward to seeing the bairns, of course. I've missed them.'

'Me, too. It will be so good to be home,' she said, leaning back in her seat. 'To be honest, I can't wait to get away from this place.'

He changed gear and accelerated. Everything was fine. He had to stop being so paranoid. He was enough. Wildflower Farm was enough. He was being stupid.

Chapter 7

The front door banged.

'Did you get the yow?' Eden called, as she ran the iron along one of Eliot's shirt sleeves. He'd taken the quad bike, with the trailer attached, to collect one of his strays from a fold on the moors, following a call from a neighbouring farmer who had found her among his own flock.

Her welcoming smile died when he entered the kitchen and she saw the look on his face. 'What's up?'

'Daisy's birthday card.' Eliot slapped an envelope on the table, sank into the chair and shook his head. 'Found it on't doormat. She's sent it back unopened. Can't believe it.'

Eden put down the iron, her eyes warm with sympathy, knowing he would feel guilty.

'She's still raw, Eliot. She's been through a tough time. Give her some space and things will get better.'

'Will it?' He gave her a stricken look. 'Maybe, if I'd been more supportive, all this need never have happened. She could have stayed at Crowscar if I'd helped more. What if this isn't what she wants? What if this is Tom pushing her?'

Eden sighed, switched off the iron, and walked over to where he sat at the kitchen table, his head in his hands. She began to massage his shoulders, feeling the knots of tension under his shirt.

'He's her big brother and he loves her. I'm sure he wouldn't force her to do anything she didn't want to do. And, besides, she needed this. Her dad's being cared for properly in that nursing home, and she's close enough to visit him without having to take care of him herself. She must be exhausted. Leeds may not be the ideal place for someone like Daisy, but it will give her a chance to decide what she wants to do next. It might do her the world of good, and it will be nice for her to get to know Tom all over again. She hasn't seen much of him for years, has she?'

'I know, I know.' He caught hold of her hand. 'But if I'd been kinder...'

His voice trailed off, and Eden moved round and sat on his knee. 'If you'd been kinder, it would actually have been cruel. You know how Daisy feels about you. If you hadn't made it plain to her that there could never be anything between you, she'd have hung around, wasting her life, waiting for something that would never happen. At least, this way, she gets the chance to move on, make a new life. You mustn't blame yourself.'

He gazed at her through troubled eyes. 'I feel bad for her.'

'Of course you do, because you're a good man. But you can't help the fact that she loved you, and you didn't love her in the same way.'

'She's bin through so much.' His voice was harsh, and Eden stroked his face, knowing that no matter how many times she tried to make him feel better, he would always feel responsible for Daisy.

She was his best friend's kid sister, and had loved Eliot since she was a child, staying loyal even when he married Jemima, and flying to his side when his wife was killed in a car accident, when George was only four weeks old. Without Daisy, Eliot wouldn't have been able to manage with the farm and three young children, but that didn't mean he had to live a lie, did it? He wasn't responsible for her feelings, and he'd never led her on, made her believe there could be anything between them but friendship.

Eden felt sorry for her, too, especially since her father had become unwell and prone to falls. She knew Daisy had cared for him the best she could, until it became too much, and she'd reluctantly agreed with her brother that a nursing home was the only safe option. Since Tom lived in Leeds, and Daisy couldn't manage Crowscar Farm alone, even if she'd wanted to, it seemed to make sense to put their father in a nursing home in the city, and for Daisy to stay with Tom.

Eliot had offered to help her sell off the stock, even keep the farm going if she wished, but she'd rebuffed all his offers of help. Instead, she'd sold off the livestock, locked up the farm and left without a word of goodbye. Since she'd discovered his feelings for Eden, she wanted nothing more to do with him. At least she still had her brother. Eden hoped she would find happiness, for her own sake, and for Eliot's. He had enough guilt buried within him.

'Tom should have come back here years ago,' he burst out. 'Can't believe he left her to deal with their dad by herself. She needed his support. When did he get so selfish?'

'You said he didn't get on with his father; that the old man treated him badly.'

'He did, but so what? That were nowt fresh. He treated every bugger badly, including Daisy. She still stood by him, didn't she? It was all right for Tom, making his new start in Leeds. How could he not care what he'd left behind? Why didn't he hate himself for leaving her to cope with the old man all by herself? If she'd been my sister, I'd have felt that bad for leaving her with him, I'd have come straight back and taken everything off her shoulders, soon as I heard he was ill. He abandoned her to cope alone. Why didn't she let me help her, for God's sake?'

His voice had risen, and she wrapped her arms around him and kissed his forehead. 'Maybe this is his way of trying to make it up to her — inviting her to stay with him, I mean. What will happen to Crowscar Farm now?'

'Not much left of it,' he said. 'All the stock's been sold on. It's still the old man's, after all. He may be frail, but he's not lost his marbles. Can't see him agreeing to it being sold, any road. Afterwards, when he's gone, they may sell it or even rent it out, I suppose. Maybe,' he added hopefully, 'Daisy will come back and farm it herself. I could help her set it up. Least I can do.'

'You have to stop this,' she said.

'Stop what?'

'This guilt thing you've got going on. You seem to feel responsible for everyone and everything. Look, Daisy is a grown woman, and if she needed help — I mean, really needed help — she'd ask for it. She knows you'd give it to her. You've made that very plain. If she doesn't want to ask you for that help, that's her decision. Stop trying to carry everyone's burdens for them.'

'I don't!'

'Yes, you do. Look how long you've struggled with Jemima's death, even though it was an accident. And then you feel guilty about George, because he's not yours, as if that was your fault!'

'Well, how's he going to feel about it when I have to tell him? And then there's the girls. How will they react?'

'Stop worrying about it. It's a long way off before we have to tell him, and I'm sure all the children will realise how much you love them and how much you sacrificed to keep them all together, safe and happy. Then there's me.'

'You?'

'Don't deny it. You feel guilty about me starting up this new business. Like I'm going to be some sort of wage slave or something.'

'Well, it will be bloody hard work, won't it?' He glanced towards the window, as if he could see the builders, plumbers and electricians who were out there, putting the finishing touches to the barn conversions. In a few days, they'd be leaving, once the work had been inspected and signed off. Eden intended to start work on the painting, and she'd already ordered the bunks and kitchen equipment. He wasn't sure she realised what a big project she was taking on.

'I've never minded hard work, Eliot. I trained to be a chef, remember? I worked in the kitchen of The Red Lion for years, and believe me, working for someone like Gavin was hardly a walk in the park. Not to mention all the years I worked for Cain and Honey. Being here, building something for our family, isn't work. It's a privilege, and I can't wait to get started.'

He sighed and rested his head on her chest. 'What did I ever do to deserve you?'

'Guess you got lucky.' She laughed and hooked her finger under his chin, lifting his face to hers. 'So, no more guilt trips, okay? Daisy might love life in Leeds and have a far better time than she ever had at the farm, with her father breathing down her neck. So, let her get on with it and stop fretting. Agreed?'

He nodded. 'Agreed.'

She shook her head, knowing that he wouldn't be able to help himself. Well, maybe she had some news that would distract him for a little while, at least.

'There's something I have to tell you,' she said, hesitantly. 'I'm not sure how you're going to react.'

'Oh, hell, what now?' He shrugged. 'Go on, then. You'd best tell me and get it over with.'

'It's Cain,' she said. 'He's coming up to see us, and he's bringing Jed and Emerald with him.'

'What!' Eliot looked horrified. 'What the hell for?'

She knew how he felt. They'd only just got a bit of normality back in their lives after months of upheaval — workmen, council officials, not to mention the huge lorries that had regularly pulled into the farmyard, as a new access road was constructed along the side of the beck. It led to the back of the barns, where a brand-new car park now waited for its first occupants. It had been a nightmare, and had caused a great deal of mess, noise and frustration — particularly for the children who no longer had the freedom to run outside as they wished. They were closely guarded due to the number of strangers around, as well as the traffic.

Eliot was adamant that if he'd known how bad it was going to get, he'd never have started the damn project. Now, at last, they were through the other side and they'd been so looking forward to peace and quiet again. All they needed were more intruders — and Carmichaels at that. Hardly Eliot's favourite people.

'He wants to discuss the wedding, he said.' Eden frowned, feeling it was all a bit odd. When she'd got the phone call, it had thrown her. She'd assumed Cain would simply post them a cheque towards the cost, but to her surprise, he announced he was visiting the farm to start making plans. She couldn't say she was happy about it, and the fact that he was bringing Jed and Emerald with him was disturbing, to say the least. Jed was okay, but Emerald was... Well, she was Emerald.

Eden had felt sorry for her, and still did in a way. On the other hand, she couldn't help feeling that it was no wonder Honey and Cain weren't exactly close to her. She was quite a difficult person to like.

She wished she could tell Cain not to bother, that she didn't need his help and, as much as she was grateful for, and touched by, the generous offer, she only wanted a simple, quiet wedding. Something for her and Eliot and the children, and maybe her parents and Beth. She didn't need a fancy wedding dress, or a big party, or a huge cake.

She'd longed to say that at the hotel, but something in Eliot's face had stopped her. She knew he wanted her to have those things. It seemed to matter to him, for some reason, and she knew he wouldn't be able to afford a big wedding for years. He didn't need that pressure on top of everything else, so she'd agreed, but it had been with a heavy heart.

She'd kind of hoped that Eliot would change his mind and tell her they'd have to settle for a simple wedding after all, but he hadn't. On the contrary, he'd gone on and on about it the following morning at the hotel, telling her what a great idea he thought it was, and how kind of Cain to step up like that. She couldn't let him down when it had clearly been a huge relief to him, and, God knows, he had enough to worry about.

'I hope he doesn't think he's taking charge,' she added. 'It may be his cheque book, but it's our wedding after all.'

Eliot narrowed his eyes. 'But you're looking forward to it? The wedding, I mean?'

'Of course!' It wasn't an outright lie, she thought. She *was* looking forward to being Mrs Harland at last. It was what they'd have to endure to finally be husband and wife that worried her. 'I'll give Cain's credit card a good battering and pick the loveliest dress in Yorkshire.'

He smiled. 'You do that. Well, I suppose if they're coming, there's nowt we can do about it. But God knows where they're going to sleep.'

'Oh, don't worry about that,' she reassured him. 'They've booked rooms in The Paradise Hotel in Kirkby Skimmer from Saturday. They're not staying in the farmhouse.'

'Thank God for that,' he said. 'Happen I'll be out and about in the fields and won't see them at all.'

'Nice try,' she said, laughing. 'But you're going to have to be involved, too. You *are* the groom, after all.'

'S'pose so.' He grinned. 'You're looking much happier today. Everything okay?'

She flushed, feeling awkward. 'Of course. Why shouldn't it be?'

His eyes searched her face, and she did her best to hide the guilt that was tearing her apart.

'Dunno. You've been a bit — distant lately.' He gave a short laugh that only revealed how worried he was and made her feel even more wretched. 'Wondered what I'd done wrong.'

'You've done nothing wrong,' she assured him. 'Stop worrying.'

'You can tell me you know,' he said, clearly trying to sound nonchalant about something that was preying on his mind. 'I won't be offended.'

'Stop over-thinking things.' She kissed him, wanting so much to convey to him how much she loved him, and wishing she could find the courage to put things right between them.

Eliot's arms tightened around her. 'You do know the house is empty? Girls at school, George at nursery... We're all alone.' His eyes expressed a mixture of nerves and hope.

'So we are,' she acknowledged. 'But aren't you far too busy to spare another five minutes for me?'

'Five minutes!' He sounded offended. 'Come on,' he added, jumping up and grabbing her as she almost fell to the floor. 'If we're going to be swamped by bloody Carmichaels any day now, we need to spend every spare moment we have together. Reckon I can give you ten minutes of me time.' He winked and took her hand.

'Wow, Eliot,' she teased. 'You mean, we're going to do it twice?'

He gave her a knowing look, and she almost crumbled in front of him. She knew that look, all too well. She had a funny feeling the builders would be waiting a while for their elevenses that morning.

****

Eliot couldn't get the ticking of the clock out of his head. His heart thudded along in time with it as he stared at the ceiling, knowing the moment had come at last and there was no more denying the facts.

Beside him, he heard Eden's breathing, still shallow and rapid from their exertions.

It had been good, physically — it always was — but there was something wrong, he could feel it. She wasn't herself with him any longer; she hadn't been since the wedding. He didn't want to know, yet he knew he couldn't put it off again. It was eating him up inside. He just had to find the words...

'Eliot, there's something I have to tell you.'

Her words came out in a rush and his heartbeat speeded up. She sounded afraid, even ashamed.

He took a deep breath. 'I know.'

He felt the mattress dip slightly beneath him as she turned over onto her side to face him. 'You know?'

'I know there's summat you need to say. I don't know what it is, but I know it's bin coming for weeks.'

She was quiet for a moment, then she sat up, pulling the duvet around her naked form as if she no longer wanted him to see her body. He daren't look at her anyway, too worried about what he'd see in her eyes.

'I'm ever so sorry,' she said, and he heard the weight of shame in her voice. 'I didn't know how to tell you.'

He contemplated the light shade above the bed for a moment, then he sat up beside her and faced her.

'Tell me what?'

Eden looked sickened, he realised. There was genuine pain in her eyes. What had she done? What was she so afraid of? He put his arms around her, pulling her to him.

'It's okay. Whatever it is, it's okay.'

84

She shook her head, pulling away from him. 'You can't say that. You don't know.'

'I don't care,' he said desperately. 'It doesn't matter.'

'It was at the hotel.' Her words tumbled out in a torrent and she couldn't look at him. 'When we went into the kitchen to meet the staff, remember?'

A vision of Jemima and James Fuller flashed through his mind, tumbling around in his bed while he was out on the hills, working. He thought about Eden heading into the kitchen, Jed behind her. He'd kissed her hand, hugged her.

He pushed the thought away fiercely. Eden wasn't Jemima and whatever she was about to tell him it couldn't be as bad as that. She wouldn't do that to him. Something else was wrong, but what? What was she so ashamed of?

'If I tell you this, you have to promise me that you won't tell anyone else.'

He frowned, bewildered. 'I'm not following, my love. What happened at the hotel?'

'Please, Eliot. Promise me.'

He shrugged but nodded. 'Of course. If you don't want me to say anything, I won't. Promise.'

She looked pale. 'I should have told you this that night, but I didn't have the words — or the courage.'

'You can tell me anything,' he assured her, meaning it. She was trembling, and he couldn't stand to see her like this. He reached out for her again, and this time she allowed herself to rest against him, not resisting as he held her close and stroked her hair. 'Whatever it is, we'll deal with it.'

'What if I'm not the woman you think I am?' she whispered.

He half-laughed. 'Not again! You weren't the woman I thought you were when we first met, remember? Don't tell me you've got a third identity?'

He wanted her to laugh, too. She was scaring the life out of him.

'I didn't tell you because I didn't want to see the look in your eyes when you found out what I did.'

Her voice was barely audible, and he tried to pull away from her to reassure her, but she clung to him.

'Please, stay there. Let me say it while you can't see my face and I can't see yours.'

He resumed stroking her hair. 'Go on, my love. Say it.'

'When I went into the kitchen to meet the staff, there was someone there. Someone I used to know. Turns out he's now head chef at Chessingborough House. Done very well for himself.'

She sounded quite bitter, and not like Eden at all.

'Right.'

'His name's Ryan and — I used to work with him.'

Eliot realised he was holding his breath and exhaled slowly. 'O-kay.'

What was she going to say? That she'd felt some sort of spark upon seeing him again? He couldn't believe it. Wouldn't believe it.

'Eliot, didn't you ever wonder why I ended up working in a place as grotty as The Red Lion?'

Embarrassed, he admitted he hadn't given it much thought.

'I didn't pay much attention to it, that night I came to get you. I was too focused on bringing you home. Nowt else mattered.'

He squeezed her and was relieved when she grasped his hand and laughed. 'I remember. I thought you were never going to tell me what you wanted.'

'I'm no good at stuff like that, I've told you.'

'No, well. I kind of know how you feel now,' she admitted. 'The thing is, Eliot...' She hesitated, then shook her head and pulled away from him.

As she turned to face him, he saw the bleak expression in her eyes and wanted nothing more than to take it away, make it all right. Whatever she'd done he'd forgive her. It didn't matter. Only they mattered.

'The thing is, I was involved with Ryan. We — we had an affair. He was the sous chef at a restaurant in Bath and I was the pastry chef there. We clicked from the start. He was so kind to me. He was fifteen years older than me, and I — well...'

Eliot didn't want to know. He swallowed. 'Aye, I get the picture.'

'We were involved for over a year,' she admitted. 'We had to keep it quiet. There's a lot of jealousy and friction in a restaurant kitchen and personal relationships between staff were frowned upon. Ryan didn't want to jeopardise his job, or mine come to that, so we were careful. Very careful.' She closed her eyes for a moment as if remembering it all. Eliot didn't want her to remember.

'Eden, are you — are you saying...?'

He couldn't finish the sentence. If she'd fallen for this bloody cook again, well, he didn't know what the hell he *could* say. A voice in his head was screaming at him that, of course she hadn't. She was his. She loved him, he knew it. No one could come between them, not now. Yet what else could it be? Having a boyfriend years ago was no crime. He'd have been amazed if there hadn't been other men. Eliot himself had had a wife, for God's sake. So, what else?

Light began to dawn. 'Eden, are you saying he was *married?*'

Her eyes flew open.

'I didn't know,' she garbled. 'I swear I didn't. Not at first, anyway. No one ever talked about their personal lives — there wasn't time, to be honest. And, like I said, we were so careful because he'd told me it could make things difficult at work. I had no reason to suspect him, well, not really. And by the time I did...' She stared at him with wide eyes. 'Please don't hate me.'

He shook his head, relief flooding through him. So that was her guilty secret?

'Why the hell would I hate you?'

'Because of Jemima. Because you've been through it all and I don't want you to think I'm like her, or James Fuller. When I found out, I wanted to end it. I *tried* to end it. He told me they were married in name only, that they hadn't got around to a divorce but that they lived separate lives. I believed him.' She hung her head. 'I suppose, I wanted to believe him.'

'Right.' He didn't know what else to say, waiting for her to continue.

'Then I saw them together in town, arms around each other, looking like any other couple in love. Thing is, deep down I knew. All the out-of-the-way places we visited, the cancelled dates... I was lying to myself because I didn't want it to end. When I saw them that day, it woke me up somehow. I ended it that evening, and I left the restaurant immediately. I couldn't get work in Bath, so I moved home to my parents' house, and that's when I got the job at The Red Lion. It was a dive, really, but it was an income, and it felt like the sort of place I deserved. I hated myself so much. I mean, me, the other woman! It makes me sick to my stomach to think about it, and I've tortured myself for years about it.'

'But you didn't know!' Eliot took hold of her hands. 'It wasn't your fault. You're not bloody James Fuller, or Jemima. You were innocent in all that. It was him — that man. He were to blame, not you.'

'But his poor wife.'

'Aye, well. I reckon it's him as should be carrying the guilt about her, not you. You've got enough on your plate.'

'I don't know if she ever found out. It torments me sometimes.'

'Don't let it,' he advised. 'It's past and done.'

'You won't tell anyone, will you? I'd die of shame.'

He cupped her face with his hands. 'I swear to you, what's between you and me stays that way. No-one'll find out from me.' He paused. 'Did he say anything to you? At the hotel, I mean.'

She tutted. 'He couldn't even look at me. I saw his face when I walked through the door. He was horrified. We didn't speak to each other. Honestly, I have nothing to say to him and, quite clearly, he'd rather forget all about me.'

Eliot frowned. 'Then why were you so afraid to tell me?'

'Because I'm not the woman you thought I was,' she admitted tearfully. 'I didn't want you to think less of me, after everything you've been through.'

'You're exactly the woman I thought you were,' he told her, kissing away her tears. 'Kind, honest, decent. Sort of woman who hates the thought of hurting anyone and would never knowingly do so. *My* woman.'

'Still?' she murmured, gazing up at him. 'After everything I've told you?'

Eliot lowered her gently onto the bed and smiled down at her, his own eyes feeling suspiciously damp.

'Always,' he promised.

Chapter 8

Beth and James hovered by the front door, watching for the first sight of a car.

'He's bloody late, as usual,' tutted James, checking his watch. 'Bet you anything you like he gave us the wrong time on purpose. Him and his power games.'

Beth didn't answer. She felt queasy, waiting for the arrival of her in-laws. As if things weren't tricky enough, now she was going to have to put up with David's lewd jokes and bad temper. No doubt he'd be barking orders at them within hours. Then there was Deborah. Oh, God.

She swallowed, imagining being on the receiving end of one of her mother-in-law's *looks* — looks that left her in no doubt that she was a failure and a huge disappointment to the Fullers. Well, she thought, trying to muster her courage, if they only knew what their precious son had done in their absence, they might see things differently.

She glanced at James as he stood in the doorway, peering down the drive. She'd thought him attractive once, she remembered. In fact, when she'd first met him, she'd been bowled over by his good looks. He had fair hair, blue eyes, and a charming smile, and he was always immaculately dressed. She'd believed she was the luckiest woman alive when he'd asked her to marry him. Funny how things changed.

Since she'd discovered his affair with Jemima, she'd done her absolute best to forgive and forget. Maybe it would have been easier if he hadn't fathered a baby with Jemima. Maybe if they'd been able to have their own children, the pain would have eased a little. It wasn't as if he hadn't tried to make it up to her. He was always buying her little presents and taking her on holidays.

The one thing he didn't seem willing to do was the only thing that mattered to her. Why wouldn't he discuss other options regarding their desire to become parents? Sometimes, she couldn't help but wonder if he was as keen on the idea of having children as she was. He didn't seem to have any yearning to be part of George's life, after all, and how could he help himself?

She'd asked him once, almost afraid of the answer, terrified that he would confess that he longed to have his son living with him and had only turned him away for her sake. But he'd been quite firm that he didn't regard the boy as his own.

'He's Jemima's,' he'd said with a shrug. 'I know it sounds harsh, but the whole thing was a ghastly mistake, and George reminds me of that fact. He's better off with Harland. I don't feel like his father, and I never will.'

She'd been stunned at his assurance but had to admit she'd also been relieved. She couldn't have borne it, really, if he'd wanted George back, and she knew it would break Eliot, which was the last thing she wanted. He'd been a good friend to her. He'd coped with a lot and helped her deal with the fallout of their spouses' affair. She didn't want to make things difficult for him, after everything they'd been through together.

Standing there in the hallway of Thwaite Park, she realised that no matter how many gifts or holidays James showered her with, she didn't feel the same about him any more, and nothing she tried made any difference to that fact.

He'd broken her trust, and she couldn't seem to get past that, no matter how much effort they both made. There was something about him, something that nagged away at her. She didn't know what she could do about it. Maybe time would heal, eventually. Other women got over their husband's affairs. It wasn't as if she was the only one, was it? So, what was she complaining about?

'They're here.' James took a deep breath as the Mercedes swept up the drive of Thwaite Park. He reached for her hand. 'You okay? You look a bit pale.'

'I'm fine,' she assured him. 'Just a bit nervous.'

'Don't let them intimidate you,' he said. 'They're only my parents, after all. Not royalty.'

'Hmm.' She forced a smile, and followed him as he stepped outside, waving to the occupants of the car as it drew to a halt in front of the grand Regency house.

'Luggage!' David sounded like a sergeant-major issuing orders as he called across to his son, who dutifully obeyed and ran down the stone steps to the boot of the car to collect their bags.

Beth hated David's voice. It always sounded angry. James had told her, many times, that it was just the way he spoke, and didn't mean anything.

'He's a toothless tiger,' he'd assured her. 'Ignore the tone. He doesn't intend to sound so angry, it's just his way.' Funny, but he didn't even sound convinced himself.

Beth felt her stomach flip over as Deborah climbed out of the car, looking as immaculate as always. Her brown hair was beautifully styled, her face exquisitely made up, and her petite figure swathed in an expensive, well-cut navy-blue wool coat. She wore red shoes that must have had heels of at least four or five inches, and a red bag that, no doubt, had cost more than Beth's entire monthly shopping bill. She gave James a faint smile, then turned an icy stare on Beth.

'Deborah,' Beth managed, 'how lovely to see you again.'

'And you.' Deborah turned away, apparently losing interest in her daughter-in-law immediately. 'I hope the heating's on, James. It's freezing here.'

James and David exchanged glances and laughed.

'Nothing changes, I see,' James said. 'You're always cold, Mother. Don't worry, we turned it up for you.'

Deborah sighed and headed up the steps, brushing past Beth as if she were invisible. Beth clenched her fists, forced her mouth into a smile, and followed her into the sitting room. She'd been quite wrong. It wasn't going to be tricky at all. It was going to be hell.

****

Jed gazed down at the stunning vista before him and whistled. 'Wow, it's amazing! I'd forgotten how beautiful England can be.' He glanced across at his sister, who was bent double, taking deep breaths by the side of the road. 'You feeling any better, Emerald?'

She straightened, pushing the hood of her Parka coat back to reveal a pale face. 'A bit. I can't believe I got travel sick. That never happens.'

'It's been a bit of a winding road, and maybe you're not used to being in the back seat?' He smoothed the fake fur around her hood. 'You can go in the front and I'll climb in the back the rest of the way? Okay?'

She nodded and went to stand beside him. 'It's very peaceful here, isn't it? You know,' she added, nodding at the valley before them, 'in a few months these meadows will be bright with wildflowers. Buttercups, eyebright, red clover, bistort, pignut...'

He was impressed. 'How the hell do you know that?' he asked.

She gave him a smug look. 'I'm a child of nature, Jed. I told you. Honey may know every shoe designer from here to Paris, but I'll bet you anything she couldn't tell a poppy from a petunia.'

'You're probably right.' He put his arm around her. 'Thought we weren't going to sweat over Honey, any more? We had a deal, remember?'

She nodded. 'Sorry. Force of habit.'

'I know, I know. Guess it's gonna take you some time to accept things. Have you thought about therapy?'

She stared at him, a wary expression in her eyes. 'What sort of therapy?'

'You know, a psychologist or a psychotherapist. Anyone's who's anyone has their own therapist back home. There's no shame in it.'

She shuddered. 'No thanks. Anyway, I've had therapy, if you must know. Proper therapy. I'm a work in progress so don't worry about it. Can't say this is helping, though.'

'What, coming to the Yorkshire Dales?' he shook his head,

93

astounded. 'I would have thought it would help a hell of a lot. How can you not feel contented here? It's — God, it's paradise.'

'I mean all this chasing around after Eden,' she said, scowling. 'All this fuss over someone who isn't even related to him. I can't think why she matters so much that he'd leave his home to come all the way up here. Don't they know how to Skype, for heaven's sake?'

Jed said nothing, feeling it best not to admit to Emerald what their father had confessed. Cain found Emerald's presence deeply uncomfortable and was struggling with the fact that she'd decided to stay on at his Cotswolds home indefinitely.

'She's proper annoying,' he'd confided. 'And she keeps banging on about this business proposition. Like I'm gunna give in to that! Bin there and done that with Honey, and I ain't falling for it again. Got a cheek, if you ask me. I owe her nothing. It's not like she's starved for years, is it? Cost me a bleeding fortune in maintenance, that one. Yet she reckons I owe her big time! Can you believe it?'

Jed could believe it all too well, having listened to Emerald's rant at their father which had started within an hour of them arriving at his house in Upper Bourbury.

'You set Honey up in her own shop,' she'd pointed out, pouting her lips. 'And she's lived here with you for years getting everything she wanted at the click of her fingers. Why should she get it all? And it's not as if I'm asking for a handout to spend on a new car or a flashy holiday, is it? It's a business proposition, after all. I'll be self-supporting before you know it. I could even save you money in the long term.'

'I'll believe that when I see it,' Cain snorted. 'Look, Emerald, forget it. Honey tried to pull this one on me and look what happened there. She never made a penny profit in all the years she had that shop, and it was a drain on me cash. Contrary to what you kids believe, I ain't a bottomless pit you know.'

'If that's true, how come you're paying for the wedding of a former employee?' Emerald folded her arms and glared at him.

Jed had winced as Cain had blundered about, falling straight into the trap. 'Eden ain't just a former employee. She's bin like family, and I want to help her. She deserves a nice wedding.'

'Right, so Eden's *like* family and therefore you're happy to waste a fortune on her, making her happy, but my happiness counts for nothing, even though I'm your *actual* daughter. Says it all, doesn't it!'

Cain had admitted to Jed that he could see her point, but he still felt her so-called business idea was a joke.

'A retreat? She's one sandwich short of a picnic if she thinks I'm forking out for New Age weirdos to lie in the lap of luxury, burning candles and listening to that crappy hippy music. Finding themselves! For God's sake, they ought to get a grip, get a shower, and get a bleeding job.'

Sick of hearing Emerald's persistent whining, he'd come up with the plan to escape to Skimmerdale, away from her relentless earbashing, using the wedding plans as an excuse. He'd been horrified when Emerald announced she was coming with him.

'Why would you want to go all the way to Skimmerdale?' he'd demanded. 'You don't even like Eden!'

'Well, I'm quite sure I can be of some help,' she said. 'What do you know about weddings? You may have been married three times, but I'll lay a pound to a penny that you had nothing to do with organising any of them.'

'And you've organised a wedding before have you?'

'No,' she admitted. 'But I'm a woman. Weddings are in our DNA. Anyway,' she'd added, 'you're not exactly a style icon, are you?'

Cain had been too stunned to argue. Bleeding cheek of her! She seemed to live in jeans or maxi dresses and ankle boots. She was hardly likely to feature in Vogue any time soon.

'Besides,' she'd continued, 'if you think you're buggering off and leaving me you can think again. You've hardly spent any time with me these last twenty odd years. You owe me your company, at least, even if you are too tight to invest in my business idea.'

'What do I do?' Cain had demanded of Jed. 'I can't stand a week alone with her up in the wilderness.'

'Why don't you give her what she wants then?' Jed reasoned. 'Would it kill you to listen to her plan? Look, I get that right now it's an ill-formed, half-baked idea, but if you helped her, maybe between you you'd be able to develop it into something workable. And if you do that, she'll be so busy with setting it up that she'll leave you alone. Plus, she could never say you don't care enough about her again. Anyway, don't you think you owe her?'

'For what?' Cain demanded. 'I paid my way with her. I gave Cassandra a flaming fortune, and Emerald never went without. Gets a monthly allowance from me, even now. I mean, look at her, Jed. She's in her late twenties and she's never had a job! What does that tell you? Tells me she's bone idle, like her mother. You know what I reckon? She don't know the first thing about running a retreat. Bet she can barely run a bath. This isn't about her wanting her own business. This is all about revenge on Honey, and I ain't having it. Emerald needs to get over this jealousy stuff and get a grip. If I give in to her, I won't be doing her no favours. She'll just end up screwing it up and feeling even worse. Meanwhile, I'll be a few hundred grand poorer. Nah. She's had all she's getting off me. She's bleeding lucky she still gets her allowance, like some daft kid. '

'From what I can gather, she was hardly living in the lap of luxury as a child. And her mother seems to have been a little bit, er, strange.'

'You're not wrong there,' Cain admitted. 'Proper loony tunes she turned out to be. Mind you, no doubt that's all my fault, too.'

'Well, you did break her heart,' Jed pointed out.

'Whose side are you on?'

'I can see both sides,' Jed said. 'I feel for Emerald. She's not had a settled life, and she *does* feel pushed out and lonely. She needs to feel as if she matters to you. Is that too much to ask?'

Cain gave a heavy sigh. 'I suppose not.' He considered Jed. 'You're quite fond of her, ain't you?'

'She's my kid sister,' said Jed. 'I don't like to think she's unhappy.'

Cain brightened. 'Great. Well, in that case, you can come with us.'

'What? Whoa! I never said—'

'If I'm stuck with her, so are you. Surely, if you care so much about her, you'll want to keep her company while I'm sorting out this wedding stuff. Right?'

Jed frowned. 'You're not really planning this wedding, are you? What do you know about them?'

'Fuck all, mate,' Cain admitted with a grin. 'I wore what they told me, turned up on the day and said the words — mug that I was. Even so, I'm gunna make damn sure that Eden gets what she wants. Eliot strikes me as someone who ain't up for anything fancy, but I don't want him scuppering her dreams. So, are you up for it? 'Cos if you won't come, Emerald can't come, and that's that.'

Against his better judgement, Jed had agreed, which was how he found himself standing at the edge of the hillside road, gazing upon a chequer board of fields in various shades of green, while Emerald fought to keep down her lunch beside him.

'Did you call your mom, tell her you wouldn't be back for a while?'

'Oh, yes.' Emerald's tone was grim. 'She was furious at first; accused me of abandoning her and telling me I was a traitor who'd been sucked in by Dad's lies. Then I told her I was still going to send her my allowance and, funnily enough, she wished me a happy holiday and hung up.'

Jed's heart ached for her, hearing the pain in her voice.

'Well,' he said, 'then a happy holiday's what we'll have. Right?' At her doubtful expression he forced himself to sound optimistic. 'It will be fun, honest it will.'

He half-believed it. He loved the countryside and being around animals. It was the prospect of being stuck between a warring Cain and Emerald he didn't relish.

'I really hope Eliot doesn't keep goats,' Emerald said.

Jed laughed. 'Kinda random. You don't like goats?' He nudged her. 'And you, *a child of nature*.'

'I *used* to like goats,' she assured him, 'until a few months ago.'

'What happened a few months ago?' he enquired, intrigued.

'Goat sodding yoga happened,' she muttered. 'God, that was a real eye-opener.'

Jed felt the laughter bubbling up inside him and fought to keep a straight face. 'Goat yoga?'

She glanced up at him, looking suspicious. 'It's all the rage,' she assured him. 'It's supposed to relax you and release oxytocin — the feelgood hormone.'

'And did it do that?' He figured he already knew the answer, judging by the way she screwed up her nose in disgust.

'It made me want to puke. My goat used my yoga mat as a toilet, and every time I bent over it butted me in the bum. Very painful. And how are you supposed to concentrate with a goat glued to your backside?'

Jed turned away, so she wouldn't see the laughter in his eyes. 'Sounds a bit weird,' he said finally.

She sighed. 'Lots of people love it. Animal therapy is very successful, and I suppose it's sort of in that category. But it's not much use if you take your yoga seriously.'

'And you do?'

'It gets me through life,' she told him. 'I can't go a day without my yoga session.'

'Wow.' Jed puffed out his cheeks. 'Poor goats had no chance then.'

'Not really. I should have known better.' She cast a glance back at the car, where Cain was sitting in the front seat, trying to hunt for Pokemon on his cell phone and letting out intermittent yells of frustration as his signal vanished. 'Talking of pains in the butt, when are you going to tell him? About the real reason you're in England, I mean.'

Jed shrugged. 'Soon. He hasn't asked. If he does, I'll tell him.' *At least, some of it*, he thought. There was no need to paint a picture — a quick sketch would suffice.

She nodded. 'Have you decided what you're going to do? I mean, you can't stay with him forever, can you?'

He took a deep breath. 'No idea. I guess I'm hoping for some divine inspiration. Maybe round here, I'll find it. What about you?'

'Oh.' She folded her arms. 'I know exactly what I'm going to do. Dad's going to invest in my business, and I won't stop nagging at him until he does.'

Chapter 9

'July! That doesn't give us much time, does it?' Emerald gave Eden a pitying look. 'Really, Eden, if you're going to do this properly, it takes at least six to twelve months of planning. It's already March.'

'I don't much care if it is,' Eden said. 'Eliot and I met at the end of July, exactly two years ago. I want to celebrate that fact with our wedding. Don't forget, we have to work around the farm. We've got to find a gap in the diary before winter sets in. Trust me, we don't want a winter wedding. We might never be able to make it out of Wildflower Farm to get married at all, so you'll have to go with me on this.'

She seemed about to say something else but clamped her lips shut, as if suppressing the words.

Emerald could guess what they were. *What's it got to do with you, anyway?* Eden was quite transparent, and evidently wasn't happy that Emerald had turned up to help. In fact, from the way she was acting, it had become quite clear that she didn't particularly want a big wedding at all.

As Eliot sat there, looking more and more depressed, Emerald felt a spark of mischief ignite. Neither wanted what Cain was offering, but both thought they were doing the other a favour by accepting.

It was obvious to her, from her dealings with Eliot, that he was a proud man, and having her father pay for the wedding would be killing him. Not to mention the fact that he loathed fuss and social gatherings. The only reason he would possibly agree was for Eden's sake. No doubt he thought, like Cain, that she deserved the best, and was swallowing his pride to make sure she got it.

For her part, Eden clearly wanted a quiet wedding, but was trying to save Eliot the expense and worry. It was too funny.

The fact that Cain was oblivious, and thought he was doing them a favour, would have been the funniest thing of all, if it wasn't so damn annoying that he was happily forking out for this fiasco, when he wouldn't put a penny towards her own business.

She scowled at her father as he sat, scribbling words on a piece of paper. Dates, venues, costings... He was being thorough, she thought, the bitterness coursing through her. God, she hated Eden. *Look at her sitting there, all innocent and cow eyed.* What the hell did someone like Eliot see in her?

She saw him shifting impatiently in his chair and thought he was wasted on that scheming bitch. She wondered what his first wife had been like. Probably another schemer since she was related to Honey. Men were such idiots, sometimes. She'd have thought Eliot would have wised up by now.

'I think Eliot needs to get back to work,' she said, giving him a sympathetic smile. 'Don't you think we've kept him away from the farm for long enough?'

His brown eyes flashed her a look of gratitude which quite turned her knees to jelly.

'Aye, that's true enough. If you don't mind, I want to get on with mending walls in lower fields before the owd girls come home.' He turned to Eden. 'You can manage without me, can't you?'

Eden smiled. 'Of course. You get back to it, and we'll work through this lot.'

He nodded and left the farmhouse, shutting the door behind him, and no doubt heaving a massive sigh of relief as he made his way across the yard.

'What old girls are coming home?' Cain enquired, sounding puzzled.

Eden laughed. 'Our elderly ewes. We send them to a farmer

further south to take care of them over the winter. It's too harsh for them round here in the bad weather. They're coming back in a couple of days to reacclimatise before they lamb in April.'

'Get you,' Cain said, sounding admiring. 'You know all the lingo now, don't you? Proper farmer's wife.'

'Not yet, she isn't,' Emerald reminded him. She jumped, startled, as something brushed against her leg. To her relief, she discovered it was a rather beautiful seal point ragdoll cat, with huge blue eyes, and not the rat she'd feared.

'Aren't you gorgeous?' Emerald reached down and scooped the cat up, gratified when it settled comfortably on her lap. Who'd have thought such a stunning cat would live on a farm? She glanced around the large, glossy kitchen, having to admit to herself that it was far classier than she'd expected. Evidently someone, at some point, had shown great taste. She could almost see herself living here. With Eliot by her side, it wouldn't be so bad, surely? She could see it now — feeding baby lambs with a bottle as Eliot looked on proudly and told her how wonderful she was and how much he loved her.

'So, you've got your heart set on a church? Are you sure?'

Her father's voice snapped her back to reality. Cain sounded disapproving, which wasn't surprising, considering his complete lack of faith or belief in any kind of afterlife — a fact that his fans would find most bewildering, given his backlist of songs which read like a tribute to Satan and all the demons of hell.

While his more ardent fans hailed him as a king of the underworld, Cain dismissed all talk of anything supernatural with a wave of the hand and a firm, "When you're dead, you're dead, and thank God for it". He never seemed to see the irony of that statement, but that was her father all over. He wasn't the sharpest tool in the box.

'It seems to be important to Eliot,' Eden murmured.

Emerald raised an eyebrow. Really? She wouldn't have put Eliot down as a religious man, either. She wondered what was behind his desire to make his vows in the house of God.

'But is it important to *you*? It's as much your wedding as his,' she said, thinking the more trouble she could stir up between them the better. Why should Eden get the perfect man? If she could cause her a few bumps in her perfectly smooth, straight road through life, well good. Her own journey had been a bloody nightmare — full of sharp bends and whopping big potholes. Let Eden hit some obstacles for once.

'If it makes him happy, I'm all for it,' Eden assured her, and Emerald fought down her irritation. They were the perfect couple, weren't they? So thoughtful and considerate towards each other. It was sickening. The cat purred, and Emerald was pretty sure she was agreeing with her. Cats were highly intelligent creatures after all.

'So, you need to get onto the vicar, then,' Cain was saying. 'If you're sure you want it here, I mean? Wouldn't you like to get married nearer to your parents? The church in Lowminster is cracking, and I'm sure—'

'This is my home now,' she said. 'I've made my life here, and I'm happy here. There's a lovely little church in Camacker, and the vicar's a nice man. I'm sure he'll be able to fit us in. It's not as if there are a lot of weddings round here.'

'So, what about the reception? Now, hear me out on this. Seeing as you refuse to come back to the Cotswolds, I was thinking of a hotel near here. Ashington Hall's only a few miles from where we're staying, and it's got a good-sized function room. I had a gander online 'cos I was gunna book there 'til I saw the prices, but they do quite a few wedding receptions there, apparently, so they know what they're doing. We could— '

His voice trailed off as Eden shook her head. 'Thank you, Cain, but Ashington Hall! It's far too big and grand. The village pub has a room and—'

'The village pub! Good God, Eden, what sort of a wedding is this? What's the point of getting married if you ain't gunna push the boat out? You want a church wedding, right? Well, you need to invite a good few people then, because otherwise the place'll be all dark and bare. Nothing spookier than a half-empty church. All them creepy echoes and shadows. Fair makes my skin crawl.'

'How odd, since you don't believe in an afterlife,' Emerald said. She smiled at Eden. 'Maybe you could get married at Hallowe'en.

Then it wouldn't matter if the church was as quiet as a tomb.'

'For gawd's sake! This is supposed to be the happiest day of their lives. I won't have it. At the very least you deserve the function room at The Paradise, and I don't want no arguments. I know you're trying to save me money, but you don't have to worry about it. I'm more than happy to pay.'

'Aren't you a lucky girl?' said Emerald, not bothering to keep the sarcasm from her voice. Was her father deliberately trying to upset her?

The door opened and Jed strolled in, carrying a little boy in his arms. Behind him walked two young girls, all dark curls and flashing brown eyes, like their father.

'You've found Bella,' said the youngest girl, looking impressed. 'She doesn't usually sit with strangers. She must like you.'

'The feeling's mutual,' Emerald admitted, glancing down at the cat on her lap. 'She's gorgeous.'

'We've been showing Jed Flora,' said the eldest girl, as Eden removed a reluctant George from Jed's grasp. 'He loved her, didn't you?'

'Cute pony,' Jed confirmed. 'In fact, I reckon she's the prettiest pony I've ever seen.'

The girls beamed with pride and Emerald smirked. *All right, all right, don't overdo it, brother dear.* She watched as he took his seat at the table, and the two girls crowded round him. He was good with children, and she smiled as George demanded to sit with him.

Eden laughed and handed him back, and Jed sat him on his knee, bending his head to talk to him.

As he glanced up, her smirk dropped. Something in his eyes twisted her heart — a bleakness that quite wrenched her. What was wrong with him? She knew why he'd come back to England, but there was something else. Something he wasn't telling her. She was so concerned that, for a moment, she forgot to be hateful to Eden and found herself saying please when she was offered a cup of tea.

As she looked away from her brother, she realised, with surprise, that her father was also watching him. Maybe he wasn't as stupid as he looked. He seemed thoughtful, considering Jed's expression. She had a feeling that tonight was going to be the night that Cain finally asked the question Jed had been dreading.

****

'So, what's this really all about?'

James handed his father a glass of whisky and took a seat opposite him. They were in the snug at Thwaite Park — a small, cosy room with dark red walls, a log burner, and squashy leather sofas. It was their favourite room during the colder months, although, during the summer they much preferred the sitting room along the hall — a large, bright space painted in a summery shade of yellow, with French doors that opened out onto the lawns.

He watched as his father took a sip of his drink and leaned back in his chair, a smug grin on his lips. His father was in his early sixties now, but he was still a figure of authority. There was never any doubt as to who was in charge when he was around. James realised that things were going to be quite different now that he was home, and the thought wasn't an altogether pleasant one. He'd been used to doing things his way. Now David Fuller was back, it would be all about him. It was always all about him.

'There must be some reason for leaving London,' he probed. 'I must say, I can't imagine why you'd want to leave Barnes behind. It's a lovely area, and Mother seemed very happy there. She said it was a friendly little community, and that there was a real village feel to the place. Anyway, I thought you were enjoying your life of leisure?'

'You thought wrong then.' David shot him a look of disgust. 'It's very overrated, you know, being retired. Oh, in theory it's all very well. No more meetings, or accounts, or deadlines. In reality it's boring as hell. I was itching to get back up here. I've missed this house. I've missed Yorkshire.'

'London wasn't to your taste?'

David hesitated. 'London has never been to my taste. Barnes — became uncomfortable.'

There was quiet for a moment as he took another sip of whisky, and James gripped his own glass a little tighter. No doubt his father had been up to his old tricks, and some woman had got too clingy for his liking. He wondered if his mother knew. Somehow, he rather thought she must do. She always seemed to find out, almost as if she had a sixth sense about such things. Yet here she was, still by his side, still calm and cool and unruffled.

James thought about Beth. When she'd found out about Jemima, she'd been far from cool. She'd sobbed hysterically, and he'd worried she'd never smile again. Even now, things weren't right between them, and he didn't know what else he could do. Truthfully, he was growing tired of feeling guilty, tired of trying to think of new ways to make it up to her. He wondered at his father's strength. Why did he never seem too worried when his affairs were discovered? Guilt certainly never seemed to weigh him down or cause him to lose any sleep.

'That's the thing with these *friendly communities*. Everyone knows your business.' He felt rather brave, going as far as that. Better not push his father too far.

David swilled the whisky in his glass and sighed. 'I quite liked where we lived but, truthfully, your mother wasn't herself there. Anyway, it served its purpose. Time to look to the future now.'

'And what might that involve?'

'Oh,' David waved his glass in the air, 'who knows?'

Something in the way he said it made James nervous.

He watched, feeling unaccountably anxious as his father stood and walked over to the window. 'You've nothing in mind then?'

David was staring out over the lawn. 'What do you see out there?'

'The garden.' James wondered if his father was quite all right. He strolled over to join him, trying to see what it was his father was seeing.

'The garden, yes, and acres of prime Yorkshire Dales land. All ours. You understand that, boy?'

James tried not to show his annoyance. He hated it when his father called him *boy*. He was thirty-five, for God's sake.

'Well, obviously. It's beautiful. We're very lucky.'

'Yes, we are. I've roamed these gardens since I could walk, and I've loved this house all my life. I've travelled to many places, and I've stayed at many of our other properties, but this one, this one is special. I knew I'd come back here one day. It's where I belong.'

David cleared his throat, as if embarrassed by his show of emotion. James wished his father would display the same depth of feeling towards his own son some time.

He jumped as David spun round to face him. 'So, no sign of a child yet then?'

James felt his cheeks start to burn. 'Not yet, no.'

David nodded. 'Not looking very hopeful, is it?'

'Oh, you know. Early days.'

David flashed him a look of irritation. 'You appear to have lost your sense of perspective if you think it's still early days.'

'No need for that, surely?' James said, struggling to keep an even tone.

'You think?' David pushed him aside and headed back to the sideboard, reaching for the whisky decanter. 'Saw your Aunt Kathryn and Uncle Scott in London last month.'

James frowned. What had that got to do with anything? 'Oh, how are they?'

'Gloating, as per usual. Did you know your cousin Owen's wife's pregnant again?'

James swallowed, knowing where this conversation was heading. 'No, I didn't. Can't say I keep in touch with them.'

'Don't blame you. My God, that bloody Kathryn's a cow. Really rubbing it in about having a third grandchild on the way. Your mother was quite upset. She's longing to be a grandmother you know.'

'Is she?' James was surprised. 'She's never mentioned it.'

'Not to you, maybe. Doesn't want to put pressure on you, obviously. But I know for a fact that she can't wait, and having Kathryn and Scott going on about their precious Samson and Delilah — yes, honestly! Can you believe that, for fuck's sake? — and then this new baby on the way... Christ knows what they're going to call this one. The mind boggles.' He strolled back

107

to the armchair and sat down, whisky glass clutched in his hand. 'You do understand the implications of this, boy?'

'Implications?'

'For God's sake!' David sat back in the chair, almost spilling the whisky. 'Use your noggin! Kathryn and Scott have three grandchildren. Your mother and I have none. At this rate, we're never going to have any, and you know what happens then. When you die, this house, the family fortune, will pass to Owen or, if he's already dead, to his children. Your grandfather's will was very specific about that. It's not to go outside the immediate family and they're the only immediate family left. You need to do something about this.'

'I don't see what I *can* do about it.' James protested, wondering what his father was suggesting. 'What does it matter anyway?'

David's eyes widened. 'What does it matter? Are you seriously telling me you don't care if Thwaite Park and all our other properties go to that jumped up little tosser?'

'The way I see it, when that happens, you and I will be dead and buried, so who cares who gets it then?'

'Really?' David's face was almost purple. Clearly, he didn't share James's view. 'And what about your precious wife? Suppose you die ten, twenty years before she does. Where does that leave her, or don't you care about her either?'

'Of course I care—'

'Selfish!' David drained his whisky glass and slammed it on the armchair in disgust. 'Didn't think how it might affect others if you died young, did you? The consequences of that don't bear thinking about.'

James slumped. Now he could see what his father was worried about. It all made sense.

'I'm sure it won't come to that,' he assured him. 'Rest assured,' he added, 'I've no intention of dying young.'

'Idiot.'

His father's muttered response made him feel like hurling his own glass across the room. He pictured it for a moment, feeling some satisfaction at the thought of his father's shock, but dismissed the image with some regret. He would never have the nerve.

'I presume you've investigated the matter?'

'Investigated what matter?'

'Are you deliberately trying to annoy me? The matter of your apparent inability to father a child. Have you had tests?'

'Oh. Yes, yes we both have.'

'And?'

'And there's nothing wrong with either of us. It's one of those things apparently. Some couples aren't compatible, and it seems we're one of those couples.'

'Hmm.' David frowned. 'Then maybe you should rethink the situation.'

'Rethink what situation?' James couldn't see what else his father wanted him to do. He couldn't conjure a baby up out of thin air.

'The Beth situation. If you can't get *her* pregnant, maybe you could manage it with another, *compatible* partner.'

'Are you talking about surrogacy?'

'I'm talking about divorce. There's still plenty of time. You're young enough to get another woman, and it's not as if you and Beth are exactly love's young dream.'

'What do you mean by that?' James spluttered.

'Oh, come on. I've got eyes in my head, haven't I? I can see that the relationship between you two has gone downhill quite drastically. There's no love there any more, that I can see.'

'You don't know what you're talking about!' Fear, in a funny way, made him brave. The thought that his marriage was in such a dire state that his own father had noticed it was terrifying, which spurred him into an aggressive response that he wouldn't normally have had the courage to give. 'Beth and I are fine. Absolutely fine.'

'If you say so.' David didn't sound convinced. 'So, the doctors ruled it out then?'

'Not ruled it out, no.' James was cautious. He didn't want to raise his father's hopes. On the other hand, he wanted to get him off his back. 'They said the longer it went on, the less likely we were to conceive.'

'Right.' His father sounded thoughtful.

James waited, hardly daring to breathe.

'Very well, we'll leave it at that for the time being.' David waved his hand airily at James, and he heaved a sigh of relief. The subject was closed — at least for now.

****

'Them barns are coming on in leaps and bounds.' Cain nodded approvingly as Eden shut the door behind them. Together, they wandered along the side of the beck before entering the farmyard, heading back towards the house. 'Reckon you've got a viable little business on the cards there, Eden. When do you reckon on opening?'

'We're hoping to get the bunk barns open for the May Bank Holiday.' she said. 'It's taken so much longer than we anticipated. It's been eighteen months since Eliot first started looking into this, can you believe? Planning permission was a nightmare, and then waiting for the building firm we usually use to schedule us in. At least the remaining work's only cosmetic now. The builders have finished the bunk barns. They're just doing some maintenance work on the other outbuildings now. The electrics are done, and it's passed building regulations and safety checks, so it's a case of plumbing in the bathrooms and kitchen sinks, decorating and furnishing the place and adding those finishing touches.'

'What's with them picnic tables?' he asked, nodding at the newly arrived outdoor furniture that was currently piled up outside one of the barns.

'Going to put them by the beck so walkers can have a sit down. I'm planning to offer drinks and cakes, or cream teas to them. It's all extra income after all.'

'Let's hope the weather improves then,' he said, shivering. There was an icy blast around his vitals. The cold in this place seeped straight through to your bones. It was no place for a man of his age.

'Walkers don't seem to feel the cold,' she said, with what sounded like admiration.

110

'Crackers, the lot of 'em. Still, good news for you. You'll make a fortune,' he said.

'I doubt that.' She smiled. 'We're just hoping to make any sort of profit. Truth is, we've sunk every penny into it, and if it doesn't work... Worse still, it will be all my fault. It was my bright idea after all.'

'It's a great idea,' he reassured her. 'All them daft bleeders in their hiking boots, tramping through the hills. They're gunna want a sit down and a cuppa, ain't they? Nowhere else round here is there? And the bunk barns idea... I mean, it ain't my cup of tea, sharing a room with a load of strangers, but walkers are funny onions. They'll doss down anywhere.'

'Thanks.' Eden sounded offended and he laughed.

'You know what I mean. Bit long in the tooth to spend a night in a dormitory, but when you're out tramping the dales and you want a bed for the night, I reckon this is just the job.'

'I think so. We researched it carefully. We were considering making a handful of larger en-suite rooms and charging more, but it seems people are happy to spend a night in a youth hostel type environment. Cheap and cheerful. The main barn will sleep sixteen and the smaller one twelve.'

'You ain't gunna be cooking for them all?' he asked, horrified at the thought.

'No. At first, the plan was that I'd offer bed and breakfast, but we realised I wouldn't have the time. The barns will each have a kitchen and dining room, so they're fully self-catering. I've got all the kitchen equipment and stuff on order. Libby had the bright idea, the other day, of making up picnics, so people can buy a basket of food and drink to take with them on their walks. That might be a useful side-line.'

'You're going to have your hands full,' he observed. 'You sure you can handle it all on your own?'

'I think so. We're asking guests to bring a sleeping bag and pillowcase with them, to save on laundry. We'll provide a sheet and pillow. I'm trying hard to cut down on work, and I've looked at loads of other bunk barns to see what they offer. I think we can compete.'

'But you've got the kids to see to,' he pointed out. 'Aren't you taking on too much?'

'The kids are at school, or with the childminder,' she said. 'When they're not, they pitch in and help either me or Eliot, anyway. They're ever so good. Even George has his jobs to do. It will be okay, Cain, don't worry.'

'I hope you're right, darls. I'd hate to see you struggling. Seems like an awful lot of palaver for a few quid.'

Eden pulled a face. 'Maybe so, but that few quid could be the difference between make or break for us. We have to try.'

'Things that bad?'

She opened the farmhouse door and ushered him inside. As they wiped their shoes on the doormat, she said, obviously trying to sound casual, 'Not exactly a thriving business, sheep farming. It's tough to make a living from it these days, but we do okay.'

'Hmm.' He frowned, then put his arm around her. 'If you ever need any help, you know where I am. I mean, I ain't no sheep farmer, but I can always put a few quid your way, if you need it. You know that don't you?'

'What a saint,' came a voice from the end of the hall, and Cain groaned inwardly as he glanced up and saw Emerald standing there, arms folded and a face like thunder.

'Don't start,' he warned her, sick of hearing her whining pleas for cash.

Eden looked uncomfortable. 'I'll put the kettle on,' she said, pushing past Emerald and heading into the kitchen.

'Yeah, you do that,' Emerald said. She put her hands on her hips and glared at her father. 'Well?'

'I ain't discussing this again,' he said, following Eden into the kitchen, a protesting Emerald following him. Cain's heart sank when he saw Jed standing there, too. That was all he needed. He only hoped the lad hadn't come here for round two of their argument. There'd been quite enough rowing going on last night. Gawd knows what the other guests at The Paradise Hotel had thought.

****

Beth pulled into the farmyard at Wildflower Farm, her heart sinking as she spotted a vintage Rolls Royce parked beside Eliot's Land Rover, Eden's Nissan, and the builder's van. So, they had visitors, and rather grand ones at that. Maybe she should leave. Go home.

She ran a weary hand over her face and sighed. Home. It hardly felt like home these days, with David prowling around and Deborah avoiding her. She felt awkward, on edge. It was their house, after all, and she was the intruder. Very much so. Clearly, eight years of marriage to Deborah's son hadn't changed that.

It was even worse than she'd imagined. David was behaving very oddly. He kept looking at her with a definite query on his face, and James was being strange, too. Evasive. Shifty. Something was wrong but, as usual, she was the last to know what it was. With Deborah barely managing to exchange two words with her, Thwaite Park wasn't somewhere she felt comfortable any more, and Wildflower Farm was becoming more appealing by the day.

She knocked on the farmhouse door and waited. A movement caught her eye, and she laughed as a large, reddish brown hen strutted over to survey her. 'Hello. Are you visiting, too?'

The hen stared up at her in disapproval, and she was suddenly reminded of her mother-in-law. It wore the same expression that Deborah permanently wore. *I'm not even good enough for a chicken, evidently.*

She heard the door open and turned, expecting to see Eden or one of the children standing there. Instead, a young man with fair hair, a wide smile, and the kindliest blue eyes she'd ever seen stood before her. He was tall, even taller than Eliot, and broad, with tanned skin and white, even teeth. Yet, he wasn't traditionally handsome. She would have said his face had character, rather than that he was good looking, but there was something about him. Something instantly appealing, and far too attractive for her peace of mind.

She gaped up at him for a moment, not able to speak.

The man's smile faltered, and he cleared his throat. 'Can I help you?'

She swallowed. He was American. Well, that was the last thing she'd expected to find in a remote farmhouse in the Yorkshire Dales. A tall, attractive American man. You never knew what the day would bring.

'I'm — is Eden in? Or Eliot?'

He blinked for a moment, as if he hadn't understood what she said, then he shook his head slightly, as if clearing away brain fog, and nodded. 'Sure. You are?'

Who was she? Oh yes. 'Beth. Beth Fuller.'

He held out his hand. 'Pleased to meet you, Beth Fuller. I'm Jed Carmichael.'

'Pleased to meet you.' She shook his hand, almost gasping as what felt like an electric shock shot through her fingers. Through a daze, the name registered. 'Carmichael? You're Honey's brother?'

'That's right. You know Honey?'

'Not really,' she admitted. 'I know of her, obviously. After the other year...'

Her voice trailed off, not sure how much he knew of Honey's escapades the summer before last.

His laughter told her that he knew it all, and she warmed to him as he said, 'Yeah, she was kinda bad, wasn't she? But it all worked out for the best, right?'

'Right. Absolutely.' She realised he was still holding her hand and blushed. What the hell was wrong with her? She felt like a schoolgirl gazing up at some gorgeous pop star whose poster she'd had on her bedroom wall for months.

'I'm so sorry for leaving you on the doorstep. What am I thinking? Come in, please.'

He let go of her hand and moved aside, allowing her to pass. She hoped he didn't see her trembling. He would think she was peculiar.

'Eden's in the kitchen,' he told her. 'You might want to rethink your visit, though.'

'Oh?'

'Let's just say, things are a little tense in there. You know the way?'

'I know the way,' she assured him. As she headed up the hallway, she was all too aware of his presence behind her. My God, the air was crackling. Was she having a mid-life crisis, or something? She gradually became aware of the sound of raised voices coming from up ahead and realised the American hadn't been joking. It sounded a little heated in the kitchen, and not in the usual way.

As she walked into the kitchen, she spotted Cain Carmichael, whom she recognised immediately, arguing with a rather beautiful blonde girl who, she realised, was probably the American's girlfriend. Damn.

Eden, meanwhile, was heating something in a pan on the hob, while making cups of tea and casting wary glances at the clock on the wall.

Jed murmured in her ear, 'Told you, didn't I?'

Beth gulped. 'So you did. Seems like I've walked into a war zone. What on earth's going on?'

Chapter 10

Cain shook his head. 'I've told you, Emerald, it ain't happening. Look, I know what you said about it being a proper business, but I don't see it. I can't imagine people paying good money to sit in a field and chant. I mean, I just can't. Most of the types you'd attract ain't got two pennies to rub together. Bleeding drop-out hippies. It wouldn't work, and I've been there before, with Honey. Her shop never made a pound profit in all the years she had it. Cost me a fortune to indulge her and make her feel she was doing something worthwhile. I ain't making that mistake again.'

'You haven't listened to a word I said!' She stamped her foot in clear frustration, and Cain shook his head, his irritation growing when Jed came to stand beside her. 'I know what I'm doing, and I have lots of friends who can advise me. I want to make a living from something, not be dependent on you for an allowance. Why won't you take me seriously?'

'Dad, I don't see why Emerald has to pay the price for Honey's mistakes.'

'I might have guessed you'd be on her side, as usual. What are you doing here anyway?' he demanded.

'I called a cab and came to collect my little sister. We're heading back to the hotel to pack. I think we've both been under your feet for long enough, don't you?' His voice was even, but there was unmistakable tension there.

Cain sighed. 'Look, you don't have to go yet. Wait until

116

tomorrow and we'll go back to my gaff together, talk things through properly.'

They all looked up as Eliot opened the back door. He stared round at everyone, and Cain saw the look of dismay in his eyes. Bloke's face was an open book. You could tell at a glance what he was thinking, and it wasn't usually complimentary, come to think of it.

'I think we talked things through enough last night, don't you?' Jed's voice brought his attention back to the matter in hand, as his son put his arm around Emerald. 'You know, Dad, I get that you're disappointed in me. I get that you wanted me to follow in your footsteps and be some great rock star—'

'It's not about me,' Cain protested. 'You're a gifted guitarist, a cracking songwriter, and you're in a good band. I don't get why you'd quit now! All those years of trying and you finally get the right line-up, a bloody good record deal, and you cut a brilliant album that's selling by the shedload, and you decide that's enough, you're out. I don't understand, and I think you're making a massive mistake.'

'I don't want to be in a band. Honestly, I don't think I ever did. I wanted to get your approval, and I thought that was the way to go. All those years of striving to make it work kind of fed the illusion, somehow. But when it happened, when I finally got what I thought I wanted, I realised it meant zilch to me. It's not the life I want. It doesn't matter.'

'Doesn't matter!' Cain was bewildered.

'Your soup will be ready in a minute,' Eden interrupted, laying a hand on Eliot's shoulder. 'And I've got some scones for you all to try afterwards. Thought I'd better get some practice in.'

Cain saw Eliot grasp her hand, but he didn't look as if even the prospect of grub had cheered him up. Miserable bleeder. Like he had anything to be miserable about! He ought to try living Cain's life.

'Doesn't matter?' he repeated, focusing again on Jed. 'What do you mean, it doesn't matter?'

'You see? That's the difference between us! You can't see how I could think that, because it means the world to you. To me, it was something to do because I didn't know what else I wanted.'

'So, what *do* you want?' Cain demanded.

'I have no idea,' Jed admitted, sounding tired. 'All I know for sure is, I had to get out of that life. I had to get away and start again. I'm still looking, but I'm sure I'll find it.'

'Huh. If you say so. Left it a bit late, haven't you? You're thirty-four, for God's sake. You should have found it by now.'

'Yeah, well, the thing is, Emerald's only in her twenties, and she wants to stand on her own two feet, not rely on you, but you're not listening to her. I would have thought you'd be happy that she wants to make her own way in the world and would want to help her do it.'

'Make her own way in the world?' Cain snorted. 'Oh, yeah. After I fork out a barrow-load of cash first to set her up. And, anyway, she don't even know how to run a retreat. It's all airy-fairy arty-farty crap. When she's got a proper idea, then I'll listen to her.'

'Or you could listen to her first, while she explains what she's hoping to achieve, and then you could help her come up with a real plan.'

Cain's eyes narrowed. 'Got it all worked out, ain't ya?'

'Absolutely. You don't want to repeat the mistakes you made with Honey, and I get that, but I'll bet your bottom dollar you didn't have any say in her business. Bet you left it entirely to her, right?'

'So?'

'So, Emerald's not just asking you for money. Can't you see that? She's bored, she wants something to do. She's got a vague notion of what she could do but she doesn't know how to go about it. She wants your input, your guidance. She wants you to be her *father*, for Christ's sake.'

Cain bristled. What the hell did he mean by that? His kids would be the death of him, no doubt about it. He turned his head as he suddenly registered that Eden and Eliot were staring at him.

'No more nagging at me, okay?' he said, holding up his hand as Emerald started to say something, 'I ain't rushing into anything. As for you,' he said to Jed as his son sank into a chair, 'you're gunna need a job. I ain't keeping you for nothing, either, and since you seem determined to stay in England for the time being, you'd better figure out what it is *you* want to do with your life pretty damn sharpish. Right?'

Jed nodded. 'Right.'

'Jeez, what a pair you are.' Cain sighed. 'So, you'll stay? Both of you, I mean? And you'll come back home with me tomorrow?'

He watched as Emerald and Jed exchanged glances. As they nodded, he felt a strange surge of relief. He would feel bad if they parted on such bad terms. He supposed he was being over-emotional because Honey was still on honeymoon and he missed her. Probably.

'Them scones sound good to me, Eden,' he said, sniffing the air hungrily as she dished out soup for Eliot. 'And who are you when you're at home?' he added, noticing for the first time that a stranger was in their midst. The young woman was sitting at the table, opposite Jed, watching the scene before her with evident bemusement.

'Beth! I'm sorry, I couldn't get a word in edgeways.' Eden put the pan in the sink and took another mug from the cupboard. 'Cup of tea for everyone, and a bit of peace and quiet. You must think you've walked into a madhouse.'

'Just a bit. What on earth's going on?'

'Looks like you and me have walked into some family drama, Beth.' Eliot scowled and lifted his spoon. 'Like bloody Piccadilly Circus in here lately, what with the workmen and building inspectors and everyone else.'

'Meaning us, I suppose,' Cain said. 'Bleeding ungrateful. We're only here to sort out your wedding, which, by the way we don't seem to have got very far with. We need a proper meeting or it's gunna be a fiasco.'

'Goodness, and we wouldn't want that, would we?' Emerald muttered.

'Cup of tea,' Eden said, handing Cain a large mug.

'Bit rude, if you ask me.' Cain continued.

'I'm sure Eliot didn't mean to be rude,' Eden said, flashing her partner a meaningful look. Eliot appeared suspiciously unrepentant to Cain. 'Cherry scone anyone?'

'I think Eliot has every right to be annoyed,' Emerald said, picking up Bella and cuddling her tightly. 'Have you got any plain scones? I hate cherry scones.'

'You would.' Cain tutted. 'Anything to be awkward.'

'Sorry. I'm afraid you'll have to do without,' Eden said.

'Oh, I'll have to make do then,' Emerald replied. 'I'll pick the cherries out.'

'What's he got to be annoyed about?' Cain demanded. 'Eliot, I mean? Seems to me he's got it made, what with me forking out for his wedding. And he doesn't even have to lift a finger to organise it, which is a good job, seeing as he clearly couldn't give a shit what goes on.'

Eliot slammed his spoon in the bowl and soup splashed onto the table. 'I never said that!'

'You didn't have to, mate. Every discussion we've tried to have, you've been conspicuous by your absence. Always sumfink wants doing somewhere, ain't there?'

'Of course there is. I work on a bloody farm. You think the place grinds to a halt 'cos you want to talk about which bloody flowers we should have?'

'Quite right, Eliot,' Emerald soothed.

'Let's calm this down,' Eden said, hurrying to the cupboard and taking out a tin which, no doubt, contained the scones. 'We're all clearly stressed, so it's not a good time to talk about this.'

'And when will be a good time?' Cain queried. 'Sorry, Eden, but it's got to be said. You deserve a decent wedding and you're gunna get one, and that means organisation. But we're getting nowhere fast 'cos miladdo here is always otherwise engaged. I know, I know,' he held up his hand, 'he's a farmer and farmers are busy. I get it. But it don't solve our problem, does it? I have to go back to Upper Bourbury soon, and things are still completely up in the air.'

'I'm sure me an' Eden can organise our own wedding,' Eliot grumbled.

'I'm sure you can, mate,' Cain said, 'but what sort of wedding, eh? 'Cos it seems to me that Eden's got enough on her plate, what with the house and the kiddies to see to, not to mention this new business to get ready and then run, and we all know how busy you are 'cos you've just told us.'

'Dad, I really think—'

'I don't much care what you think, Jed. This needs doing properly, and we've got a matter of days to sort it out. Bleeding July. Have you ever heard the like? Next spring would've made more sense, but no.'

Beth took a deep breath. 'Wow! All this tension! I came here because it's pretty miserable at home and I wanted to be among friendly faces,' She flicked her long, dark hair over her shoulder. 'I think I'd have been better off at Thwaite Park.'

'Sorry, Beth.' Eden gave her a feeble smile. 'One of those days.'

'It's always one of them days round here lately,' Eliot muttered, dipping bread into his soup. 'Never a minute's peace.'

'If it's any consolation,' Beth replied, 'no one rows at home; it's all stony silences or sarcastic comments. You have to really care about someone to bother to argue, don't you?'

They all looked at each other, as if considering her words. Cain supposed she was right.

'Reckon you're onto something there, although it has to be said, Emerald would start a war with the Dalai Lama if she couldn't get her own way.'

Emerald gasped. 'I might have known it would come back to me!'

'You can't deny it. Sick of hearing about these business plans of yours.'

'It clearly means a lot to her,' Beth said. 'Sorry,' she added, as they all turned to stare at her. 'I don't want to interfere.'

'Then don't,' Emerald said coldly, stroking the cat like some Bond villain.

Cain wanted to tell her to shut her cakehole, but she had a point. Who was this interfering bird, anyway? Like he didn't have enough women telling him what to do.

'The thing is, as a completely impartial outsider, it seems to me that the answer to all your problems is staring you in the face.'

She took a sip of her tea and Cain wanted to scream. What the hell was she talking about? Luckily for him, Emerald was already demanding answers.

'Well, isn't it obvious? Emerald wants a business to run but doesn't have any experience that leads you to trust her with an investment. Eliot and Eden want to get married but haven't got time to organise a wedding. You, Cain, want to be able to head home, knowing the wedding is in good hands and plans are progressing nicely. So, why doesn't Emerald stay here, and take over as wedding planner? I'm sure she's been to enough of these events to know what's good and bad, and she would be on hand to liaise with both Eden and Eliot as and when they're available. Wedding planners are worth their weight in gold. We paid ours a fortune. If Emerald can pull this off, then I'm sure you'll have more faith in her ability to make a plan and stick to it, organise things and balance a budget. Of course, it's just a suggestion. Feel free to ignore me.' She leaned back in her chair and smiled at them all.

The entire kitchen fell silent as everyone digested her suggestion. Cain considered the matter. The girl had a point. He supposed it would get Emerald off his back, which was something, and it would shut Jed up, too. And, of course, it would ease the tension between Eliot and Eden, while making sure they had a proper decent do. He had a feeling that, left to themselves, Eliot would settle for the smallest, quietest wedding possible, and Eden would go for the cheapest so as not to waste his money. If only his own kids were so thoughtful, he mused.

'I suppose it's one solution,' he conceded. 'If you're really set on making your own living, Emerald, then here's as good a place as any to start. And you had enough to say about Honey's wedding and all that was wrong with it, so I reckon you must know sumfink about them.'

Emerald looked as if she didn't know what to say, which was unusual for her.

'Emerald?' Jed's tone was gentle.

She turned to him, looking stricken. 'But it would mean staying up here, in Yorkshire!'

'And?' Cain's face darkened. You couldn't win with some people.

'It's — well, it's so far away from — from everything.'

'Ungrateful little bleeder,' Cain muttered. 'I can't win with you, can I?'

'Happen she was hoping to be a bit nearer her dad,' Eliot muttered. 'Can't blame her for that, can you?'

What did he mean by that? Was he saying Cain was exiling her, or something? As if Emerald would care! All she wanted was to get her eager mitts on his money, like every other woman he'd ever known. If she wasn't so keen on Yorkshire there must be another reason, and if she was anything like Honey, he could guess what it was.

'I know what you're thinking, Emerald, but you can keep your 'air on. I know it feels like the back of beyond, but it ain't that far from the shops really,' he said. 'There's a Harvey Nicholls in Leeds, you know. I'm sure you'll find plenty of places to buy your clothes and whatnots.'

Eliot tutted. 'I don't think—'

'It's a great opportunity, Emmy,' Jed murmured, squeezing her hand. 'And you're grateful. Right?'

Emerald looked at Bella as if asking for help, and Bella stared back at her as if giving her opinion.

Evidently, the cat had more common sense than his daughter, because Emerald sighed and said, 'Yes. Yes, of course. Thanks, Dad.'

Jed nodded. 'Good call, Dad.'

'Hang on a minute.' Cain held up his hand. 'I ain't finished yet. I've been burned before by Honey. It was a big mistake, leaving her to get on with doing things the way she wanted. And I know you and your streak of mischief. Put it this way, this wedding will be a test. Do it right and I'll seriously consider investing in business premises for you. Get you all the equipment, everything you need to make a real go of this retreat lark. Screw it up and you can forget it, right?'

Emerald frowned. 'But the premises won't be in Yorkshire?'

Cain hesitated. Yorkshire seemed like a pretty good idea to him. It was far enough away to get some peace and quiet from his daughter, for a start. Still, he'd better give her some reason to make an effort, he supposed.

'Wherever you like,' he conceded. 'Although, I ain't paying fancy London prices, so you can forget that.'

'I don't want to be in London,' she assured him. 'I want somewhere rural and peaceful.'

'Good. So that's sumfink we agree on then. Do we have a deal?'

Emerald bit her lip, then nodded. 'Okay. Deal.'

'That's great news,' said Jed, beaming at them both.

'I'm very glad you think so, because you're going to be staying up here to help her.'

Ha! That wiped the smile off his face. Serves him right.

'What? But I don't—'

'Look, you're her big brother, and I know you'll keep an eye on her. Plus, you ain't got anything better to do right now, have you? Given that you've quit the band and you're refusing to go back to the States. Besides,' he gave Eden and Eliot a sympathetic look, 'these two have got enough on their plates, and they're going to need a hand with this new business of theirs. So, the least you can do is help them out while this venture gets off the ground. Eden, you'll be glad of the help, yeah?'

Eden swallowed, not looking at Eliot. 'Of course.'

'Great. So, Jed, it's up to you but I ain't keen on Emerald staying here without you to watch her. Are we agreed?'

He watched Jed glance at Emerald, who was staring up at her brother, an undisguised appeal in her eyes. Cain knew that Jed couldn't disappoint her, and sure enough he didn't.

'Fine. Agreed.'

'That's that sorted then.' Cain leaned back in his chair and folded his arms.

Cain saw Eden and Eliot exchange nervous glances. He knew they wouldn't be so keen on having Emerald around, and he couldn't blame them, but frankly, he was past caring. With one fell stroke, he'd found a home and a job for his troublesome son and daughter, and best of all, he could go back home with a clear conscience, knowing he'd done his best for them and that they'd parted friends. All in all, Cain considered today a good one. He only hoped Marcus wouldn't be on the phone next, demanding

Cain set him up in his own venture. Knowing his offspring, he wouldn't be in the slightest bit surprised.

****

'I'm simply saying that you're spending too much time round there. How do you think that looks?'

Beth could hardly believe what she was hearing. Was James serious? 'I don't care how it looks! And looks to whom? Who else cares? Why should I stop seeing them just because—'

'*Them*? Don't you mean *him*? You always did have a soft spot for him, didn't you? Don't think I hadn't noticed. All that gushing about what a perfect father he is, how hard he works, how decent he is. Pass me the sick bucket.'

His scornful expression enraged her. 'How dare you! How can you say that to me, of all people! A soft spot for *him*? Well, you had more than a soft spot for his wife, as I recall.'

James's eyes sparked with fury. 'Don't you dare bring that up. It's ancient history.'

'Ancient history? Maybe to you! I have to live with it every day. I've had to try to forgive and forget, haven't I? Move on. Pretend it never happened, that you never betrayed me with that woman.'

'Beth, I'm warning you, shut up. We agreed when we were in New York that we'd never discuss this again.'

Shut up? Who the hell did he think he was talking to? 'And it's as easy as that, is it? Sorry, am I making you uncomfortable? How inconsiderate of me.'

'I've told you, if you're going to keep on about it, there's no point in our being together. We can never make it work if you're going to keep throwing it back in my face.'

'But—'

'I'm not listening to this any longer. We had an agreement that we'd let it go and move on with our lives. If you can't do that then we may as well call it a day. Your choice.'

As James pulled open the door, Beth flinched inwardly at the sight of her mother-in-law hovering in the hallway.

'Good morning!' Deborah's smile dropped as James pushed

past her without so much as a muttered apology. Beth was still quivering with rage. Deborah turned slowly to look at her and raised an eyebrow in enquiry.

Beth crumbled inside. 'I'm so sorry, Deborah. I'll — I'll go after him.'

Deborah's lip curled. 'Very well. If you must.' She turned and headed into the kitchen where, just seconds later, Beth heard her slamming cupboard doors and banging crockery with an alarming lack of control.

She hurried after her, anxious to appease. 'I'll try to calm him down. It was my fault. I'm sorry.'

Deborah grabbed her bowl and pushed past her, heading into the dining room without a word. Evidently, she couldn't stand to look at Beth another moment.

****

James was nowhere to be found. As Beth wandered along the footpath, hands in her coat pockets, she wondered why she was even bothering to look. In fact, she wasn't sure she *was* looking. It was an excuse to get out of the house, away from her mother-in-law's clear disapproval. She came to a fence and climbed the stile, barely registering the fact. Jumping down, she continued to walk along the track, her thoughts swirling in her mind, unclear and unformed — as if someone had stirred up a pond with a big stick and left mud clouding the water. She couldn't make sense of anything. It felt as if she had the weight of the world pressing upon her, and she didn't know what to do about it.

All around her the beauty of the landscape worked to soothe her troubled soul. She paused a moment, gazing out across the fields. She closed her eyes and took a few deep breaths, hearing the chirruping of birdsong, and the gentle sound of a breeze rustling the leaves on the trees. Skimmerdale was waking up after its long winter sleep.

Whatever James thought, she'd no intention of stopping her visits to Wildflower Farm. It was only going there that kept her sane. Being around Eliot and Eden was essential for her. They were her anchor, reminding her what a normal relationship looked like. Oh, they weren't perfect, they had their disagreements and their difficulties, but they were a team, and they loved each other deeply. As for the children — Ophelia and Liberty were such bright girls. They were very different in their personalities, but equally delightful to be around. Ophelia with her bluntness, humour and mischief, and Libby with her kindness and consideration and gentle nature.

Then there was George, of course. Despite being no relation to Eliot and bearing a strong resemblance to both his natural parents, he'd already mastered Eliot's scowl and some of his mannerisms to perfection, and he'd frequently demonstrated Libby's kindness and Ophelia's mischief. It was hard not to take to him, even though a part of her flinched every time she saw him.

She loved the Harland family, and her visits to them were the only bright spot in her week, especially now that her in-laws were back. She was glad some of the pressure had been taken off Eliot and Eden, with Cain paying for the wedding, Emerald organising it, and Jed being around to help get the bunk barns ready and lend a hand on the farm. Eliot would be glad of his help when lambing came around, she was sure, no matter how much his face said otherwise at the moment.

She found there was a hint of a smile on her face. She couldn't deny she'd felt a surge of relief to discover Jed was Emerald's brother, not her boyfriend, and he would be staying around for a while. That was good. She hoped she'd bump into him again. He seemed nice.

Nice? She laughed inwardly. That wasn't the word that sprang to mind whenever she thought about Jed. He'd had a startling effect on her, and it was most unexpected. And quite scary, if she was honest. Although... She sighed. It had been rather lovely, too. It felt like she had a secret inside her, something that was just hers. Something that no one else knew about, that she could summon up when things were getting too much. Like today.

She carried on walking, finding the path through the woodland to the village. She'd go home the long way around. It was the first real sunshine they'd had so far this year, and there was no hurry. Far from it.

As she headed out of the copse and into the sunlight again, her heart did a sudden skip and her legs felt hollow. Oh, God!

'Hey!' Jed's smile was warm and easy. 'Beth. Fancy seeing you here. You on your way to the village? I've been exploring. I figured if I'm gonna be living here a while I'd better get my bearings.' His smile faded, and his eyes filled with concern. 'Are you okay? You look real upset.'

'No, no. That is, yes, I'm okay.' She swallowed. 'Just had a row with the husband.'

Why had she said that? What did she want to go and remind him of the fact that she was married for? What was she thinking! Of course, she had to remind him. More than that, she had to remind herself.

'Ah. Right. I won't probe,' he said, holding up his hands. He glanced around, clearly feeling awkward. 'Emerald and Dad are at the farmhouse, making lists, so I escaped. She's finally coming around to organising this wedding. I guess she'd be happier if it was happening further south but, you know. It is what it is. It's great to see her smile, but there are only so many discussions you can listen to about buttonholes and favours. She's got big plans, that's for sure. I figured it was time I headed out and left them to it. I was just in the village.' He grinned. 'It's real cute — like something out of an old English movie.'

She looked over his shoulder and nodded. 'I suppose it is. One takes it for granted. I've been here so long now that I've stopped noticing.'

'Wow, I can't imagine that. I hadn't realised how much I missed England 'til I came back. I'd forgotten how beautiful it is.'

She shivered. 'I suppose it depends who you're sharing your little bit of England with.'

'You could be right,' he mused. 'I guess if you're having a hard time with — whoever — you don't notice the bigger picture.'

'Right now, I'm sharing my bit of England with my in-laws and it's so hard.' She bit her lip, wondering why she was spilling her family secrets to someone who was, when all was said and done, a stranger.

'I'm real sorry to hear that. Families, huh? Who'd have 'em?'

Beth nodded, noticing his dimples, and the way his hair flopped rather untidily. He was wearing a battered brown leather jacket, jeans, and Timberland boots, and there was a chunky watch on his wrist. No ring, though, she thought, wondering why that made her feel happy.

'I don't get on with them. David's a bully and a tyrant,' she admitted. 'Although, his wife scares me more.'

'In what way?'

They were walking now, heading towards the village. Jed didn't seem to mind that he was doubling back on himself. Beth was aware that she shouldn't be discussing James's family with this stranger. It was disloyal, and she usually guarded against disloyalty, no matter how much they hurt her. With Jed though, it didn't seem to count somehow.

'She disapproves of me,' she said. 'And you know, that makes me feel far worse than David's bossiness or downright rudeness. Somehow, it hurts more.'

'Why the hell would she disapprove of you?' he said, sounding genuinely baffled. 'You're kind, compassionate, attractive, smart. What more does she want from a daughter-in-law?'

Beth realised her face was burning. Kind, compassionate and smart? Lovely compliments. But attractive? Did he really think so? God, she was shallow.

'What she wants,' she admitted, 'is someone who is good enough for her precious son. And I seem to fall far short of that. I don't know what it is I've done wrong. I try very hard to please him, to please them all, yet it never seems—'

She broke off as her voice cracked, and she blinked away the tears, feeling ashamed of herself. He put his arm around her, his voice gentle.

'Hey, take it easy. Some people you can't please, no matter what you do. That's because there's something wrong with *them*, not with you. Maybe, you should stop trying. Maybe, you should start living your life to please yourself. What have you got to lose?'

He was right, she realised, looking up at him. More than that, there was a bleakness in his face that made her think he'd learned that lesson the hard way. She wondered what had happened to him. He'd left the band, she remembered. Cain had said — what had he said? That Jed had refused to go back to America. She wondered why he would want to stay in England when he'd had a life in the States that had been so successful.

She'd Googled him when she got home, startled to realise that he'd been lead guitarist and vocalist in Raven's Wing, a band that had had major success with their first two albums recently, and that there was fevered, and rather anguished, speculation among the fans in America as to his whereabouts, and whether or not he'd officially left the band. Why would he walk away from that? What had hurt him so much? Because she was certain something had. She felt something stir inside her, and as he looked back at her, she felt a strange and unexpected connection to him. It was probably a good thing that they'd reached the fork in the path.

'I'm going home via the village,' she said, with some reluctance. 'You need to go the other way towards Wildflower Farm.'

'Right. Sure. Well, remember what I said,' he told her. 'Stop trying to please them. Be yourself. Yourself is more than good enough.'

She would remember that, she thought, as she turned away from him. She would hold that piece of advice in her heart, and whenever James got petulant, or David got angry, or Deborah gave her one of her withering stares, she would think to herself, *I am Myself, and Myself is more than good enough.* One day, if she thought it often enough, she might believe it.

Chapter 11

'This is gunna take some painting.' Cain wrinkled his nose in dismay as he surveyed the barn, Emerald by his side.

'I don't know why they don't hire professional decorators,' Emerald said with a shrug. 'As if Eliot hasn't got enough to do already!'

'Hmm. Your concern for Eliot's welfare is touching, I'm sure. Don't forget he'll have Jed to help him out.'

'Even so.'

'They won't take no money off me to help, and decorators cost money. Reckon they've had to cut corners on fittings as it is. I saw Eden looking through a bathroom website yesterday. Talk about basic.'

Emerald tutted. 'We're talking about hikers here, Dad. How grand do you think they'll expect it to be? So long as the toilet flushes and the shower's hot, they should count themselves lucky.'

'Hah! Easy for you to say. Bet you've got gold taps and a bidet in your gaff.'

Emerald pulled a face. 'You must be joking! I've had years of being carted around from hovel to hovel while Mother dearest absorbed the atmosphere of her historical novel backdrops. When you've washed your clothes in a stream and shit in a bucket a few times, you're grateful for the most basic of mod cons.' She sighed. 'This may be a mere hostel for walkers, but it's still better than most of the places I've lived in. Warmth, a hot shower, and a flush toilet. That's perfection in my eyes.'

'Did you really do that?' Cain's eyes were wide. 'Shit in a bucket, I mean?'

'It was either that or venture outside in the howling wind and rain to do it behind a tree. Funnily enough, a bucket seemed like the best option.'

'Bleeding hell.' He shook his head, feeling stunned that his daughter had been brought up in such a savage fashion. His own childhood home had an outside toilet, but at least it had flushed. 'I'm so sorry, Emerald.'

She seemed surprised at his admission, and evidently wasn't sure how to respond. 'It's okay.' She shrugged. 'Now, shall we take a look inside?'

As they opened the door, Jed walked up behind them. 'Inspecting the place? I was about to do the same.'

'Hell's bells, where do you start?' Cain said, staring around. 'You're gunna have your work cut out here, mate. Top of the list seems to be the plumbing,' he added, giving Emerald a sympathetic look.

She didn't see it. She was gazing out of the far window, and he followed her gaze, his eyes taking in the gently sloping fields and the distant sparkle of sunlight on water as the rays reflected off the River Skimmer. He wondered how he'd never noticed this side of his middle child before. Why hadn't he known what kind of childhood she'd had? Why had he allowed Cassandra to take her away and been content to wash his hands of her?

He'd known his second wife was a bit of a fruit loop. She was too wrapped up in herself and her own wants and needs to take proper care of their daughter. He'd known it, deep down, but he was trying to do the right thing by Marcus and Sandy at the time, and he was still battling with Lowri over his eldest two. Emerald had been a casualty of war, he supposed, and felt a stab of shame.

'Looks like Jed's gunna be well and truly occupied here,' he said carefully. 'You do know that, right?'

'Of course. I'm not stupid,' Emerald said.

'And that means the wedding planning is gunna be down to you.'

Emerald's eyes narrowed. 'What are you saying? That I'm not up to it?'

'No, no.' He shook his head. 'I have to go home tomorrow. I'm doing that guest appearance on some stupid panel show. Don't ask me why. Oh well, at least I'll be back in the studio soon.' His eyes lit up at the thought of it.

'Studio? You're recording new stuff?' Jed sounded surprised.

'Bin asked to feature on a track on Sun King's next album,' he preened.

Emerald gaped at him. 'Even I've heard of Sun King. They want *you*? What on earth for?'

Cain scowled, his guilt over his daughter vanishing like vapour. 'What do you mean, what for? Bleeding cheek.'

'Dad's good,' Jed said hastily. 'His voice is excellent, and he's a master at what he does. Sun King are wise to ask him to be involved. Good luck with it, Dad.'

Cain felt a little soothed and remembered why he'd started the conversation. 'Point is, between the panel show and the studio, I got other things to sort out, so I ain't going to be here.' Too right, he did. Several charity functions for some cause or other. He couldn't remember offhand what they were in aid of, but it looked good if he attended and donated. That knighthood was within his grasp. He could almost touch it. 'That's why I've asked Eden if you two can stay at the farm.'

'What! What on earth for?' Emerald looked appalled.

'Because it's one hell of a trek between The Paradise Hotel and here and, well, it would be a dummy run for Eden, an' all. There's a guest room for you, Emerald, and Eden's gunna make up a bed in the attic for you, Jed. Bit basic, but it's okay, and it will give her the chance to find out how she copes with everything before that new venture of hers opens for business. I've got a feeling it's gunna be too much for her, and she needs to find that out now, before she's taken the bookings. Having two guests to run around after, on top of her family, will be a great trial run.'

'Great,' Emerald snapped. 'So, we're bloody guinea pigs for your precious Eden. Might have known.'

'It's not a bad idea,' Jed soothed. 'In fact, it could work out well.

The farm's pretty cool, and we've both got a lot to do, so it makes sense to be on hand. Come on, it's gotta be a lot more comfortable than staying in the hotel, right?'

'Well, you would say that,' she snapped.

'Meaning?'

'Meaning we can all see that you fancy Eden like mad. No wonder you want to stay with her.'

'What? Are you crazy? Where the hell did that come from?' He shook his head, bewildered.

Cain scowled. 'You'd better not get any ideas in that direction,' he warned. 'She's happy with this Eliot fella, and even though I think she could do better than landing herself with all this worry and hard work, I know for a fact that he thinks the world of her. Plus, there's them little kiddies to think of, so no funny business. Right?'

Jed's face was a picture of indignation. 'She's a friend! There's nothing more to it than that. I like Eliot, so why would I—? Jesus, why am I even defending myself? This is stupid. I have no intentions towards Eden at all, okay?'

'Hmm. Glad to hear it. So,' Cain looked from one to the other, 'you're happy to move in there? Do the trial run and help the Harlands out?'

Emerald and Jed exchanged glances.

Jed nodded. 'Fine by me. Emerald?'

She pursed her lips, thinking, but seemed to accept that she had no choice. 'I suppose so.'

'Good. Now let's bugger off back to The Paradise. I'm flaming starving.'

****

James recognised the look on his father's face. The determination in his eyes, the tight line of his mouth. His heart sank. Why had he been summoned?

'Sit down.'

James obeyed, wondering what the hell was in store for him now.

'I've been giving the matter some thought, and I've concluded that we haven't got time to sit around and wait for nature to take its course,' David said. 'Beth's thirty-four now. Fertility in women starts to decline in the mid-thirties, so there's no time to lose. Now, I know you said you've had tests, but I think you should see a top specialist. To that end, I've been doing some research, and I've found the perfect man. It's an exclusive clinic and it will mean a few trips to London, but—'

'No!'

James wasn't sure who was most startled at the sound of his vehement refusal — himself or his father. David's eyes had opened so wide his eyebrows were almost scraping his hairline.

'No?'

'I — I don't see any need for this. As I've said before, we've seen specialists.'

'But they weren't private specialists, were they? You get what you pay for in my experience. This chap—'

'I'm sorry. I must be clear about this. There's no need.'

David stared at him for a moment, his lips moving soundlessly as he surveyed him with undisguised amazement. Then he turned away, gazing out of the window so James couldn't see his face. Not that he wanted to. He knew his father well enough to know the matter wouldn't end there.

'Something you want to tell me, boy?'

James felt a prickling sensation as tiny beads of sweat appeared on his forehead. He was aware that his stomach was behaving in a peculiar fashion, leaving him nauseated. His mouth felt dry. He'd kill for a whisky.

There was a long silence, then David turned to face him. 'Well?'

James swallowed. 'I don't know what you mean,' he began, but he saw his father's eyes narrow and he shut up.

'This is a marvellous opportunity, and you're refusing to take it.' David sat down and glared at him. 'What are you keeping from me?'

The temptation to run was overpowering, but James knew he wasn't a six-year-old child any more. He had to stand up to his father, for once. 'I'm not sure I know what you mean,' he said, trying to keep his voice steady.

'Really?' His father leaned back in the chair and steepled his fingers under his chin, his eyes unblinking as he stared at James. 'Don't take me for a fool, boy. If you seriously wanted a child, you'd be willing to try anything. You haven't even attempted IVF for five or six years. Why not? What's going on? And don't even think about lying to me.'

James closed his eyes. This was it. The moment he'd dreaded for so long, but had always known, deep down, was inevitable. He could only hope his father had an understanding side, although he hadn't seen much evidence of it.

'Some years ago, I made a decision.'

'What decision? Well? Spit it out.'

'I made the decision that I didn't want children. To that end, I took steps to ensure I never had to worry about it.'

'Steps? What the hell are you — are you telling me you had a vasectomy?' David's voice had risen to a squeak. Clearly, the idea was preposterous.

'That's about the size of it, yes.'

David's mouth fell open. He seemed unable to speak for a moment, and James felt a fleeting stab of satisfaction that he'd managed to take the wind out of his father's sails for once, however uncomfortable the outcome was going to be. And he was under no illusions that it would be very uncomfortable indeed.

David's fingers drummed the arm of his chair as he made an obvious effort to absorb this new information. James waited for the explosion but, when it came, his father's response was subdued.

'Why on earth would you be so stupid?'

James leaned back heavily in the armchair. 'Because I realised, some years ago, that having children wasn't something I wanted.' He didn't feel able to admit out loud that his own childhood had been so overshadowed by his bully of a father that he felt no great urge to recreate it with his own offspring. Besides, what did he know about being a father? He had no real interest in learning, either. His life was pretty good as it was, with no ties or responsibilities. He and Beth had spent the last two Christmases in New York. They'd been on a cruise. Would they have been able to indulge themselves so easily if they'd had children hanging around them? Of course not but try explaining that to Beth. Hormones had overtaken her powers of reasoning many years ago.

'I take it Beth doesn't know?'

James blanched. 'No, she doesn't. And I'd appreciate it if it stayed that way.'

'I'll bet you would.'

'It's none of your business anyway,' James ventured.

He realised immediately he'd gone too far. David's face was that of an angry gremlin as he leapt from his chair and loomed over James like the shadow of death.

'Don't get clever with me! Your wife is under the impression that you and she are trying for a baby. You must know that she gets her hopes up every single month, so how do you think she'd feel if she knew that you had a vasectomy years ago?'

James hung his head. He could imagine all too well what she'd say, which was why she must never find out. It would finish them, no doubt about it.

David hovered over him, a diabolical presence that made him feel sick to the stomach. How could he even begin to explain to his father?

'Have you any idea what you've done?' David shook his head, clearly bewildered at this unexpected turn of events. 'Kathryn and Scott will love this. Owen — bloody Owen, of all people — will be rubbing his hands in glee. They've hit the jackpot. Everything we have, this house, the other properties, the furniture and paintings, all going to their grubby paws, you fucking idiot. Well,' he glared at James, 'you won't be so smug when I tell Beth what you did. That's for sure.'

'You wouldn't!' James leapt to his feet. 'For Christ's sake, you're my father! Where's your loyalty?'

'Loyalty?' David almost spat at him. 'After what you've done? To me, to your mother, to your wife? Don't you dare talk to me about loyalty. You've ruined everything, you stupid bastard!

Everything!'

He turned, as if about to leave the room. James panicked. Beth was upstairs. David would find her, tell her the truth, destroy her, destroy their marriage. He couldn't allow that.

'Wait! There's something you don't know.'

David paused. 'Something else? Jesus! What more could there be?'

James swallowed hard. He couldn't believe he was going to have to reveal the truth to his father, of all people. 'There's — I mean, I do — I mean, I have an heir.'

The effect on his father was startling. He dropped into a chair, face pale, never taking his eyes off his son. 'An heir?'

'Some years ago, I had an affair,' James mumbled.

'Speak up, boy!'

'I had an affair, with a local farmer's wife. Although, she wasn't just a farmer's wife. She came from a good family — so good, they disowned her for marrying beneath her. She and I, we fell in love. Sort of.'

'Huh. *Sort of.* Go on.'

'She got pregnant.' He shook his head, the memory of her announcement even now making him sick. 'When Jemima told me,' he admitted, 'it was the worst possible thing she could have said. I wanted it to be her husband's, but she told me there was no chance. She'd spun him some cock and bull story about them sleeping together one night when they'd been drunk, but she knew deep down that he wasn't fooled.'

'I still don't see why that made you have the snip. So, your bit on the side was pregnant. That didn't rule out having a child with your wife, did it?'

'It made me think.' James was sweating. He was sure his throat was closing up. 'I didn't want a baby with Jemima. And then, I realised. I didn't want a baby with anyone. I liked my life as it was. Jemima started to change, and not just physically, although God knows that was bad enough. Her attitude altered. She got clingy and annoying. I thought, what if Beth got like that, too? And for what? Some squawking kid who'd demand everything and give nothing.'

138

'Yes, I had one like that,' David growled.

James gritted his teeth. 'Some people aren't meant to be parents, and that's that. I'm one of them. Anyway, what if it happened again? What if I got Jemima pregnant a second time? She was using contraception but look how that worked out. And what if—'

Maybe he shouldn't go that far. It would probably sound far worse than he meant it to. But his father's gaze was drilling through him again and he was almost certain the old man could read his thoughts.

'What if you had another liaison? What if a later affair resulted in another child?'

Damn! He really could read his thoughts! James mopped his forehead.

'I'm not saying I was planning another affair. I'm saying, *what if*. These things happen, after all. One never intends to start a — a dalliance. You must understand, surely? Did you never have these worries?'

'Unlike you, boy, I took precautions and never left it to the woman. If you're going to make a habit of this sort of thing, you'd better learn the lesson right now that you can't trust them. Biggest bargaining chip in the world, a baby. Got you over a barrel then, haven't they? You have to make damn sure they can't get their claws into you, and the first lesson, the absolute golden rule, is never leave contraception to the woman.'

'Yes, well, it won't be a problem now, will it?' said James, pouting. He hated being made to look a fool by his father, especially when he realised he had a point. He should have made sure Jemima wasn't lying. For the first time, he began to wonder if she'd done it deliberately. Well, if she had, she'd paid the price for that, hadn't she?

'Are you still seeing her? This Jemima woman?'

'No.' He ran his hand over his eyes. 'She was killed in a car accident when George was a few weeks old.'

David sat up straight. 'Then where is the boy?'

'He's with Harland — that's her husband. He lives at Wildflower Farm, their sheep farm, with Harland and his fiancée and Jemima's two daughters. He's happy enough.'

'But you said Harland didn't believe George was his?'

'He doesn't, but when Jemima died it was a mess. Chaos. And I had Beth to consider. She'd just discovered the affair and she was in pieces. I couldn't expect her to welcome Jemima's son to the house, could I? Harland registered George as his own, and there was an unspoken agreement that George would, to all intents and purposes, be his son. It was for the best.'

When his father made no comment, he said in a rush, 'So you see, I didn't want to find myself in that situation again, did I? Which was why I took steps to ensure I never did. George is a Harland now, and Beth and I are working on our issues. The last thing she needs to know is—'

'That her husband is not only a cheat and a liar but a snivelling coward, too.' David shook his head. 'Putting her through the anguish of craving for a baby, knowing that every month will bring disappointment, but being too selfish, too gutless to confess.' His lip curled in obvious disgust. 'No doubt she knows nothing of the others, either.'

James could feel his face scorching. 'Others?'

David smirked. 'Did you really think I didn't know? This Jemima certainly wasn't your first, was she?'

'Look, I do love Beth. I don't want you to think that I don't. It's just that—'

David held up his hand. 'I don't want to hear it. I have no interest in your extramarital affairs. I couldn't care less if you sleep with a different woman every week. What of it? That's not the problem.'

'It isn't?'

'Of course not. The problem is that you, you idiot, have no heir, and never will now.'

'George is my heir,' James said. 'Everything will go to him. See? I did think about it.'

'George? George is a Harland now, for God's sake!'

'Of course he isn't. Look, whatever the circumstances right now, he's got our blood in his veins. He's a Fuller. I'll make sure he inherits everything. Beth keeps gabbling on about adoption, but I won't have it. Someone else's kid making a claim on our estate! No chance. George is entitled to his inheritance and he'll get it.'

'And so will the Harlands.' David shook his head. 'You are such a bloody fool.'

James bristled. 'What's wrong with leaving everything to my own son? The way I see it, it's win win. George gets to be brought up by Harland, so he's no bother to me, then he gets the estate when I die so my conscience is clear, and George gets his reward for living on a sheep farm all those years.'

'And what will a farmer's son understand about managing this house, running the businesses, investing wisely? Nothing, that's what! He'll spend it all on flaming sheep!'

'Sheep?'

'Who the hell do you think Harland will leave Wildflower Farm to, eh? Bits of girls, or the boy he's raised as his own?'

'Well, I—'

'By the time George is an adult, he'll think, eat and sleep farming. When he gets his hands on our money, he'll waste it all doing up Wildflower Farm and expanding his own business, with no thought to ours. What else can you expect? He won't want to live in a house like this! It will be beyond his comprehension. The entire fortune will be dwindled away on fucking ewes and tups and keeping that damned place afloat.'

James hadn't thought of that. He couldn't think of anything to say. Not that it mattered. David was already up and pacing the room, muttering curses under his breath, and hardly in the mood to listen. James began to feel quite indignant. 'Look, I was unlucky, but come on, you're a man of the world. You can't criticise me when you've had plenty of affairs yourself.'

'Let's get one thing straight, boy.' David stopped and fixed him with a murderous look. 'Who I screw is my own business, as who you screw is yours. Point is, I did my duty and provided an heir. You, on the other hand, even fucked that up. Now it's us who are screwed. You understand?'

James nodded dumbly.

'There's only one thing for it,' David continued. 'We need to get

141

custody of George.'

The room seemed to grow dark for a moment. James blinked and took a deep breath. 'You *are* joking?'

'Do I look as if I'm joking?'

'But Harland's name is on the birth certificate!'

'Good. He falsified a document. That will look bad on him.'

'We can't do this!'

'Give me one good reason.'

James felt quite sick. 'Beth,' he murmured. 'She'll never forgive me. She really likes Harland. They're friends.'

'Friends? Are you serious? So, you're in touch with George?'

'Not me, no. Harland won't let me near the place, not that I'd want to go near it anyway. But he and Beth have always got on. She thinks the world of him.' Didn't she just! 'To give him his due, he's a good father. Taking George away would break him.'

'Good. An added bonus then. As for Beth, she'll have to come round eventually. Surely, even she wouldn't want to deprive a man of his son?'

'But she knows I don't want him! I've made that very clear to her over the years.'

David sat, his expression thoughtful. 'Hmm. We're going to have to be very clever about this. If we go in all guns blazing, the danger is it will blow up in our faces. Beth might back Harland in court, and you can bet your life the Harlands will use every trick in the book to keep hold of the boy.'

He leaned back in his chair, his fingers drumming the arm again. James felt as if he were in some sort of nightmare. How had he got involved in all this? If he could turn the clock back, he would, whatever the price. Jemima hadn't been worth all this trouble in the end. He wished he'd kept his hands off her.

'The women hold the key,' David mused. 'If we can get your mother and Beth onside—'

'My mother!' James felt a wave of dread wash over him at the thought of telling her his sordid secret. 'And Beth will never be on my side about this.'

'She will if she truly believes you want George back.'

'She'll never believe that!'

'Then you'd better polish up your acting skills and make her believe it, hadn't you? Now, your mother... Yes, she'll have to know, but we'll have to tell her when the time's right. And knowing your mother, she'll want to see him, want him in her family. Of course, it will mean telling her that there'll be no more grandchildren, and George is her only shot.'

'I can't tell her about the vasectomy! She'll tell Beth.' James felt close to tears and tried to remain calm. His father would have no truck with emotional outbursts.

'We don't need to mention that. It's pretty clear that something's wrong when you've been trying for a baby all these years. When she hears about George, she'll assume it's Beth's fault, which is even better when you think about it. She'll feel even more sorry for you, deprived of a child, and will want to get George back for you.' He smirked. 'Yes, I can see this plan taking shape. What is it they say? Softly, softly, catchy monkey.'

James rubbed his forehead. 'George seems happy with Harland. He has a family, sisters...'

'And here he'll have his father, his grandparents, and a lifestyle that Harland could never give him in a million years. Look, this is for the boy's own good. He's only — what? — three, four? He'll forget all about Wildflower Farm in a year or two, and by the time he's an adult it will be nothing but a dim and distant bad dream. He'll be a Fuller, through and through.' He narrowed his eyes at James. 'All this is your fault. You've brought it on yourself, left us no choice. Now, we need to make a plan, because this has to be done carefully. We need to have everything in place before we pounce. Take that look off your face! This is going to happen, boy, whatever you say. You'd better get used to it.'

Chapter 12

'I'm terribly sorry,' Eden said. 'I know it's not much but—'

'Hey, it's fine,' Jed assured her. He glanced around the attic room and smiled. 'It's warm and dry and,' he dropped onto the bed and bounced a couple of times, 'the bed's comfortable enough. Look, I won't be up here much. I've got my work cut out, painting the barns with you and helping Eliot on the farm.'

'You don't have to do that, you know,' she said.

'I figure it's the least I can do,' he said. 'Besides, I want to keep busy. The more work I have to do, the better.' His voice trailed off and he was quiet for a moment, then looked up at her and smiled. 'Good job you have a spare room for Emerald, though. I doubt she'd appreciate being put in an attic.'

'You'd be surprised.' Emerald's voice cut through the sudden silence that had descended as Eden viewed Jed and thought that there was a sadness there that he was desperately trying to hide. As Emerald joined them in the attic, she tried not to pull a face.

She swung round and forced a smile instead. 'Oh. So, you'd have been happy up here? Perhaps Jed should take the guest room, after all.'

'All I'm saying,' Emerald drawled, 'is that I've lived in even worse hovels than this one.'

Eden glared at her. Emerald's baby blue eyes met hers in a challenge.

'The attic's not that bad,' Jed said hastily. 'I've never been scared of spiders either, and hey, I have a whole floor to myself! Result. Have you seen your room, Emmy?'

Emerald nodded. 'Yeah. It's okay, I suppose. I can just about squeeze my yoga mat in so that's something.'

Eden's mouth tightened, but she was determined not to rise to that woman's goading. July couldn't come soon enough. The quicker this bitch left Wildflower Farm, the better.

'Right,' she said, 'now that you've seen where you'll be sleeping, let's go downstairs, shall we? I'm sure Cain is ready for a cup of coffee.'

'Could use a coffee myself,' Jed said, smiling at her.

In his blue eyes, she detected a trace of sympathy, and something else — a plea for patience, perhaps? She understood that he was protective of his younger sister, but Emerald wasn't easy, and Eden wasn't a saint. She hoped she could keep the lid on her feelings while the two of them were staying.

Cain had turned up at the farm that morning, having unexpectedly returned to Yorkshire following his recording of a panel show. He'd headed straight to Wildflower Farm, begged for a cup of tea and some cake, and demanded to know what was going on with the wedding plans, and how far the work on the barns had progressed.

'Stop fretting, Dad,' Jed said, laughing. 'Look, we're onto it, okay? Leave it with us. You have to start trusting us or you're going to be a nervous wreck. Or are you intending to head back to Yorkshire every few days to check up on us?'

'You must be joking. Takes forever to get here,' Cain said. 'You can't blame me for worrying, though, can you?'

'Thought you were going into the studio with Sun King,' Emerald said. 'Or did that fall through?'

'No, it didn't fall through, cheeky git. I'm going back tomorrow, as it happens. Looking forward to it.'

Knowing Cain of old, Eden had thought she detected a trace of nerves in his voice. He may be looking forward to getting back in the studio, but he was also fearful. Not that he'd ever admit that, of course.

When she entered the kitchen with Jed and Emerald, Cain was

sitting at the table, his eyes wide with astonishment as Ophelia sat opposite him, telling him all about her success at last year's gymkhanas. Eden grinned to herself as Ophelia provided every detail, dazzling Cain with equine information that he clearly didn't understand or care about.

'Wow,' Jed said, slipping into a chair beside the excited ten-year-old, 'you sound like an expert. Are you taking part in any more shows? I'd love to come and watch you.'

'Oh yes,' Ophelia confirmed. 'There are a couple of local gymkhanas, and then there's the Skimmerdale Show at the end of August. That's fantastic. But I expect you'll be gone by then.'

'I expect we will,' Jed said. 'But there's nothing stopping me from coming back to watch, is there? Is it just you taking part, or does your sister ride, too?'

'Libby's very good,' Ophelia admitted, 'but she looks a bit daft on Flora now. She's too big for her really.' She eyed Eden hopefully. 'We need another pony. A bigger one.'

Eden patted her on the head. 'Yes, we've talked about this, haven't we? As soon as we can afford it, we'll do what we can. Give us the chance to get this business up and running, eh?'

'I did think,' Ophelia said, 'that Dad would have used some of the proceeds from Gideon to buy a pony.' She turned to Jed. 'Gideon was our prize tup. We sold him for a fortune t'other year.'

'Tup?' Jed queried, frowning at Eden.

'Ram,' she explained. 'He was the overall champion at the Skimmerdale Show, the summer before last. Eliot did do quite well with him at the sale. Nevertheless,' she said, giving Ophelia a stern look, 'we made it very clear that every penny of that was needed to put into this new venture. What did we say?'

'All right, all right.' Ophelia sighed. 'It's nothing to me, is it? It's Libby I feel sorry for. She loves riding, but her feet proper dangle now. Reckon it's a bit harsh, that's all.'

Eden bit her lip and turned away before Ophelia noticed her smile. Ophelia was a very forthright and opinionated person, and Eden could see her point about Libby, but she was perfectly aware that the timing wasn't right yet and was playing to an audience. Did she really think appealing to her in front of Jed and Emerald would make a difference? Little monkey.

'Heavens, don't give up now, Ophelia. You may be getting somewhere.'

Eden spun round as Emerald addressed the little girl. 'Please don't encourage her,' she said, trying to keep a lid on her temper. The last thing she needed was anyone giving Ophelia more ammunition.

'But it would be a missed opportunity if she didn't persist,' Emerald said, staring unblinkingly at Eden, while affectionately stroking Bella who was, as usual, sitting on her lap. 'I mean, she has a captive audience here. My father obviously takes a personal interest in you and your family, and I'm sure it wouldn't take much to persuade him to stick his hand in his pocket for a new pony. How many ponies did Honey have, Daddy dear?'

Cain looked a bit dumbfounded as Eden seethed.

'After all,' Emerald continued, addressing Ophelia, 'nothing means more to him than your soon-to-be-stepmother's happiness, and I'm sure he'd want to remove yet another burden to that happiness by fulfilling your dreams.'

Eden glared at her. 'We wouldn't dream of asking Cain to buy the children a pony,' she snapped.

Ophelia looked thoughtful. 'I don't know so much, Mum. It would solve everything, wouldn't it?'

Emerald giggled. 'I do like you, Ophelia. As children go, you're quite entertaining.'

'Can it, Emerald,' Cain growled.

'Stop stirring up trouble,' Eden said. 'We've told the girls already, when the time's right we'll get them a pony.'

Emerald rolled her eyes and leaned towards Ophelia. 'Prepare for a long wait, kid,' she said in a stage whisper. 'In my experience of parents, there's always something more important than you. Children wait in a *very* long queue.'

Ophelia looked pretty fed up and Eden was trembling with anger. If Ophelia and George hadn't been in the room, she'd have told Emerald exactly what she thought of her.

Dimly, she heard Jed telling Ophelia to take no notice, that

Emerald was winding her up, then Cain grasped her arm and said, 'Can I have a word with you, Eden? Outside.'

Shooting Emerald a filthy look, she followed him into the garden and closed the door behind them. Before she could even open her mouth, Cain threw up his hands.

'I know, I know. She's a pain in the arse. You don't have to tell me.'

'Why have you landed her on me? Seriously, don't you think we have enough to cope with, without her giving us grief every day?'

'I know, Eden, but the truth is I don't know what else to do with her.' Cain leaned against the wall and gave a heavy sigh. 'I feel sorry for her and—'

'Sorry for her! You're as bad as Eliot. He said the same thing. What is it about her that she can be a total bitch and still twist men around her little finger?'

'She ain't had a great life, and that's my fault. I didn't realise how crap it had been until recently. I left her to the cruel fates, also known as her mother, and she had a proper weird childhood. Bin dragged from pillar to post and Cassandra was too self-absorbed to pay her much attention. Thing is, I feel like I should make it up to her.'

'Then *you* spend time with her,' Eden suggested.

'Bleeding hell, no way. What would I have to say to her? Thing is, you worked miracles with Honey. Now, come on, was there anyone worse than that little git when you first came to stay with us? But look at her now. A happily married woman. Down to you, that is.'

Eden shook her head. 'Flattery will get you nowhere. You know as well as I do that it was down to Teddy. Honey fell in love and he brought out the best in her. It had nothing to do with me. Nice try, though.'

Cain sighed. 'But you could cope with her, Eden. I never could. I was always out of me depth with me kids, and I'm sodding drowning with Emerald. All I want is for her to spend some time living with a nice, normal family, so maybe she can start to think like a nice, normal woman.'

Eden tutted. 'Good luck with that.'

'She needs some good influences, that's all, and let's face it, I'm hardly that, am I?' He pursed his lips and considered. 'She seems to think a lot of Jed. He's the only one of her siblings she cares about. And she also seems to like Eliot. Between the two of them, they might be able to bring out the best in her. I mean, they're both ordinary, decent blokes. I'd like her to be around them. She's bin brought up by a single mother who, well quite honestly, lived in cloud cuckoo land.'

'She's a nightmare, Cain, and I've had enough of ungrateful little madams. I had years with Honey. I thought all that was behind me.'

'I know, Eden, I know.' He gave her an apologetic look. 'Just, can you try? For me? She's drifted along for too long now. She needs a purpose. This retreat thing — personally, I think it's codswallop, but it means a lot to her. Must do if she's willing to stay here and plan your wedding for you. I want her to give it her best shot, but she's going to need help to do that. She needs to learn some responsibility, and I need to know I can trust her. I'm asking you, as a favour to me, just let her do this, eh? I know she's a moody mare, but you'll get a cracking wedding out of it, and I'll be forever grateful.'

Eden felt like kicking the garden wall but managed to stop herself. A broken foot wouldn't help anything, would it? She should tell Cain to stick the money, then she'd owe him nothing. She'd always said she'd be happy with a registry office wedding and she'd meant it. It was the marriage that mattered. Then she thought of Eliot, and his stubborn insistence that they have a church wedding and a proper reception afterwards. She slumped, defeated.

'You'll give her a chance?'

'Doesn't seem like I have much choice, does it?' Eden gave a big sigh. 'I suppose so. But she'd better stop with the bitchy comments. I don't want the girls picking up on it, thank you very much.'

'Good girl,' Cain said, beaming at her. 'It's all gunna work out a treat. I can feel it in me water.'

****

'I guess you're really up against it, ha?'

Eden swung round, paint roller in hand, as Jed strolled up behind her. 'You could say that, yes.' She gave him a rueful smile. 'It wasn't planned, but then, you never can plan these things exactly. There are so many variables. Planning permission, unexpected structural problems, how many cups of tea the builders require per hour.'

She'd be glad when they'd finished. Right now, they were fixing a rotting loft floor in one of the barns and replacing some slates on the roof of the old stables. Once that was done, they'd be gone at last. She felt as if they'd practically moved in to Wildflower Farm.

He laughed. 'Per hour?'

'You've been in America too long. The British are awash with tea. It's what keeps us going.'

'Fair enough. So, you want this place up and running by early May, right?'

Eden pulled a face. 'That was the dream, but whether or not it will happen is debatable. We've only got a matter of weeks now and there's this place to paint and furnish.'

'Well, if it's any consolation, the flooring's all done in the smaller barn's dining room and kitchen, and it looks great.'

Eden gave him a grateful smile. 'Thank you so much, Jed! That's saved Eliot a job. Oh, and thank you, by the way, for sorting out the website and Facebook page for me. I wouldn't have had a clue.'

'Every business needs an online presence, and it's not that hard when you know how. I learned a lot when we started the band. I see the picnic tables are already in place beside the beck. Are you going to start serving drinks and cake before the bunk barns are done?'

'We thought we may as well start at Easter. At least it will be a bit of income at last. If we can make this work, it will be a weight off our minds. A wish come true.'

'Well, if anywhere can make wishes come true it's Wildflower

Farm. Look how Emerald got her wish at last.'

Eden raised an eyebrow. 'Does Emerald ever *not* get her wish?'

'You'd be surprised.' He folded his arms, thinking. 'Emerald came off worst out of all us kids, I reckon. Me and Scarlet, we got whisked off to the States, which seemed like the end of the world for a time but worked out pretty well. Marcus—' he laughed, 'well, Marcus is the most normal person ever. He's real happy with Janette and his little life at the bank, and good for him.' As Eden watched, a shadow fell across his face. 'Did Dad tell you Janette had a baby girl? Three days after the wedding. Six pounds twelve ounces. Mom and baby doing great.'

'Yes, he did. He's planning to visit them soon. Isn't it lovely?' Eden smiled, wondering why she had an odd feeling that the news had affected Jed more than it should. 'Justin is such a nice kid. It will be great for him to have a little sister.'

'Yeah. It will.' He shrugged. 'Anyway, as I was saying, Honey got all Dad's time and attention and pretty much ran rings around both her parents, from what I've heard. Emerald, meanwhile, got shipped off with her mom, who is, shall we be kind and say eccentric? She's stayed in the worst places and never got to settle anywhere for long. I think she's more vulnerable than she lets on.'

'Emerald! Vulnerable?' Eden spluttered with laughter. 'If you say so.'

'I know, I know. She hides it well. I think she just wants her dad, at the end of the day.' Jed held out his hand. 'So, pass me the roller and I'll get to work.'

'You're sure a superstar singer is up for this?'

He gave her a wry look. 'Sure I am. This place needs fixing up and I figure Eliot's far too busy to help much, so who else you gonna call? I'm at your service ma'am.' He gave a mock salute and she laughed.

'That's very kind of you, Jed, I'm sure.'

'Aye, right kind.'

Eden's heart leapt as Eliot walked into the room. 'Hello, you! What are you doing here?' She glanced at her watch and gave a yelp. 'Blimey, is that the time already? I'll fix you some elevenses.

Jed, would you like a sandwich or something? Keep you going until lunchtime.'

'That would be great, thanks.' Jed smiled at Eliot. 'I've finished the kitchen and dining room floors in the next-door barn, and it's looking good, if you want to take a look. I'm giving Eden a hand painting here now. It's all coming together. I reckon you'll do a roaring trade.'

'That's the plan.' Eliot's voice was strangely flat.

Eden peered at him. 'Are you okay?'

'Me? I'm grand. Just hungry is all. Could murder a cup of tea.'

'Coming right up.' She squeezed his arm as she hurried past him, calling to Jed that she'd bring his elevenses over in a few minutes. At least, she thought with some relief, there was help at hand at last. She could hardly expect Eliot to paint when he worked so hard on the farm, and she couldn't for the life of her imagine Emerald rolling up her sleeves. Thank goodness for Jed.

****

Eliot was beginning to wish he hadn't come back to the house for food. Firstly, finding Eden in the barn with Jed had made him feel uncomfortable, although he didn't like to dwell on the reasons for that. He knew he was being pathetic, but the way they'd been laughing together made him uneasy. Jed was a rock star, for God's sake, with an American accent and plenty of money. More than that, he had a way with him, an ease about him. He could talk to anyone. Eliot couldn't help but feel resentful and he was annoyed with himself for it.

As if that wasn't bad enough, he'd followed Eden back to the farmhouse, only to be pounced on by Emerald, who was taking her wedding planner duties deadly serious.

'I've been into Kirkby Skimmer this morning, and look what I've bought,' she trilled, waving a pink leather Filofax in his face. 'I'm already filling it up with my to-do list, and I've ticked something off already. I've made an appointment for you to speak to Mr Edwards.' She beamed at them both as Eliot and Eden exchanged nervous glances. 'He's the vicar at St Mary's in

Camacker.'

'Yes, we know who he is,' Eden muttered.

'What do we need to speak to him about?' Eliot said, feeling nervous.

'Well, what do you think?' Emerald giggled and tapped him on the arm. 'For goodness' sake, Eliot, you wanted a church wedding! You can't reserve a slot online, you know. It's not like booking an optician's appointment. You have to speak to the vicar in person, and you'd better be on your best behaviour.'

'Why? Is it like an audition or summat?' Eliot was already grumpy, and this wasn't helping. Like he didn't have enough to do already. When was he supposed to find time to visit a bloody vicar, for God's sake?

Emerald tilted her head, watching him curiously. 'I'm guessing you didn't have a church wedding first time around?'

He saw Eden glance over at him and give him a sympathetic smile. She knew how much he hated talking about his first marriage.

'No,' he said. 'Registry office. Straight in and out.'

'Not very romantic,' Emerald observed.

'No. It weren't.' And look how it had turned out, he thought bleakly. Which was why he wanted it to be different this time around. He wasn't bothered about all the stuff that went with it—the clothes and the party and all that malarkey. He could happily have done without it if it wasn't for the fact that Eden deserved her special day. But the actual wedding mattered.

This one was forever, after all. It couldn't be anything else.

'So, this time you have to make an effort,' Emerald said, making huge assumptions about his previous wedding. He opened his mouth to contradict her, but seeing her bright smile and shining eyes, he couldn't bring himself to tell her off. She meant well, after all.

'Aye, you're right, I suppose, and it'll be worth it. So, when do we see the vicar?' He was aware that Eden was staring at him in amazement and tried not to look at her.

'Thursday morning. Ten o'clock. Hopefully you can get the date pinned down and then we can crack on with this wedding.'

'Great.' He risked a glance at Eden who was now rummaging, quite noisily, in the bread bin. 'Isn't it, my love? Good news that we can pin down a date.'

'Oh, wonderful.' Eden reached for some plates and gave Emerald an exaggerated smile. 'Cheese or ham, Emerald?'

Emerald pulled a face. 'I don't suppose you have any smoked salmon?'

Eliot rolled his eyes. The girl really knew how to push it. She was her own worst enemy.

Chapter 13

The vicarage was an attractive stone house overlooking the River Skimmer. Beside it, basking in unexpected late March sunshine, St Mary's stood in a pretty churchyard, bright with the first of the daffodils.

'Like something from a children's book,' Eden mused, gazing up at the spire which reached into clear skies. 'I mean, seriously.' She shook her head. 'Look at this place. It's perfect.'

Eliot smiled at her. 'Right place for us to get wed, then.' He nodded towards the front door of the vicarage. 'You ready for this?'

'It'll be all right,' she assured him. 'Mr Edwards is a lovely man. Very kind. I'm sure he'll be all right with us.'

'Not him I'm worried about,' Eliot replied. 'You remember his wife, I take it?'

Eden giggled. 'How could I forget? The champion of the Dales.'

Mrs Edwards was a keen baker. She entered her cakes and pies at every local competition, and always, without fail, won. It was generally believed that no one dared to downgrade her, even to second place. Mrs Edwards could be a very fearsome woman when she chose.

'It will be all right,' she assured him. 'If you're absolutely sure you want this? The whole church wedding thing, I mean?'

'No doubts whatsoever.'

'Come on then. Let's get it over with.'

They both took a deep breath and headed up the path towards

the door.

It turned out that Mrs Edwards, when not in competition mode, was a rather charming woman. Eliot and Eden exchanged astonished glances as she ushered them into her husband's study — a large, square room with long windows overlooking a neat little garden. A faded, rather thin carpet covered the floor, and the furniture was dark and badly scuffed. There was a strong smell of furniture polish, and Eden could see that someone — probably Mrs Edwards herself — was very house proud, despite the shabby appearance of the room.

The vicar's wife fussed around them, congratulating them and plying them with tea and cake, while her husband rifled through his diary and tried to find a suitable date.

Eden could feel Eliot's discomfort as the vicar expressed his condolences on the loss of Jemima.

'How wonderful that you've been given a second chance at love, and how marvellous that you've chosen to seal that love in our little church.'

She squeezed Eliot's hand as she felt him squirming with embarrassment. She knew how much of a hypocrite it made him feel when people showed sympathy towards the widower, although, personally, she thought he'd earned that sympathy. He was far too hard on himself, she reflected, never thinking he deserved any compassion.

'And having to look after three little children like that, all alone.' The vicar was shaking his head. 'So sad, so sad.'

Mrs Edwards mopped her eyes with a handkerchief. 'Terrible. Terrible.'

'I had a lot of help,' Eliot protested, clearly unable to bear all this praise. 'People are very kind.'

'Ah now, there's a lot of truth in that.' Mr Edwards nodded. 'When darkness falls, there's always a light to help us see. The Lord works through his flock, guiding them towards the path of kindness and compassion.'

'Aye, well...' Eliot shrugged, clearly not knowing how he was supposed to respond.

'The good shepherd leads his sheep to safety through the

wildest of storms.'

'Hmm.'

'And if anyone knows about leading sheep to safety, it's Eliot,' Eden said, beaming at the vicar.

'What? Oh yes!' He smiled back. 'Another good shepherd, eh?'

'Dunno about that.' Eliot obviously wished he could change the subject.

Eden decided to do it for him. 'So, there's no impediment to us getting married in church?' she queried.

Mr Edwards peered at her over his glasses. 'Impediment? Should there be?'

'I mean, with us not being regular church goers.'

He smiled. 'Oh, I see. No, you're not, are you? I've never seen you at any of our services, Eden, and it's such a pity. I think you'll be delighted by our beautiful church. And, Eliot, I haven't seen you for — hmm, when was the last time?' He considered the matter. 'Oh! It must have been at your wife's funeral. Goodness, that's four years ago or so, isn't it?'

Eden turned to Eliot, shocked. 'Jemima's buried here?'

'In our little churchyard. Didn't you know?' Mr Edwards glanced from her to Eliot, looking a little nervous.

Eliot had his head down. 'Does it matter? This is our local church so—' He broke off and shrugged.

Eden supposed, in the scheme of things, it didn't matter, and it was quite true that this was their local church, so of course Jemima was likely to be buried here. It hadn't occurred to her, and she couldn't help but wonder why Eliot would want to be married at St Mary's, given that his ex-wife would be lying just feet away from where they said their vows.

'I'm not one for Sunday services,' Eliot burst out, 'but it matters, doesn't it? Having a church wedding. Somehow, it makes it more real.'

'Oh, I quite agree,' Mrs Edwards said, pushing another slice of cake towards him. 'Do you know, I've actually heard of people getting married underwater. Now, I ask you! What sort of a wedding is that, for heaven's sake? It makes a mockery of the whole thing. Who would get married underwater?'

157

'The Little Mermaid?' Eden suggested, nibbling at her chocolate cake. Hmm. It was rather good. Maybe Mrs Edwards did deserve her many awards and rosettes after all?

'And the amount of bookings the hotels in the area get,' Mr Edwards added. 'I have a friend who's a registrar, and he travels all over the Dales marrying couples in different locations.' He sighed and shook his head. 'There's no problem with you getting married in church, my dear. Let's face it, if I refused to marry parishioners who didn't attend on a Sunday morning, there'd be no weddings held here at all. Most of my congregation are over seventy and, with the best will in the world, I can't see many of them wanting to walk down the aisle any time soon.'

He flicked through another few pages of his diary. 'You said July?'

'Early to mid-July, if possible,' Eden said. 'I know it's quite short notice, but we want to get it done before harvesting.'

'Not at all. How about the second Saturday of the month?'

Eden looked over at Eliot. He nodded. 'Sounds grand.'

'Excellent. Now, morning or afternoon?'

'Afternoon,' Eden said as Eliot proclaimed, 'Morning.'

Mrs Edwards tittered. 'Ooh, dear. We seem to have some marital discord here and you're not even married yet.' She gave Eliot a beaming smile. 'Bride's prerogative, my dear.'

'Best to learn to give in from the off,' Mr Edwards assured him.

As Eliot raised an eyebrow, Eden said, 'Do you have any idea how long it's going to take to get myself and the children ready? You weren't in Honey's suite when we were getting made up and having our hair styled. It's a big deal, you know.'

Eliot tutted. 'Happen Honey needed more help than you will. You always look grand, makeup or no.'

Mrs Edwards tittered. 'Ooh, what a romantic man you have there, Eden.'

Eden grinned as Eliot glowered. 'Don't I just. I'm such a lucky girl. Even so, why morning?'

'Well,' Eliot sounded uncomfortable, 'we're up at the crack of dawn, aren't we? We'll only be hanging around waiting.'

She could see the tension in his face. He was already nervous, and it would be a nightmare for him on the actual day. He was sacrificing enough to give her this wedding.

She turned to Mr Edwards, smiling. 'Is there anything around half ten? That's a good compromise.'

'Is it?' Mrs Edwards sounded doubtful.

'Oh yes. Eliot's quite right. We're up so early that what's morning to most people feels like mid-afternoon to us, anyway.'

'Ten-thirty it is then,' Mr Edwards said, pencilling it into his diary.

'Great.' Eliot placed his cup and saucer on the nearby coffee table and got to his feet.

'Not so fast, young man,' Mrs Edwards admonished. 'We're not finished yet.'

'Eh?' Eliot looked at them all, clearly baffled. 'Thought we were done.'

'We need to go over certain things. We've only just begun.'

'I know a song about that,' Eden said, trying to lighten the mood. Poor Eliot, he was itching to leave. If only he'd agreed to a quick registry office do, he wouldn't have had to endure any of this. This big, fancy wedding was obviously more important to him than even she'd realised. It must be, because why else would he want to be married in the very place where he'd said goodbye to Jemima?

Chapter 14

Emerald wasn't impressed with The Wedding Dress Shop, the only bridal shop in Kirkby Skimmer. The name had warned her that its owner wasn't blessed with much imagination, but when she beheld the selection of white meringues that were on sale, her nerve nearly deserted her. She wanted to run, but a little voice told her to stay put and be sensible. As much as she fancied Eliot, as much as she loathed Eden, she had every intention of making this wedding a success. Her future depended on showing Cain that she had a business head on her shoulders. Maybe, just maybe, if she could win his respect, she would also win his love.

Having said that, she'd wondered briefly if the wedding would go ahead at all a week ago, when the happy couple had returned from seeing the vicar.

She'd been searching for her tote bag, which she'd left hanging over one of the kitchen chairs. Libby had informed her that Eden had moved it into the boot room, which seriously annoyed her. She'd stormed into the little room off the hallway and grabbed her bag, which was on a hook next to the children's coats and had been about to leave when she heard some murmuring coming from the garden, outside the window. Moving closer, she'd strained her ears to hear what was being said, realising that Eliot and Eden had returned and wondering why they were in the garden instead of coming into the house. Her heart had leapt when she realised that, unbelievably, they were arguing!

'You put me in an embarrassing position,' Eden was saying. 'How could you let me walk in there without knowing it's the same church?'

'I never thought,' Eliot replied, sounding tense.

'Never thought? About something as weird as that?'

'Nowt weird about it.'

'But there is! Doesn't it bother you, really?'

'Look, it's a new beginning, that's all. It feels right to me somehow.'

'What do you mean?'

There was a long silence and Emerald began to wonder if they'd moved away. She was about to risk opening the window a little wider to look out for them when Eliot replied.

'Last time I were in that church, it felt like the end of the world. I couldn't see a way forward for me or my bairns. Look where I am four years on. I suppose—' He hesitated a moment then ploughed on, 'I suppose I want to turn a page. Turn something with bad memories into something good. It's like — I dunno — like showing the world I've done it. That I've put it behind me and I'm happy again.'

Emerald pulled a face. Yuk! How soppy was that. She knew Eden wouldn't be able to stay angry at him now.

Sure enough, there was a bit of mumbling and then Eden said, 'It's okay, sweetheart. I do understand, and if you're happy with this then I'm happy, too.'

'You're sure? I don't want to force you. We can look for another church if you really don't feel comfortable.'

'No, no, honestly. Besides, it's a beautiful church and it will be a lovely day. It will be *our* day.'

'Completely,' he replied.

Then there was the unmistakable sound of kissing and Emerald couldn't stand it any longer. She'd left the boot room, thinking they were the most nauseating couple she'd ever come across.

Now here she was, acting the part of wedding planner for a woman she couldn't stand. Her father had her over a barrel. She so wasn't in the mood for this.

As a smartly dressed brunette headed over to her, Emerald

forced a smile which wavered somewhat as the assistant peered at her with evident disdain, and far more haughtiness than her poxy little business gave her any right to. Big mistake.

'May I help you? What exactly are you looking for?'

'Take a wild guess,' Emerald replied, waving her hands in the general direction of the racks of wedding dresses. 'It's not a new telly, is it?'

The woman gave Emerald a withering stare. At least, she attempted to. It seemed to occur to her, however, that she was wasting her time. Emerald could not be withered so easily. Instead, she seemed to decide to resort to insults.

'Hmm. Let's see. Around a size eighteen or twenty perhaps?'

Emerald wouldn't give her the satisfaction of a denial. 'It's not for me.'

'Oh?' The woman sniffed. 'Then for whom?'

'My client.' Emerald saw the woman's expression alter immediately.

'Your client?'

'Yes. I'm a wedding planner and I was hoping that this shop would be one I could recommend to several of my clients. However, now...' She let her voice trail off, leaving the implication hanging in the air for the stuck-up bitch to chew on.

'Doesn't your client wish to choose her own dress?'

'This is a reconnaissance mission. I'm scouting the area for suitable suppliers. I must say, we're not exactly spoilt for choice, are we?'

'We *are* the only bridal dress shop in Upper Skimmerdale,' Miss Hoity-Toity admitted. 'However, I can assure you, we have a wide selection of some of the finest gowns. We're also able to order in dresses that our ladies may have seen in a magazine, for example, and taken a fancy to.'

'Really?'

'Oh, yes. And we also employ a wonderful dressmaker, who is more than capable of customising any gown to suit our ladies' requirements.'

'Hmm.'

'Perhaps your client would like to attend the wedding fayre at

The Paradise Hotel?'

Emerald pulled a face. 'Frankly, I'm not overkeen on The Paradise. Whoever named it has been a bit ambitious if you ask me. When is this fayre?'

'Two weeks' time in The Gainsborough Room. There are going to be lots of exhibitors there, and we'll have a selection of our finest gowns on display for your client to peruse.'

Emerald considered the matter. 'I suppose there'll be a men's outfitters there, too?'

'Several.'

The thought of Eliot in a morning suit and cravat was making Emerald feel quite hot.

'Perhaps,' the woman continued, 'you'd like to take a flyer?' She handed her a glossy leaflet which bore the image of The Paradise Hotel on the front. It looked quite grand and not at all as shabby as it appeared in real life.

'If the photographer who took this picture is at the fayre, I'll hire him on the spot,' Emerald said. 'Anyone who can make that dump look so classy might even be able to make my client presentable.'

The woman raised a well-plucked eyebrow and Emerald cleared her throat. 'I'll take this to show my client and, hopefully, we'll see you there.'

The woman nodded and showed her to the door.

'You're not going to be the only wedding dress company at the fayre?' Emerald queried, holding the door open.

Miss Hoity-Toity gave her a half-defrosted smile. 'I understand there will be several others, although from further afield, obviously. This shop would be much more convenient for you.'

'Yeah, well.' Emerald beamed at her. 'You have to wade through a lot of shit to find a nugget of gold, but it's always worth it.'

She marched out of the shop, slamming the door shut behind her.

****

Emerald decided not to go straight home. It felt good to be

walking on actual pavements again and made a pleasant change to look at shop window displays rather than grass, stone walls, and the odd black-faced sheep. It was also rather a relief to be breathing in fresh air. At Wildflower Farm she daren't even open her bedroom window because the pungent smell from the farmyard quite took her breath away. She couldn't imagine why no one else noticed it.

It wasn't as if she could escape downstairs, either. The Harlands' retired sheepdog, Tuppence, suffered frequently from wind. Libby and Ophelia thought it hilarious to see Emerald gasping for breath, while Tuppence lay watching her, not in the slightest bit perturbed that she'd just turned the air putrid. That dog definitely had something wrong with it and Emerald didn't think any amount of chakra balancing or crystal therapy would help. In her opinion, the animal needed exorcising.

She caught sight of her reflection in a shop window and tutted. Size eighteen to twenty! She was a fourteen to sixteen, tops, and she could carry it well. That woman was a complete cow. Emerald had barely scrounged any of the children's Easter eggs at all, but she was beginning to think she may as well have eaten the lot for all the good it did her.

'Watch out!'

The shout hardly registered as Emerald collided with someone. Embarrassed, she stared up at a smartly dressed man who, unfortunately for him, had been carrying a cup of coffee in his hands. He was no longer carrying it. He was wearing it.

'Oops,' she said. 'Sorry about that.'

The man dropped the empty cup and frantically wafted his shirt away from his skin. 'Bloody hell. Why didn't you look where you were going?'

Emerald didn't like to admit that she was too distracted by her own reflection. Instead, she switched on a dazzling smile and handed him some tissue paper from her bag.

'It's like that film, isn't it? You know, *Notting Hill*.'

He gaped at her, clearly astonished, as he blotted the liquid from his shirt. 'Are you for real?'

'Though, of course, you're not Hugh Grant,' she said.

'And you're no Julia Roberts,' he pointed out, rather rudely she thought. 'Anyway, didn't he spill orange juice? This is coffee. Bloody hot coffee.' He looked down at the stains on his shirt and pulled a face. 'As if I haven't got enough to worry about.'

'I said I'm sorry,' Emerald reminded him. 'There's no need to go on about it.'

The man looked as if he were about to launch into a verbal attack, but then his eyes skimmed over her and she saw his whole stance alter. To her surprise, he grinned and held out a hand. 'You're quite right. No need at all. James. James Fuller.'

Cautiously, Emerald shook his hand. 'Pleased to meet you, James Fuller.'

He waited, then when she added nothing else, he said, 'I suppose you have a name?'

'You're quite right,' she said. 'I do.'

He looked taken aback, but seemed to decide to let it go, unlike her hand, which he held onto. 'May I buy you coffee? To apologise for my overreaction, and my rather rude comment about you not being Julia Roberts.'

Emerald considered. She was in no hurry to return to Wildflower Farm, and it was rather flattering to be asked out for coffee by an attractive man. He was a bit too smooth for her liking, but even so. Besides, she was starving. 'Make it lunch and you have a deal,' she said, extricating her hand from his grasp.

'Fair enough. Have you tried The Daffodil Café? It's quite decent.'

'If you say so,' Emerald said. 'Although, I'm learning that the Skimmerdale meaning of decent is usually absolute shite.' She stooped down and picked up the empty coffee cup. 'I hate litter. Put this in that bin, please.'

James Fuller looked astounded but obeyed. 'Of course. Well, this way.'

Grinning to herself, Emerald followed him down a little side street, where he ushered her into a cosy little teashop. The place was every bit as twee and cramped as she'd expected, but it didn't stop her ordering The Daffodil Café's upmarket version of a fishfinger sandwich, with a side order of chips — served in a wire basket — and a gingerbread latte.

James, who had restricted himself to a black coffee and a toasted teacake, looked quite astounded as she tucked in with gusto. Evidently, he wasn't used to seeing women eat.

She noticed he was wearing a wedding ring. No doubt his wife lived off liquidised lettuce fed through a tube in her veins. She knew so many women like that, not least her own sisters. It was the only possible explanation for their pencil-like figures which, in her opinion, were hideously unattractive.

As her own father had so charmingly put it at the wedding, as he watched one of Freya's bony cousins rattling towards them to give fake greetings, 'I've seen more fat on a greasy chip.' Even so, it was a bigger compliment than being called meaty. That still rankled, but she was determined he wasn't going to get to her any more. Stuff him.

'Well,' she said, pushing away her empty plate with some regret, 'that was rather nice, considering.'

'Considering what?'

'Considering we're in a backstreet café in a small town at the arse end of England.'

He looked a bit annoyed. 'Kirkby Skimmer has everything you could possibly need, and the Yorkshire Dales are incredibly beautiful and very popular. This area has a lot to offer.'

'I'll take your word for it,' she said, 'although, as soon as my business here is concluded, I'm hoping to get as far away as possible.'

'You're here on business?' His interest was obviously piqued. 'What sort of business?'

'You're very inquisitive. Do you always grill strangers this way?'

'Only the ones who are pretty enough to be taken out for lunch.' He smiled. 'Don't look so cynical. I was merely asking a question.'

'Hmm. If you must know, I'm a wedding planner.'

He grinned. 'Really?'

'Does that amuse you?'

'The whole wedding planner thing amuses me,' he admitted. 'We had one for our wedding, and I swear I could have done a better job of it myself for half the price. These huge, fancy weddings are such a waste of time and effort.'

'Everyone deserves the fairy tale, don't you think?'

'Frankly, I think it's self-indulgent claptrap, but I wish you luck. I take it you're working for a local couple?'

'Yes, I am,' she said, feeling annoyed that he'd already poured cold water on her brilliant new — if temporary — business venture. 'At least, they're from Skimmerdale, but not this town. They live on a farm near Beckthwaite.'

He frowned. 'A farm near Beckthwaite? You don't mean the Harlands, by any chance?'

'Yes.' She narrowed her eyes. 'You know them?'

'Yeah, I know them.' He considered this information. 'So, Eliot and Eden are actually going through with it. I never thought they'd get that far.'

Emerald's stomach fluttered hopefully. 'Really? Why ever not? They're love's young dream, aren't they? Quite sickening.'

'On the surface maybe, but there's a lot of baggage there, Miss —' His eyes lingered on her face, and she saw a distinct gleam in them. She felt a little frisson of excitement. He was no Eliot Harland, but he wasn't bad looking, and after all, it was ages since any man had looked at her in that way. Yes, he was wearing a wedding ring, but what the hell. It was only a harmless flirtation, after all. It would never go any further.

'Carmichael,' she said. 'Emerald Carmichael.'

'Carmichael?' She wasn't sure if it was the lighting in the café, but she was sure his pupils dilated. 'I don't suppose you're related to Cain Carmichael?'

She sighed. Great. Another fan of her father's. Bloody hell, and when she'd finally started to enjoy herself. 'Yes, I'm his daughter, but if you think I'm going to get you his autograph or—'

He shook his head. 'It's not that. I've just put two and two together. I knew you were staying at Wildflower Farm with your brother, but I didn't realise you were also the wedding planner.'

Emerald stared at him. 'How do you know I'm at Wildflower Farm with Jed?'

He pushed his own cup away. 'You met my wife recently. Beth?'

'Beth? She's your wife?' Emerald tilted her head to one side, considering. They seemed a pretty unlikely couple, in her view. 'Well, this whole wedding planner business was her idea.'

'It was?'

'Yes. Didn't she tell you? Eliot and Eden don't have the time to organise a wedding, and I — er, I was looking for a business opportunity. Beth suggested I take over the planning of their nuptials, so we could all get what we wanted.' She frowned. 'I'm surprised she didn't say.'

'She mentioned that you and your brother were staying with the Harlands. Other than that...' He shrugged. 'We don't discuss them much.'

'Oh?' Now her own interest was piqued. And why was that she wondered. Considering how close Beth seemed to be to Eliot and Eden, it was odd that she didn't discuss them much with her husband. Come to think of it, she'd never mentioned him, and Emerald had never seen James Fuller at the farm either, even though Beth seemed to visit regularly. There was a story there, she was sure of it.

His finger circled the rim of his coffee cup. 'The Harlands and I have little in common.'

'I can imagine.'

'What's that supposed to mean?'

'Well, you don't seem the sheep farm type,' she observed. 'And since Eliot and Eden seem to think about little else, I shouldn't think you have much to talk about.'

She gave an inward shudder. Life at Wildflower Farm had become even more dreary lately, with the imminent lambing season. She'd been quite appalled the other day to open her bedroom curtains and see Eliot and Eden herding what looked like thousands of sheep through the farmyard into the huge barn opposite the house. Apparently, the elderly ewes and first-time mothers-to-be were going to lamb indoors. Emerald couldn't see what all the fuss was about. Sheep had been giving birth since — well, since forever. She sometimes thought the Harlands deliberately made it seem harder work than it was.

'I wouldn't have had you down as the sheep farm type either,'

James said. 'Yet you obviously get on with them.'

'I never said I got on with them,' she said. 'At least, I certainly wouldn't say I got on with *her.*'

The gleam in his eye had returned. 'You mean Eden?'

'Saint Eden, surely?' She tutted. 'It doesn't matter.'

'Oh, but it clearly does.' He smiled at her. 'She's annoying, isn't she?'

Emerald felt soothed. Finally, someone else could see it. 'Yes, she bloody is, but no one else seems to get it. They all think she's perfect, and she's not.'

'Oh, I know she's not. I could tell you some things about Miss Robinson.'

'Really? Like what?'

'You do know how she and Harland met?'

Emerald wrinkled her nose. 'Of course I know. My darling sister blackmailed her into pretending to be her, so she could run off and shag some married man.'

'Hmm. Blackmailed her indeed. Don't you think she could have said no? I hardly think she's a paragon of virtue. And then she went behind Harland's back to let Beth see the children, even though he specifically told her not to.'

'What?' Emerald found it hard to believe that Eden would go against her precious Eliot. 'Are you sure?'

'Positive. At the time, Eliot wanted the children to have nothing to do with Beth, but Eden felt sorry for her and sneaked them out to meet her. Not just once, either, but on several occasions. I told Beth she was wrong to do that, but she wouldn't listen. I almost felt sorry for Harland, especially when I realised he'd fallen for her.' He shook his head. 'There's another side to Miss Perfect. I wouldn't trust her as far as I could throw her.'

'Really?' Emerald was warming more and more to this man with every word he uttered. 'Me neither. Eliot deserves so much better than her, but he's blind to her and, even worse, so is my father. Do you know, Dad's even paying for their wedding?'

James leaned forward, elbows on table, chin propped in his hands. 'You're kidding!'

Emerald's eyes widened. 'Wow, your wife doesn't talk to you

much, does she? Big church wedding, all paid for by Cain Carmichael.'

'Why is your father paying for it?'

'Because Eden has him wrapped around her little finger and, let's face it, they can't afford it. They're always broke and—' She stopped, frowning. 'I probably shouldn't be saying all this stuff. Dad would kill me and it's not fair on Eliot. He's a decent sort. For a farmer,' she added hastily, in case he was more perceptive than he appeared.

'I'm sure he is decent, deep down. Of course, I doubt very much that Daisy would agree.'

'Who's Daisy?'

'Daisy is a local woman. When Eliot's first wife died, she stepped in and kept Wildflower Farm afloat. Did everything for him — cooked and cleaned, cared for his children, all so he could get on with earning a living.'

'Another saint,' Emerald said grumpily.

'They had an understanding, if you get what I mean.'

Emerald stared at him. 'An understanding? You mean, Eliot and this Daisy were—'

'In love and set to marry. Oh, there was no official announcement, but it was known throughout the village.'

'What happened?'

He sighed. 'What do you think happened? Eden came along and pushed Daisy well out of the picture. Turned Eliot against her, wrapped him up in her web of deception. Poor Daisy was heartbroken. She cleared off to Leeds. Couldn't stand seeing him around, flaunting his new relationship.'

'Bloody hell! I had no idea! She really is a bitch, isn't she? Eden, I mean.'

'I'm afraid Eliot has no idea what she's capable of. Love is blind, as they say. You know, Miss Carmichael—'

'Emerald.'

'Emerald. You know, Emerald, I've enjoyed being with you this afternoon. It's made a real change for me. Maybe,' he placed his hand over hers, 'we could do this again some time?'

Emerald looked down at his hand, noting it was his right one and not the hand with the wedding ring gleaming on one finger.

'I don't think so,' she said, removing her own hand and reaching for her bag.

He looked surprised, evidently not used to rejection. 'Why on earth not?'

'The question, surely, is why on earth would we? The only thing you and I have in common, Mr Fuller, is that we both dislike Eden Robinson. It's hardly a basis for a flourishing friendship, is it? Always supposing it's friendship you were seeking, which I doubt, somehow.'

His mouth dropped open. He eyed her curiously for a moment, then smiled — a genuine smile this time. 'You're quite something,' he said, almost grudgingly.

Emerald rolled her eyes. 'And flattery won't get you anywhere.' She stood up. 'I think we're done here.'

'Think about it, Emerald.'

'It's Miss Carmichael to you, actually. Thanks for the lunch and sorry about the coffee.'

She tutted as he thrust a card into her hand. 'Take this and think about it, please, Emer — Miss Carmichael. If you change your mind, my number's right there. Just a drink or a bite to eat sometime. No strings.'

'Don't hold your breath. Bye, Mr Fuller.'

She left the café, thinking what a bloody nerve he had and how all men were the same. Except for Eliot, of course, which was just her luck. Trust her to fall for someone so doggedly devoted, so loyal and straightforward. Fancy him falling for someone like Eden! At least James Fuller agreed with her on that little matter.

She smiled to herself, remembering the glint of lust in his eyes as he'd leaned over to hand her his card. He had a damned cheek, especially when they'd been discussing his wife. Even so, she ignored the waste bin at the end of the street and tucked the little card into her coat pocket. Just in case.

171

Chapter 15

'But you see what I mean, don't you?' Ophelia tugged at Jed's arm as they stood in the yard, admiring the rather pretty pony before them. 'Look at her feet! Aren't they dangling?'

Libby's feet were a little below the pony's girth, he had to admit, but he didn't want to get involved in Ophelia's second pony campaign. He figured Eliot and Eden had enough on their minds without worrying about buying a new pony.

'It's not that bad,' he fudged. 'And ponies are very strong. I'm sure Flora has no trouble carrying Libby.'

'That's not the point,' Ophelia said. 'Point is, she looks proper daft.'

'Oh, thanks, Ophelia.' Libby glared at her sister. 'Good job there's no one around to laugh at me then, isn't it?'

'No use having a go at me.' Ophelia shrugged and patted Flora's dapple-grey neck. 'It's Mum and Dad you need to be having a word with. I can't fight all your battles for you.'

It had occurred to Jed to offer to buy a pony for the girls himself. He could certainly afford it, and it had seemed like a good way to thank Eden and Eliot for their hospitality. Luckily, he'd run it past Cain first, and his father had soon put him straight.

'Eliot ain't the sort you can do that for,' he'd advised. 'Them's his kids, and he's proper defensive over being able to buy stuff for them. Leave it to him to sort out and stay well clear.'

Jed had taken his advice and was trying hard not to let sentiment get in the way of common sense. 'So, are you going to help me paint the dormitory today or are you too busy riding?' he said.

The girls looked at each other. Ophelia pulled a face. 'Really?' Libby said, albeit reluctantly, 'If you need our help...'

Jed laughed. 'I'm kidding. Go on, get yourselves out of here.'

They looked relieved. 'See you later, Jed,' they called as Flora clip-clopped out of the yard and they headed into the fields.

Jed was entering the barn when he heard someone calling hello. He turned, his heart doing a most unexpected skip as he took in the sight of Beth, pretty as a picture in cropped jeans and a floral cotton shirt.

'Hey! Great day isn't it?' He grinned to himself as he realised he'd already fallen into the habit of discussing the weather with everyone he met. His English roots were wrapping themselves around him, slowly but surely. It wasn't a bad thing. 'If you've come to see Eden she's gone into Harrogate. Something to do with kitchen supplies.'

'Oh, right.' Beth looked a bit lost. 'Has she taken George with her?'

'Nope. He's at the birthday party of one of the kids from nursery.' He glanced at his watch. 'I said I'd pick him up when they're done, since Eliot's so busy, but I've got a couple of hours yet, so I was gonna carry on painting the dorm.'

She seemed wistful, somehow. 'I suppose I should go home then,' she murmured, sounding reluctant. Then her face brightened, and she said, 'Unless, of course, you wouldn't mind some help.'

'You?' He couldn't help but laugh and was rewarded with narrowed eyes and folded arms.

'What do you mean by that?'

'Sorry but, seriously? Have you ever painted anything before?'

Beth admitted, obviously embarrassed, that she hadn't, which didn't surprise him. He doubted she'd ever been without money in her life. Her sort of folks had the cash to pay people to do such menial tasks for them.

Not that he blamed her for that. He'd never been short of money either, and any work that his family had needed doing they could have hired help to do it. Luckily for him, two of his stepfathers had been hands-on kind of guys and had taught him the value of — and the fun in — doing the work for yourself. At least he had that to be grateful for, he mused, even if they'd turned out to be prize jerks in other ways.

He surveyed Beth thoughtfully. Maybe it would do her good to get stuck into hard graft. She always looked so lost and unsure of herself. Whatever it was that was weighing her down, getting down and dirty with a paintbrush might do her the world of good. Speaking of which...

'I don't want you to get paint on that nice top you're wearing,' he told her. 'Wait there.'

He rushed back into the house and shot up the stairs to his attic bedroom, where he rummaged among his belongings to find an old, rather creased checked shirt. Okay, it needed ironing, but it was clean. He ran back downstairs and into the kitchen, stopping to collect something from a dish on the windowsill, then he crossed the yard and handed the garment to a bemused looking Beth. 'Put this on. It'll protect your own clothes.'

She raised an eyebrow but did as he said, shrugging on the shirt and fastening the buttons. It buried her, but it would do the job.

'I grabbed this, too,' he said, handing her a scrunchie. 'One of Eden's. I figured it would be better to tie your hair up.'

'You think of everything,' she said, smiling as she gathered her hair into a ponytail. 'There. Do I look okay?' She spread out her arms and did a little twirl.

Jed thought she did more than that. She looked real cute. Beth was always a picture of elegance and sophistication, with her flawless skin, large, dark eyes and long brown hair. Seeing her in this rather odd outfit, her hair tied up, it was like seeing her for the first time.

Something tugged at his heartstrings, and he felt a fleeting surprise. It had been ages since that had happened, and he hadn't expected it to happen again for a long, long time.

'You do,' he managed. 'I guess I'd better show you how to paint.'

She laughed. 'How to paint! How hard can it be?'

'Oh, you have a lot to learn,' he said, shaking his head and leading her into the dormitory, where cans of emulsion, rolls of masking tape, and paint pads, trays, brushes and rollers were stacked up against the wall.

Beth looked around, obviously taking in the size of the room, and he saw the first trace of doubt in her eyes. Somehow, he knew he'd not manage to get much painted that afternoon, what with trying to show her how to get a flawless finish. It didn't matter. Some things were more important.

****

Cain's throat felt sore. Slumping into the white leather sofa in his lounge, he sucked on a lozenge and reflected on the miserable day he'd had.

It had all started so well. Sun King were an up-and-coming band, earning growing respect from insiders in the industry, and gaining more fans every day. Working with them would introduce him to a whole new generation, as well as boosting their credibility and getting both parties some welcome publicity — at least, that was the theory.

They'd seemed a nice bunch of lads at first. A bit wet behind the ears but he'd met worse. One of them had pissed him off a bit by telling him his grandad was a huge fan of Cain Carmichael's music — his sodding grandad! — but other than that, all seemed well. The song they were working on wasn't exactly a rock classic, but Cain supposed it would be popular with the bits of kids who listened to their music. Sun King, it seemed, could do no wrong anyway.

When it came to his turn to lay down vocals, he'd given it everything he had. He was convinced he'd done a cracking job, but a few takes later he was beginning to wonder if there was any pleasing them.

The worst bit was, he sounded a hell of a lot better than those little shits, with their reedy voices and nasally tones. Anyone with even one ear for music could tell that. Yet he'd seen them, muttering to each other, rolling their eyes and exchanging amused looks, as if he was some sort of joke. Like they were doing *him* a favour!

One of them — Kent, he said his name was and a proper Kent he looked, too — said he thought Cain wasn't *getting it*.

You'll bleeding get it in a minute, mate, Cain thought, trying not to scowl. 'Trust me, I've bin around long enough to know how to sing a fucking chorus,' he'd snapped.

They'd all looked at each other, then over at the producer, who'd suggested another take.

'You're not interpreting our lyrics,' one of them grumbled. Quentin, his name was. Honestly! Cain didn't know what musicians had come to. They drank mango smoothies and snacked on hummus and crackers. There wasn't a joint or a bottle of Jack Daniels to be had. He wasn't having any fun at all.

'Listen, kid,' he'd grumbled, 'I'm singing this pap to the best of my ability, and I'm sure all your teenybopper fans will be only too happy to *interpret* your precious lyrics when they stick your CD on and—'

He'd realised his mistake immediately and hadn't needed their incredulous looks and snorts of derision to confirm it.

'CDs!' Dominic had groaned and shaken his *casually styled* hair that had, no doubt, taken his stylist several hours to perfect. 'Jesus, what century are you from?'

'Nobody buys CDs these days,' Kent informed him pompously. 'Everyone downloads.'

'So why bother making CDs then?' Cain challenged them. 'You wanna be careful before you start dissing people who buy a CD, mate. You might find yourself alienating half your fans.'

'I doubt it,' Dominic said, looking at Cain with a sneer, as if he could smell something rotten nearby. 'None of our fans are over fifty, for a start.'

'Anyone who listens to this tosh is probably under five,' Cain retorted, stung. Who did they think they were, anyway? Cheeky little gits. Five minutes in the industry and they thought they knew it all. He'd hung out with Mick Jagger, got pissed with Rod Stewart, gone on the pull and trashed hotel rooms with some of the best in the business. He didn't need this shit.

It was only the thought of his manager, Derek, that stopped him from punching them in the nose and walking out. He'd promised him he would behave, give it his best shot.

'This could be a great opportunity, Cain,' Derek had warned him. 'Don't fuck it up.'

So, he'd bitten his lip as they complained to the producer and whined at their manager and then demanded to know why there weren't any more nibbles. Nibbles! He'd never heard the like. He remembered the recording sessions he'd had with his own band. Singing through a cloud of smoke, stoned out of his head, empty beer cans and overflowing ashtrays everywhere, sexy blondes draped around the studio, eyes heavy with the effects of marijuana, the familiar and comforting odour of whisky and weed, stale perfume and vinegary fish and chips. He sighed fondly. Such happy memories. These kids had no idea.

He'd been glad to call it a day and head home. Swallowing the lozenge, he made himself a cup of coffee and stuck two slices of bread in the toaster. The truth was everything had changed. The good old days were gone, and life had moved on, leaving him behind. He didn't belong in this weird music industry any more. He didn't have the heart for it, truth to tell. He stared at his distorted reflection in the shiny steel cooker splashback, remembering how he'd stuck out like a sore thumb next to the squeaky clean, makeup free, fresh-faced members of Sun King. They looked like students on a work experience jaunt. He felt old, worn out. Foolish.

Yep, he thought, buttering the toast despondently. That's exactly how he'd felt. Like some relic from the past who was only there to laugh at.

He remembered, at Honey's wedding, how Marcus had almost passed out in relief to discover his father wasn't wearing much makeup and had obeyed orders by wearing a suit, rather than leopard skin leggings.

He thought about Rex, looking a sight in his own suit, those stupid teardrops tattooed on his face. Hadn't he looked a prick! Thank God Cain's own tattoos were more discreet. His children would really have something to be embarrassed about otherwise.

Not that they weren't embarrassed enough. He was aware that they considered him to be outdated. He supposed he was, in a way. Even Rodders had abandoned the leopard skin. All the old rockers were more sedate these days, more respectable.

Was he really a joke? Was it time to abandon the old ways, act his age? Would his kids appreciate it if he did? He knew Honey thought his hairstyle was hideous, for a start, and even Jed had suggested that he tone down the makeup. His new granddaughter, Florence, had started howling the minute he'd picked her up, and Janette had hurriedly removed her from his arms. Had the eyeliner scared the kid? Maybe, just maybe, he should think about having a makeover. New hairstyle, new look, new clothes. Did he dare?

Of course, if he did that, it would show Rex Scotman up. Now that git *was* stuck in the past. Sun King would have had a field day with him. How would it look if Honey's father cleaned up his act, got respectable, and left her father-in-law to look like some museum exhibit? He'd bet she'd be delighted with him. Hmm.

Cain chewed his toast. Try as he might, he couldn't imagine receiving his knighthood from the Queen looking the way he did now. Her Majesty would think he was some sort of weirdo, with his kohl eyeliner and bleached mullet. If he wanted to act the mature, responsible adult, who donated to charity and deserved a knighthood, perhaps he should look the part.

Maybe that was why he hadn't got his knighthood yet? He couldn't imagine any other reason. He'd pretended to care about loads of good causes, and he'd given buckets full of cash to the Party. There had to be a reason, and he could only think of this one.

It was time he took some advice on image. God knows, he had enough contacts. Yeah, sod it. He would show Sun King, his kids, every numpty who had ever taken the piss, that he was modern, progressive and relevant. Fuck 'em all.

****

178

Dinner at Thwaite Park that night was eaten, not for the first time, in almost total silence. James wondered how it was that four people, so closely related and living under the same roof, could be so distant with each other. It seemed there was little to say, no conversation to be had.

His mother was prodding at her salmon, showing as much interest in it as she'd taken earlier in her soup.

His father was bolting down his food while simultaneously scanning the newspaper. Now and then he grunted, rattled his pages and scooped up another potato.

Beth was chewing asparagus, a thoughtful look on her face. James wondered what she was thinking. At least she looked a bit happier, which was a bonus. He was sick of seeing her moping around the house with her usual mournful expression. Come to think of it, she'd seemed a lot brighter lately. He would have to find out why. It had better not have anything to do with Harland, that was all.

James put down his knife and fork and pushed his empty plate away. 'That was delicious. Thank you, Mother.'

Deborah raised an eyebrow. 'For what? I only told Mrs Ketley what to cook, I didn't do it myself.'

'Yes, well, even so.' He tried not to feel irritated. She was a hard woman to be pleasant to, sometimes. 'Would you excuse me? I have some work to be doing and I'd like to get on with it.'

It was a lie, but he'd say anything to get away from the uncomfortable atmosphere in this room, with only the occasional clatter of cutlery and the ticking of the old grandfather clock to break the silence.

His father put down the newspaper at last. 'Actually, I need to talk to you, so shall we go to the sitting room?' He scraped back his chair, gathering up his newspaper at the same time.

James was dismayed. 'You haven't finished your dinner yet,' he pointed out.

David tutted. 'I've eaten all I can of that. I hate fish, as your mother should know.'

James glanced sympathetically across at Deborah, his eyes widening as he noted a distinct twitch of amusement on her lips.

Then it was gone, and he blinked. He must have been mistaken, surely?

'Very well. If you really need to speak to me now.'

'I do.' David gave him a meaningful look and James sighed inwardly. He could well imagine what this was about. At least he had one thing to tell him, something to please him at any rate.

David threw open the French doors as soon as they reached the sitting room, taking deep lungfuls of fresh air. Outside, the weakening rays of the evening sun still managed to warm the gardens, as the first of the season's butterflies and bees hovered around the flower beds, performing a last dance before bedtime. It was only early April, but the weather had been kind for the last few days. Not that his mother thought so. She spent her evenings in the snug, wood burner blazing away as if it were the depths of winter.

'So, have you anything to tell me? Any news?'

David didn't believe in beating around the bush. There was only one thing he needed from his son, and he wasted no time in getting to the point. James was relieved he'd had that meeting in Kirkby Skimmer the other day. It had been most fortunate. 'I have, actually. I met Emerald Carmichael.'

David frowned. 'Cain Carmichael's daughter? How did you manage that?'

James felt quite smug. 'I spotted her in town and — shall we say — I engineered a little accident.'

'What sort of accident?' David sounded alarmed.

James smiled. 'Nothing to worry about. She was busy gawping at her own reflection in the shop window and far too enchanted by it to notice me, until I bumped into her and spilled coffee all over my shirt.'

He would never have gone that far if the coffee hadn't been lukewarm, he thought. He'd been planning to throw it away, so it was no loss, and it'd had the desired effect.

'Of course, I made out that it was her fault for not looking where she was going. She was most apologetic. We ended up having a drink together in a café.'

And the rest! The girl could certainly eat. No wonder she was so plump. She was bordering on fat, not his usual type at all. Although, he had to admit, she was stunningly pretty, and refreshingly natural-looking.

'So what? What's that got to do with anything?' David sounded grumpy. Evidently, he wasn't impressed. James bit down his annoyance.

'So, we got talking. She's quite chatty and rather naïve. She was open about what's going on at Wildflower Farm. For instance, Harland and his fiancée are getting married, and she's been hired as the wedding planner.'

David swung round, tutting impatiently. 'How is that good news? The last thing we need is for them to seem even more secure, more settled. We need the Harlands to look unstable, not like love's young dream, for God's sake.'

'But that's my point,' James said, trying his best not to sound snappy although, God knows, his father was pushing it. 'Emerald Carmichael is the best placed person to ruin their wedding, and she could also be useful to us in other ways.'

'What ways?' David sank into the chair opposite James and frowned. 'I'm not following.'

'Emerald,' said James, leaning forward and eyeing his father with some satisfaction, 'has a crush on Harland. Oh, she didn't say as much, but reading between the lines and seeing her soppy expression when she talked about him — well, it was obvious. He certainly does attract them,' he added bitterly, thinking of his own wife's not infrequent visits to Wildflower Farm. You couldn't tell him she'd developed a sudden passion for sheep and chickens. Something was drawing her there, and he could make a very good guess what — or rather who — it was. 'Not only that, but she despises Eden. That's Harland's fiancée. As far as Emerald's concerned, she's a prize bitch who has bewitched poor, innocent Harland, and conned him into falling in love with her. There'd be nothing she'd enjoy more than breaking those two up, and how good would that look when this case goes to court, eh?'

He sat back, waiting for David to congratulate him on his cleverness. Instead, his father rolled his eyes. 'Is that it? So, have you got her onside? Have you made arrangements to meet up with her again? Is she going to help us?'

James felt his face heat up. Damn! Trust his father to ruin the moment. 'I gave her my card,' he told him, realising how feeble it sounded. 'She'll call me, I'm sure of it.'

'So that's it? One drink in a café, one business card handed out, and suddenly all our problems are solved?'

'Look, Emerald's clearly harbouring a major grudge against Eden — not only because she fancies Eliot, but because Cain Carmichael adores Eden and is even paying for their wedding himself. Emerald's furious about it. I reckon she's going to want to cause as much mischief as possible for her. If she can split Eden and Eliot up, I think she'll go for it. She wants Eliot for herself, that much is obvious, but more than that even, I think she wants to punish Eden. What better way to do it? And if she joins forces with us, we can make it happen, I'm sure of it.'

'Hmm.' David nodded. 'And if the Harlands go through a split — as acrimonious as we can make it — a judge is going to pretty much see us as by far the best choice for George.' He rubbed his chin thoughtfully. 'You know, I don't see why we don't move now. A birth certificate can be amended. All it would take would be a DNA test. Once that's sorted out, there'd be nothing to stop you applying for custody. He's your biological son and you must have rights.'

James shuddered. 'I've told you, if we rush into this it will go horribly wrong. For a start, Beth will be against the idea. She doesn't want me to have George, and she'd see it as a betrayal of Harland. She's far too close to — that family — to go against him like that. She would probably go so far as to defend him in court, tell the judge that I never wanted George. She'd make me out to be an uncaring father. We could easily lose the case. Plus, she'd never forgive me. She'd leave me, no question.'

'Pity you weren't so considerate of Beth's feelings before you had your vasectomy,' David muttered.

James swallowed down his anger. He was getting used to doing that whenever his father was around.

'The point is, there are far too many people in this village who adore Harland and would be willing to stand up in court and tell the judge what an amazing father he is. Think about it, he'd look like a saint, bringing up the son of an unfaithful wife and the man she betrayed him with. How bad will it make me look next to him?'

'But in law—'

'We need Beth onside,' James said firmly. 'And the only way to ensure that is to take our time to convince her that I'm genuinely missing George. Then I need to convince Mother that I want my son back, wind her up so that she goes after the Harlands and Beth can blame her for taking action, not me. You know Mother. When she really wants something, she's like a dog with a bone, and you say she wants a grandchild. It's the only sure-fire way to win this. With Beth and Mother working with me to get my son home, and Emerald working against the Harlands for us, making them look unstable and unsuitable, we can't lose, and what's more, we'll have the villagers and my wife on our side, rather than furious with us and causing trouble for us. You must see it makes sense?'

He could see in his father's face that he knew he was right but hated the fact. David never liked to give James credit for anything. It went against everything he stood for.

'Huh. This is going to take ages.'

'It doesn't matter how long it takes, as long as it happens, does it?' James hesitated, wondering if he dared to push it, having just won a small victory over his father. On balance, he decided it was worth the risk. 'Look, are you sure about this? Can't we drop it? I don't want George back, you know. I'm not the paternal type, and Harland is doing a good job of bringing him up. I can't say he's not, much as I'd like to.'

David glared at him, then marched over to the bureau in the corner of the room. Taking a key from his pocket, he unlocked the drawer and rummaged around for a moment, before removing a letter. Scowling, he handed it to James. 'Read this and then tell me if we should drop it.'

James scanned the letter, his spirits sinking as he realised it was from his uncle Scott. More boasting as he announced the birth of a second grandson, Solomon. Eight pounds six ounces and, apparently, the spitting image of Aunt Kathryn — poor little sod. Scott had ended the letter with a casual enquiry as to whether there was any sign of a grandchild for David and Deborah, pointing out what a shame it was for them, and what a blessing the grandchildren were, enriching their lives so much. *And what a blessing to have an heir and two spares lined up, should James fail to live up to his duties* was the subtext. No wonder his father was so desperate to get George back. It was almost enough to make him want to rush over to Wildflower Farm and stake his claim right there and then — almost.

'Your son is coming home to Thwaite Park,' David told him, through gritted teeth. 'Those brats get their hands on this place over my dead body.'

Chapter 16

Beth was curled up on the sofa in the sitting room, book in hand, trying hard to concentrate on the story she was supposed to be reading. She'd gone over the same paragraph several times now and couldn't for the life of her remember what it was she'd read. The truth was, she acknowledged, she was too busy making up her own story in her head — a romance, featuring a lonely, bored housewife and a sexy American singer with fair hair, an amazing physique, and the bluest eyes she'd ever seen in her life. Her stomach fluttered as she closed her eyes, the story unfolding in her imagination with disturbing clarity. She ought to be ashamed of herself. She wondered why she wasn't.

'Something amusing you?'

Beth jumped, startled at the sound of James's voice. She felt heat sear through her cheeks. Thank God he couldn't read her mind. 'No, no. Just daydreaming. It's this book. Very good.'

He gave the cover a cursory glance, clearly losing interest. 'I've made you a coffee,' he said, handing her a mug.

She took it, surprised. Since when did James make her a drink? 'Thank you.' She eyed him uncertainly. 'Is there something wrong?'

'Why should there be anything wrong?' He sank down beside her.

Beth involuntarily tensed and edged away from him, taking care not to spill the coffee on Deborah's white sofa. She put her book on the coffee table and cradled the mug in her hands, eyeing

James warily. 'I don't know. You seem a bit — odd.'

'Odd?' He shook his head, smiling. 'I'm not sure how to take that.'

'You know what I mean. Since when do you make me a coffee? And since when do you come and sit with me in an afternoon? Come to think of it, you're not usually at home. Are you feeling all right?'

'I'm fine, fine. Don't worry about me.'

Beth thought, with some shame, that she wasn't. She was curious, that was all. It was a very different thing.

'Not going to Wildflower Farm today then?'

The question came out of the blue and threw her. Wildflower Farm was never discussed in this house. It was a taboo subject. On the rare occasions when Eliot's name was mentioned, it was before, during or following a row, or said in icy tones. The words Harland and Wildflower Farm were practically swear words at Thwaite Park. 'No. Eliot and Eden are up to their necks in lambing, and I didn't want to get in their way.'

'Ah. I thought there must be a reason since you're usually there nearly every day.'

Beth sighed. 'Not this again. Are we going to have yet another argument? Because if we are—'

She felt a tremor of shock as his hand rested on her thigh. 'I don't want to argue, darling. It was a simple question, which you answered. End of.'

'Oh.' She sipped her coffee, wondering if she was having some sort of weird hallucination. None of this conversation felt real.

'How is everyone at the farm, anyway?'

Okay, so this was beyond weird! Beth narrowed her eyes. What was James up to? 'Everyone's fine. Busy, of course, what with the bunk barns to get ready, and the wedding to plan, all on top of lambing season. Everyone's taking it in turns to spend the nights in the lambing shed, so they're all exhausted.'

'Oh yes. And then there are all the children to care for. Must be hectic.'

'Yes. Yes, it must.'

James sipped his own coffee. 'How — how is little George?'

186

Beth stilled, her heart thudding in her chest. 'George?' What on earth was he doing, asking after George? Not once, in all these years, had he ever enquired about the little boy. 'George?' She repeated it, not quite sure that she'd heard him right.

'Yes. George. Is he doing okay? How's he getting on at nursery?'

She blinked, confused. 'He's okay. He starts school in September.'

James nodded. 'Yes, I suppose he's at that age now. Amazing. And is he doing well? Does he like going to nursery?'

'He does. He's got lots of friends there, anyway.'

'Excellent. I'm glad to hear it.' He didn't sound particularly glad. He sounded quite wistful, in fact. Beth's heart skipped again. She put her mug on the table beside the book and fixed her husband with a stare. 'James, what's this all about? You never ask after George.'

'I know, I know. Delicate subject isn't it? I don't know. I suppose it's because my cousin Owen and his wife have had another baby boy. It makes you think, doesn't it?'

Beth's hand flew to her mouth. 'Are you saying — are you having second thoughts? About having a baby, I mean?'

He gave a mirthless laugh. 'Having a baby? That's not exactly working out for us, is it?'

'No, but...' She hesitated, almost afraid to voice the question. 'Are you perhaps thinking that we should explore other options?'

'Other options?'

She turned to face him, unable to keep the eagerness from her voice. 'Another round of IVF, perhaps?'

Her stomach plummeted as he tutted and drained the last of his coffee before slamming the mug down on the hard, wooden floor. 'Don't you think I've got enough to worry about without all this IVF and adoption stuff you keep going on about? We gave the treatment two chances, remember? It didn't work. And what you seem to forget is, I already have a son. A living, breathing little boy who I never get to see and can never have any contact with.'

She took a sharp breath. He sounded so resentful, so hurt. Since when had not seeing George been an issue for him? 'You never

187

wanted to see George before,' she protested, stung. 'You had no desire to be a father to him, to have any contact.'

'How could I? How could I possibly inflict that on you when I'd already done so much to hurt you? You tell me, what sort of man would that make me?'

Beth didn't know how to respond. He'd completely thrown her. She nibbled her thumbnail. 'I didn't know.'

He slumped, clearly repentant. 'I'm so sorry, darling. I didn't mean to snap at you like that. It's been building up for ages, knowing Owen was about to be a father again and knowing I already am a father but having to pretend none of it matters.'

'I don't understand. I thought George *didn't* matter to you?'

'How could he not matter? He's my own flesh and blood. Oh, I know what I said, but it was all such a damn mess when Jemima was killed. I panicked. God knows, I'd done enough to hurt you already. I couldn't live with myself if I asked you to endure even more pain.'

'Are you honestly telling me that you care about George and miss him?' she murmured, hardly able to believe what she was hearing.

His fingers plucked at a cushion. 'I've always cared about him. I'm only human. Most of the time I push it away, try to pretend it doesn't matter. It's just sometimes...' He shook his head. 'I'm sorry, darling. Forget I said anything. It was unfair of me to bring this up. Father had a letter from Uncle Scott boasting about his new grandson. It brought it all back, stirred up the longing again. I'll be fine in a little while. It will all be back under control.' He smiled at her, but she could see it was an effort.

'Are you — are you thinking about getting George back?'

'Of course not.' James squeezed her hand. 'I know I've left that far too late. It wouldn't be fair on Harland, for one thing, and as for George — well, he doesn't know me from Adam, does he? Breaks my heart, but there it is. Don't worry about it. I've come this far and I'm sure I can carry on. Forget it.' He stood up, smoothing his trousers. 'Go on, get back to your book. I have work to do anyway.'

He leaned over, gave her a peck on the cheek and walked

towards the door, as Beth watched him, feeling too stunned to reply.

At the door, he stopped and turned around. 'Beth?'

'Yes?'

'Could you — I mean, would you keep me informed? You don't have to go into great detail, just let me know how he's doing, eh? The little things, so I can build up a picture of him. I know it's not much, but it's the best I'm going to get, and it would mean the world to me.'

'Of course. Of course I will.'

He nodded and left the room, leaving Beth sitting open-mouthed on the sofa, the book completely forgotten as she contemplated this latest twist in their lives that was far stranger than any fiction.

****

Jed stepped back and scrutinised the paintwork, checking for any smears or missed bits, or areas where the plaster was showing through the new cream paint. 'Not bad at all,' he said, feeling quite satisfied. It had been a long day, but it was worth it. The largest bunk room was looking fresh and clean and he'd made a good job of it. Tomorrow, he would start on the second largest. Maybe it wouldn't seem so daunting.

'I think you should call it a day.' Eden said, as he wiped his forehead with the back of his arm and put the lid back on the emulsion tin. 'I'm going to head over and start tea. The kids will be starving, and Eliot will be back soon. Wherever he is.'

Jed shrugged. 'Maybe he couldn't sleep with all this activity outside. Maybe he's gone for a nap in the Land Rover instead.'

'It wouldn't surprise me,' she admitted. 'But I wish he'd try harder. He's going to be up all night again with the ewes, and he needed a couple of hours rest in a decent bed.' She frowned. 'I'd have thought if he couldn't settle, he'd have come back to the lambing shed to make sure I was getting on all right.'

Jed had spotted Eliot driving off, not long after Eden had informed him that she would be in the shed if he needed her, taking over from Eliot for a while, as he was going to bed.

'I hope Emerald's survived.' Jed couldn't help but laugh. Because it was Saturday, the children weren't at school or nursery, so his sister had been roped into keeping an eye on George, while he painted, and the girls helped out in the lambing shed.

'I'm more worried about George,' Eden said. 'I can't imagine what he's been allowed to get away with today while she sat on her backside watching television or scrolling through Facebook, no doubt with Bella on her knee. That cat adores her, weirdly enough.'

'Hey, don't be too hard on her,' Jed said, wondering as he did so why he always felt the compulsion to defend her. He had no doubt that Eden was right, and Emerald would hardly have gone out of her way to entertain the boy. Even so, he couldn't help but stick up for his little sister. 'She may have been great with him. Hey, if he had any complaints, I'm pretty sure you'd have heard them from here, right?'

He could tell by Eden's amused expression that he was right. George was always very vocal in his opinions.

'I suppose so.' She stretched and yawned. 'I'll get over there and start cooking. Thanks for this, Jed. Great job. Will you be okay to clean up in here? Tea will be at least half an hour.'

'Fine, no problem. You head back, and I'll finish up here.'

She gave him a grateful smile. 'I do appreciate this, you know. It's ever so good of you to help.'

'Don't be silly,' he assured her. 'I'm having a great time.'

She gave him a knowing look. 'Sure you are.'

He laughed and waved his paintbrush at her as she headed out of the barn. Okay, this wasn't what he'd expected when he'd flown to the UK from the States, but so what? Maybe painting a bunk barn wasn't the best career move in the world, but it was what he needed right now. The bigger the distraction the better.

He collected the trays, rollers and brushes and carried them to the sink in the adjacent bathroom. His thoughts wandered, as he'd feared they would, back to America and to JoJo. What was she doing right now? The band would be gearing up for their

190

forthcoming European tour. There'd been bad feeling between himself and a couple of his ex-bandmates when he told them he was leaving Raven's Wing. He knew they were thinking commercially. He was a big part of the band, and they were afraid his departure would have a negative impact on sales of their music and on tickets. He also knew that the other band members, Ron and Shane, understood his reasons for leaving and were sympathetic to him, although sad to see him leave.

JoJo hadn't expressed an opinion. By the time he left, they weren't even speaking, which would have been unthinkable a year ago. A lot could happen in a year. He ran the paintbrushes under the tap, scrubbed out the tray, all the while picturing her standing there on stage, messed-up blonde curls, dark eyes, tiny frame somehow managing to fill the stage, so strong was her presence. Raven's Wing didn't need him. It would evolve, become JoJo's band. He had a feeling she would take it to even greater heights. It was what she wanted, after all. More than anything. Well, good for her. He realised he didn't care any more — not about her, at any rate.

'Penny for them.'

He jumped, startled, as he heard Beth's voice behind him. It was so different to JoJo's — soft and yet clipped. JoJo's drawl would fill this room. Her singing voice, so distinctive and raw, could fill a concert hall, whereas he doubted Beth would make herself heard in a living room. They couldn't be more different, he realised, as he turned and smiled at his visitor, who was looking cool and pretty and terribly English in a printed cotton dress.

'If you're here to help we were finishing up for the day,' he told her. 'Was that the plan, huh? Come over here and show willing, knowing it would be too late?'

To his horror, her eyes filled with tears and he watched, not knowing quite how to react as she fought for composure. 'Hey, Beth, I was kidding. Don't mind me. I think before I speak sometimes. I'm real sorry.'

She shook her head, gulping down the tears. 'Don't be silly. It's not you, honestly. Been a tough day and I thought — I don't know what I thought. I wanted to come here and get myself together somehow. It has that effect, doesn't it? Wildflower Farm, I mean. Sort of gives you comfort. Respite.'

He supposed it did in a strange way. But what did Beth need respite from? She looked lost, broken. There was something so fragile about her that she brought out the nurturing side of him. It was good to be needed. JoJo had never needed him, he reflected. She always had everything under control. Life on her terms.

'Is there something I can do?'

'Not really.' She laughed suddenly, her eyes still brimming with unshed tears. 'Not unless you can turn the clock back five or six years and change the course of our lives.'

Oh! If he could do that, how different would he have done things himself? There was no use wishing. It was what it was, and he had to make the best of it — as did Beth. 'I can't do that, unfortunately,' he told her, turning off the taps and drying his hands on a towel that had been thrown over the side of the newly fitted bath. 'What I can do is listen, and I'm more than happy to do that if you want to talk.'

He saw the doubt in her eyes. He couldn't blame her. She barely knew him, after all. How could she possibly know that she could trust him? How could she be aware that, even though he'd only known her for a few weeks, he was already certain that he would never let her down and wanted nothing more than to see her smile.

She had a beautiful smile, he thought. It was a pity she didn't reveal it more often. She seemed to have the weight of the world on her shoulders.

He took her arm and led her back into the dormitory, where Eden had put a couple of fold-up chairs so any workers could take a break and drink their tea in relative comfort. He unfolded them and motioned to her to take one. She sat, looking pensive as he sat opposite her. 'You don't have to tell me anything you don't want to,' he said, 'but I promise whatever you do tell me will go no further.'

'Why on earth would you want to listen to my problems?' she

queried.

'I don't know. Maybe to take my mind off my own?'

'You have problems? I thought yours were all sorted.' She sounded curious. 'You didn't want to be in a band any more, so you left, right?'

'Right. But that's just the bit in the middle. The real problem is all the stuff that led up to me making the decision, and then what happens next. I mean, what do I do now? Not much call for an ex-musician who never qualified for anything in his life. I was never one for schooling, always preferred to be outdoors riding, fishing, building stuff. Try making a resume out of that.'

She shrugged. 'Still more use than me. I did my exams. I wouldn't have dared not. Though, what have I ever done with them? I left school, went to university, got a job working for a friend of my father's, met James, married him, moved to Yorkshire and have spent the last eight years being a professional wife. Not much of a CV, is it?'

'Guess we make a real pair then.' he winked at her, then, realising what he'd said, he cleared his throat and changed the subject. 'So, what are you seeking respite from? Is there anything I can do?'

'No, I'm afraid not. Like I said, only a time machine would help.' She chewed her lip, seeming to consider whether to pursue the conversation or not. 'Did you know about my husband and Eliot's wife?' she blurted out.

He gaped at her. 'James and Eden?'

'No, no. His wife — his late wife. Jemima. She and James, they had an affair.'

He drew in a sharp breath. 'No, I didn't. Jeez, that's got to be awkward all round.' He considered for a moment. 'Is that why your husband never comes to the farm?'

'Yes. There's no love lost between Eliot and James as you can imagine. It was all very messy at the time. Still is really.'

He waited, not wanting to push her as bit by bit, she filled him in on the whole sorry story. He sat, feeling quite stunned, particularly when she revealed the truth about George.

'And Eliot took him in, brought him up as his own? Wow.' He

thought about the implications of that, and how much it must have cost Eliot to raise the child born to the woman who had betrayed him and a man he must loathe. He tried to remember if there'd been anything to give the truth away, any sort of clue that all was not as it seemed, but he couldn't think of a single instance when Eliot hadn't demonstrated that he loved George just as much as his daughters. He had to admit, the taciturn farmer had shot up in his estimation.

Then his thoughts turned to Beth and he gave her a sympathetic smile. 'That must have been so tough on you. Yet you stayed?'

It came out as a question because, frankly, he couldn't understand why she had. She didn't seem happy, that was for sure, and given what had happened who could blame her? How would you even start to get over that, when you had the living reminder of all that pain and anguish every time you visited Wildflower Farm? And yet, she did visit Wildflower Farm. Frequently. It was very strange.

'I've tried to put it behind me, really I have. I know James is sorry and I know we must move on, but it's so difficult. And now—' She broke off, staring out of the window, probably seeing nothing except whatever it was that was hurting so much.

'Now?' he probed gently. 'Has something else happened?'

'He never wanted George,' she said, her voice thick with emotion. 'Never. Not from the moment he was born. He was happy for Eliot to take him on as his own. At least — at least that's what I thought.'

'But now he's changed his mind?' Jed really hoped not. It would be a disaster all round if this Fuller guy decided he wanted his son after all. Eliot would fight every inch of the way, quite rightly, and Beth would be caught up in the middle of it all.

'He doesn't intend to fight for George,' she assured him, obviously noting the look of horror on his face. 'He knows he's left that far too late. But it turns out he's been missing his son all this time, wanting to be part of his life, and he only kept away for my sake.'

'Really?' Jed hoped that hadn't sounded as cynical as he meant it. He found it impossible to believe that someone like James

Fuller would be so noble. From what he'd heard of the guy, he did what made him happy and to hell with anyone else. His affair with Jemima was proof of that.

'So it seems.' She tucked her hair behind her ears and folded her arms. 'I've kept him away from his son all this time, as if it isn't bad enough that I—'

The tears began to fall freely. Jed was paralysed, not sure what on earth he should do for the best. He hardly knew her, after all, and she might not take kindly to him demonstrating any affection for her, but hell, she was in a real state and if it was Emerald or Scarlet taking on so, he hoped someone would be there to give them a hug if they needed it.

He threw caution to the wind and went over to her, crouching down to wrap his arms around her and pull her into a comforting embrace. 'It's okay. It's okay.' As he stroked her hair, he was uncomfortably aware that this was far from a brotherly hug. He was ashamed to admit that he liked holding her so close. Hell, this was dangerous territory!

'You don't understand,' she whimpered into his chest. 'I've already stopped him from being a father, and now it's because of me that he can't have George. Do you have any idea how that makes me feel?'

He froze. 'Stopped him from being a father? How?'

It felt like he held his breath forever until she answered, 'I can't have children. At least, we can't have children together. We've had tests, lots of them. They couldn't find anything wrong with us, said it was one of those things. We tried IVF twice but that didn't work either. Then Georgie came along, so you see, it's clearly my fault. James can't have children with me, and now he's lost his own son, all because he was putting me first. Can you imagine how bad I feel about that?'

Jed could. But he could also imagine the pain that Beth had been enduring about not having children — the pain that she'd just glossed over as if only James's feelings mattered. He was right. She couldn't be more different to JoJo if she tried. All she'd had to deal with… God, and he thought he'd had it tough!

'Are you okay?' She was looking at him, quite concerned. Her face was wet with tears, but her eyes showed anxiety now as she surveyed him. He realised he had tears running down his own cheeks and blinked, embarrassed. She seemed to have forgotten all about her own misery as she hesitantly wiped his face with her hand and stared at him with huge dark eyes, so full of conflict and pain and worry that it ripped him apart.

'Aw, Beth, how can you even ask me that? After everything...' His voice trailed off as his gaze devoured her, absorbing every detail in her beautiful face, until he couldn't help but lean towards her and press his lips to hers. It was only meant to be a way of expressing how sorry he was for everything she'd been through, when words had failed to do that. In the event, it turned out to be a way of expressing everything that had been building in him over the last few weeks, growing stronger and more certain each time he laid eyes on her.

He wouldn't have been in the least surprised if she'd pushed him away, yelled at him, told him in no uncertain terms what a louse he really was. But she didn't. And somehow, her kiss expressed everything he'd hoped and dreamed she would feel but hadn't dared believe could be true.

After some time, when a million words had been exchanged in total silence, they pulled apart and stared at each other. It was as if they'd communicated a lifetime to one another in the space of a minute or two.

'What do we do now?' she whispered, not sounding in the slightest bit sorry or regretful.

The truth was, he had no idea. Never in his wildest dreams had he imagined falling in love with someone again, after everything that had happened. And Beth wasn't just someone. She was a married woman, with all the complications that entailed. He knew he should call a halt, walk away. He was way out of his depth, and only heartache could possibly lie ahead. Yet he knew, looking at her, that he couldn't do it. Where had all these feelings come from? How had this quiet, reserved Englishwoman penetrated through all that pain and grief?

'Jed?'

He cupped her face, gazing softly into her eyes. 'I don't know,

196

honey,' he admitted. 'I've never felt this way before, and I never expected—'

She covered his hand with hers. 'I don't regret it,' she told him fiercely.

He pulled her to him and kissed her again. Maybe, in time, they would both come to regret it, but right now it felt right, and if there was going to be a price to pay, he would pay it. Willingly.

Chapter 17

The Paradise Hotel was busier than Emerald had ever seen it, though that wasn't saying much. The ground floor was almost entirely given over to the wedding fayre, with the wedding service room, the function room, and the conference suite given over to stalls and demonstrations.

Eliot, looking ridiculously sexy in a leather jacket and jeans, was trying hard to look excited, but he wasn't fooling Emerald. It was a bit sad to see. He shouldn't have to go through all this. She'd never met anyone as hunky as him, and such a gorgeous man didn't deserve this amount of stress. It was all that phoney Eden Robinson's fault.

Eden was clearly more interested than she'd expected to be. Her eyes lit up when she saw the rails and rails of wedding gowns, and she turned to Eliot with obvious excitement.

'Look at all those gorgeous dresses! We must find the gentlemen's outfitters for you.'

Eliot made a huge attempt at a smile, though his tired eyes and the dark shadows beneath them betrayed his exhaustion.

'Aye, they look right grand. Why don't you go over and find one you like and I'll have a wander round.'

'Are you okay?' Eden's excitement seemed to fizzle out. 'Maybe this was a bad idea. I told you, you could have used the time while Mickey and Adey are covering to have some sleep. You didn't need to come.'

'It's my wedding, too,' he said. 'I'm all right, any road. Lambs come every year. I'm used to it, so stop fretting.'

'If you're sure.' Eden sounded doubtful. 'You need to find a suit. Do you want me to help you choose?'

'I'll do that,' Emerald said immediately. 'You go and look at the wedding dresses, and I'll help Eliot find something suitable.'

'You help Eden,' came a familiar voice behind her, 'and I'll see to Eliot.'

Emerald groaned inwardly and turned, expecting to be faced with her kohl-rimmed, mullet-headed, leggings-wearing freak show of a father. Standing there instead was a smartly dressed man, makeup free, wearing dark trousers and a plain light cotton shirt, with short, cropped, greying hair and an alarming lack of jewellery.

Emerald was so astonished that she quite forgot she hated Eden as the two exchanged bewildered glances.

'Bloody hell,' Eliot murmured. 'Is that really you, Cain?'

The new, improved Cain shuffled, a little uncomfortably. 'What do you think?' he muttered. 'Do I meet with your approval?'

Emerald was so delighted at the change in him that she wanted to hug him, and was about to tell him how marvellous he looked when he turned to Eden and said, 'What do you think, darls?'

Emerald's stomach plummeted. As Eden assured Cain that he looked fantastic, and complimented him on his change of image, Emerald could only stand there, her hatred for the pair of them growing with every word.

Eventually, her father remembered she was there and said, 'Well? Got anything to say to me?'

Emerald scowled. 'Not bad,' she said. 'You're looking vaguely human, so that's something. Are you sure you wouldn't rather help Eden pick out her wedding dress?'

Cain's eyebrows knitted together. 'That's women's stuff, and thanks for the glowing compliments, Emerald. Proper chuffed you like the new look so much. Bleeding hell. Don't know why I bother.'

It was on the tip of her tongue to say that she knew the feeling. 'What are you doing here, anyway? Are you staying at The Paradise?'

'Yeah, obviously. I wasn't aware all this palaver was going on or I'd have thought twice, but then again, when I saw you it seemed like fate. Providence, you might say. Good job I'm on hand to keep an eye on things, eh?'

Emerald gave him one of her looks. 'You don't need to keep an eye on things. We had a deal, remember?' She hoped he wasn't about to back out now. She was going to get that retreat if it killed her — or him.

'Chill your beans, kid. I ain't gunna cramp your style. Just taking a friendly interest. Anyway, I'm only here for a couple of days so let's not argue. I thought I'd pop up here and see how you were all getting on, that's all.' He turned to Eden. 'Has Jed been pulling his weight? Not been skiving or nuffink?'

'Oh no, he's been great,' Eden assured him. 'He's been a godsend, to be honest. I don't think I could have managed without him.'

'That's what I like to hear,' Cain said, sounding satisfied, which was more, Emerald thought, than Eliot looked. He seemed irritated that Eden was singing Jed's praises. Hmm. A hint of jealousy there perhaps? Did he not trust his precious Eden? Interesting.

She turned to her father. 'Well, I suppose you're right. You may as well make yourself useful and choose the style of suit Eliot's going to wear. Don't order anything though, unless it co-ordinates with the colours on my mood board first.'

'Your what?'

'Mood board,' Eden muttered. 'She's already picked our colour scheme, and everything has to work around that, apparently.'

'Heard it all now,' Cain murmured. 'What colour are you having then?'

'Pink,' Eden said dully.

Eliot pulled a face. 'Aye. Me in pink. Imagine it.'

'Don't say it like that! With your dark hair you're going to look divine with a pink cravat. Trust me on this, I have some wonderful ideas for your wedding,' Emerald assured them. 'Now, come on, Eden, let's see if we can find you the perfect dress.'

'And don't be worrying about the cost,' Cain reminded them.

'Just pick the one you like, no looking at the price tag.'

Emerald gritted her teeth and steered Eden away before she said something she'd regret.

'I wonder what's brought his change of image on?' Eden mused, glancing back over her shoulder as Cain and Eliot headed towards the nearest gentlemen's outfitters. 'Doesn't he look different? I can't believe it.'

'I'd like to know what he's doing back here already,' Emerald muttered. In actual fact, she was pretty certain that it was because he didn't trust her, which annoyed her no end. She was doing her best to organise the perfect wedding. The wedding Cain had demanded, in fact. She *would* get her retreat.

For the next half hour, Emerald tried hard to look enthusiastic as Eden rummaged through dozens of rails of countless wedding dresses, and flicked through catalogues and watched tall, willowy models parade in front of them, demonstrating how beautiful you could look if you too were six feet tall and weighed about six stone.

Emerald thought it was criminal, and there should at least be some attempt to cater for the shorter, fatter bride. Eden wasn't exactly plump, but she was never going to look like those women. Emerald sighed. This was so dull. All she really wanted to do was help Eliot choose his suit. She wondered if he'd tried on any yet. She'd bet he looked handsome, whichever one he chose. She craned her neck, glancing around the room in the hope of seeing him, but no such luck. He'd probably gone into the adjoining room. Bugger.

Eventually, Eden found a couple of dresses she liked and took the contact details of the suppliers. Needless to say, neither was from The Wedding Dress Shop. It would mean a trip to Ripon but that wasn't too bad, and Eden planned to take Ophelia and Liberty, so they could choose bridesmaid dresses and accessories at the same time.

'Now that's done, shall we go and find Eliot?'

Let the poor man breathe, thought Emerald sulkily. 'Sure. Why not?'

Emerald was hoping for a glimpse of the farmer in a morning

suit and cravat, but, as so often in life, she was to be disappointed. When they finally spotted Cain and Eliot, they were standing in a small crowd gathered around a table, where a man in a faded suit was demonstrating a card trick.

'A magician? Are you serious?' Eden giggled as Eliot rolled his eyes.

'He's proper clever, this bloke,' Cain assured her. 'Worth considering. Keep the kiddies amused, at any rate.'

'We don't need a magician at our wedding,' Eden insisted. 'I don't even like magicians.'

The man, who was in the middle of his next trick, glared at her. Emerald smirked as Eden blushed and turned away, saying, 'I think we should look at something else. Something we need. Did you find a decent suit?'

She brushed imaginary fluff from Eliot's shoulder. *Claiming ownership* thought Emerald bitterly. It was textbook behaviour. Maybe Eden felt threatened? Hmm. Emerald cheered up a bit at the thought.

'Aye. We're going into town in a couple of weeks to get fitted.' He sounded thrilled. Not.

'Who's we?' Emerald said suspiciously.

'Me, Cain, Mickey, Jed and Adey,' he said.

'Who on earth is Adey?'

Eliot frowned. 'Lad who helps out on the farm when he can. You've met him.'

Emerald considered the matter. 'I have? Oh yes, I think I know who you mean. Why are you getting him a suit?'

'Because he's going to be an usher, like Jed is, apparently.'

Emerald felt indignant for him. Clearly, that had been Cain's suggestion. Eliot barely knew Jed. On the other hand, it would be lovely to have her brother involved.

'So, who's your best man?' Surely not her father? Even if he had finally had a haircut and a change of image, there had to be someone better than that available.

'Mickey.'

Emerald tried not to look appalled. *Mickey!* The old shepherd was positively ancient. He didn't seem to have a tooth left in his head. He would look dismal in the wedding photographs.

She forced a smile. 'How lovely. Favours!'

'Huh?' Cain pulled a face. 'What bleeding favours do you want now? Don't you think I've done enough?'

'Not that sort of favour,' she assured him. 'Wedding favours.'

Cain and Eliot exchanged bewildered glances as Eden shook her head. 'We don't need those either. It's all silly, pointless extras. All we need is something to wear, rings and a cake to cut.'

'Don't be stupid!' Cain and Emerald chorused their disapproval and then stared at each other, clearly horrified that they'd agreed on something.

'This is a proper wedding,' Cain decided, 'and you'll get what every bride should get.'

'Yes, Eden,' Emerald purred. 'There's nothing I want more than to give you what you deserve.'

Eden, it seemed, wasn't as stupid as she looked. She gave Emerald a filthy look. Emerald decided to change the subject.

'So, Dad, what's with the change of image?' She looked Cain up and down, realising that, although he was now dressed like a middle-aged man for a change, he suddenly looked an awful lot younger. A bleached mullet and a face full of makeup had aged him. She wrinkled her nose as a thought suddenly occurred to her. 'Has this got anything to do with Honey?'

'Honey? As if! That's you, with your obsession,' he said, tutting. 'Look, I thought it was time I started to look a bit more — well—'

'Your age?' Emerald suggested helpfully.

He growled. 'A bit more sophisticated, shall we say. I mean, let's face it, I mix with the cream of British society these days, and I can hardly collect my knighthood from the palace in me leopard skin leggings, can I?'

'Heaven forbid,' she agreed. 'Thank goodness that doesn't seem likely.'

'Still in good form, I see,' he said. 'Well, you might be interested to know that Honey and Teddy are back from their honeymoon.'

'I should hope they are,' she said. 'I was beginning to think they'd be celebrating their first anniversary over there.'

'Be fair.' Cain looked around at Eden and Eliot, as if pleading for backup. 'They've bin proper busy these last few months, what with the charity and the wedding to organise.'

'As if *All the Goss* didn't organise most of it,' Emerald snapped. 'But of course, poor little Honey. Deserves a two-month honeymoon in Africa, if only to rest that enormous head of hers. Must be quite wearing her out, carrying that huge ego around with her every day.'

'Oh, for goodness' sake,' Eden said, linking her arm through Eliot's as if she was determined to annoy Emerald, 'drop it.' She smiled at Cain. 'Has she been to see you? How are they? Did they enjoy the honeymoon?'

He grinned. 'Got on like a house on fire. Had a fab time. Course,' he added, sounding less pleased, 'they're living with Rex for now, which is a flaming shame. But they're looking for a house and when they find something decent, they'll be setting up their own little home.'

'Why don't you build them something in your garden?' Emerald said, hoping they hadn't all noticed the wobble in her voice. 'Then you'll never have to be parted from her again.'

Cain scowled. 'Good idea. I might suggest that. By the way, Eden, Honey sends her apologies but she's going to have to decline your invite to the wedding. She's gunna be at some fancy humanitarian awards do with Rex and Teddy in LA that week. She's ever so sorry.'

'Not sorry enough to skip the do, though,' Emerald pointed out.

As Cain glared at her, Eden hastily told him that it didn't matter, and she quite understood.

'How did the recording go?' she said, changing the subject. 'Did you enjoy yourself with Sun King? What are they like?'

Cain's demeanour changed immediately. His back stiffened, and his face took on a tight, tense expression. 'Great. We had a smashing time. Nice bunch of lads.'

'That's not what I've heard,' Emerald said. 'From what I know about them, they're a bunch of pretentious twerps without an original thought in their heads.'

'And how would you know?' Cain demanded.

'I have friends who have friends,' she said mysteriously. He didn't need to know that it was Jed who'd confided in her. Her brother, it seemed, knew everyone, whereas she knew no one. Let her father chew on that puzzle.

'You amaze me,' Cain said. 'You having friends. Who'd have thought it?'

'These favours,' Eden said. 'Can we just not bother?'

'But everyone has favours,' Emerald said. She turned to Eliot. 'What do you think?'

'If that's what folks generally have, then that's what *we'll* have,' he said, after a moment's hesitation. 'I draw the line at the magician, though.'

'Quite. Extremely tacky in my opinion, unless you've got someone classy like Dynamo.' Emerald peered up at him. 'Do you want me to try to get Dynamo?'

'No, I bloody don't,' he said firmly. 'Even if he was up for it, which I doubt, he'd cost a fortune.'

'Besides,' Cain added, 'everyone would be so busy watching him they wouldn't be looking at Eden, and we don't want that. All eyes should be on the bride.'

Emerald scowled, wondering if she could sneak Dynamo in, after all.

'Where are we at with this wedding, anyway?' Cain had stopped at a cake stall and was already helping himself to several free samples. 'What you got done so far?'

Emerald tutted. She *knew* he was here to check up on her!

'The church is booked and I'm viewing several function rooms this week.'

She ignored the groan from Eden. They'd had quite heated arguments about the wedding reception. Eden was adamant she wanted something small and informal and Emerald had reminded her that she was in charge of the wedding, something Eden herself had agreed with Cain, and that Eden should trust her, upon which Eden had pulled a scornful face that had made Emerald want to slap her.

She had a few places in mind and whatever Eden wanted, it was really Cain that Emerald was trying to please. He knew exactly the sort of wedding he wanted them to have, and she was going to deliver. It was, after all, her father that held the power to grant her health retreat wish, not Eden, or even Eliot. They would have to lump it. 'I've shortlisted the photographers, and the cars, and Eliot and Eden are going into town soon to get their rings ordered.' Emerald made a mental note to draw up a list of photographers and car hire firms, hoping her father wouldn't demand details before she got the chance to do so. Well, she'd been busy creating her mood board and making plans. Making firm bookings had been way down the list of priorities. 'Eliot's sorting the menswear, Eden and I are going to Ripon to choose the dresses and—'

'I'd rather like to go alone,' Eden interrupted, 'Well, me and the girls if you don't mind.'

'But I do mind,' Emerald said crossly. 'I'm your wedding planner, after all, and—'

'And the dresses are up to me. My choice.' Eden looked at Cain. 'I'm sorry, but my mind's made up on this. It's the one area that I don't want any involvement from you or Emerald or anyone else.'

'Except for Dad's cheque book,' Emerald muttered.

'Not even that.' Eden gave her a fake smile. 'My dad has insisted on paying for the dresses. He sent me some money the other day with the express instruction that it's only to be used for that purpose, and I'm not going to refuse him that right, whatever anyone says. So, this will be a personal thing, for me and the girls.'

Emerald looked at Cain. To her disappointment, he nodded and smiled. 'I reckon that's a lovely gesture from your dad. Nice for him to be able to do that. Good for you, Eden. You go off and have a nice day with the kids.'

'But — but—' Emerald had no idea what to say. She had total control of this wedding so far, and she liked it that way. This didn't fit in with that, at all.

'Eliot,' she said, appealing to his better nature, 'you know that I need to be there, right? I'm the wedding planner, after all. I should be involved in every step of this wedding.'

To her dismay, he shook his head. 'Not this, Emerald. This is between Eden and her dad, and I reckon if that's how they want it then so be it.'

Emerald almost stamped her foot she was so cross. She could feel her third chakra sliding out of control, the wheel spinning furiously within her upper abdomen. *Think yellow, think yellow*, she told herself. *I send love and compassion to you all.* She closed her eyes and took a few deep breaths, visualising a glowing yellow light within her solar plexus.

'Tell you what, this cake ain't half bad,' Cain said.

Emerald's eyes snapped open as he reached for another slice, earning a disapproving look from the woman who was handing out samples. 'What do you think? Are we having a fruit cake at this wedding, or one of them sponges?'

Eden squeezed his arm affectionately — a gesture which incensed Emerald — and said, 'You don't have to get us a cake, Cain. Honestly, I can bake one myself.'

'You will not!' Cain looked outraged. 'Bake your own bleeding wedding cake! What is this, the war? I'm quite sure we can buy you one and no arguments.'

'How about a croquembouche?' Evidently spotting a potential sale, the woman put down her tray and hurried over to greet them. 'They're terribly popular at the moment.'

'What the heck is a croquembouche?' Eliot looked out of his depth.

'A towering structure of profiterole balls,' she said, reaching for a brochure that lay beside a fat diary. 'Terribly popular in France and Italy, and growing in popularity here, too.'

'But this is Yorkshire,' Eliot said, in a voice that clearly ruled out a croquembouche. As he peered at the photographs she waved under his nose, it was evident that he wasn't going to change his mind.

The saleswoman obviously recognised that fact, too. 'Or perhaps, instead of one cake, a whole assortment of cupcakes instead? We do some wonderful designs. We can do almost any flavour and decorate them as you wish. You could have three tiers — each tier filled with a different flavour of cupcake. You could even have one large cake as the base and—'

'Aren't there any normal wedding cakes?' Eliot sounded weary. 'You know, a bit of fruitcake with marzipan and icing, and a plastic bride and groom on top?'

The woman reeled back, wounded. 'Really?'

'I reckon none of these will taste as good as Eden's cakes any road,' Eliot said, which only made the poor woman look even more hurt.

'How about a nice sponge cake?' Eden suggested hastily. 'The children don't like fruit cake, and I'm not terribly fond of it either.'

The woman tried to recover her composure. 'We do several flavours of sponge cake and, of course, we would endeavour to provide you with whatever style or design you wish.'

'Here, Eden, get your laughing gear around this,' Cain said, waving a dish of tiny bite-sized cake squares in her face. 'This is proper tasty.'

'Lemon and elderflower,' the woman said, wrinkling her nose in distaste as Cain stuffed four pieces into his mouth at once. 'One of our most popular flavours.'

'We don't want popular,' Emerald said. 'We want unique. Something different. Something spectacular. Something no one's had before.'

'No we don't.' Eden was eyeing the lemon and elderflower cake in the brochure. It was a pretty design with very pale lemon buttercream covering the cake, and yellow and lilac flowers sitting on top. 'This is lovely.' She looked at Eliot. 'What do you think?'

'It doesn't fit with the colour scheme.' Emerald put her hands on her hips, feeling the control of this wedding slipping further away from her with every minute. She turned to her father, appealing to his better nature. 'You said you wanted her to have the best wedding ever. How is this sort of thing going to contribute to that?'

'You ain't tasted this cake,' he mumbled, showering her with crumbs as he did so.

Emerald wrinkled her nose in disgust. He may have changed

his image, but he was still the same coarse, common individual beneath it all. She wondered why his opinion even mattered to her.

Despairing, she cast her gaze over the catalogue that lay on the counter, and suddenly let out a whoop. 'What about this one?'

Cain peered at the picture she was pointing to. It was a large, grand, three-tier structure, coated with thick white icing and decorated in a style that was rather French, with ornate swirls and little pearls. It looked like a wedding gown itself. Sitting on top was a little posy of white roses.

'Look at the flavour,' she pointed out. 'Look at the colour of the actual cake inside!'

He screwed up his eyes, trying to see properly. Too vain to wear glasses, she thought, and too cowardly to wear contacts. He was a lost cause, really.

'What's this?' he said.

'Pink cake,' Eliot said. 'Like angel cake?'

'Pink champagne,' the saleswoman said, the eagerness in her voice a reflection, no doubt, of the fact that the cake they were now discussing was far more expensive than the simple lemon and elderflower cake. 'It really is most exquisite, and the taste is simply divine.'

Eliot and Eden looked at each other.

'Perfect,' Cain pronounced. 'Just the job that. Can't beat a bit of champers and having it in your cake makes it that much more special, don't you think? We'll take that one,' he pronounced, without even so much as checking on the Harlands' opinion.

Emerald smiled to herself. Her father was such a snob. He could always be relied upon to go for the fancier option.

'Cain, it's too much,' Eden said, sounding desperate. 'Look at the price of it. Honestly, I can bake one myself.'

'You will not,' Cain said. 'This is your big day, and you're having the best. Am I right, Eliot?'

Eliot nodded. 'They're right, love. I want this to be as special as you are. This cake's right grand, and no less than you deserve.'

Emerald turned away before she revealed too much. Her loathing of Eden had cranked up another notch. Why was everyone so besotted with the woman? She was such a phoney! Why did no-one but her see that? She thrust her hands in her pockets, scowling to herself.

Her fingers curled around a piece of card and she pulled it out, curious. Then her face cleared. James Fuller! She'd almost forgotten about him. He despised Eden almost as much as she did. If anyone would understand how she felt, it was him.

She put the card back in her pocket and bit her lip, considering. Eliot was such a sweet man. He'd never said a bad word to her, and always seemed to take her side. Well, almost always. She'd never met anyone like him — except for Jed. They were very similar. Not in looks, of course. They couldn't look more different. But in personality, temperament. Jed was more confident, more outgoing than Eliot, but he had the same kindness, the same understanding. They were the only two people she'd ever known who seemed to listen to her, seemed to even *see* her. Maybe she should try to get along with Eden, if only for his sake?

She fixed a smile on her face and spun round, deciding to throw herself into the joys of ordering an extortionately expensive cake. Her smile died. Eliot had his arms tightly around Eden, and they were both smiling at the lady behind the counter as she informed them of the different types of cake topper they could have. Cain, meanwhile, was stuffing his face with more samples. Emerald glared at them all. They hadn't even noticed that she wasn't with them. It was all about Eden, as usual. She'd never felt so alone, nor so lonely. She needed a friend. Someone who understood. Thank goodness she'd kept hold of that card.

Chapter 18

Cain was starving and beginning to wish he'd accepted Eden's invitation to dinner, but since he'd already had lunch with them and spent most of the day at Wildflower Farm, he felt he'd outstayed his welcome. He had an awful feeling that if he didn't get back to the hotel, he'd be roped into doing some evening painting in the barn, and he couldn't be doing with all that. Not with his knees. And hips. And back. And neck. Jesus, he was a wreck and no mistake.

He'd booked a table for eight o'clock but regretted his decision. It was only seven and his stomach thought his throat was cut. He could hear its grumbling protests already. Maybe, he thought, he should buy himself a couple of drinks and fill up on peanuts at the bar. That should stave off the worst of it.

After showering and changing, he headed into the hotel restaurant and plonked himself on a stool at the bar. Trying to ignore the boards which listed today's specials, he ordered himself a pint of lager and coughed loudly as his stomach growled its disapproval at him. Why was he so hungry? Eden had piled up his plate at lunchtime. Emerald had been disgusted. Then again, Emerald was always disgusted.

He munched miserably on a handful of peanuts, wondering what the hell he was going to do with his problem middle child. It was weird, but the whole time he was back in Upper Bourbury he hadn't been able to stop thinking about her.

Truth was, he felt guilty. She'd been off his radar for so long that he'd almost forgotten about her, and he didn't have a clue how she'd lived her life, what she enjoyed doing, who she was — apart from obnoxious and a bit wacky, of course. That went without saying.

She was a moody mare, but there was a little nagging voice inside Cain's head that kept reminding him that, compared with his other children, she'd had a rough time, and that he'd barely spared her a thought in years. He wanted to make it up to her, but he didn't want to be made a fool of again, the way Honey had made a fool of him with her poxy little shop that had ended up costing him a small fortune. Honey had never made any real attempt to run it as a profitable business. She was a spoilt little madam, truth to tell, but Cain couldn't help but love her. And look at her now! All grown up and married and responsible. Maybe there was hope for Emerald, after all.

'Gin and tonic please.' The cut glass accent made Cain turn his head to get a better view of its owner. He was a sucker for a posh voice. It was what had led him into Freya's clutches, and look how that had turned out. The woman sitting next to him at the bar was older than Freya — or maybe she wasn't. It was hard to tell, given how much plastic surgery Honey's mother had undertaken.

The woman beside him was all natural, with fine lines at the corners of her eyes and light feathering above her lips, but she was attractive, nevertheless. She turned her head and stared at Cain and he thought she was very attractive indeed. With large, dark, almond-shaped eyes she reminded him of a Jersey cow — in a good way, of course. She was — what was the word? — elegant. Yeah, that was her. Elegant.

The woman turned away and accepted the gin and tonic from the barman with a grateful smile. He was dismissed.

Sighing inwardly, Cain resumed his musings on his daughters, and how different they were. Honey's return from her honeymoon had cheered him up. At least, at first.

When she and Teddy had turned up on his doorstep a few days ago, he'd been over the moon to see them, all tanned and happy and looking totally loved up. But Honey hadn't even mentioned his new look for ages — too busy telling him about the honeymoon. Which, he supposed was understandable. Just a bit disappointing, that's all.

And when she did finally seem to notice, it was Teddy who brought it up, not her.

Honey had looked him up and down and said, 'About time you started dressing your age. Did I tell you Rex is having laser treatment to remove those tattoos on his face?'

Then she'd launched into a long discussion about his long-time rival, Honey's new father-in-law. It was all *Rex this*, and *Rex that* until, quite frankly, he was sick to death of hearing about sodding Rex.

Honey had completely thrown herself into working for the Scotman Foundation, founded and run by — yes — Rex. Teddy worked for it, too, and the two of them had spent a great deal of their honeymoon working, rather than relaxing, sunbathing, sightseeing and doing a lot of bonking like they should have been doing. It wasn't right, he thought gloomily. Rex Scotman had always been the bane of his life, and now he'd taken Honey, too.

Depressed and feeling even lonelier, Cain had decided there and then to head north and visit Emerald and Jed for a couple of days. Maybe they'd be more appreciative of his new look.

He'd been ever so nervous when he clapped eyes on Emerald heading into the hotel conference room. What would she say about him? He'd been half eager to find out and half dreading it. Ever the coward, he'd backed out of asking her and turned to Eden instead, because he knew he was guaranteed a polite answer from her. He'd saved Emerald 'til last, and she hadn't disappointed. She'd lived up to his expectations and poured cold water over the whole thing. He wondered why he'd been stupid enough to hope for anything else.

He wished he could think of a way to put things right with her, to build some sort of relationship with her, but he didn't have a clue how to start and, to be honest, Emerald didn't seem that bothered anyway. Her priority was getting this wedding sorted so she could prove she could be trusted and then the money for the retreat would be hers. She'd grab the money and run, and he'd never see her again. No doubt about it.

It was gutting. Five kids and not one of them seemed to want or need him. He supposed he was paying the price for his life of debauchery, and for more-or-less abandoning them while he pursued his career and a string of sexy blondes. Bleeding karma. What a bitch.

'May I buy you a drink?'

Cain blinked, snapped out of his misery as the posh bird on the next stool leaned towards him, all big eyes and expensive perfume.

'Eh?' *Oh, nice one, Cain! How classy.* 'I mean, pardon?'

She lowered her lashes quite coquettishly and smiled. 'I said, may I buy you a drink?'

Cain swallowed. Was she taking the piss? Oh, of course. She'd recognised him, even with his new image, and thought he was worth tapping up for a few quid. Then he frowned, noting the expensive gold jewellery on her wrist and fingers. She didn't look short of a bob or two. Mind you, that might be why. Maybe she went around fleecing gullible rich blokes all the time.

'It's all right, thanks. I've still got half a pint.'

She nodded. 'Fair enough.' She moved her stool a little closer and held out her hand. 'Constance.'

Cain considered for a moment, then shook her hand warily.

'Jeff,' he said, wondering what her reaction to that would be. 'Jeff Moggs.'

It wasn't an outright lie, after all. Jeffrey Dennis Moggs was the name on his birth certificate. The fact that it had been legally changed when he was only twenty was neither here nor there.

Constance didn't seem to doubt he was telling the truth, and he thought maybe she hadn't realised who she was talking to after all. Perhaps she was genuine. 'I'm pleased to meet you. I was sitting here contemplating an evening all alone and it's nice to have someone to talk to, isn't it?'

Cain nodded. 'Yeah, I suppose. Are you staying here then?'

'Just for the one night. How about you?'

'Yeah. I'm heading home tomorrow.'

'Have you eaten?'

Cain shook his head. 'I've got a table booked at eight.' He glanced at his watch and felt a gloom descend upon him again. 'Wish I'd booked it earlier,' he confessed. 'I'm starving.'

Constance gave him a wide smile and he noticed she had very even teeth and a dimple in her left cheek. 'My table's booked for half past seven. Would you like to sit with me? It would be awfully nice to have some company.'

As he hesitated, she held up her hands. 'Sorry. I didn't mean to push you. You may want to be alone this evening.'

As she gave him a sidelong look, Cain felt his legs go all funny. 'No, no, not at all. I'd love to join you — if you're sure?'

'Quite sure,' she confirmed. 'I'm sure you'll be most entertaining company.'

Funny, but Cain realised he suddenly wasn't feeling very hungry any more.

****

Cain wasn't quite sure what had happened. He lay staring up at the ceiling of his hotel room, his heart pumping, his pulse racing, and contemplated how funny life was. You never knew what was around the corner.

Beside him, Constance was already getting dressed, reaching for her rather fetching black, lacy bra. Cain gulped and watched, fascinated, as she slipped the straps over her shoulders, feeling a twinge of regret as those pert little breasts of hers were once again encased in the flimsy material. She may be getting on a bit, but she had a cracking body, and boy, she knew what to do with it.

He couldn't quite believe, even now, that they'd ended up in bed together. It was all so unexpected. They'd barely even got started on their meal when the small talk had turned to out and out flirtation. Cain had found himself loosening his shirt collar, and he'd seen Constance's pupils dilate as she moistened her lips with her tongue. It had been pretty obvious they were both of the same mind.

Pushing her plate away, Constance had breathed, 'Your room

or mine?'

'Mine,' Cain murmured, thinking it was the gentlemanly thing to do.

They'd almost knocked their chairs over in their desire to reach the lift and the doors had hardly shut before they were kissing. It had been a frenzied hike to his room, then the door was locked, and they were on the bed.

My God, he thought, she'd been wild. She'd practically ripped his clothes off him. For such a posh bird she had a down and dirty side, that was for sure. She'd almost vacuumed him up. Not that he was complaining.

Cain hadn't had sex for a couple of years and his last few sexual partners had all been young bimbos who hadn't given a toss about him. They'd been in it for the money and he knew it, but it was okay because, well, what else did he have to do? They'd quite worn him out and he'd been put off sex for life. Or so he'd thought. Constance's mature beauty and her obvious desire for him with no strings attached had been a huge turn-on.

He'd remembered what it used to feel like, all those years ago, when it had been enjoyable and not a chore. He'd well and truly got stuck in. No wonder his poor old ticker was thumping like mad. He could have sworn it was drumming out one of his biggest hits, *Satan in Stilettos*. He glanced at Constance. Was that what she was? Maybe she'd filmed the whole thing? Maybe this was some sort of blackmail scam? Shit, what had he done?

'I must tell you I don't usually do this sort of thing.' She turned to him, looking different somehow — sort of shamefaced. 'Seduce strange men, I mean. It's the first time, in fact.'

'Really?' God, that sounded rude. 'I mean, I believe you. 'Course I do.'

'I was — lonely.' She shrugged. 'I suppose that sounds pathetic. I'm in Yorkshire on business and I just felt so far from home and so—'

'It's okay. I get it.' He'd seen the gleam of a gold wedding ring on her finger. She didn't need to explain. 'It was a one-off, and that's fine. It will never go any further, okay, Connie?'

She smiled at him. 'Thank you, Jeff. I must say, you were

wonderful. I've really enjoyed myself.'

Cain grinned. 'Me an' all, Connie. Me an' all.'

'I must be going.' She stood up, tucking her blouse into her skirt and glancing around for her shoes. 'I expect this is goodbye.'

'I suppose it is.'

They stared at each other, suddenly awkward. Constance bent down, easing on her shoes, then held out her hand. He shook it, feeling stupid and also a bit sad, which was ridiculous.

'Goodbye, Jeff.'

'Goodbye, Connie.'

Then she opened the door, and Cain could only lie there, wishing she would stay a bit longer, listening wistfully to the clicking of her heels as she headed down the corridor.

Chapter 19

James looked at his watch and tutted. She was ten minutes late already. He hated that. He was taking her out for dinner, for God's sake. The least she could do was turn up on time.

He sipped his water, wondering what it was that had persuaded Emerald Carmichael to call him after all. He hadn't been sure that she would, although it would've been a cold day in hell before he'd confessed that to his father. He had to admit, it had been a huge relief to hear from her. At least it would buy him a bit more time. His father was so pushy.

He glanced up, his eyes widening as he saw Emerald approaching. Well, that wasn't what he'd expected. He supposed he should have known, given the fact that she'd been wearing jeans and a parka, with her hair in plaits, that day in town, yet he'd grown so used to dates with women who dressed to kill and plastered on makeup with a trowel. Emerald was practically makeup free, her hair loose, and she was wearing a teal-coloured maxi dress with ankle boots and a denim jacket. Hardly the height of sophistication yet, somehow, she looked sensational.

James felt a familiar stirring in his loins and an excited fluttering in his stomach. He loved the thrill of these extramarital flirtations. They stirred the blood, reminding him that he was still young enough to enjoy the chase, and there was always the promise of a reward at the end of it. Sometimes the flirtations remained innocent, even if there was that frisson bubbling beneath the surface. Often, though, he got lucky, and the flirtation evolved into something much more satisfying.

He wondered which way it would go with Emerald. It was hard to tell. She didn't give much away, although he suspected that she revealed a lot more than she intended. There was a naivety and a vulnerability about her, despite her attempts to sound cool and in control. She was intriguing, and he couldn't wait to get to know her better. He stood as the waiter pulled out her chair and she sat down, nodding her thanks.

'Sorry I'm late,' she said, tucking her tote bag under her chair. 'I had to get a taxi and they're not very reliable around here.' She smiled at the waiter. 'Thank you so much.' Turning to James she queried, 'Have you ordered?'

'No, of course not. I was drinking water until you arrived.'

Emerald nodded. 'Would you mind awfully if I had a glass of water, too, until we decide what to order?'

The waiter flushed and gave her a wide smile.

'Not at all, madam.' He hurried off to do her bidding.

James grinned. 'You've got him eating out of your hand already,' he remarked. 'Well done.'

After hanging her jacket on the back of her chair, she looked at him, surprised. 'What do you mean?' Grabbing the menu, her eyes widened in delight as she scanned the dishes on offer. 'This looks amazing. I could eat a horse.'

James picked up his own menu. She was totally unaware that the waiter had succumbed to her charms and was more concerned with the food on offer. In a strange way, she was quite refreshing, if a little unsophisticated.

'Don't you have a car?' he enquired, remembering her comment about the taxi.

'I've never seen the need,' she confessed, 'so I never bothered.'

'Never seen the need!' James lowered the menu and stared at her in astonishment. 'Are you serious? You *can* drive, though?'

She leaned back in her chair, her eyes bright with amusement. 'Yes, I can drive, but I rarely do. Some of the places I've lived there wasn't even a road, never mind a car. The truth is, I've probably only driven around a handful of times since I passed my test, and I'm not very good at it.' She grinned at him. 'You look stunned. Is it so unusual?'

'Well, yes.' He shook his head. 'Most people I know own at least one car. No wonder your driving skills are a little rusty. Still,' he gave her what he hoped was a seductive smile, 'we can't all do everything, and I'm sure you have other talents.'

'Oh yes. I can read auras for a start,' she informed him.

James blinked, not sure if she was winding him up or not, but she seemed deadly serious. 'And what does my aura tell you?'

She frowned. 'Quite honestly, it's a bit murky. I suspect you have dark secrets.'

He tugged at his shirt collar. That was a bit too close for comfort.

'Are you into all that stuff then?' he said. 'You don't look like a hippy.'

Although, quite honestly, he supposed she did. Thank God she wasn't a vegan. She'd wolfed down that fishfinger sandwich at The Daffodil Café with enough relish to convince him of that.

'You sound like my father,' she rebuked him. 'Prejudice is an ugly trait, as is a closed mind. My intention, in the long term, is to open a retreat for like-minded people. Maybe you should book yourself in when it opens. You'll see for yourself what I'm really all about.'

'But all that stuff,' he protested, 'it's all a load of baloney, isn't it? A money-making invention by you New Age lot.'

'We prefer to call ourselves spiritual seekers. Besides, the term New Age is very misleading,' she said, turning a grateful smile on the waiter as he returned with her water. 'Thank you so much. We've not decided what to have yet, but we'll call you over as soon as we have.' He nodded, and she turned back to James. 'These therapies, and this knowledge has been around for centuries.'

'Hmm. Until we evolved and realised what a load of mumbo jumbo it is.'

'I think this is going to be a very short dinner date,' she said, putting down her menu.

James threw up his hands. 'I'm sorry. That was very rude of me. I've had a long and rather dire week.'

'Join the club,' she muttered, picking up the menu again and jabbing her finger at the page.

He noticed she wasn't wearing nail varnish. What an extraordinary young woman she was! He peered at her curiously. No makeup, no jewellery, no nail varnish, simple clothes. He suspected she didn't fit in very well with the sort of people her father and the rest of her family mingled with. No wonder she'd turned to all that hippy rubbish to get her through.

'It's ever so expensive in here,' she murmured. 'I think I prefer The Daffodil Café.'

'It's on me. Choose whatever you like.'

Emerald frowned. 'You've already bought me one meal. I don't see why you should pay for another.'

James couldn't believe it. He'd never met anyone like her before.

'It's all tax deductible,' he assured her. 'Honestly, I'd rather spend it on you than give it to the taxman.'

She looked suspicious for a moment but seemed to decide he was telling the truth. 'Okay. Well, in that case, I fancy the braised beef brisket and mini Yorkshire pudding with horseradish puree for starters, and the sea bass for my main course. What about you?'

James hadn't even had time to think about it. The girl certainly had an appetite for food. He wondered what her appetite for other pleasures was like. Pushing the thought away, he scanned the menu quickly as she beckoned the waiter over. As Emerald gave her order to the clearly smitten waiter, he made a snap decision.

'The game and redcurrant terrine for me,' he said, handing the menus back to the waiter, 'followed by the pan-fried calves' liver. I'm driving,' he told Emerald, 'so I'm going to stick to water, but would you like wine?'

'I'd prefer to keep a clear head, thank you. May I have some of the elderflower lemonade?'

'Of course, madam. I'll bring it straight over to you.' The waiter gave her a beaming smile, nodded at James and headed towards the kitchen.

James wondered if it were a good or bad thing that Emerald wanted to keep a clear head. It was odd, but he was suddenly unaccountably nervous. There was an innocence and honesty about Emerald that was making him feel quite hot.

'I was surprised to hear from you,' he told her. 'You made it very clear after our last meeting that you wouldn't be getting in touch.'

'No, well, I didn't intend to,' she admitted. 'For some reason, I hung onto your card, Mr Fuller. I'm not sure why.'

'James, please. Mr Fuller's my father.' At the mention of David, James inwardly shuddered. He could practically hear his father roaring in his ear to get on with it, get down to business, get Emerald onside without all this preamble. 'And I'm very glad you did.'

'I want you to know that I like Beth.'

James narrowed his eyes. What on earth was she bringing Beth into it for?

'Well, that's very nice of you. She's a good person.'

'Yes, she seems to be, although I do think her root chakra needs balancing. She's terribly jittery. I expect she gets awful digestive problems. Anyway, my point is, I want it to be clear that I'm not going to do anything to hurt her.' She leaned forward, big blue eyes gazing into his. 'I want your friendship, nothing more. You do understand that?'

James gaped at her, then snapped his mouth shut. Was she serious? He was paying for an expensive dinner, and she wanted *friendship?*

'Of course. I never expected anything else. Although,' he added smoothly, 'I'm a little surprised that you contacted me if that was the case. Surely, someone like you already has enough friends?'

She looked surprisingly vulnerable. 'Not really. I moved around a lot as a child, and rarely stayed at one school for long. That's if I went to school at all. And right now, I'm sort of isolated at Wildflower Farm, while I plan the wedding. My brother's there, of course, but he's so busy. It's lambing time and it's manic there at the moment.' She shook her head. 'Even the children have stayed up all night in the lambing shed, keeping Eliot or Eden

222

company. Jed's done a few night shifts, too, and he's also working on the bunk barns to get them ready in time for opening. I don't really have anyone to talk to. Besides,' she shrugged, 'what would I have in common with them? They're all infatuated with St Eden.'

'Ah yes. She has a way of making people fall for her,' he said. 'Never understood it myself.'

'Me neither,' she said with feeling. 'My father dotes on her, my sister's her best friend, and even my brother seems to adore her, and he's usually a man of exceptional taste.' She blushed a little. 'And Eliot deserves better. Much better.' She cleared her throat as he narrowed his eyes. 'I mean, after what you told me about him and Daisy and how she broke them up, and then all that stuff with going behind his back so Beth could see the children...' She shrugged. 'So, as you can see, I'm kind of out on my own there, so I'd like a friend who's of the same mind as me.'

James felt offended. He'd been right! It was patently obvious that Emerald Carmichael had a crush on Eliot Harland. What was it with that man? He was an ignorant sheep farmer, when all was said and done, yet the women seemed to fall over themselves, desperate to be with him. He was so annoyed that he felt like walking out and leaving her to it.

As if it wasn't bad enough that Harland had managed to persuade someone as beautiful as Jemima to marry him, there was Beth, who, despite her protests, seemed to be spending an awful lot of time at Wildflower Farm lately. There could only be one reason for that, and it wasn't due to a love of sheep. His own wife!

At the thought of Beth, he remembered the reason he'd wanted to befriend Emerald in the first place and his spirits sank. He had no choice.

'I do understand, and it will be nice to meet up and discuss our mutual loathing sometimes. I can't mention it to Beth, of course, since she dotes on Eden, too. Most perplexing.'

He was rewarded with a huge smile that lit up her face. She grasped his hand. 'Oh, thank you! I hoped you'd understand!'

Her breasts strained against her dress as she leaned towards him, and James felt an uncomfortable pressure against his trousers. God, she was beautiful! Even the cat hairs on her dress didn't lessen her appeal. She would be wasted on Harland. Surely, he would be able to make her see that? Whatever she said about friendship only, his instinct was telling him that she was looking for someone to flatter her, boost her ego. She may have said she wanted their relationship to be strictly platonic, but he sensed that she wanted him to want her, even if she had no intention of acting on it. She was a lost and mixed-up young woman, no doubt about it.

'Of course I understand, and it will be my pleasure to spend time with you.'

It really would be, too, if only he could persuade Emerald that he was much more her type and could give her a far better time than Harland could dream of.

An image of Beth entered his mind, and he pushed it away. He loved his wife, of course he did, and he would never hurt her again. But Emerald was so sexy — a beguiling mix of scheming and naïve, and those curves were to die for. Best of all, she seemed oblivious to her own beauty. He didn't see why he couldn't have his cake and eat it. This time, he would be more careful, that's all. It was just a matter of time.

****

Beth smoothed the moisturising cream into her hands and considered herself in the mirror. She didn't look any different, she thought. Somehow, she'd expected that after she kissed Jed there would be something about her — something that made her duplicitous actions evident to everyone. Maybe a huge speech bubble above her head, so that everyone could read her treacherous thoughts. Imagine if that were true! Her life would be hell right now.

Ironically, it was the first time in a long time that she *didn't* feel her life was hell. At last, she had something to smile about, even though she should be hanging her head in shame.

Did she feel guilty? Yes, she realised, she did. James had done everything he could to make it up to her for his affair with Jemima, but she'd found it impossible to forget. Their relationship had suffered as a result. Yet here she was, doing the unthinkable and falling for someone else, just as James had. Hypocrite!

She'd never expected to fall in love with another man. James had been her entire world for so long that it wouldn't have occurred to her that there could be anyone else. Yet, from the moment she'd set eyes on Jed, something strange had happened to her. She'd known from the instant she saw him that he was special, and something inside her had called to something in him, pulling them together, despite all the reasons they should have stayed well away.

After he'd kissed her — oh! She closed her eyes, remembering that kiss, and felt a flush of heat on her skin at the memory — after he'd kissed her, they'd clung to each other, as if they'd found each other again after being apart for decades. Centuries. Maybe they had. Maybe he was her lost soul mate, the one she'd been destined to find all along. She could well imagine they'd been lovers in another life. It seemed unthinkable that they hadn't. She couldn't think of James as her soul mate. She hadn't thought that for a long time, if ever.

Jed had told her he expected nothing from her, that he understood. She'd wanted to beg him to take everything from her, there and then, that nothing else mattered. Of course, she hadn't. He was quite right. She was married, for goodness' sake. They had to be sensible, practical. Yet, as they'd looked at each other, she saw something burning in his eyes that she felt within herself, and somehow, she knew that common sense and decency wouldn't hold out for long.

Maybe they'd have given in right there and then if Libby hadn't pushed open the barn door and called to Jed that his tea was ready. That had poured cold water over the pair of them all right. Good job, too, really. There was no rushing this sort of thing. She had to be careful. Hadn't she?

She groaned inwardly as the bedroom door pushed open and she saw the reflection of James in the mirror. He'd been at some business meeting in Richmond — or was it Ripon? Somewhere like that, anyway. She hadn't taken much notice. At least he wasn't drunk, since he'd been driving and would never do anything so stupid. She eyed him nervously in the mirror. He looked flushed, bright-eyed. *Had* he been drinking?

'Of course not!' He sounded indignant when she posed the question. 'You know me better than that, surely?'

'Sorry.' She couldn't help but notice there was something different about him though. She had to stop herself from flinching as he came to stand behind her and watched her in the mirror.

'You look particularly lovely tonight,' he told her.

Beth swallowed. 'Thanks.' It wasn't like him to pay her a compliment. She couldn't remember the last time he had, come to think of it. She felt exposed and vulnerable under his gaze, and wished she wasn't wearing her night things. The thin satin of her camisole top revealed far too much to his lustful gaze. She could see the gleam in his eyes and wondered when it was he'd last looked at her that way. She couldn't remember.

She almost slapped his hand away as it slid beneath her top and rested lightly on her breast. He was her husband! How would it look if she pushed him away?

'Beautiful,' he murmured.

Beth lowered her eyes, not wanting to see the leery expression on his face as he caressed her, gently at first but then with increasing pressure.

'James, what are you—?'

He grabbed her arms suddenly, pulling her to her feet. 'Come to bed.'

Oh, God! That was the last thing she wanted.

'I love you. I need you.'

Beth frowned. *Since when?*

'It's been ages.' He led her to the bed and threw her onto it.

Beth pushed him away as he lowered himself onto her. 'What the hell do you think you're doing?'

He peered down at her. 'What do you think I'm doing? Have you forgotten how you do it?'

'Just about,' she said. 'You can't push me around like this. What's got into you?'

He sat up, eyeing her with a doleful expression. 'Sorry. I didn't mean to come on so strong.' He reached out a hand and ran it softly up and down her arm, which only served to irritate her. She wanted to swat him away, like a fly. 'I've missed you. All through the meeting this evening, I wanted to get home to you. I kept imagining us doing this. It's been far too long, Beth.'

'I know.' She hung her head, guilt searing through her as he told her how much he loved her.

'There's been so much going on we never seem to have time for each other. I know it's my fault.' He sighed. 'I've been brooding about George for so long, feeling sad and missing him so much, I suppose it's placed a barrier between us, and it shouldn't have. I'm sorry.'

Beth was ashamed. He hadn't even been able to tell her how much he was suffering because of her. The least she owed him was some affection, some show of love. She reached out a tentative hand and stroked his face. 'I know. I'm sorry, too.'

James evidently took that as his invitation to proceed. Maybe, thought Beth, as she closed her eyes to shut out the image of her husband, if she hadn't kissed Jed, she would have had the strength to turn James away. As it was, the guilt and shame were eating away at her, and she felt she owed him something, anything. Even so, as James finally rolled off her and left her in peace, Beth knew that it would never happen again. She couldn't bear it. He was her husband, but she didn't want him touching her. There was no going back now

Chapter 20

It had been a busy day on the farm, with the arrival of dozens of beds and various other bits and pieces of bedroom furniture.

Eden had spent the entire day with Jed, as they lugged the items into place in the main barn, and she didn't know how she'd have managed without him. She was hot, sweaty, and worn out, and wasn't looking forward to cooking dinner.

It was with some gratitude, then, that she accepted Jed's offer to take the children into Kirkby Skimmer and buy them dinner in The Monk's Haven — a child-friendly pub in the town that was well-known for serving delicious and hearty meals that would even manage to fill Ophelia up.

'Are you serious? That would be fantastic, and the kids would love it,' she said.

'It would be my pleasure. Hey, why don't you and Eliot come with us? Emmy's off in Leeds again, so why not?'

Eden considered for all off five seconds. 'Thanks, Jed, but we'll pass.'

'But why not?'

She grinned at him. 'Because Emmy's off in Leeds again, and Adey's taking a turn in the lambing shed tonight. You see?'

Evidently, he did, because he turned a fetching shade of pink and laughed. 'Sure, I get it. Well, I can't blame you. I guess you and Eliot haven't had much privacy lately. Fair enough. I'll get the kids out of your way and make sure we linger over dessert.'

The children had, as Eden predicted, been beside themselves with excitement to head into town for a meal at a pub, and after she'd washed and changed George into something presentable and persuaded the girls to get themselves cleaned up and dressed nicely, too, they all headed off, leaving Eden to grab a quick shower before Eliot finished work. She decided not to bother cooking. For once, they would have a takeaway. She would wait until *afterwards* and then make her order. Who knew how long it would be before they needed food? Hopefully, Eliot would be hungrier for something else.

Hearing the door slam shut, she hurried downstairs and peered into the kitchen, pleased to see Eliot standing by the sink washing his hands.

He turned as she closed the door behind her, his smile dropping into an expression of amazement when he realised she was stark naked except for a bath towel wrapped around her, her hair soaking wet.

'What the—?'

'The children are in town with Jed,' she told him. 'They're eating out and won't be back for hours. And Emerald's in Leeds. We have the house to ourselves, and Adey's on shift with the lambing, so we can spend some time together at last.'

Eliot swallowed. 'We can?'

'We can.' She eyed him nervously, suddenly not so sure he'd be up for it. Things had been distinctly off-key lately, and they hadn't been setting the world alight in the bedroom department. Maybe he wouldn't be in the mood? Maybe he'd gone off her? Maybe—

She gasped as he grabbed her and pulled her to him. 'You're serious? We're all alone?'

She nodded, smiling up at him, as she saw the light of desire in his dark, tired, eyes. His lips sought hers, and she melted inside, overwhelmed with relief that he still wanted her, and burning with need for him. She'd missed him. They'd been so busy lately that she hadn't realised how much.

Without saying a word, he took her hand and led her up the stairs, halting on the landing outside the bathroom. 'I'm filthy' he told her, a wicked smile on his face. 'Look at the state of my clothes.'

'They *are* disgusting,' she confirmed. 'Perhaps you'd better take them off immediately.'

He obeyed, dropping them to the floor while keeping his eyes on her the whole time.

She shivered in delight as he stood naked before her. At least it was obvious that he wanted her as much as she wanted him. He moved slowly towards her and gently unwrapped the towel from around her, letting it fall around their feet. His arms went around her in its place, and he held her gently to him, kissing her neck.

'Trouble is,' he murmured, 'it's not just my clothes that are filthy. *I'm* right filthy, an' all.'

'Are you?' she said, closing her eyes as his lips traced tiny kisses across her collar bone.

'Aye, and now that I've touched you, I'm afraid you're filthy, too, which means...'

She opened her eyes and saw him watching her, and the need in him almost took her breath away.

'What does it mean?' she managed, with some difficulty.

'It means you're going to need another shower now. Maybe we should get one together. What do you think?'

'I think it's the only right thing to do,' she confirmed.

He led her gently to the shower cubicle and opened the door. She stepped inside, and he made to follow, then paused. His eyes searched hers, a look of intensity in them that made her quiver.

'I've missed you that much, Eden,' he murmured.

She smiled. 'Let's get reacquainted,' she suggested, and it was very evident that he needed no further invitation.

****

'I brought you your dinner today, did Mickey tell you?'

Eliot half-paused in climbing out of the bed, then continued without looking round. 'No, he didn't.'

'Probably because then you'd have found out he'd eaten your sandwiches,' she said. 'Where were you?'

He flung open the wardrobe door. 'Oh, took a stray back to Garbutt's Farm.'

'Mickey never said.' She frowned. 'In the Land Rover? Why not the trailer?'

Eliot hesitated. 'Right. Must've been a different time then. That's right, I remember now. I heard Granny Allen hadn't been well, so I popped round to hers to see if she were all right.'

Eden nodded. 'Oh. And was she?'

'Aye.' He tutted. 'You know Granny Allen. Indestructible.'

Granny Allen was an old lady who lived in Beckthwaite, and was no relation to anyone in the village, despite her honorary title. She was also rather lacking in personal hygiene. Few people were brave enough to venture over her doorstep.

'But didn't you have anything to eat?'

Eliot pulled on a pair of jeans. 'I weren't hungry.'

Eden's voice was anxious. 'Are you okay?'

He spun round and smiled at her. 'Fine, my love — except that I'm bloody starving now, which I suppose serves me right. I'm ready for me tea. Can't remember the last time we had a takeaway.' He reached into the wardrobe and pulled out a clean shirt. 'I'm looking forward to it. I feel right spoilt tonight.'

'You deserve it,' Eden told him. She straightened the duvet and patted it approvingly. 'There. You'd never know that five minutes ago it looked like there'd been an earthquake in that bed.'

'Felt like one an' all.' Eliot grinned at her. 'We certainly made the earth move tonight.'

Eden dropped onto the bed. 'I was a bit worried you wouldn't be up for it,' she admitted.

Eliot frowned and sat beside her, hooking his arm around her shoulders.

'What are you on about? Why wouldn't I be?'

She shrugged, feeling awkward. 'Things have been a bit distant between us lately, that's all. We don't seem to get much time together, and I was a bit worried we were drifting apart.'

He looked down at the carpet, seeming to consider his words carefully.

'Happen things have been a bit difficult lately, but that's got nothing to do with how I feel about you. You know that?'

She bit her lip, nodding, but didn't reply.

Eliot looked stricken. 'You have to know that, my love? It's everything else — you know, the farm and money, and the pressure of getting the business up and running, and worrying about you overdoing it, and—'

'And this wedding taking over our lives?'

He shook his head. 'It's not taking over our lives. And any road, it'll be worth it.' He sighed. 'It doesn't help that we've had a houseful of Carmichaels to deal with, an' all.'

'Two of them!' She laughed. 'Although, I must admit, Emerald does feel a bit like ten people. She's quite high maintenance.'

'Cain's been here a fair bit an' all,' he pointed out, 'and then there's Jed, who seems to be everywhere I turn these days.'

'But he's so useful,' she protested. 'He helps me out with the barn, and you can't deny he's been a godsend to you, too. He certainly seems to pull his weight, and he enjoys the farming life very much. You can't complain about Jed.'

Eliot tutted. 'I can complain about anyone I like.'

He rolled his eyes as she gave him one of her looks.

'All right, all right, I s'pose you're right. He's useful to have about the place, and he's a grafter, I'll give him that.' He rested his forehead against hers. 'Doesn't mean he's not in the way, though. Let's face it, they all are. I can't wait until it's just me and you again.'

'And three kids,' she reminded him.

'Or even four,' he said quietly.

Eden pulled away, staring at him. 'Four? Are you serious?'

He shrugged. 'I'm not putting any pressure on you, my love. Just that, you've not had one of your own and I wondered—'

Eden tilted her head. 'Those three kids are like my own. I hope you know that.'

'Of course I do. I'm not saying that. But — would you like a baby?'

'I suppose I would, yes. We've never really talked about it, have we? I thought, maybe you'd got enough on your plate with the three you've already got.'

232

'Nowt I'd like more than to give them a little brother or sister,' he assured her, smiling. 'The more the merrier. And I'd love us to have a baby together, if that's what you want, too?'

'I'd love it,' she murmured. 'In fact, I can't think of anything I'd love more.' She smiled. 'Maybe we should wait until after the wedding, though?'

'Happen you're right,' he agreed. 'Summat to look forward to, though, another bairn around the house.'

'And lots of fun making it,' she pointed out.

'Aye, there is that.' He grinned and nudged her. 'I knew you couldn't get enough of me.'

'All right, big head!'

'Can you deny it?'

She couldn't, and he knew it. Laughing, they held each other tightly, glad to be on familiar territory again.

'Fancy doubting me,' he soothed. 'You're a daft ha'porth.'

'I suppose I'm a bit insecure,' she admitted, feeling stupid.

'Insecure? What in God's name have you got to be insecure about? It's me that's punching above my weight, as Mickey and Adey remind me every day!'

She nudged him. 'As if! And I mean, since I told you about — well, you know. Me and Ryan. I've worried you think less of me.'

Eliot sighed. 'Eden, love, I've told you, it makes no odds to me. Look, you were young, and you made a mistake. You're not the first woman to be taken in by a married man, and you were nowt but a bit of a lass. I don't even think about it, and neither should you. All that matters is me and you and our future together. Right?'

She blinked away her tears and smiled. 'Right.'

He patted her knee. 'Good. Now, if that takeaway dun't arrive in the next five minutes I'm going to ring up and complain. A man could fade away and die of starvation. I must have burned off three thousand calories in the last hour.'

'Oh, there he goes again,' Eden laughed. 'Showing off. You really are—'

She broke off as the front door slammed. They stared at each other, dismayed.

233

'Peace is over,' Eliot whispered. 'Happen that's the kids back.'

A voice called from the bottom of the stairs. 'Anyone home?'

Eden groaned. 'Oh, God, it's Emerald. Brilliant. So much for our evening alone.'

Eliot put his hands on her shoulders and eyed her fiercely. 'We might have to share a takeaway with her, but the most important thing is, we got the chance to be together at last — properly together. We must do this more often, Eden. Whatever it takes. Our relationship *has* to come first. Forget all this rubbish going on around us, okay? We have to make time for *us*.'

She nodded. 'Absolutely. I love you, Eliot.'

'Oh, lass. I wish you knew how much I love you,' he told her, stroking her hair.

'Yoo hoo!'

'We'd better go downstairs,' Eden said with a heavy sigh. 'But I'll tell you now, she's not sharing *my* onion bhaji. Not for anything.'

Chapter 21

'You're sure you don't mind doing another shift?' Eden handed Jed a mug of tea and eyed him anxiously. 'You've been working flat out all day in the barns and I'm getting worried about you. We'll be charged with slave labour at this rate.'

Jed laughed. 'Honest, I'm fine. Let's face it, Eliot's beat.' He nodded over to where Eliot was slumped, asleep, in the armchair, oblivious to the sound of the television, or the argument Libby and Ophelia were having over which programme to watch.

Eden's expression softened as she watched her sleeping fiancé.

'Look at the state of him,' she murmured. 'He hasn't even had his tea yet.'

Jed smiled. 'He looks like he's got some god-awful disease,' he said. 'Either that or he's a heavy smoker on an industrial scale.'

Eden laughed as she followed his gaze to Eliot's hands, which were stained yellow from the iodine he used to treat the newborn lambs' navels as a precaution against infection — always a risk with indoor births.

Not only was Eliot having to deal with all the usual farm work, but he had the additional tasks of feeding and watering the sheep in the lambing barn, cleaning out the pens, as well as overseeing the birthing process. He was out at five-thirty each morning, taking feed and bales of hay to his outdoor ewes, and to check for any new lambs that had been born in the night. Last thing before he went to bed, he would patrol the fields again, checking things were all right, scouring the flock for more lambs. Eden often joked he was like a midwife on call, since everywhere he went, he carried his delivery kit of antiseptic spray, antibiotics, supplements, feeding tubes, bottles and syringes. Life seemed to be about sheep and lambs, and precious little else.

The farming life could be very harsh, and Eden had developed a strong stomach, accepting as necessary the skinning of a dead lamb in order that its fleece could be placed over a live orphaned lamb, with the hope that the dead one's mother would be fooled into thinking her baby was still alive and allow him to feed from her. Often, it worked, but not always.

But there were compensations. When the mothers accepted the lambs, for one, and when life returned to a little creature that seemed beyond hope — such as that very morning when Eden had watched, amazed, as Libby revived a lamb she'd been convinced had no chance. It was completely still and silent, lying on the floor of the pen, and Eden had given up hope. Eliot and Libby, however, had other ideas.

'Go on, love. Do what you can,' Eliot had said, nodding at his eldest daughter, with complete confidence.

Libby had rubbed the lamb roughly with straw, then she'd cupped her hands and blown gently into its mouth. When the little creature took its first breath, father and daughter had exchanged looks of such pride that Eden had found tears running down her cheeks. The lamb was one of triplets, and while the other two had seemed big and healthy, this one was delicate.

Libby had taken it into the house, and even Emerald had been moved by its story. George had named the little lamb Tiggy, and she was currently lying in a basket in front of the fire, her tiny body swathed in blankets. Eden and the children took it in turns to feed her with some of her mother's colostrum, using a syringe, and Eden had been amazed when Emerald had hesitantly offered to take turns. Maybe there was hope for the woman, after all.

Even so, the lion's share of the work fell on Eliot, especially as she and Jed were having to split their time between helping on the farm and getting the bunk barns ready, so she was grateful whenever anyone offered to take a turn with the night shift. Adey had done a few, and even Mickey had done a couple, but Eliot didn't like to put on Mickey at his age, and nine times out of ten he ended up staying in the barn with him, as much to keep an eye on the old shepherd as the ewes.

To make matters worse, the brief interlude of sunshine had ended, and mid-April was bitterly cold. When Eliot got back from his final tour of the farm each night, he was freezing. Eden often wondered how anyone could work so hard, in such difficult conditions, and earn such little reward. If there was any justice in the world, Wildflower Farm would be so financially secure that the bunk barns would never have been necessary. This, however, was the real world, and they needed the extra income. It would soon be May. In less than three weeks, the first guests would be arriving to stay. Eden felt exhausted just thinking about it.

'Are you gonna wake him up to eat?' Jed asked, sipping his tea as he watched the sleeping Eliot.

'No. Let him sleep while he can. I'll warm his tea up for him when he wakes up.' She yawned. 'So much for starting our cream tea business up early.'

'You've had enough to do,' he told her.

'Yeah, you could say that. Stupid idea. I should have thought, with the lambing season, that Easter was out of the question. I suppose I was desperate to start bringing some money back in, rather than paying it out.'

'The barns will pay their way,' he assured her, hearing the worry in her voice. 'You'll see. You know what? You look beat, too. You've never stopped these last few weeks. Get an early night, okay?'

'I will. I don't know if I'm coming or going these days.' She slumped in the chair. 'Thanks, Jed. Oh, did I tell you, Beth's coming round later? She rang up to ask after Tiggy, and she offered to sit with you in the barn for a couple of hours later. She's smitten with the lambs and she's desperate to see one being born. Would you mind?'

Jed's face was neutral, so she wasn't sure whether he minded or not, but his voice sounded pleasant enough. 'Sure, why not?

Doesn't her husband mind her being out this evening?'

'No idea,' she said. 'I never ask about him. It's safest to avoid the subject of James Fuller at all costs.'

'Why does everyone hate the guy so much?' Jed murmured, clearly aware that the children were sitting in front of the television and might well be listening in.

Whether they were or not, Eden had no intention of revealing family secrets to Jed, as nice as he was. 'Oh, he's not a kind man,' she said with a shrug. 'Sly, manipulative, selfish. Beth deserves better. I suppose that's what makes it worse. She's such a lovely person, don't you think?'

Jed drained his mug. 'Yeah, I guess. She seems okay to me, anyway.'

'Oh, she is, Jed. I hope she gets to see a lamb born tonight. It will cheer her up. Although—' She broke off and Jed peered at her curiously.

'Although what?'

'Nothing. Forget it.' She'd been about to say that witnessing any birth might be a painful reminder to Beth of her own sad situation, but that was none of Jed's business. He didn't need to know anything about their friend's personal life, after all.

****

'Five lambs and no problems,' Jed said, with obvious satisfaction. 'That's what I call a result.'

He looked at Beth, whose eyes were still shining with excitement as she watched the latest arrivals staggering around on dainty legs. Within minutes they were suckling at their mothers. Two sets of twins and a single lamb — four of them female. It was the most moving thing they'd ever seen.

'I'll have to go,' she said, glancing at her watch and pulling a face. 'He thought I was mad when I said I wanted to be here to watch the lambing for a couple of hours. He'll be even more suspicious if I stay longer.'

'Suspicious?' Jed felt a mixture of hope and anxiety at the thought. 'He's suspicious of us?'

She shook her head. 'Not us, no. I don't think he's even remembered you're staying here. No, it's Eliot. He's convinced I have a thing for him.'

Jed leaned back against the wall of the lambing shed and folded his arms, surveying her in amusement. 'Really? Wow, you kept that quiet. And do you?'

She laughed. 'Of course not! Eliot's my friend. If anything, I see him more as a brother than a lover. I don't think of him in that way. I never have, as fond as I am of him.'

'His accent's not as sexy as mine anyway,' Jed drawled.

'That's debatable actually,' Beth said, wrinkling her nose as she pretended to give the matter some serious consideration. 'The Yorkshire accent is rather earthy and manly if you ask me.'

'That's outrageous,' Jed said. 'You can't say you don't find my accent just as manly!'

'Between you and me,' she teased, 'neither of you can hold a candle to an Irishman. Now *that's* an accent!'

Jed knew he was beaten. He'd never met a woman yet who didn't love an Irish accent.

'Okay, fair enough,' he said. 'But I claim second place and that's final.'

She laughed and shuffled over to sit beside him. 'I've enjoyed this last couple of hours,' she said. 'Being with you, all alone like this. I wish I didn't have to go home.'

'I wish it, too,' he said softly. 'I miss you. I was so glad when Eden said you were coming over tonight. I'd been kinda worried I'd scared you off.'

'Scared me off?'

'When I kissed you like that. Bit intense for a first kiss, huh?'

'Not at all,' she breathed. 'It was perfect.'

'Beth—' he hesitated, not wanting to pressure her in any way, 'it meant a lot to me. I mean, I wasn't just saying it at the time. *You* mean a lot to me. I don't know what it is about you, but it feels right, you know?'

'I know. I feel the same.'

'I wasn't sure. You don't strike me as the kind of girl who makes a habit of this.'

'Never! I've never so much as looked at another man since I met James. I've been hurt so badly by infidelity that I never thought, not for one moment, that I'd be contemplating it myself.'

'Contemplating it?' He reached out a hand and found hers waiting. Their palms pressed together, and she looked down at them, clearly trying to formulate what she wanted to say.

'In my mind, I suppose that kiss was cheating,' she admitted. 'It was hardly innocent, was it? I mean, there was an awful lot of feeling in it — on my part anyway.'

'And mine,' he assured her. 'Beth, I don't want to push you into doing anything you don't want to do—'

'But I want to!' she burst out. 'I know that sounds awful, and I'm so ashamed of myself, and I feel so guilty for James, but it's all I can think about. I want to be with you, Jed. Really be with you. I'm sorry. I must sound shameless.'

'Beth, I've been driving myself crazy wanting you,' he murmured. 'If you're shameless, then so am I, but I don't feel like it. This isn't some passing attraction, is it? This is real. You can feel it, can't you?'

'Yes,' she admitted. 'And it scares me to death. I've never felt like this about anyone before — *anyone*. I've been trying to tell myself it's lust and it will pass, but somehow, it's like I was meant to meet you. Right from the first moment I saw you on the doorstep of the farmhouse, I *knew*. I — I can't stop thinking about you, Jed.'

He pulled her onto his lap and wrapped his arms around her waist. She stared into his eyes, as if desperately trying to communicate to him all the things she longed to tell him. Gently, hesitantly, their faces moved ever closer, until his lips crushed hers and everything else was forgotten.

'I want you so bad,' Jed gasped, 'but this isn't the time or place. It's not right.'

'I don't care,' she begged. 'Honestly, I don't.'

It took every ounce of self-control he possessed to pull away from her.

'You deserve better than the floor of a lambing shed,' he told her. 'Besides,' he added with a wry smile, 'we don't wanna startle the sheep and set them all off in labour.'

Beth's chest was heaving, and he forced himself to look away before he did something totally irresponsible and selfish.

'I'll think of something,' he told her. 'I promise.'

Beth took his hand and placed it on her breast, leaving him powerless to resist. 'There's an old stone barn just beyond Barton's Copse,' she told him between kisses. 'It's never used these days, but it's safe and out of the way. Meet me there tomorrow?'

'A barn?' Jed wanted to be strong. He wanted their first time to be perfect. An old barn hardly seemed the most romantic place. But every cell in his body seemed to be screaming for union with hers, and he knew he couldn't say no. In any case, he would make it perfect wherever they were. How could it not be? They were meant to be together, after all. He gasped as her tongue flicked his and knew he was lost.

A few minutes later, she scrambled to her feet and brushed straw from her clothes. 'Tomorrow morning? What time?'

Jed thought fast. He would be up until around six when Eliot took over. He'd hurry back to the house, have a quick shower and a change of clothes then head out again. They would all assume he was in bed, anyway. 'About seven?' he said doubtfully, not sure she'd be awake at that time, or if she could even sneak away.

'I'll be there at quarter to,' she promised, smiling.

Then she was gone, and Jed fell back against the wall feeling dazed. There was a lot more to Beth than the quiet, demure, rather shy woman he'd first met, that was for sure. A hell of a lot more. He couldn't wait to find out what other surprises she had in store.

Chapter 22

Cain loaded his suitcase into the boot of his hire car. Since he was incognito, he'd left his beloved Rolls Royce at home and taken the precaution of driving to Skimmerdale in a run-of-the-mill saloon. Waste of time, really, and he'd known it when he made the arrangements. He was an idiot.

He slammed the boot shut and climbed into the car, feeling the gloom settling on him. *Well, what did you expect? No fool like an old fool*, he thought bitterly. It was stupid to even hope that he'd bump into Constance again, yet he hadn't been able to help himself.

Ever since that crazy evening with her, he'd not stopped thinking about her. If only he'd had the foresight to get her number. Even her surname would have helped. As it was, he had no idea where she lived and no way of contacting her. Yet, like the old fool that he was, he'd found himself heading up to the Dales again, without even telling anyone he was coming, and hiding away at The Paradise Hotel in the vain hope that Constance would have returned, too.

It was crazy, and he knew it. She'd only been in Yorkshire for business and there was nothing to suggest she would be returning any time soon — if ever. Even if she did, Yorkshire was a big county. She could be staying anywhere. It was highly unlikely that she'd be at The Paradise Hotel on the very day that he booked in, now was it? Even so, Cain had spent the last two nights in the restaurant, lingering over food he had no appetite for, scanning the bar hopefully for a glimpse of an elegant brunette with almond eyes and legs to die for.

Now he'd finally accepted that it was a waste of time, so he'd checked out and was heading home. He didn't even intend to call at Wildflower Farm. He wasn't in the mood for more of Emerald's moaning. He wanted to go home and pretend he'd never met Constance. If he could only get her out of his brain, that is.

Driving out of the gates, Cain headed down the lane that led to Kirkby Skimmer town centre, cursing as he realised that it was market day, and the town was unusually busy. The streets were packed with parked cars since the market had taken over the square where people usually parked. He steered the hire car at a crawling pace down a narrow, cobbled lane, keeping an eye out for anyone stepping out from between the parked cars that lined both sides of the lane. He had no patience for this and blasted his horn as a car door opened and a driver stepped out onto the road, a few cars ahead of him.

His mouth fell open as the driver turned to look at him, and his heart began to drum frantically. Without even glancing in the rear-view mirror to see if there was anything behind him, Cain turned off his engine and leapt out of his car.

'Connie!'

It was a stupid thing to do, he realised afterwards. She could have been with someone — maybe even the husband he was convinced she had, given the ring on her finger. How would they have explained that?

Luckily for him, fate seemed to be on his side. She was alone, and to his relief, her face lit up at the sight of him.

'Jeff, darling!'

He felt stupidly delighted to be called darling, even though he was aware that posh birds like her used the term willy-nilly. Everyone was a darling as far they were concerned—well, to their faces anyway. He remembered Freya air kissing people, almost on a daily basis, gushing, 'Darling, how lovely to see you!' then muttering to Cain that she hated them and hoped they'd get run over by a steam roller on their way home.

Even so, the sparkle in Connie's eyes told him she was genuinely pleased to see him, and he could hardly wipe the smile off his own face.

She tottered towards him, and he realised she was wearing black knee-high boots with a four-inch heel, at least. She was still half a head shorter than him, and he had a sudden crazy urge to protect her. Protect her from what? She probably had a much better life than he did, for Christ's sake.

'What on earth are you doing here?'

Cain realised he was blushing — a most unfamiliar sensation. 'Er, had to nip back on business. What about you?'

'Oh, me too. What a coincidence.' She bit her lip. 'So, er, are you staying at The Paradise?'

'I just checked out,' he admitted, suddenly cursing his impetuous decision to give up so soon. 'Are you booked in there?'

'Er, no. A little guest house a few miles away. What a shame. We could have had a drink together or something.'

The implication hung in the air.

Cain swallowed. 'Are you busy then?'

Connie glanced around and shrugged. 'I was killing time before heading home. Business concluded so I thought I'd do some shopping for an hour or two.'

'Oh, right. Well.'

They stared at each other, and Cain saw the gleam of desire in Connie's eyes. It lit a fire deep within his belly. Sod it, it was worth a shot. She could only say no, after all.

'I don't suppose — I mean, I could always book a room for one more night?'

She raised an eyebrow. 'You could?'

'I could, if I needed to. I mean, we could spend the afternoon there. What do you think?'

She eyed him steadily. 'I'm married, Jeff.'

Cain's heart sank. 'I know. Sorry. Like you said, it was a one-off.'

Connie hesitated. 'I suppose — that is, what he doesn't know won't hurt him.'

Cain's heart lifted. 'Well, exactly.'

'I want to make it quite clear that I don't normally do this sort of thing. You're the first. I've never cheated on my husband before.'

'I believe you, Connie. You're a lady. Anyone can tell that.'

'And it's strictly no-strings? No expectations, no demands. Just sex?'

Cain shivered in anticipation. Was he dreaming? This was the perfect scenario.

'Absolutely. Just sex.'

She smiled softly. 'It *was* rather good, wasn't it?'

'You're not wrong there, Connie. I'd forgotten I could enjoy meself like that, truth to tell, and we seemed to — you know — gel. Right?'

'Oh, we did,' she murmured. She winked at him and turned towards her car. 'I'll follow you to the hotel,' she called over her shoulder. 'Go and get that room booked!'

Cain almost fell back into his car. Life was suddenly looking very promising indeed.

****

James found his mother sitting in the snug. Why she persisted in using that room during the summer months he had no idea. She was the only person who ever used that room outside of deepest winter. Anyone would think she liked being alone.

She was sitting in one of the huge, winged armchairs, curled up with a glass of wine, staring into space. She seemed rather annoyed by his arrival which wasn't a good start. Great. Just what he needed. His stomach lurched with anxiety as he geared himself up to tackle the knotty subject of his illegitimate son. Evidently, his distress was apparent in his face.

'What is it?' She leaned towards him, showing an unusual concern for his wellbeing.

He swallowed, trying to gather his courage. 'I — I need to talk to you. To tell you something.'

'Oh?'

245

'Some time ago — years, actually — I did something I'm not particularly proud of.'

His mother picked up her glass of wine again and took a sip, eyeing him suspiciously. 'Really? You intrigue me.'

James licked his lips. 'I made the mistake of getting involved with another woman.'

She arched an eyebrow. 'You mean you had an affair?'

He flinched. 'I hate that word.'

She smiled at him. 'Oh, I *am* sorry. What would you prefer me to call it?'

Was she being sarcastic? 'Well, I'd call it a big mistake, personally. It was with a local woman, Jemima. She was rather beautiful, and so charming. She was from a good family, but she made the mistake of trapping herself in a loveless marriage with a man who didn't understand her.'

His mother tutted. 'Poor thing. Thank goodness you came along.'

'Er, quite.' James eyed her nervously. 'Anyway, the thing is, the relationship continued for over a year and only ended when — well, she was killed, rather tragically in a car crash.'

He watched as she took a gulp of her wine. The silence seemed to stretch on forever. Eventually, she said, 'Why are you telling me this, James?'

'Because—' He glanced around the snug, as if someone was hiding in a corner, spying on him. 'Because the relationship resulted in the birth of a child. A boy. My son.'

She slammed her wine glass on the table and stared at him. 'A son? But — where is he? Who is he?' She folded her arms and frowned. 'How do you know he's yours? How do you know he isn't her husband's child?'

'Because she didn't sleep with Harland — with her husband — for ages. Long before she got pregnant. And, anyway,' he added, rather shamefaced, 'you only have to look at the boy to know he's mine. It's quite easy to tell.'

His mother was clearly shocked. She stood and began to pace the room, as if trying to absorb this new and most unexpected information. 'What's his name? How old is he? Where does he

246

live?'

'His name's George.' James eyed her, obviously wary of her response. 'He's four, and he lives with Harland at their farm.'

She stopped pacing. 'But why? Why does he live with him? Surely, with this Jemima dead he should be living with you?'

James flushed. 'When she died, it was all a bit of a mess. It had all come out about our liaison, and there was the shock and the grief, as well as practical details to address. Harland registered George as his child and it was sort of assumed that he would take care of him, along with his own two children.'

His mother looked incredulous. '*Sort of assumed?*'

'Well, thinking about it rationally, it seemed to be for the best.'

She sank into the chair, staring at him in confusion. 'Best for whom?'

'For everyone.' He felt rather embarrassed, thinking how it must sound to her. 'Look, you have to understand how chaotic everything was back then. Beth wouldn't have been able to deal with me bringing home Jemima's baby, and then, was it fair to George to take him away from his two sisters? I didn't know anything about bringing up children, whereas Harland had already got two children and some experience. You do understand, don't you?' When she didn't answer, he ploughed on. 'But now things have changed somewhat.'

'In what way?'

He sighed, reaching out his hands to grasp her own. Her hands were icy cold.

'I miss him, Mother. That's the sad truth. Oh, I've seen him a few times, but things aren't easy. Harland is growing ever more protective of him, the older he gets, and as his looks change and his resemblance to me becomes more obvious, he is — understandably, I suppose — keeping him close. He won't let me go to Wildflower Farm, although Beth's welcome. She sees George regularly, but she doesn't really mention him. I can't blame her, of course. It's all been terribly difficult for her.'

'So, Beth knows about George?'

'From the first,' he admitted. 'She suffered a great deal.' He hung his head. 'I behaved appallingly, Mother. I'm ashamed of myself. But George—' he looked up at her, trying to appeal to whatever maternal instinct she still possessed, 'George is my son. Whatever's happened, whatever I've done, whatever I've deserved, that doesn't change, does it? He's my boy, and I want to see him, be part of his life. I don't know what to do.'

His mother took a deep breath and held his gaze, as if she were trying to read his mind. 'Why are you telling me all this now?'

'I don't know.' He shook his head. 'It's been getting harder and harder to bear, and I had no one to talk to, to confide in. Now that you're back, I've wanted to tell you since I saw you. I didn't know how to go about it. I know you've always wanted a grandchild. You've probably longed for baby news as much as I have.'

Although, it had to be said, she'd hidden it well. Who'd have thought it? His cold, distant mother had a maternal streak after all, even if it had skipped a generation.

'So, you *do* want children then?' She sounded surprised. 'Only, I wasn't sure. I knew you were trying some years ago, but then nothing happened. I thought, maybe only Beth wanted them.'

'Certainly not.' He sighed. 'It doesn't look as if it's going to happen, unfortunately. We've more-or-less given up hope. Even IVF failed, so...'

'So, George might be your only child.'

He saw tears in her eyes and reared back, astonished.

'I'm so sorry.'

'What do I do, Mother?' he pleaded, emboldened by her unexpected show of emotion.

'We fight for him,' she announced, standing up. 'He's your son, and this Harland man had no business registering him as his own. We need to see a solicitor, find out our rights, where we go from here. Harland needs a few things making very clear to him. George is a Fuller, and it's time he knew it.'

My God! She actually bought it! James could hardly believe his luck.

'Oh, Mother.' He gave her a grateful smile. 'I just *knew* I could count on you.'

Chapter 23

Cain lay on his back, his eyes closed to the afternoon sun, which beat down mercilessly upon him. Beside him, Connie gave a contented sigh, and Cain thought, *this is the life. It really is.* He couldn't remember a time when he'd felt happier, which was a rather scary thought.

'Isn't it beautiful here?' Connie's voice warmed him as much as the sunshine, and he opened one eye to take in the sight of her, lying close beside him, her breasts rising and falling with each breath, making the blood stir in his loins all over again.

He half wished he'd refused her suggestion that they spend the afternoon exploring Skimmerdale Abbey. He'd far rather be in bed, exploring every inch of her delectable body instead, but she'd seemed so keen to do something different that he hadn't wanted to say no. He hoped she wouldn't go straight back to wherever it was she was staying after they left here. He'd made damn sure his hotel room was neat and tidy, just in case.

'It's nearly a thousand years old, you know.'

'Fancy.' Cain wasn't one for abbeys and castles and the like, though even he could appreciate the stunning beauty of this abbey's golden ruins, perched on a high hill called Mikkel Rigg, overlooking the river and the market town of Kirkby Skimmer. It was a Cistercian abbey, according to the guidebook, although that meant little to him. He should've paid more attention to history at school — to anything at school, come to that. 'Oh, gawd, look at that.'

Connie sat up, shading her eyes with one well-manicured hand. 'A school trip!'

She looked delighted to see the children, which wasn't an emotion Cain shared. That was all he needed — a group of sticky-fingered, whining kids tramping around him. He sat up, too, surprised to see a wistful expression on Connie's face. He wondered if she had children. He'd never asked, as she'd never asked him. It was an unwritten rule. They didn't discuss their private lives.

After that second meeting, when they'd rushed back to the hotel and torn off each other's clothes, they'd realised that whatever the circumstances of their individual lives, they wanted to continue to meet up.

'For sex only,' Connie had said hastily, and Cain had readily agreed. That was the arrangement. It was strictly a sexual relationship, and boy was it flourishing.

Cain had suggested that, every fortnight, he book a room for three nights at the hotel, somewhere they could be together for a few precious hours each day. Connie had checked her diary and assured him that she could keep to that arrangement, and so they'd begun their — affair, he supposed, given she was married. It had given him a new lease of life, all those afternoons together with little conversation and lots of action.

Except — except there had been little snatches of conversation the last couple of times. Not much, but enough for Cain to learn that she was married to a businessman and the marriage wasn't a happy one, and for Cain to admit that he'd been married three times and each time had ended in a bitter divorce, that he'd had an illegitimate son, many affairs, and had made a complete mess of his love life. He'd been a bit worried that Connie would be put off him by his revelations, but there was something about her that made him want to be honest with her, and she seemed to appreciate that. He supposed, in the long run, it made no difference to her. She wasn't asking for commitment after all.

The schoolchildren couldn't have been more than eight or nine. They carried little workbooks and looked hot and bothered as the teachers dragged them around the ruins of the abbey, pointing out various facts to them and making them jot down notes in their books.

'Oh, to be that young again,' Connie sighed.

Cain frowned. 'Really? I'd hate it.'

She lifted an eyebrow. 'Why? Didn't you have a happy childhood?'

Cain thought about it. 'Suppose it was all right, in the sense that my mum and dad were decent enough. We didn't have two pennies to rub together, though. You should have seen our house. It got pulled down in the end. Two tiny bedrooms, a little front room and a kitchen, no bathroom. Just a tin bath hanging from a nail on the wall of the yard, and an outside lavvy. Proper shabby.'

Connie laughed. 'Oh, it sounds like my grandparents' house! I remember being ushered into the front room because Grandad was getting a bath in front of the fire in the parlour! Gran always wore a pinny, and she was always baking or cleaning. She was so houseproud, bless her. They didn't even have running hot water. They had to boil a kettle every time. You wouldn't believe it now, would you?' She nodded at the bored-looking schoolchildren. 'They wouldn't be able to imagine it.'

'Don't know they're born these days,' he agreed. 'Do you know, I was watching a programme the other day and these kids were on about food. They didn't know that potatoes grew in the ground! One kid nearly chucked 'cos he said he'd seen an egg come out of a chicken's bum. Can you Adam and Eve that? I mean, what's the world coming to?'

Connie sighed. 'I'm afraid there's still an awful lot of poverty and ignorance. Most people these days have bathrooms and running hot water, but many children are, even now, crammed into houses that are too small or living in those high-rise flats in the inner cities. They never see a blade of grass, so how are they to know where their food comes from? Do you know, some children have never even seen a sheep! It's unbelievable.'

'Kids round here are the lucky ones,' Cain said. 'They get to grow up in this beautiful countryside, surrounded by animals, breathing in fresh air. Shame all kids don't get the same opportunities.'

He thought about Libby and Ophelia. Every time he went to Wildflower Farm, they were either riding, or collecting eggs, or helping their dad with the sheep. They'd have hated to live in a high rise flat, and who could blame them?

'Absolutely.' Connie shivered, drawing up her knees and resting her chin upon them. 'It's been a lovely afternoon, Jeff. Sometimes, I wish our time together never had to end.'

Cain looked at her, surprised. She'd never said that sort of thing before. It stirred something deep within him, and he batted the feeling away, suddenly afraid. 'Well, we've got a couple of hours left. Do you want to go back to the hotel room?'

She closed her eyes, and he wished he'd never said it. She would think he only wanted her for sex. Then he tutted to himself. *She* only wanted *him* for sex! That was the whole point. So why did he feel so guilty about it?

'Or we could go to the café, have a cup of coffee and a slice of cake?' He glanced over at the complex behind the abbey, where the tearoom and gift shop were located, as well as an exhibition room, displaying the history of, and artefacts from, the abbey's eventful past.

Half of him wanted her to take his hand and drag him back to The Paradise for an hour or two of unbridled lust, but the other part of him wanted to sit with her a bit longer, chat to her, get to know her a bit better. The truth was, he liked her. He liked her a lot. Despite her casual approach to her marriage, he thought she was a decent, honourable sort of person, and in a weird way he trusted her. He would like to know more about her. It scared him, truth to tell.

Connie gave him a beaming smile. 'Would you mind? That would be splendid.'

Cain hauled himself to his feet and held out a hand to her. 'Your wish is my command.'

Connie took his hand and stood, smoothing her dress. 'Thank you, Jeff. You're such a gentleman.'

Cain didn't feel much like a gentleman. He was feeling increasingly bad about keeping his true identity from her, but felt he'd gone too far now. He should have told her on that second meeting, but he hadn't and now it seemed too late. What would she think of him for lying to her all this time?

The café was a large, light building, with glass windows all round giving a panoramic view of the abbey and its surrounding lands.

Connie ordered lemon drizzle cake and tea, and Cain had chocolate cake and a black coffee. They took a seat by the window and chatted amiably about the weather, the beauty of Skimmerdale, and a little more about their respective childhoods. Cain noticed that Connie talked only of her grandparents, and never mentioned her parents. He wondered if she'd lived with them instead. Clearly, she'd had the same sort of upbringing as he'd had, but, like him she was obviously wealthy now. She'd probably married well. As the conversation wound around his own father's job, selling scrap metal, and her grandfather's job on the docks, Cain couldn't help himself.

'And what about your husband? What does he do?'

Connie flinched, and Cain wished he'd kept his big mouth shut. 'It's okay,' he said hurriedly, 'forget I said that. You don't have to tell me anything.'

She stirred her tea thoughtfully. 'But clearly you're interested.'

'I'm not! At least,' he added uncomfortably, 'I suppose I am a bit. It's only natural though, innit? I mean, I've got to say, I feel a bit bad about the bloke, considering what I'm doing with his wife.'

'He doesn't own me!' Connie snapped, and Cain reared back, shocked.

'I know, I know. Sorry.' He took a sip of coffee, wondering how to put things back on a civilised footing. He hated this sudden distance between them.

'I'm sorry, Jeff,' she said eventually. 'I can understand you being curious, of course I can. But you know, you shouldn't feel guilty about sleeping with me. Believe me, he's hardly been an angel throughout our marriage.'

Cain dropped another lump of sugar in his coffee. 'You mean he cheated on you?'

He gaped at her as she nodded. 'Is he mad? Why would anyone cheat on someone as smashing as you?'

She laughed. 'Didn't you admit to cheating on your wives? I'm sure they were equally *smashing*. Why does anyone cheat on their partner?'

Cain squirmed, realising she had a point. Lowri *had* been smashing, and so had Freya to start with. Cassandra had always been a bit batty. He had no idea what he'd been thinking of there.

'So, he had an affair, too?'

She tutted, putting down her teacup with a clatter. 'If only! I could have dealt with that. No, he didn't just have an affair, Jeff. He had multiple affairs, dozens of one-night stands. God knows how many women he's slept with behind my back. And if you think he regrets it, or that he's sorry, you'd be very wrong. I've never had a word of apology or remorse from him and I truly believe, if anything, he's quite proud of himself.'

'Jesus.' Cain shook his head, stunned. Poor Connie. No wonder she'd needed something outside her marriage. Some small comfort against her husband's disgusting behaviour.

'It's not revenge, if that's what you're thinking,' she said, her eyes flashing defiance. 'And it's not a distraction from what he's up to either. This has nothing to do with him. Nothing! This is for me. It's *all* about me for once in my life.'

'I never — I didn't think it was, love.' Cain squeezed her hand gently. 'Sounds to me like you've been put through the wringer. I'm sorry.'

'Don't be,' she murmured. 'One gets used to it eventually.'

'But you shouldn't have to.' He hesitated a moment, then ploughed on. 'Are you worried that's he's doing it again?' Cain felt deeply uncomfortable, asking the question. 'Sleeping around, I mean?'

Connie bit her lip, evidently considering her reply. 'Not at all,' she said eventually, and Cain noticed that her nails were digging into her palms.

'But you must have some doubts? I mean, the bloke's got some track record. Not the type to start keeping it in his pants, is he?'

'I can assure you he's most definitely keeping it in his pants now,' she said.

Cain heard the bitterness in her voice and saw the tears in her eyes. 'Aw, Connie, love. Don't cry.'

'I'm not crying,' she protested. 'I don't do crying, and if I did, I certainly wouldn't waste any tears on *him*. He's not worth it. He's never been worth it.'

Cain looked around nervously. 'Sorry, love. I didn't mean to upset you.'

'You haven't upset me.' She lifted her chin. 'Why shouldn't you know? I owe him nothing. The truth is, I know that my husband isn't having an affair, because he's not capable.'

'Not capable? I don't get ya. Seems more than capable to me, going by his past — oh.' He lifted an eyebrow. 'You mean, he ain't capable physically?'

She took a deep breath. 'Hasn't been for over a decade now.'

'A decade!' He leaned back in his chair, staring at her in amazement. 'You mean, you haven't — for ten years?'

She wiped her eyes. 'No.'

'Jesus. You poor cow.' Cain thought two years had been bad enough.

She glared at him. 'You're not feeling sorry for me, are you?'

Cain ran his finger around his shirt collar. 'I wouldn't bleeding dare, Connie. What I don't get is, if it's been going on this long, why ain't he been getting any help? You know, Viagra or sumfink.'

'He did get some once. From the internet. It gave him a pounding headache and bloodshot eyes. He leered over me like a vampire, with all these horrid red veins popping out from his eyeballs. It was disgusting. And it didn't do anything for him, anyway. I'm not convinced they were the real thing. You can buy any old rubbish from the internet, and how do we know they're the real deal?'

'But why not go to the doc's? Get the proper stuff?'

Connie pushed her cup of cold tea away and shook her head. 'That's just it. That's what I can't forgive.' The tears were running down her face and she wiped them away. 'I understand that men become impotent. I get it, really, I do. What I can't forgive is that he wouldn't do anything about it. He wouldn't go to a doctor's, or a counsellor. Too proud. Too afraid to admit that he could be less than perfect, or that this self-proclaimed stud could be anything other than super fertile. He kept promising me he'd get help, but he never did. And there's been nothing...' She shook her head, trying to regain control. 'I mean, ever since the problem started, he turned his back on me. Literally.'

She looked at Cain, her eyes wide with desperation. 'There are other things you can do, aren't there? I mean, even if you can't have full sex, there are ways to show love to one another. Lots of ways. Lots of things. But he — he dismissed me. It was as if I was of no use to him any more. And what I wanted, what I needed wasn't important. He'd decided that our physical intimacy was over and there was nothing I could do about it. I had to live with it. But I didn't *want* to live with it! I may have fallen out of love with him a long time ago, but we were still married, we still had some sort of relationship, even if it wasn't hearts and flowers. And I have needs. I'm not dead yet. It's not fair, is it? *Is it?*'

She seemed to realise that her voice had risen and glanced around, but no one was taking any notice of her. Cain felt awkward, wondering how on earth he could make her feel better when she'd been through such a horrible time.

'I'm so sorry,' she murmured. 'Far too much information. I apologise.'

His hand covered hers and he leaned towards her.

'Not at all, love,' he murmured. 'You obviously needed to pour all this out. Reckon it's been burning away inside you for years, and no wonder. I'm really honoured you chose to share it with me.'

She looked into his eyes and gave a faint smile. 'Thank you, Jeff. That's very kind of you.' She wiped her eyes and composed herself. 'You know, really, he did me a favour.'

'He did?' Cain couldn't see it himself.

'Oh, yes. Somehow, when we were having an intimate relationship, it kept us bonded. Or rather, it kept me bonded to him. It's peculiar, but when he cut that bond, it broke the spell.

For the first time, I seemed to step out of the relationship and look at it from an outsider's perspective, and I realised how stupid I'd been, and how little he cared about me throughout our entire marriage.'

'Does anyone else know about this? I mean, that you and your husband don't—'

She shook her head. 'Nobody. Nobody knows. It would kill him. He makes very sure that we always share a bedroom.' She wrinkled her nose. 'Although, when he does finally come to bed in the early hours of the morning — hoping I'm asleep, no doubt — he turns his back on me immediately and is asleep within minutes.'

'Connie,' Cain squeezed her hand, 'no offence, love but — what the fuck are you doing with him?'

Her eyes widened as if she'd never asked herself that question before. He wondered what her reasons were. Why *was* she with him? What was keeping her there? Some misguided sense of loyalty? Fear of a future without him? The unknown? Or was it simply cold, hard cash?

'I don't know,' she whispered. 'All I know is I'm so tired. And I'm so sad. I've been lonely for so long. I can't even remember the last time he kissed me or gave me a cuddle. What kind of marriage is this?'

A rogue tear escaped her eye, rolled down her cheek and leapt to freedom, landing on the tablecloth.

Cain put his arm around her. 'What kind of *life* is this?' he murmured. 'Maybe it's time you started to be happy again, eh? And maybe you need to figure out exactly what's keeping you tied to this jerk. You deserve better, Connie, and I swear to you, you can do this. There's a big wide world out there. Time you explored a bit of it, eh?'

She smiled at him through her tears. 'I expect you're wondering what on earth you've got involved in,' she said. 'I must sound so miserable, so needy. I expect you can't wait to escape.'

Cain stroked her hair and kissed her lightly on the cheek. The terrifying truth was her confession hadn't put him off her at all. In fact, if anything, it had only made him want her more.

But he was no good at relationships, and they always ended the same way, with the woman demanding a small fortune from him and a whole load of bitterness and acrimony. He couldn't face all that again, which was why he'd jumped at the chance of a no-strings, sex-only fling.

This wasn't turning out at all as he'd expected. What the hell was he going to do about it?

Chapter 24

It was just two days before the first guests arrived. Eden was in the larger bunk barn kitchen, making an inventory of all their new equipment — a task that, for some reason that Emerald simply couldn't fathom, made her squeal in excitement as she reeled off the list of appliances and gadgets to a clearly bemused Eliot.

Emerald had excused herself and gone to help Jed instead, and the two of them were making themselves useful in the smaller barn, putting together the bunks, and hanging curtains. At least, Jed was putting together the bunks and Emerald was holding the curtains in her hands while staring in some bewilderment at the plastic hooks that came with them and trying to fathom out how to slot them in.

'You'd think there'd be some sort of instructions with these,' she grumbled.

Jed looked up and grinned. 'You've never hung curtains before?'

'Why would I?' she demanded. 'Anyway, you needn't look so smug. Have you?'

He had to admit he hadn't. 'But, come on, how hard can it be?'

Emerald sighed and dropped onto the floor beside Bella, who'd ventured out of the house for probably the first time in her life to be with Emerald. Emerald couldn't help but feel flattered. The cat didn't seem particularly fond of anyone else at Wildflower Farm, but she'd really bonded with her. At least someone loved her.

Sitting cross-legged, she eyed the curtain hooks dubiously. 'It's a bit complicated,' she said. 'What?' she added, starting to laugh as Jed gave her a wry look. 'Don't look like that! You think I'm stupid, don't you?'

'Believe me, Emmy, that's the last thing I think,' he assured her. 'How are you supposed to know what to do if you've never done it before? Do you want me to help?'

'No. You've got enough to do. Maybe I'd be better helping you put those bunks together.'

He puffed out his cheeks. 'Not if we don't want our guests to sue us for injuries when their beds collapse.'

She raised an eyebrow. '*Our* guests?'

He turned away, tightening the bolts with an allen key as he muttered, 'You know what I mean.'

'You really like it here, don't you?' she said, watching him thoughtfully. 'On the farm, I mean. You feel right at home.'

He nodded. 'I guess I do, yeah. I spent years on my first stepfather's ranch, and I loved it there. He raised cattle and we had horses. It was a great life. Of course, it didn't last, 'cos Mom met stepdad number two and had moved in with him before you could say store card, which surprised no one. She was growing very bored of country life and Walt had a fabulous house in New York, and, in the end, cattle couldn't compete with trips to the theatre, and all those department stores, and a credit card with practically no limit. But I really missed the life. Being here—' he looked around, as if seeing fields and hills rather than cream-painted walls, 'it kind of reminds me of that life. I'd forgotten how much I loved it. The fresh air, the wide-open spaces, the animals. I feel happier here than I have in years.'

Emerald sighed. 'It *is* beautiful,' she admitted. 'But it's so remote, isn't it? So far away from — everything.'

He stood, stretching his back as he surveyed the finished bunk. 'I guess so, if by everything you mean Dad.'

Emerald scowled and grabbed the bag of curtain hooks from the floor. Giving them a vicious yank to open the bag, she tutted as the plastic split and the hooks tumbled to the floor. 'I didn't mention Dad.'

'You didn't have to,' he said softly. He rubbed his back and dropped the allen key on the bedside cabinet he'd put together the day before. 'I guess home is about a lot more than countryside and scenery, right? It's people. People we love. People who love us.'

'Which is probably why I've never felt as if I had a home,' she admitted. 'Mother was never the loving sort. She called me yesterday, by the way. She'd battled the elements to get to the village and rang me from the post office. Wanted to make sure I was transferring my allowance this month, and to ask me if Dad was involved with anyone. She didn't even ask how I was. Not that I expected her to. She never noticed me, even when I was a kid. Too busy channelling Flora McDonald or whoever. I wanted—' she sighed. 'I don't know what I wanted.'

'Oh, I think you do,' he said.

Emerald shrugged. 'Anyway, what about you?'

He raised an eyebrow. 'What about me?'

'You said home is about people we love, who love us. Where's your home? Who are your people?'

Jed said nothing, and Emerald watched as he made a great show of gathering up the various bits of packaging and tools.

She waited a few moments, then said, 'Is America still your home? Deep down, I mean. I know you're avoiding the place right now, but in your heart...'

Jed hesitated, then shook his head. 'No. America's not my home any more.' He watched her for a moment, as if considering how much to tell her, then sank onto the floor beside her. 'I can't see me ever going back there. England's my home now. I'm glad to be back.'

'And your people?'

He smiled. 'I'm in touch with Mom and Clint, and Scarlet and Luke, if that's what you mean.'

'It isn't,' she said brutally. 'And I think you know that perfectly well.'

'Wow, you take no prisoners.' He reared away, grinning. 'Okay, well, I guess the truth is, my home was definitely America for some years, but now it's not. Now, my home is here, and I'm

261

finally starting to settle again.'

She narrowed her eyes. 'And would that have something to do with a certain lady of the vicinity?'

Jed distinctly flushed, and Emerald's heart sank. So, she was right! She'd hoped she was imagining it. Okay, she really wanted her brother to be happy because, whatever had gone on in the States had clearly made him very miserable indeed, and she'd been delighted to see the colour returning to his cheeks and the sparkle to his eyes. But, really, falling for Eden was about the worst thing he could do. That bitch would string him along and break his heart. Besides, Eliot would kill him. She scooped Bella into her arms and kissed her between her ears, eyeing her brother worriedly.

'How did you—'

'I've got eyes. You're very transparent, to be honest. You need to be careful, Jed. Have you forgotten she's taken?'

He searched her face, seeming to be looking for signs of approval or otherwise, trying to decide how much to confide.

'We love each other,' he said. 'It's that simple.'

'Except, it isn't simple at all, is it?' she pointed out, wondering how Eden had managed to hook her brother so completely, and why he wasn't more concerned about destroying Eliot and those precious kids he seemed to adore.

'Emmy, I know it's a mess,' he said, 'but she's not happy. If she was do you really think she'd have looked twice at me? She's not that sort of woman. I swear, she's never done this before.'

'That's her story,' Emerald muttered. 'How do you know she doesn't make a habit of it?'

His expression changed. His eyes darkened, and his brows knitted together. Emerald thought that, when it suited him, Jed could glower almost as fiercely as Eliot.

'Because I know her. I'm telling you, this is the first time, and the last. Beth and me are for keeps.'

Emerald nearly choked with shock. Beth! Since when? My God, she'd really got that wrong, hadn't she? But James! What about poor James? 'You're really serious about her? It's not just a fling?'

Jed gathered up the curtain hooks and gazed at them as if they were suddenly fascinating. 'I really love her,' he said in a low voice. 'I can't help it, Emmy. There's something between us that we can't fight. It's like,' he looked up at her, his eyes shining suddenly, 'we knew it the moment we met. As if we'd been waiting for each other.' He laughed. 'I know. It sounds crazy, huh?'

Emerald swallowed. She'd been thinking how beautiful it sounded, and how lucky Jed and Beth were to have experienced such a feeling. But there was James to think about. She didn't know how to feel about it all.

Then she remembered the look on Jed's face that day of Honey's wedding. She recalled the tired eyes, the defeated expression, the weary posture. She remembered how worried she'd been about him, how she'd wondered who had hurt him. She looked into his eyes and saw the love and excitement shining from them, and suddenly it wasn't difficult at all.

'I'm happy for you,' she said, mentally apologising to James. 'I hope it works out for you.'

'You mean that?' He looked thrilled, as if her blessing really counted for something.

Emerald gulped, cuddling Bella tightly. 'Yes, of course I mean it. I want you to be happy, Jed. You're my big brother and I — I love you.'

She almost gasped out loud as he reached out and pulled her towards him, enfolding both her and the cat in a huge bear hug. 'Thank you, Emmy. That means more to me than I can ever tell you. I love you, too.'

As tears pricked at her eyes, Emerald vowed there and then that, no matter how kind or nice James Fuller was to her, Jed and Beth were going to make it. Nothing was going to stop them.

****

Eden was glad to get out of the post office. She had enough to do with the imminent arrival of the first guests at the bunk barns, and she'd wanted to get straight back home after dropping Ophelia at school and George at Mrs Thompson's. She could have done without the long queue.

Emerald could have got the stamps for the invitations, she thought crossly. She went out enough times, and it wouldn't have killed her to pop into a newsagent, supermarket or post office, depending on where she was, and get a few booklets of stamps.

And it had cost a fortune! She rarely posted anything, so had no idea how much the cost of sending a letter had gone up recently. All those invitations to post. Crazy, really. After all, most of them were going to people in the village. She could have shoved them through their letterboxes. Or got Emerald to, at any rate, she thought, smirking at the very idea.

'Ah, Eden, my dear.' Mrs Edwards swooped down upon her with little warning. She glanced down at the bundle of envelopes in Eden's hand and beamed at her. 'Are those the wedding invitations? How lovely that you're doing it properly. Do you know, some people invite guests by email or text these days? How disgraceful is that?'

She nodded approvingly at the thick envelopes. 'They look like good quality,' she said.

'They are,' Eden said, remembering the cost of them. Just because Cain was footing the bill didn't mean it was okay to waste money on unnecessary things, in her view, although Emerald was adamant that her father wanted them to have the best.

Best for whom? Eden was beginning to wonder.

'The wedding plans are coming on nicely then?' Mrs Edwards beamed. 'All on schedule?'

'I think so,' Eden said, adding honestly, 'our wedding planner's dealing with most of it. We just have to turn up.'

'Goodness. A wedding planner! How very modern of you,' Mrs Edwards said, looking a bit baffled.

'Isn't it,' Eden said glumly. 'I must go, Mrs Edwards, I've got such a lot to do today.'

'Of course, dear. It was lovely to see you again. Such a coincidence.'

'What is?'

'Well, I can go weeks, months without seeing either of you, but

I bumped into Eliot yesterday and then you today. How odd.'

Eden wrinkled her nose. 'You bumped into Eliot yesterday? Where?'

'Didn't he say? Oh, well, why would he? In Camacker, dear. I was getting off the bus from Kirkby Skimmer and I saw him getting into his Land Rover. He was parked not far from the vicarage.'

Eden frowned. 'Did he see you?'

'Oh yes, I waved, and he waved back. Anyway, I'll let you get off. I have lots to do myself.' She leaned forward and whispered, 'I have a doctor's appointment.'

'Oh. Oh, well, I hope everything's okay,' Eden said, flummoxed.

'Oh, I'm sure it will be. When we get to a certain age, we have to expect some things to start giving up, don't we?'

'Er, I suppose so. I'll bear that in mind for future reference,' Eden said.

As Mrs Edwards hurried off, she checked through the invitations one more time, making sure they all bore a first-class stamp.

'Right, no going back now,' she muttered, and shoved them, a handful at a time, into the post box. Suddenly, it all seemed very official.

****

'I now declare this bunk barn officially open. May God bless her and all who stay in her.'

Jed grinned and cut the ribbon, to the cheers of Eliot, Eden, Beth, Mickey and Adey, not to mention whoops of joy from the children.

'We're gunna be rich,' Ophelia told George, who raised his arms in the air and yelled, 'Yay!' at the top of his voice.

'Let's not get too carried away,' Eden said, with a wry grin. 'Although, I did two cream teas yesterday, so that's a start.'

'It'll soon pick up,' Beth said. 'The weather's beautiful at the moment, and if it continues this way, I think you'll be swamped before you know it.'

'I saw loads of leaflets getting picked up from't' village shop,' Adey volunteered. 'Plenty of hikers were having a good nosy through them. If they pass that info onto their mates, you'll have loads of bookings, right enough.'

'Let's hope so,' Eliot said, raising his glass of beer to his lips. 'We're sunk if this dun't pay off.'

'It will,' Eden assured him, her fingers crossed tightly behind her back. She caught Beth's eye and gave her a rueful smile. Beth was all too aware of the precarious state of their finances. It was she who had persuaded them to have the leaflets printed and had gone into the village to beg Mrs Tucker at the shop and Jill and Dave at The King's Head to place them on their premises, so any passing hikers would find them.

Together with Jed's work on the website and Facebook page, and advertisements in various magazines for hikers and Yorkshire tourists, they were certainly getting their business known. Now it had to work.

'Glass of champagne, Jed?' Eden held up the bottle as Jed strolled over to the picnic table and joined them, having safely returned the scissors to the farmhouse, away from George's eager grasp.

'Don't mind if I do,' he said. 'Now that I've done my official duties, that is.'

'Fancy us having a genuine rock star cutting the ribbon on our little bunk barn,' Eden giggled. 'We should have called the local papers.'

Jed gave her a knowing look. 'And you know what would have happened if you had. You'd have looked like crazy people, 'cos I'd have been long gone.' He gave a sigh of satisfaction as she filled his glass with champagne — a gift from Cain.

'You don't miss it then?' Adey asked, curious. He'd been overwhelmed when he'd realised who Jed was, having been quite a fan of Raven's Wing himself. 'I'm gutted you've left. Your guitar playing is legendary.'

Jed raised his glass in appreciation. 'Thank you kindly, young man,' he said, as if he were ancient. 'No, I don't miss it. That is, I miss playing music, but my guitars are at Dad's, and I'll be picking them up again real soon. The other side of it — no thanks. From now on, music's gonna be purely for pleasure. No business involved.'

Eden noted the brief glance he gave Beth, and the hint of a smile she gave him in return. Something about the way they looked at each other made her sit up and take notice. Hmm. Interesting. Not that anything could come of it, of course. Beth was far too loyal and too timid to go against Fuller. Sadly, she would be in his clutches forever.

'This champagne's delicious,' Beth said. 'It was kind of Cain to send it.'

'You're not drinking it?' Jed shaded his eyes as he peered up at Eliot, who was halfway through a pint of beer.

'Not keen on it,' Eliot admitted.

'Tha's drinking women's stuff,' Mickey sneered, nodding at Jed's glass of champagne. 'Tha should try some of this ale. Make a man of ya after all them years in foreign parts.'

Jed laughed. 'Thanks, Mickey. I'll bear that in mind.'

'Nowt like a pint of ale on a sunny day,' Adey said, smacking his lips together appreciatively.

Eden's finger slowly circled her glass. 'I hope you're not getting too fond of it,' she told him.

Adey looked startled. 'Eh? What do you mean by that?'

'Well,' she said, 'the other day! Dragging Eliot off to Camacker for a pint at The Shepherd's Crook. What was wrong with Beckthwaite if you had to have a drink?'

'Told you,' Eliot interjected, 'he's partial to Lusty Tup beer and they don't serve it at The King's Head.'

Adey's mouth dropped open as he looked from Eden to Eliot. 'Eh?' was all he seemed able to manage.

'T'other day,' Eliot said, sounding irritable. 'When we bumped into Mrs Edwards in Camacker, remember?'

'Oh. Oh, aye.' Adey took another gulp of his beer. 'Forgot about that. Sorry, Eden. I'll not do it again.'

Eden watched him through narrowed eyes. It was what she'd suspected, as Eliot mumbled his excuse to her when she told him about bumping into Mrs Edwards. She hadn't even been asking why he was in Camacker, she'd merely mentioned it out of interest, but his weird reaction had set her mind racing, and she hadn't believed a word about Adey wanting to drink a particular beer. There was no doubt that Adey knew nothing about Eliot's trip to the village, and Mrs Edwards hadn't mentioned seeing him anyway.

Slowly, she sipped her champagne. The question remained, what was Eliot doing in Camacker? And more importantly, why was he lying to her?

Chapter 25

Beth replaced the receiver and picked up her notepad. Running a line through the last name on the list, she heaved a sigh of relief. Thank goodness that job was over. There had been a lot of unhappy people who had fully expected to be returning to Thwaite Park for the annual open day in August — owners of fairground rides and attractions, food vendors, and local dignitaries particularly. Mr Edwards had seemed most put out, although he'd been somewhat soothed when James had assured him there would be a hefty donation to the local charities who usually benefitted from the event.

Thwaite Park was a beautiful Regency mansion set in acres of sculpted lawns, neat paddocks, and well-managed gardens. Carefully decorated and furnished in keeping with its age, it was known throughout Upper Skimmerdale as probably the grandest private residence in the area. The family at *the big house* were expected to contribute to local life, and for many years they had. There was no longer a large team of servants working in the house and grounds, but apart from Mrs Ketley there was still a handful of gardeners from Beckthwaite and the surrounding villages who helped to keep the outdoors in its neat and tidy state. More than that, the family hosted many charity events throughout the year, and the open day was the pinnacle of Thwaite Park's year.

A donation to charity wasn't the same as bringing a whole community together for a day of fun, festivities, and fundraising, and Beth cursed David Fuller for his arrogance and posturing. It wouldn't have cost him anything to allow the open day to go ahead, but last night he'd dropped the bombshell that he didn't want visitors in his grounds, and that the open day was to be cancelled for the foreseeable future. In her view, it was simply another way of demonstrating who was boss.

The open day was very much James's project, and she had no doubt that David was reminding him that, now that he and Deborah were back, things would be done their way, not his. She felt a pang of sympathy for her husband, quickly followed by another enormous stab of guilt. Running her hand over her eyes, she tried to push it away, but failed. How could she be happy with Jed when she had this dark cloud hanging over her? How could she be so selfish, so cruel? She'd had no idea this was the sort of person she was, nor that she was capable of such deception, so many lies.

Was this, she wondered, how James had felt when he was involved with Jemima? Did it cause him as many sleepless nights as her affair with Jed was causing her? Did the guilt eat away at him, too? She could almost feel sorry for him, knowing now how hard it was. Was it worth it?

The answer came to her before she'd even finished asking the question. Being with Jed was worth anything. She knew there was going to be a huge price to pay for their relationship, but she also knew, deep within her soul, that she would pay it willingly. She wished she didn't have to hurt James at the same time.

As if her thoughts had drawn him near, she looked up to see her husband walking towards her, a half-smile on his face. 'Have they given you a rough time?'

'Sorry? Oh!' She glanced down at the notebook and shook her head. 'Not really. Well, most of them were okay. There were bound to be some who took it badly. They'd just got used to being here every year, after you started it up again, hadn't they?'

'I know. It's going to make it bloody difficult to get them back next year,' he said, sitting down beside her. 'That's if we go ahead next year,' he added gloomily. 'The way it's going, we might never hold the event again.'

Beth put down her notebook. 'You think your parents will stay then?'

'I can't see them going anywhere,' he admitted, sounding far from pleased about it. 'Father's definitely got plans...' His voice trailed off and he stared into the distance, clearly worrying about something.

Beth reproached herself fiercely as it crossed her mind that, if David Fuller was planning to hang around, her relationship with Jed was a real blessing. She would need something — someone — to get her through life at the house. That's if she stayed, of course.

For a split second, she imagined herself and Jed, living far away from the Fullers, but she dismissed the image. Jed had never suggested anything permanent, and anyway, how could she abandon her husband to this dreadful life with his awful parents? It was impossible.

'I need to talk to you, darling.'

Beth blinked, dragged back to the present as James took her hand.

'Don't tell me your father's done something else,' she said, trying to ignore the inclination to throw off his grasp. What on earth was wrong with her? She was struggling to endure his touch lately. She was a horrible person, she really was. She peered up at him. 'What is it? You look dreadful.'

Whatever he wanted to say she could tell it wasn't pleasant. She had a brief panic that he knew about her and Jed but dismissed the thought. He wouldn't be holding her hand if he did.

'This isn't easy for me,' James said, and she had a sudden flashback to the moment when he'd finally admitted his affair with Jemima, on the day she'd died. It had probably been the worst day of her life.

'Why don't you tell me?' she said, trying to sound calm. Whatever it was, it couldn't be as bad as that day. Nothing could.

'It's about George.' His grip on her hand tightened, almost as if he knew she wanted to pull away from him. She forced herself to stay still, waiting. 'I want to see him. I want to be part of his life.'

His voice seemed to echo from far, far away. From that day, over four years ago, when he'd informed her that he had a child. A tiny baby, four weeks old. A poor, motherless scrap of humanity, born into a dreadful, terrible mess.

'You can't,' she murmured. 'You can't do that.'

'He's my child,' James said, his voice wheedling. 'I don't want to hurt you, Beth, really I don't, but—'

'It's not about me,' she said, her tone rising in panic. 'What about Eliot? What about George? You can't do this to them!'

At the mention of Eliot, she saw his face darken. 'Harland has had my son for over four years. Don't you think it's time I got to see him? For God's sake, who does he think he is? He won't even let me visit the boy. What right has he got to—'

'He's got every right,' she snapped. 'Where were you when George was left without a mother? You didn't want to know! Couldn't be bothered. Where would George have been if Eliot hadn't put aside all the terrible things you'd done to him and taken that poor little boy in?'

'If Harland hadn't wanted him, then of course I'd have—'

'Would you? Because I don't think you would! You can't turn up out of the blue and decide you want to have access to him! What about George? Have you even thought about him in all this? He thinks Eliot's his father! Oh, for God's sake!'

James glared at her. 'I let Harland keep George to himself for your sake, not mine! You were far too fragile and unstable to ask you to bring another woman's child up, let alone Jemima's. What was I supposed to do? It was you or my son, and I chose you. I put you first.'

'How big of you,' she muttered.

'Yes actually, it was,' he said, his voice angry now. 'I knew I couldn't have both of you, and you were the one I decided to focus on. And haven't I spent the last four years trying to make you happy?'

She couldn't deny it. He had.

'Trips to New York, cruises, a new car, anything you wanted you got. Now, didn't you?'

'Do you really think that's all it takes? Holidays, possessions!

272

Do you think that puts it right?'

'For God's sake, Beth, what more could I do?'

'You could have done the one thing I wanted you to do,' she said, tears running down her face. 'You refused to try IVF again, or even look into adoption, yet here you are demanding rights to George.'

She choked on a sob as the injustice hit her, along with the realisation that she had been weak. She should have forced the issue, not let him move along at his own pace, which had been practically stationary. She should have been tougher, demanded that they investigate other options or else.

Or else what? Would she ever have left him? She didn't know the answer to that question. All she knew was that something had changed irrevocably between them, and there was no going back.

Maybe it was down to Jed and the way she felt about him. Maybe it was finally growing up, seeing things the way they really were, rather than the way she wanted them to be. Maybe it was the threat of hurting Eliot and George, destroying the Harlands for what? Because James wouldn't take to George, not really. He'd never shown any interest in him before. Whatever his motives now, she couldn't sit back and allow him to throw a grenade at Wildflower Farm. She just couldn't.

'Not this again,' James said, scrambling to his feet. 'For God's sake, it always comes back to this. I was talking about George, not some mythical baby that we may or may not ever have. Right now, I have a son, and I want to be part of his life. Are you going to help me or not?'

She stared up at him through blurry eyes. 'Help you?'

'You're friends with Harland,' he pointed out. 'You could pave the way, make him see that this is important to me.'

'Oh no.' Beth shook her head. 'I won't help you in this, James. I can't. And if you go ahead, I'll—'

He frowned. 'You'll what?'

She let out a strangled sob. 'It will be the end of us. Can't you see that? I'm sorry but—'

He sat beside her and grasped her hand again. 'All right, all right.'

His voice was soothing, and she detected a trace of fear in it as he stroked her wrist with his thumb, making her cringe inwardly. 'I'm sorry. I didn't mean to upset you. It all got out of hand.'

He leaned back on the sofa, his face ashen. 'If it worries you that much, we'll forget it. At least for now. I'll back off, think it through properly, okay?'

She blinked away the tears, feeling another vicious wave of guilt. She couldn't see a way through this mess at all. James wanted to be part of George's life, and she'd already stopped him from doing that for four years. How could she deny him it even now? Yet she knew that if he pursued this, it would destroy Eliot and turn George's world upside down, not to mention Libby's and Ophelia's who had no idea that George was only their half-brother. How could she please everyone? How could she make everyone happy?

She could almost hear Jed's soothing voice, murmuring to her that it wasn't her problem, that she wasn't responsible for other people's happiness. He was always so understanding, and he always knew how to lift the burden from her shoulders. Yet, somehow, she didn't think he could help her this time. How could he, when her love for him was yet another huge burden she had to carry, along with everything else?

****

Dark clouds were gathering above Wildflower Farm as Beth entered the yard that afternoon. She thought how appropriate that was. With the mood she was in and the events that had taken place that morning, she wouldn't have been in the least surprised if it were pouring down with rain, and lightning was ripping the sky in half, at the very least. In the distance, she could hear the girls giggling and calling to each other from the paddock. They must be riding Flora.

She wondered if Eden was in the barn or the house. She decided to try the house first and knocked at the door, her stomach churning, the familiar feeling of guilt swirling around in there along with nerves as she contemplated telling Eden what had occurred at Thwaite Park, and the anticipation that she might see Jed. It was a most uncomfortable mixture, and she felt quite sick as she stood there, wondering how she was going to break the news.

Of course, she'd considered not telling anyone what James had said. It would be easier to believe that he meant it when he said he wouldn't pursue the idea of seeing George, and it would make sense for her to stay out of it. She was, after all, married to James, and it wasn't fair to ask her to be involved. Even so, as she'd sat there on the sofa, long after James had wandered off to do something else, it had finally occurred to Beth that she couldn't keep this news quiet. Whatever his promises, she had to give Eden some warning, just in case. She couldn't bring herself to tell Eliot, but Eden would surely know what to do for the best.

As the door opened, Beth felt her stomach practically take off and fly out of her mouth, as Jed stood there, his face split by an enormous smile at the sight of her. 'Hey, you.'

'Hi,' she murmured, almost shyly. She realised she was smiling, too, and felt bad. She wasn't here to enjoy herself. She had business to conduct. Important business. 'You okay?'

He glanced behind him then his eyes scanned the yard. Seeing no one, he pulled her to him and kissed her gently, his fingers lightly twisting her hair. She allowed herself to put all thoughts of George and James and Eliot aside for a few glorious moments and lost herself in his kiss.

'I've missed you,' he murmured against her lips.

She almost pointed out that he'd only seen her the day before yesterday, but she didn't. The truth was, she'd missed him, too, and every hour she wasn't with him hurt. His eyes fixed on hers, expressing all the love and longing that she returned, and she melted against him, wanting nothing more than to stay in his embrace forever.

'I missed you, too,' she whispered.

He gasped and held her tightly, seeming unable to bring her close enough to him. She could feel him hard against her body, and her own desire for him heated up to boiling point. As his

275

lips pressed against hers again, she forgot about everything except the comfort of his arms around her, the fresh, clean scent of him, the softness of his beard against her chin, and the way his kiss made her feel as if she were falling through space, unaware and uncaring of anything else.

'Who is it, Jed?'

Eden's voice calling from the kitchen plunged them back to reality and they pulled apart, breathless.

Jed exhaled deeply. 'It's Beth,' he replied.

'Oh, come in, Beth!'

Beth wasn't sure she could move. Her legs felt distinctly shaky. Jed stroked her cheek. 'You'd better come in,' he whispered. 'But, hey, I need to see you. Properly, I mean.'

'I know.' She felt a shiver of delightful anticipation at the thought. 'But when?'

'How about I book us a room at The Paradise?'

Beth's eyes widened. 'You're serious?'

'It's not right, all this hiding in barns. We deserve better. You deserve better. I want to spend some time with you — real, quality time. I want us to enjoy being together properly. What do you say?'

Beth could hardly say a word. The thought of enjoying Jed was making her speechless. She merely nodded, and he smiled. 'Come on, we'd better go in or she'll wonder what we're up to.'

Dumbly, she followed him into the kitchen, where Eden was preparing dinner, or tea as the Harlands called it.

'There you are!' she said, smiling as they entered the room. 'I thought you'd changed your mind and gone home.' Her smile died. 'Are you okay? You look ever so flustered.'

Beth blushed as Jed strode over to the sink and filled the kettle with water. He'd already learned that the first thing anyone did upon arrival at Wildflower Farm was drink tea.

'I'm — I'm fine, thanks.'

'Are you sure?' Eden frowned. 'You don't look right.'

Beth took a deep breath. It was as good a time as any, she supposed. 'I have some news for you, Eden, and you're not going to like it.'

Eden put down the potato peeler and Jed turned off the tap. They both stared at her in concern. 'What is it?'

Beth sank into one of the chairs and tapped her fingers on the table, considering where to start. In the event, she decided the best way was to be brutally honest. It was no use sugar coating the pill.

'It's James,' she said, aware that Jed had straightened and was now staring intently at her. 'He told me this morning that he wants access to George.'

Jed turned to look at Eden who was standing still and silent. She'd gone quite pale and he hooked an arm around her shoulders, clearly recognising her shock. 'You okay?'

'But why?' Eden whispered, not taking her eyes off Beth. 'Why now?'

Beth swallowed. 'He's — he's been talking more about George lately,' she confessed. 'He admitted he's missing him. Apparently, he only let George go out of consideration for me.'

She couldn't look at Jed now, fixing her gaze instead upon the scrubbed pine table.

'He assured me he wasn't interested in changing the status quo,' she added hastily, 'or I'd have mentioned it sooner. Only, this morning, he said he couldn't carry on the way things were. He wanted to see his son and — and he wanted me to approach Eliot to help him.'

She heard Eden make a funny sort of noise and looked up quickly, seeing her friend slump against Jed.

'And is that why you're here?' Eden's voice was harsh. 'To convince Eliot?'

'Of course not!' Beth rose to her feet and hurried towards Eden, who was now eyeing Beth suspiciously. 'I'd never do that, and I told James so. I said I'd never ask Eliot to allow him to see George, and I wanted no part of it.' She cast a fleeting glance at Jed. 'I told him, if he pursued this, it would be the end of us.'

She saw Jed's eyebrows raise and looked away hurriedly.

'He backed down then, said he wouldn't do anything for now. He's going to think it through. I'm so sorry, Eden, but I thought I should warn you. I don't know if he'll forget all about it or if

277

he'll decide to go for access, but I thought you should be prepared.'

Jed hugged a shaken Eden to him. 'Are you gonna tell Eliot?'

It didn't seem to occur to Eden to ask how Jed knew what was going on. She was evidently too upset to remember that, as far as she was aware, Jed had no idea that George wasn't one of Eliot's children.

'I can't,' she whispered. 'I just can't. This will kill him.'

'It may come to nothing,' Beth said, desperate to soothe her friend. 'You know how flaky James is. He knows how I feel about it. It may be enough for him to drop the matter entirely.'

Eden nodded. 'Perhaps.'

'I'm sure it will be all right,' Beth said. 'But if I hear anything, anything at all, I'll tell you straightaway. I promise.'

Eden reached out a hand and grasped Beth's. 'Thank you, Beth. I don't know what we'd do without you.' She shook her head. 'This can't happen. I can't imagine what Eliot would do, how he'd react. It's his biggest fear.'

'I know,' Beth said. 'Really I do. That's why I told you, not him. No need to worry him while it's all up in the air. Unless,' she added, 'you think he should know now.'

Eden paused, then slammed her hands on the worktop. 'No! No, he's not to know. Why make him miserable when it may all come to nothing? And it will come to nothing, won't it?' Her eyes held an appeal to Beth. 'Don't you think?'

'I'm sure it will,' Beth assured her. After all, James had backed down when she'd threatened to leave him. He wouldn't risk their marriage, not after all he'd done to try to repair it. 'He knows how I feel, and he won't go against me. I'm sure of it.'

From outside, barely audible, came the low rumble of distant thunder.

Jed's eyes met hers, and she realised that he was as aware as she was of their terrible dilemma. James might back off while he was desperate to keep Beth happy, but if he ever discovered that she was having an affair with Jed, all that concern would be out of the window. There was even more at stake now. As if the fallout of discovery wouldn't have been bad enough, it seemed the fate of the Harlands depended on their affair remaining a secret. How much more could they risk?

****

Eliot wiped his eyes with the back of his forearm. The rain was pouring down and his hair was dripping wet through. He'd be glad to get indoors. A nice hot shower, a hearty tea, then an evening curled up on the sofa with Eden and the kids. He smiled, then his smile faded as he mentally added, *and Jed and Emerald plonked on the armchairs, swapping anecdotes about programmes I've never heard of and don't give a monkey's about.*

It was getting on his nerves now, having the two of them around so much. All right, they were polite enough to him — Emerald was downright gushing towards him, although she was less pleasant to Eden, who wasn't much nicer to her, to be fair — and Jed certainly pulled his weight around the farm and with the barns, while Emerald was working flat out on this wedding stuff, but even so. He longed for the day when they headed home to the Cotswolds and left the Harland family in peace.

Apart from anything else, he thought grumpily, it was putting a stop to him and Eden having, what he termed, *adult time.* They'd tried to be as quiet as possible, but Eden was paranoid about Jed being above them and Emerald across the hall and, he had to admit, it wasn't doing much for his libido either. Apart from that one night when Jed had taken the kids to the pub for tea, they hadn't had any fun in ages, and he missed it. He missed Eden.

At the thought of exactly how much he was missing her, he raised his head to the sky and let the rain pour down on his face. With any luck it would wash away his longing, although he wasn't completely convinced it would work. He glanced down at his sheepdogs, Lug and Jake, who were sitting by his side staring up at him in surprise.

'Think I'm crackers, don't you?' Eliot said with a grin. 'Happen you're right. Why else would I be standing out here getting soaked, eh? And it didn't even work. Oh well...'

Sighing, he opened the door of the farmhouse and, following

his usual routine, he removed his boots and carried them to the boot room, hanging up his jacket and grabbing a towel from the laundry basket to rub his hair dry. Lug and Jake joined Lug's grandmother Tuppence, who was busy devouring her tea. Tuppence lived in the house full-time, but Lug and Jake would have their food then, later, he'd take them over to the barn, where they slept with the Jack Russells, Fagin and Dodger — most excellent ratters. As the dogs began to eat the food that Eden must have put out for them, Eliot put down the towel and headed into the kitchen, bracing himself for a roomful of Carmichaels.

He was surprised to discover that only Eden and the children were in the kitchen. Well, that made a welcome change. He couldn't hide his pleasure as he ruffled the girls' hair and planted a kiss on George's head.

'Where is everyone?' he enquired.

Eden grinned, knowing exactly who he meant. 'Emerald's gone into Leeds. Something to do with the wedding.' She rolled her eyes. 'She said not to expect her back until tomorrow, as she might as well stay over. And Jed's in Harrogate. He said he's meeting some friend there —something to do with the music industry. Don't ask me what. He won't be home until tomorrow either.' She gave him a meaningful look. 'We've got the house to ourselves tonight.'

Eliot whooped, then threw his arm around her waist and whirled her round to face him.

She laughed, waving a ladle in the air. 'You're making me drip the casserole everywhere! Ugh,' she pushed him away, clearly not meaning it, 'you're wet through. Your hair's dripping all over me.'

'Well, in case you hadn't noticed, it's chucking it down out there,' he said, nodding towards the window. 'I just dried me hair with a towel any road. How bad can it be?'

She put down the ladle and ran a hand through his curls. He saw the expression on her face change as her eyes met his, and the blood pumped through his veins as he recognised the reflection of his own longing in their depths. For a moment they stared at each other and he felt the familiar tug of desire for her.

'Skimmerdale Show schedule's come for you, Dad.'

Ophelia's voice cut through the air, slicing open the bubble that he and Eden had been in. He blinked as Eden picked up the ladle again, and he saw her swallow hard as she turned back to the cooker.

Repressing a sigh, he smiled at his daughter. 'Oh, aye? Have you opened it?'

"Course not!' She looked most indignant and he decided not to mention the fact that she'd been happy enough to open it last year. Evidently, the telling off she'd received then for opening his mail had taught her a lesson.

'Good lass.'

'And there's another letter for you, too,' Ophelia continued, giving George a filthy look as he flicked bread and butter at her. 'Pack it in, George, or I'll give you a clip round the ear!'

George grinned but knew her well enough to down weapons.

'Meanie,' he told her, then quietened when Eden gave him one of her looks. 'All right. Sorry, Mum.'

'It's from a solicitor,' Ophelia continued, scooping up the little squashed bullets of bread that George had been firing at her. 'Do you think we've come into money?'

Eliot laughed. 'I doubt it.' He glanced round at Eden, surprised to see her standing perfectly still, as if frozen. 'Do you know about this?'

She shook her head. 'I didn't know there was a letter,' she said, her voice sounding shaky. 'You never said, Ophelia.'

Ophelia shrugged. 'Forgot. I found them on the mat when I were heading out to clean the hen house, so I shoved them on the bookcase in the hallway. Do you want me to fetch them?'

'Maybe we should eat first,' Eden said, making a lot of noise as she slapped the plates down on the worktop with a resounding clatter.

Eliot raised an eyebrow. 'Spuds aren't even mashed yet,' he pointed out. 'May as well see what's what before you serve it.' He gave her a quick kiss on the cheek, not daring to risk any more. 'Hey, don't look so worried. No one's suing me,' he assured her. 'Leastways, not that I can think of.'

He laughed, but she could barely manage a feeble smile in return. Weird.

He washed his hands then sat down at the table beside Libby, who, as usual, had her head buried in a book. 'Owt good?' he enquired, nudging her.

Libby smiled up at him, a sweet-natured, gentle girl who had stolen his heart from the moment he saw her in Jemima's arms at the hospital. A tiny baby of only five pounds six ounces, she'd had dark hair, a red face, and solemn eyes which surveyed him knowingly, as he took her in his own arms and gazed at her in wonder. He'd wanted to be at the birth, but Jemima didn't agree with it, insisting that she didn't want him to see her in such a state and that he could wait outside until all the messy business was over with. Liberty Jane Harland — his firstborn child and a beautiful soul.

She waved the paperback in his face and he laughed. 'Oh, a pony book. Might have guessed. Do you ever read owt else?'

She considered the matter. 'At school. And I do have some other books, you know. But nothing's as good as a pony book.'

'Aye, I know, love.' Eliot sighed, thinking he really needed to organise his finances and get her a pony. Flora was too small for her and she deserved her own pony. He needed things to go well with the barns, and at the Skimmerdale Show, of course. Speaking of which...

'You got that schedule, love?'

Ophelia returned to the table and handed him two white envelopes, one bigger than the other. 'The schedule and the will.'

'Will?'

'I reckon someone's left you summat. Why else would a solicitor be in touch with you?'

Why else indeed? Eliot winked at her and slit the first envelope. 'Here you go,' he said, handing her the show schedule. 'You can have first dibs on that. No doubt you'll be wanting to enter plenty of events.'

'Great! Thanks, Dad.' Ophelia grabbed the brochure and began to flick through the pages, all thoughts of wills and inheritances gone from her mind.

Eliot gave her an affectionate smile then turned to the other envelope. *Hebblewhite and Wilson, Solicitors, Richmond.* Hmm. So, what did they want? He pulled out the sheet of paper within. It was thick, expensive paper. Whoever this firm were, they didn't skimp on stationery. Smoothing the letter down, he began to read.

At first, he didn't take in exactly what was being said, yet the mere mention of George's name gave him a hollow feeling in the pit of his stomach. His heart began to thud, and he read the letter a second time, slowly, taking every word in. Hardly able to believe what he'd read, he raised his head and looked across to Eden. She was standing by the cooker, watching him, her face pale with dread.

It was as if she knew. But how could she? No one could have known. No one could have predicted this, surely? Of all the reasons a solicitor might have been writing to him, this was the last one he'd have expected.

And yet, hadn't it been the thing he'd most dreaded for the last four years? Why had it shocked him then? Maybe because Fuller had done such a convincing job, over George's lifetime, of seeming not to care about the little boy at all. Yet here he was, suddenly, it seemed, remembering who George's biological father was after all, and demanding custody. Eliot screwed up the letter and held it in his fist.

'No money then?' Ophelia sounded disappointed, but Libby looked concerned.

'You all right, Dad? It's nothing bad, is it?'

Eliot managed a faint smile. 'Course not. Just junk mail. Nothing important at all.'

'Pah! Back to the drawing board for that pony, Libby,' Ophelia remarked, not even glancing up from the schedule.

Libby gave Eliot a curious look, but he managed to sound calm as he responded to Ophelia's comment with a casual tut and a shake of the head.

'Happen I'll go up and have a shower while tea's getting cooked.'

'But it's nearly ready.' Eden's voice sounded strained as she stared hard at him.

'Aye, but I feel filthy. I need to get this muck off me.'

Didn't he just! He could hardly wait to get out of the room and headed up to the bathroom as fast as he could, dropping the crumpled letter on the bed, throwing off his clothes, and stepping into the shower with relief.

He spent a good ten minutes scrubbing away at his skin, as if trying to wash the fear away, too. The memory of all Fuller's promises, all Beth's assurances, assaulted his mind as he rubbed shampoo into his hair and closed his eyes, letting the hot water pour down upon him.

Various scenarios flashed through his mind: Facing that loathsome man in court; hearing a judge tell him that George wasn't legally his and there was nothing he could do; Fuller arriving at Wildflower Farm to claim his son; George in the back of Fuller's car, his little face twisted in fear and bewilderment as a strange man took him back to Thwaite Park, to be separated from his family forever. And — hovering in the back of his mind, refusing to depart — Eden's face as she stood at the cooker, watching him.

He thumped the tiles and turned off the water. Wrapping a towel around his waist, he strode into the bedroom, stopping dead at the sight of Eden sitting on the bed, her eyes large with anxiety, the crumpled letter in her hand.

'You knew.'

It wasn't a question. Her expression had given her away from the moment she'd heard about the letter from Ophelia. He hadn't wanted to believe it.

'Not for sure,' she almost whispered. 'I hoped I was wrong but—'

'But what?' His voice was harsh, and he saw her flinch. Guilt. He recognised that emotion, all right. 'Why the hell didn't you tell me? Warn me? How long have you known?'

'Eliot, sit down.' She patted the bed beside her, but he didn't move. Sighing, she smoothed the paper. 'I'm so sorry. Beth seemed to think it had blown over, that he'd backed down.'

'Beth? *She* told you?'

Eden held out her hand, but he ignored it.

'She came to see me,' she admitted. 'James had told her he wanted to be part of George's life, but I never expected this!' She waved the letter at him. 'I don't think Beth did, either. She said access, not custody!'

Eliot felt sick. 'I thought Beth was my friend. I thought—'

'She *is* your friend! Believe me, she told James in no uncertain terms that if he persisted in trying to get access, their marriage would be over. She thought she'd done enough to dissuade him. He backed down.'

'If she thought that, why bother telling you? And why didn't she tell *me*, more to the point?'

'Because she didn't want to worry you! She wanted to tip me off that it had crossed his mind, but she honestly thought she'd scuppered it. And she only said access. I don't think it even occurred to her that he'd want full custody of George.' She looked down at the letter, shaking her head. 'I can't believe this. I'm so sorry, Eliot.'

'You should have told me.' He sank down onto the bed beside her at last, and she tentatively stroked his wet shoulder, her eyes soft with compassion. 'I might have been able to do something. Stop him. It might not have come to this.'

'If Beth's threats to end the marriage didn't work, I don't see what you could have done,' she said gently. 'You must know she'd never do anything to hurt you. This isn't Beth's fault.'

'No.' He clenched his jaw in anger. 'We all know whose fault this is.' He sat for a moment, staring at the floor as a million thoughts flitted through his mind. 'They're demanding a DNA test. What do I do, love?' He lifted his head and gazed at her through blurry eyes. 'Please tell me, what do I do?'

She put her arms around him, and he allowed himself to be held, drawing comfort from her embrace. She didn't seem to mind that he was wet, and he didn't care that he was cold. He needed her beside him. His worst nightmare had come true, and he didn't have the first idea how to fight back.

Chapter 26

Jed stretched lazily and smiled up at the ceiling, a gesture of gratitude to some invisible Cupid, as if he were hovering above the bed. Beside him, Beth slept, her dark hair a raven's wing across the pillow. Raven's Wing. As the thought of his band and — more sharply — JoJo entered his mind, he half-froze, steeling himself for the familiar stab of pain. It was a joyful relief when none came. He took a deep breath. It all seemed so long ago, so far away. He would never forget, but it seemed finally he'd moved on. Accepted the unacceptable. Was time the healer, or was it love?

He shifted carefully onto his side, gazing at the woman who had mended his heart. Her lashes cast shadows on her high cheekbones, and her lips were slightly parted as she breathed deeply and evenly, dreaming of who knew what. He was tempted to kiss her, but he didn't want to disturb her. Let her sleep. She looked so contented, so peaceful. The frail, nervous woman he'd first encountered upon his arrival in Skimmerdale was a world away from the passionate, strong woman he'd spent the afternoon with. They'd talked, they'd eaten, they'd laughed, and they'd loved, and finally fallen asleep in each other's arms, happy beyond measure, neither of them dwelling on the fact that this was one night and real life waited outside the doors of their hotel room.

'Where did you tell him you were?' He'd asked the question, then wished he hadn't, as thoughts of James briefly pervaded their bubble of bliss.

She'd avoided his gaze. 'I said Eliot and Eden were shopping for wedding things and had decided they'd like to stay out for dinner, so had asked me to babysit for them, and that, as they were going to be back late, I may as well stay over.'

'And he was okay with that?'

'I've done it before,' she said. 'I stayed at Wildflower Farm overnight when they went to your sister's wedding.' She shrugged. 'Anyway, he's hardly likely to go to the farm to check up on me, is he? It's the one place in the world I know he'll never go.'

'You think he's suspicious?'

'Not at all.' For a moment, a note of bitterness crept into her voice. 'I'm the good wife. The dutiful woman who never lets her husband down, no matter what.' She shook her head. 'Can we stop talking about him now, please?'

It was the only sour note in the whole day, and he was happy to drop the subject. He'd soon put the smile back on her face, and she'd made him forget everything — all the troubles of his past, the fact that she had a husband at home, that whatever they had it couldn't continue this way forever. At some point, soon, Beth would have to make a choice. He wanted to believe she would choose him, but deep down he wasn't so sure. She was a loyal person who took her marriage vows seriously. How could he compete with the guy who had put the ring on her finger, even if he was a prize jerk? Not only that, but they had the Harlands to consider now. Keeping James in the dark was imperative if he wasn't going to try to get George back.

Jed glanced at the clock. Only eight o'clock! They hadn't even had dinner yet. They should go downstairs, get something to eat. Or maybe they should order room service? He grinned to himself. Yeah, that would be much better. Dinner in bed, with the best kind of dessert to follow. He wondered if he should risk waking Beth, or should he order while she slept?

The sudden buzzing from her cell phone on the bedside table came as a shock, bursting the bubble as the outside world rudely intruded. She'd put the phone on silent but hadn't turned off the vibrate setting. Now the phone shuddered on the table, almost accusingly.

'Beth? Beth, honey.' He shook her slightly, anxious that it might be James. The last thing they needed was for him to start worrying about where she was.

Beth's eyes fluttered open and she stared at him, looking confused. 'What? Oh!' She smiled at him, and he smiled back. 'Hey. Sorry to wake you, but your phone's ringing. Well,' he corrected himself, 'it's vibrating like crazy anyway.'

'Oh.' She lunged for the phone. 'It's Eliot,' she said, sounding worried. 'God, I hope James hasn't rung up asking for me.'

'Would he do that?' But she'd already answered the call and he saw her frown as Eliot's voice blasted from the phone, so loud that Jed could hear every word.

'Eliot, calm down! I don't understand—'

She fell silent, listening intently to what he was trying to tell her. Jed listened too, his demeanour changing as he recognised that trouble was afoot.

'Of course I didn't know! He mentioned that he was thinking of asking for access to George, but I told him that if he did that our marriage would be over. No, of course not! He said he understood and that he'd back off. No, he's never mentioned it again.'

She glanced at Jed, her forehead creased with anxiety. 'I only told Eden because I thought she should be aware, and I didn't want to worry you unless it was absolutely necessary. If I'd thought he meant it I would have warned you, of course I would! How can you even ask me that?' She bit her lip, her eyes growing large. 'Are you serious? Custody? He never mentioned custody. He said he wanted to see George but — of course I'm sure! Eliot, I'm sorry, really I am. Yes, yes, I'll speak to him about it. Yes, tonight. Of course I will. I promise. I—' She held out the phone and stared at it in anguish. 'He hung up on me,' she murmured. 'Eliot hung up on me.'

'He's scared,' Jed said, reassuringly. 'He only got mad out of fear. When he calms down, he'll realise it's not your fault.' *And he'd better damn well apologise for talking to you like that.* 'What you gonna do? I mean, you said you'd talk to James tonight.'

'And I must,' she said. She flashed him an apologetic look. 'I'm so sorry. This isn't how it was supposed to be, but I have to talk to him, find out what on earth he's thinking.'

'You told him if he persisted in this, your marriage was over,' Jed reminded her. Did it make him a total heel that he was finding hope in all this mess? Maybe Fuller had done the hard work for him. Beth would never forgive the guy for this, surely? 'Seems to me some things matter more to him.'

She stared at him and he cursed himself for being so crass. Now was not the time for point-scoring.

'I'm sorry. What are you going to do? I mean, how can you ask James about this when you're supposed to be babysitting for Eliot?'

She shrugged, gazing at her phone while she tried to work something out. 'I'll say they got back early and found the letter. That they've just opened it.'

'He'll expect you to come home to talk about it.' Jed felt sick with disappointment and sick at himself for being so selfish. It was their one chance to spend the night together and now it was over. He would have to drive her home.

But Beth shook her head. 'I'll tell him I don't want to see him, which is quite true. He'll know how angry I am anyway, so he won't be surprised if I decide to stay out. I'm not going home tonight.'

'Beth,' he hated himself for asking but couldn't help it. 'Where does this leave us? After what he promised...'

She took a deep breath. 'Why don't you go downstairs and get us a table for dinner? I'll make the call while you're out.'

Jed knew he was dismissed, and she was trying to be as polite as possible about it. He couldn't blame her. She had enough on her mind without catering to his insecurities and needs.

Ten minutes later, he entered the restaurant, where a friendly waiter showed him to a table and handed him a menu. Jed scoured it without taking anything in. What was it with him anyway? Why did he always end up being the one sounding needy and demanding? Why did the women he fell in love with

289

always turn out to be the ones calling the shots?

He put down the menu, angry at himself. Beth was nothing like JoJo, and this wasn't her fault. He'd known she was married when he started all this, and it hadn't prevented him from kissing her. From arranging this evening together. From falling in love with her.

He stared out of the window, seeing people hurrying by on their way to who knew where. Couples, arm in arm, out in the open, unafraid of being seen together. Would he and Beth ever be like that? Would they ever be free to love? Because he did love her, and he knew she loved him, too. She wasn't the type for a quick fling, a casual affair. He knew by the look in her eyes that she had feelings for him. The question was, how strong were those feelings? And did she still have feelings — other than loyalty — for her husband?

'Hey.'

He smiled to himself upon hearing her greeting. She was picking up his speech patterns, mimicking his own regular greeting to her. She'd better watch that, he supposed.

'Hey yourself. How did it go?'

Beth sank into the chair opposite him and gave him a tight smile. 'Not great.'

'You got through to James then?'

'Eventually.' She frowned. 'It was odd. I rang him at home, but it turned out he wasn't there.' She gave an involuntary shudder. 'Deborah answered. She said he'd gone out for the night and she had no idea where or who with, so I called his mobile. He was in a foul mood, right from the off. I don't know what was wrong with him, but it wasn't about George, I'm sure of that. When I mentioned it, he sounded like he'd forgotten all about it.'

She broke off as a waiter returned to enquire if they were ready to order. Since neither had even looked at the menu, they ordered a glass of wine and promised the waiter they'd make a decision very soon. He gave them a gracious nod and headed off to fetch their wine.

'Anyway,' Beth lifted the menu and held it open without even glancing at it, 'he said he'd had business in Leeds and was on his way home. He wasn't happy that I called him about the letter, I can tell you that much. Demanded to know whose side I was on.'

'Whew! That guy has some front. He knows whose side you're on about this. You made it very clear.'

'I know, as I reminded him. He got quite huffy. Said it wasn't his idea and he hadn't charged in like a bull in a china shop. It's not even his solicitor.'

'Then whose—'

'Deborah's.' Beth wrinkled her nose. 'He told Deborah, and she's decided they have to fight for custody. James is quite upset about the whole thing. He says he tried to persuade her to drop the matter, but then Deborah got quite emotional and said George was her only grandchild, and likely to remain her only grandchild, and she had a right to get to know him.' She swallowed, and Jed placed his hand over hers, squeezing it sympathetically. 'James is stuck between a rock and a hard place. He said he didn't want to upset me or back out on our agreement, but then his mother cried, and he's never seen her cry, and he felt he had no option but to go along with her wishes.'

Jed raised an eyebrow. 'You're not buying that?'

Beth looked helpless. 'I don't know. I can't imagine he'd do this after all this time unless there was someone else pushing him, and Deborah can be very determined when she wants something.' She tucked a stray lock of hair behind her ear. 'I couldn't believe he would see a solicitor after ignoring George for four years. I thought there had to be something — someone — in the background, stirring all this up. It would be Deborah. Of course it would.'

'So, you're gonna let him get away with this?' Jed tried to keep the incredulity from his voice. She was clearly blind to Fuller's deviousness.

'I can see why he felt he had no choice,' she said. 'When your own mother is in tears of course you're going to want to do something to help. And I can understand Deborah wanting to see her grandson. But the custody thing is a whole different matter, and I told him so.'

'And what did he say to that?'

'He got very angry and said he was sick of me taking Eliot's side over his and I should get my priorities straight. He asked me to come home, so we could discuss the matter properly.'

'And?' Jed waited for her reply, praying she'd held out against him.

'I told him no way did I want to discuss the matter while we were both so angry, and I would see him tomorrow. He got quite insistent and said if I didn't come home, maybe he'd go to Wildflower Farm and drag me back.'

'He said what?' Jed was incensed. 'Who the hell does he think he is?'

'He didn't mean it,' she said. 'He was sounding off. He does that when he's in the wrong. He gets all defensive. I called his bluff anyway. I told him by all means to go the farm. I said Eliot was in exactly the right mood to meet him.' She gave a wry smile. 'That changed his mind. He said he'd see me tomorrow and hung up.'

'Did you call Eliot back?'

She took a deep breath. 'Indeed I did.'

'I'm guessing it didn't go well?'

'You could say that. I tried to explain it was Deborah pulling the strings, but I think he was past listening. He's in a real state. He told me he'd thought I was a friend, but clearly he'd been wrong about that, and to stay away from Wildflower Farm.' Her lip trembled. 'He hung up on me again.'

'He did what?' Jed quivered with rage. 'Wait 'til I get my hands on him! Who does he think he's talking to! He's got no right—'

'He's in pain, Jed,' Beth said, 'and he's scared. You have no idea how long he's dreaded this day, or how much George means to him. I understand how he's feeling, really I do.'

Jed shook his head. 'You're a kind soul, Beth. I'm not sure I'd be so forgiving.'

'You would if you knew him like I know him. We've been friends a long time. I know what he's been through, remember? This will be killing him. Poor Eliot.'

The waiter returned with their wine. 'Are you ready to order now?'

Jed glanced at Beth. 'We can go up to our room if you're not hungry. Or if you want to go home—'

She gave him a determined smile. 'Not at all. This is our night and we're going to enjoy it. Let's have a look at this menu.'

****

Emerald pushed open the farmyard gate, surprised to see the lamplight shining from the living room window. At that time of night — eleven o'clock — the Harlands were usually fast asleep in bed, and she knew Jed was out.

She grinned to herself, wondering how his night of passion with Beth was going. He'd confided his plans to her and had seemed so excited. She hoped things would work out for them. Her smile faded, and she frowned. She shouldn't really wish for that, given Beth was James's wife, but then again, he'd made it quite clear, that evening, that they were hardly happily married. If they were, he wouldn't have made his feelings toward Emerald so patently obvious.

She shivered as she approached the farmhouse door, remembering the dreadful awkwardness of the evening. She'd played dumb when James told her that Beth was babysitting for the Harlands and asked her why they hadn't approached her to mind their children, given that she was living with them.

'Heavens,' she'd trilled, 'as if they'd ever trust me with their precious offspring! And, really, do you imagine I'd have said yes to a whole day and evening alone with the little — darlings?'

He'd had to admit he couldn't really see her as the babysitting type. 'So, what will you do while Beth's caring for the kids?'

'I don't know,' she admitted. ' I shall find something else to occupy me. I may go into Richmond or something. See a film perhaps.'

'And what about your brother? Doesn't he qualify as a babysitter either?'

Emerald had thought fast. 'He's going to Harrogate that day. He's meeting up with some of his musical contacts. They're discussing the possibility of working together at some point, so he won't be back until the following day.'

It had been a stroke of genius, in her opinion, and she'd passed the suggestion for an alibi onto Jed, who had used it on Eliot and Eden. So, James was pacified and had come up with a suggestion of his own. 'Since Beth's going to be away all night, why don't we take the chance to get away from here? Have some fun. We could still see a film, if that's what you want, and get some dinner.'

Emerald thought that sounded like a wonderful plan. For one thing, she'd relish the chance of going somewhere different, for another it would give her the chance to keep James occupied, so he didn't bother Beth while she was away with Jed. 'Excellent idea! I'd enjoy that. Where did you have in mind?'

'What about Leeds? We could make a whole day of it. Do some shopping, have lunch. What do you think?'

Emerald thought. She could see no reason not to make a day of it, and Leeds did have a huge variety of shops, after all. Surely, there'd be something to interest her? There was one thing worrying her, though.

'As friends, you mean?'

He'd widened his eyes, looking astonished. 'Of course as friends. I wouldn't dream of suggesting anything else.'

She'd nodded. 'Oh, well, in that case. Yes, why not? It will be fun.'

And it had been, she thought, rummaging in her bag for her key. They'd had a wonderful day in Leeds, and James had been surprisingly accommodating while she dragged him around various shops with weird and wonderful names that had quite obviously bemused him. The heavy smell of incense that pervaded each one of them had apparently given him a headache, but he stoically waited while she sniffed oils and candles, flicked through books, and admired various items of jewellery, bearing symbols and motifs that clearly mystified him.

'What on earth are you doing now?' he demanded, as she closed her eyes, hand hovering over a shelf packed with boxes of stones.

'Waiting for a crystal to choose me,' she explained.

She'd heard him tut, but he hadn't said a word as her hand

finally closed over a stone and she opened her eyes, smiling as she realised she was holding a chunk of yellow citrine.

'Perfect,' she told him. 'It releases negativity, attracts abundance, and helps with manifesting a goal. Just what I need.'

James rolled his eyes. 'If you say so,' he said. 'Now, would you like to go somewhere normal? Like Harvey Nichols or somewhere like that?'

Emerald wondered if he had any soul at all. He'd offered to buy her some Louboutin shoes, but she'd refused, politely but firmly. She hardly thought that was appropriate. Besides, she preferred the lump of citrine, bought for less than the price of a coffee, but infinitely more interesting than shoes.

They'd had a light lunch, then caught a movie which had been surprisingly funny and had made them both laugh out loud. They'd left the cinema in a very good mood and headed to the restaurant in a rather expensive hotel, where James had made reservations.

It was during dinner that he'd got a bit odd, and his whole attitude seemed to change. They hadn't even been served the main course when James informed her, in what she imagined he thought was a seductive tone, that he'd ordered room service for them the following morning, so they wouldn't have to leave their room for breakfast.

'*Our* room? Don't you mean *your* room? Or my room, even, but certainly not *our* room.'

He'd smiled at her and said, 'Oh, come on, Emerald. We're both grown-ups. We know what's going on here, don't we?'

Emerald was appalled. 'I thought we were here as friends?'

'As friends?' James had gaped at her, clearly astonished that she'd believed his line. 'You were serious?'

'Of course I was bloody serious! You're a married man, for God's sake!' Emerald pushed the thought of Beth and Jed away for a moment and clung to her new-found morality. It was far more comfortable than accepting the main reason she couldn't possibly think of sleeping with James Fuller — that she simply didn't fancy him, and she only had eyes for Eliot.

No matter how pleasant or charming James might be, he wasn't in the same league as the dark and deeply masculine farmer, and never could be. Why Eliot was so appealing to her, she couldn't say. He certainly wasn't her usual type, and he was hardly big on flattery, or even conversation, but there was something irresistible about a tall, rugged, man's man, with a heart of gold and a streak of genuine kindness in him. Eliot might not say much, but he was always sympathetic to her and seemed to truly understand how she felt.

Plus, she'd seen him with his children, and couldn't deny that the obvious depths of his love for them was a huge turn-on. Maybe it was because Cain had been so sadly lacking in parental skills that she found the thought of a man who was an excellent father so appealing. James simply couldn't compete. No man could.

'I seem to have got this all wrong,' James muttered, pushing away his half-eaten starter of poached oysters.

'Yes, I rather think you have.' Emerald hurriedly mopped up her own starter of lobster tails in butter sauce and glanced regretfully at the menu, thinking of the two courses she was going to have to miss out on. 'I should be going.'

'You don't have to go. Can't we discuss this?'

'I really think,' Emerald said, 'that we should perhaps leave it for today, don't you? Obviously, we're at cross purposes and I don't think now's the best time to discuss our relationship. Let's leave it and cool off.'

She wanted to escape, quite frankly. Why had she ever believed he wanted nothing from her but friendship? She was an idiot! But then, to be fair, not many men seemed that interested in her. She supposed she should be flattered. She *was* flattered. If Eliot hadn't been in the picture, she'd probably have dismissed the thought that James was married, if she was being honest. He was a good-looking man in his own way. She could do a lot worse. But he wasn't a farmer with flashing dark eyes and raven curls and unbearably kissable lips. She had to go home.

'I'm very sorry.'

James threw his napkin on the table and half rose. 'I'll take you home.'

Emerald held up her hand in horror. 'No, not at all! Stay the night. You've ordered your meal and you've booked a room. I'll get a taxi.'

'A taxi!' James looked astonished. 'From here to Beckthwaite? Have you any idea how much that will cost?'

Emerald hadn't, but she had Cain's credit card sitting in her purse, so she wasn't overly bothered. 'It really doesn't matter, and I'd much prefer it if you stayed here and finished your meal. Please don't worry about me. I'll be fine.' Her tone was firm, and James evidently recognised she meant what she said, as he sat down again looking quite glum.

Emerald had waited outside the restaurant, hovering in the doorway and scanning the street for an approaching taxi. Luckily, it didn't take long, and she was soon on her way home, accompanied by a delighted taxi driver who obviously couldn't believe his luck at landing such a whopping fare.

As Emerald let herself into the farmhouse, she decided she would have to have a chat with James and clarify the situation. She'd have to be fair but firm. She wasn't looking for any sort of romantic entanglement with him. The truth was, he'd been nice to her and she'd needed that — had responded to it. Maybe she'd responded too much.

She frowned. Was this *her* fault? Had she led him on in some way? Then she tutted. He was the one who was married, and she couldn't remember ever making a single seductive or suggestive remark. He was obviously trying his luck.

She wished Eliot would try *his* luck.

Talking of Eliot ... Emerald was taken aback to discover he was still up, despite looking desperately tired. He was glaring at the television as if it was being offensive. Emerald glanced over at the screen. Since it was one of George's Disney DVDs playing, she hardly thought it merited that murderous expression.

'You're back then?' He barely looked in her direction, and Emerald tried very hard not to feel hurt. Something was bothering him. 'Thought you were out for the night.'

'I was thinking of it,' she admitted. 'In the end, though, I decided to come home. I got a taxi.'

'Huh.' He gave an absent nod, and Emerald thought he must really be distracted. Any other time he would have thrown up his hands in horror at the thought of spending all that money on a taxi from Leeds.

'Is something wrong?' she queried. 'You look ever so — well — *odd*.' The word she was searching for wasn't really *odd*, but she didn't like to offend him by choosing grumpy, miserable, angry, grouchy, pissed off, or his own favourite expression, *mardy*.

'Happen you'd look a bit odd an' all if you'd had the news I've had today.' His tone was flat, but at least he was responding. Emerald felt quite cheered.

Bella uncurled herself from the armchair where she'd been sleeping and padded over to Emerald, who automatically crouched down and rubbed her between her ears.

'What's happened?' Had he found out something awful about Eden? She could only hope. Maybe the woman had done the decent thing and called the wedding off? No, that would be too much to ask. She had to be realistic.

'Dun't matter. Forget I said owt.' He stood, looking defeated.

Emerald forgot all about point-scoring. She stood, too, placing her hand on his arm.

'Seriously, Eliot, what is it? You look dreadful.'

He eyed her dubiously for a moment, then he sighed and sat down again. 'You may as well know, since you're under this roof and can hardly avoid hearing about it. Reckon it's gunna be a big topic of conversation round here. Mind,' he added warningly, 'I don't want this going outside the house, you understand? This is Wildflower Farm business and no one else needs to know. Right?'

'Of course,' Emerald agreed, feeling increasingly worried for him. 'Whatever you say.' She felt ridiculously flattered that he was trusting her with this big secret, whatever it was, and sank into the sofa beside him, trying to dismiss the instant frisson of excitement she experienced as her arm brushed his.

'This is hard for me to say,' he told her, and she squeezed his arm in sympathy, leaving her hand in place for far longer than necessary. 'Fact is, very few people know the truth about this.'

He ran a hand through his curls and Emerald swallowed hard. 'It's about George.'

Emerald was so surprised she dropped her hand. 'George? What's he done?'

'He a'n't done owt,' Eliot snapped. 'Unless you count being born into a right bloody mess, poor bairn.'

Emerald blinked as she tried to translate. 'I'm sorry, I'm not following.'

'There's no easy way to say this, so I'll come straight out with it. Georgie — he's not my lad.'

His eyes stared into hers, almost challengingly, as if he were daring her to say something flippant. Emerald couldn't reply for a moment, she was so astonished. Of course, thinking about it, George was nothing like Eliot, or his sisters who shared their father's dark curls and deep brown eyes, but she'd simply assumed — when she thought about it at all — that he took after his mother.

'Then whose child is he?' she managed eventually. 'Is he adopted?'

'Nah!' Eliot tutted. 'He's Jemima's son, all right. Jemima's and James Fuller's.'

Emerald's mouth dropped open. 'James Fuller! You mean, he slept with your wife?'

'Weren't much sleeping going on, from what I can gather,' he said bitterly. 'At it like rabbits for over a year, and Georgie is the result.' He rubbed his chin. 'So now you know.'

Emerald was quiet for a moment, digesting this unexpected piece of news, barely noticing when Bella leapt onto her lap. So, James had form? Foolishly, she'd flattered herself that she was the first woman he'd been tempted by since his marriage to Beth. Clearly, she was one in what was probably a long line. She should have known. When was she ever that special?

To her surprise, she realised tears were pricking her eyes. Why on earth was she so upset about it? *I'm not upset*, she told herself fiercely, *just disgusted that I let myself believe he wanted me.*

Men, after all, never wanted Emerald. It was just the way it was. And what did she care, anyway? She didn't want him either. Still, the humiliation scorched her face, and she blinked away the tears, staring down at the contented form of Bella until she regained control of her emotions.

'I'm sorry,' she said at last. 'It must have been so difficult for you.'

'Aye, you could say that.' He gave an abrupt laugh. 'He was only four weeks old when Jemima died. Fuller didn't want to know him. I took him on, and I've loved that lad as my own ever since.' He glared at her, as if daring her to contradict him. 'No one can say I've treated him any different to my lasses.'

'I'm sure they couldn't,' she agreed. 'But I'm not sure why you're telling me this now?'

Eliot blinked, clearly realising that he hadn't made himself very clear. 'Letter came today from some fancy solicitor,' he told her, his voice sounding choked. 'Fuller wants custody of my lad. He's going to take Georgie away from me.'

Instinctively, Emerald put her arm around his shoulders. 'Oh, Eliot. I'm so sorry. But why? What on earth's made him change his mind?'

'No one ever knows with James Fuller.'

Eden's voice made Emerald glance around, but she didn't move away from Eliot. To her dismay, though, he more-or-less shrugged her off.

'I was telling Emerald about the letter,' he said, quite unnecessarily, as it was pretty obvious what they'd been discussing.

Eden shot her a look of pure venom, which quite cheered Emerald up.

'It's awful,' she said, her voice loaded with sympathy. 'I can't believe it. Have you contacted James Fuller? Asked what's going on?'

As if! She knew perfectly well that Eliot loathed James and the feeling was mutual. At least this cleared up what the bad blood was between them.

'No, but we contacted Beth,' Eden said as she curled up in an armchair opposite them. She was wearing pyjamas with a picture of Winnie-the-Pooh on the front. How seductive. Not. 'She got in touch with him. He reckons it wasn't his idea, but his mother's. She's found out about George and she'd determined to get him back.'

'Makes no odds whose idea it were,' Eliot snarled. 'Fact remains, they want my lad and they're not getting him. No bloody way. And Beth keeping quiet, giving me no warning, when she could have tipped me off about it days ago, didn't help.'

'She did that?' Emerald screwed up her nose, surprised. After what James had told her about Beth getting Eden to let her see the children behind Eliot's back, maybe she shouldn't be so surprised, though. It occurred to her that maybe Beth wasn't as sweet and innocent as she made out. Maybe Jed should tread carefully.

'Told Eden,' he said. 'I wasn't important enough to be told, apparently.'

Eden sighed. 'You know it wasn't like that. I've told you, and so has she. She was trying to protect you. She didn't want to worry you unnecessarily. She thought she'd dissuaded James from going ahead or she'd have told you straightaway.'

'She should have told me straightaway no matter what,' Eliot snapped. 'I can't forgive her for this. I could have got a solicitor onto this days ago. Caught us on the back foot now. I can't trust her any more. She's a Fuller, when all's said and done, and any truce we had is over. This is war.'

Emerald frowned. So, it was okay for Eden to keep it from Eliot to stop him from worrying, but not Beth? How was that fair? And Eden was saying nothing to defend her so-called friend either. Look at her, sitting there as if butter wouldn't melt! Once again, little-Miss-Perfect had got off scot-free while others suffered. Could that bitch do no wrong?

As Eliot rubbed his face, clearly stressed, Emerald pushed all thoughts of hatred for Eden away and focused on the matter in hand. So, James Fuller thought he could make a fool of her? Thank God she hadn't fallen for his lies. How bad would she be feeling now if she *had* slept with him? Well, he wasn't going to get away with making an idiot of her, nor of threatening Eliot's happiness.

'You're going to need a solicitor,' she told Eliot. 'A good one.'

'Oh, aye. Like we can afford that,' he said, throwing up his hands in despair.

'Maybe you can't, but I know someone who can,' she said, taking out her mobile phone. 'I won't take any arguments,' she added as he began to protest, 'and once he knows what's going on, neither will my father. James Fuller won't know what's hit him.'

Chapter 27

Cain couldn't believe his luck. He'd been wracking his brains all week for an excuse to head back up to Yorkshire, without making Connie feel that he was pressuring her. After all, it had only been a week since their last meeting. He didn't want to come across as needy, but now he could truthfully tell her he was here on business. He didn't have to mention it was family business, after all, and for some reason it was important to him that there was an element of truth in his words. He didn't like lying to her. She'd had enough of being lied to. This was a godsend, giving him a legitimate reason to be back in Skimmerdale.

As he drove through Kirkby Skimmer, heading towards The Paradise Hotel, the blood pounded in his veins at the thought of meeting up with Connie again. It had felt like forever.

He'd thought about texting her many times, but he'd always managed to stop himself from doing so. He didn't want to come across as clingy. Besides, what could he do about his unexpected longing to be with her? Not much use when he was in the Cotswolds and she was in — well, wherever the hell she was. Although they'd exchanged phone numbers, they'd sort of reached an agreement that there'd be no contact between them unless he was in Skimmerdale. Well, now he was, and he couldn't wait to dump his stuff in his hotel room and send her a message. First, though, there was the little matter of James bleeding Fuller to deal with.

Cain could hardly believe what Emerald had told him on the

phone and had insisted that Eden speak to him to confirm what was said. It hadn't pleased Emerald at all, but he didn't care. This was way too important to act upon without getting to the truth of the matter. Eden had, however, explained concisely that this Fuller bloke was, indeed, George's natural father, that he was threatening court action to obtain custody of the little fella, and that Eliot was beside himself.

Well, that wasn't surprising. Who'd have thought it, though? He'd kept that quiet. They all had. Well, no one was going to drop this bombshell on the Harlands and run. Not while he was around. They'd had enough to deal with.

Having unpacked, showered and changed, Cain finally allowed himself the pleasure of sending a text message to Connie:

⊠ Guess who's back in town! Fancy another trip to Paradise? J xxx

He stared at his phone for a good five minutes, but no response came. What if she'd gone off him? What if she'd found someone else in his absence? He dropped onto the bed, wondering what it was that horrified him the most — the thought of her shagging some random geezer, maybe in another room down the corridor, perish the thought, or how desolate the fact that she may have moved on made him feel.

None of that lark, Cain, he told himself firmly. *This is fun. There's plenty more fish in the sea.*

'Maybe so, mate,' he muttered to himself, 'but I ain't exactly dangling the best bait these days. Flaming lucky to have landed a catch like Connie.'

He threw a last, despairing glance at the phone, which remained resolutely silent, then grabbed his jacket and shoved the obstinate gadget into his pocket, where it immediately began to vibrate against his hip.

Cain nearly dropped the damned thing in his hurry to read the message, then scowled and shoved it back in his pocket as he registered that it was from Emerald:

⊠ Are you in Yorkshire yet? We're waiting for you so don't let us down!

Not so much as a kiss! Emerald wasn't the emotional sort, he thought. He wasn't sure she knew how to show affection. He'd certainly never witnessed it. He wondered if she was more loving towards her mother but couldn't imagine she would be. He thought it would be almost impossible to give hugs and kisses to someone whose lifestyle choices forced you to shit in a bucket.

It seemed to take forever to drive to Wildflower Farm, and the continued silence from his jacket pocket made the journey drag even more. He was relieved to pull into the farmyard at last and had recovered enough from his despair to hope that Eden had done some baking. He could fancy one of her cheese scones, or ginger cake squares. No one could bake like Eden. He wished he'd appreciated her skills more, back when she was working for him.

'Cain!' Eden threw open the door, as if she'd been looking out for him, which gratified him somewhat. 'I'm so grateful you came. It's really good of you.'

She embraced him and murmured in his ear, 'Go careful. Eliot's very touchy about this and if he seems a bit narky with you, ignore him.'

Ignoring Eliot when he was being narky was a gift Cain had already cultivated, so he merely squeezed Eden's arm and followed her into the farmhouse.

Expecting to find a house full, he was surprised, and a bit miffed if he was being honest, to discover that the kitchen was empty. Eden ushered him into a chair and immediately began to make him a cup of tea, which is what Eden always did.

'How about a slice of coffee and walnut cake? Or I've baked some of the ginger cake you love if you prefer?'

Cain sagged against the back of the chair, feeling soothed. 'Now you're talking, darls. A square of that will do nicely — two if you can spare them. I need to stock up while I'm here.'

Eden grinned and reached into the top cupboard, taking out a large vintage-style cake tin, cheerily decorated with pictures of cupcakes. She passed it to him, and he peered in, delighted to find it full of the delicious ginger cake squares he so loved. Helping himself to a couple of squares and nodding his thanks as Eden placed a small plate in front of him, he took a bite of the cake before he'd even thought to enquire where everyone was.

Eden managed to decipher his words through the cake. 'Jed's in the lambing shed. They're tagging and marking the lambs, ready to turn them outside, but they know you're on the way, so they'll be in any moment. Emerald's disappeared. She muttered something about having something to do and then left.'

'Bleeding cheek of her!' Cain took out his mobile phone and waved it at Eden. 'She's the one who texted me, demanding that I get my sorry arse here on time, and she's only done a bunk! I'll never fathom that girl.' He cast a sly glance at the screen of his phone, but it showed no texts had been received. Bugger it.

'Tell me about it,' Eden said, rolling her eyes. 'I have to say, Cain, she's a nightmare to live with. I mean, Honey was horrible, too, but at least she had the excuse of being younger. Emerald's twenty-seven, for goodness' sake. She should have learned some manners by now.'

'Yeah, I know. I reckon Cassandra failed to teach her any at all,' he said with a big sigh, then shovelled half a cake square into his mouth. 'You know,' he added, through a mouthful of ginger cake, 'I really do appreciate you keeping her here for me. Gawd knows what I'd have done with her. Can you imagine me and her clashing at home?' He shuddered and swallowed. 'Don't bear thinking about — living with Emerald.'

'No,' she said sarcastically. 'It doesn't.'

'How's she getting on with this wedding lark anyway?' he enquired, looking longingly at the cake tin and wondering whether he dared risk another square. He didn't want to be accused of being greedy, after all. 'Everything going to schedule?'

Eden looked as if she wasn't sure quite how to answer. Eventually she said, in a voice heavy with meaning, 'I believe so.'

Cain peered at her. 'You don't sound too thrilled about it.'

'It's just—' Eden handed him his mug of tea, '—to be honest, she doesn't tell us much. She created this mood board, as I told you before, so we know the colour scheme. We know the wedding reception's at The Paradise Hotel, and we've seen a sample of menus. Other than that… we don't know which menu she chose, what car or photographer we're having, nothing really. I didn't even get to choose my own bouquet. She's keeping us in the dark. She's taken all the fun out of it.'

'But it's your wedding!'

'Try telling our Wedding Planner Supreme that. She knows it all and she's doing what's best for us. It's like that programme where they keep it a secret from the bride, only in this case the groom's none-the-wiser either. This is your fault you know.'

'Mine?' Cain was wounded.

'You remember you told her that she was to make all the decisions for us because we had enough on our plates? Well, she took that literally, so thanks a lot.'

'Jesus. I meant for her to tell you what she'd done!' Cain was appalled. He'd only meant for Emerald to take the weight from their shoulders, not keep the details of their own wedding from them. Little git. Maybe he'd made a big mistake giving Emerald that credit card. This could be the hippy wedding from hell.

He could see it now — psychedelic wedding outfits, daisy chains instead of headdresses, a genuine nineteen-sixties Volkswagen camper van instead of a limo, and some beatnik weirdo with a Beatles haircut and a string of love beads taking the photos with his Box Brownie. Nah! This was going to be a nightmare. He'd have to set Emerald straight.

As if his thoughts had conjured her up, his middle child walked through the kitchen door, carrying a bulging bag on her shoulder.

'You're here,' she said, which Cain thought was stating the bleeding obvious. 'I didn't think you'd make it so soon.'

'Evidently,' he said, 'since you couldn't even be bothered to be here on time.'

Emerald's face fell, and he saw the welcoming light in her eyes die, to be replaced by a cold stare.

'Hello to you, too.'

'Never mind all that. I've bin hearing from Eden that you're taking over this wedding and doing everything you want without keeping them in the loop. Well, you can pack that in right now. I ain't having no hippy dippy types ruining things for Eliot and Eden, and that's a fact.'

Emerald gaped at him. 'Hippy dippy types? What on earth are you talking about?'

'Don't be giving me no flannel, Emerald. I know you and your weirdo mates. All that crystal therapy and wacky baccy and joss sticks. This is their wedding, not yours. It's to be done with taste, right? It ain't gunna be no freaky love-in, so whatever you've got planned, forget it.'

Emerald drew herself up in clear indignation. Cain was reminded of a swan that had once threatened him when he got too near its family, while out fishing on Freya's father's lake. It had reared up out of the water, flapping its wings at him quite threateningly. He'd nearly shit himself, while Freya, who was smoking a fag a few feet away, dressed in hideously expensive country casuals, had almost pissed herself laughing at his panic. Now his daughter was fixing him with the same alarming stare. Cain gulped.

'For your information I've gone to great pains to ensure this wedding will be everything that Eliot and Eden could wish for, while also taking account of *your* specific demands.' She slammed the bag on the table. 'And these are for you, by the way. I went to the village to get some for you, since Eliot doesn't have any in the house.'

Cain peered into the bag and was surprised, and a little ashamed, to see eight cans of his favourite beer inside. She'd lugged them all the way from Beckthwaite? 'Er, well, that's —'

He broke off as his phone beeped, and his heart began to thump most erratically. He grabbed it and almost proclaimed out loud at the sight of Constance's name on the screen, but luckily remembered himself in time and clamped his mouth shut.

'Oh, you're very welcome!' He was vaguely aware of the sarcasm in Emerald's voice, but he was too busy reading the message to pay much attention:

✉ If anyone can take me to Paradise, it's you. Just say when. C

Cain felt a familiar tingling in his nether regions. Suddenly, the wedding plans didn't seem important any more. 'Er, where were we? Oh yeah, so, this business with the custody battle. What's the state of play?'

Eden fished in a drawer and brought out a letter, which she handed to him. Cain read it in silence trying to put thoughts of the lovely Constance out of his head in order to concentrate. Dimly he was aware of Emerald flouncing out of the room. Evidently, he'd ruffled her feathers. Just like that evil swan.

'I still can't believe it,' he said, shaking his head as he handed the letter back to Eden. 'You kept all this very quiet, didn't you? Fancy Eliot not being George's dad! Can't believe it.'

'It wasn't my place to tell anyone,' she pointed out, 'and besides, he's quite paranoid about people finding out. He seems to think that if it becomes general knowledge, somehow that will make George less his.' She sighed. 'He's suffering badly, Cain. If there's anything you can do—'

'I can tell how bad it must be for him. The fact that he's agreed to me paying for a solicitor says it all,' Cain said.

'Well, you can imagine how it would be if someone wanted to take one of your children away from you.'

He could, and the thought wasn't an altogether unpleasant one. Anyway, hadn't his ex-wives and girlfriends all done that to him? Lowri, Cassandra, Sandy — they'd all whisked the kids off out of his life. Even Freya had taken Honey for a while, though she'd soon given her back when she'd had enough. This though was different. He could see how it would affect Eliot Harland, and how much impact it would have on the whole family, not least those little girls of his.

'I take it the kids don't know?'

She shook her head. 'Of course not, and we want it to stay that way for as long as possible. It's too much for them to take in. They're so young.' She looked at him through eyes bright with tears. 'Do you think you can help, Cain?'

'Well, the first thing is to get a good solicitor around here, and

I'm pretty sure that will be easy to do.' He hesitated. 'I don't suppose this James Fuller is the sort that could be frightened off? Only, I do have contacts—'

'Cain!'

He shrugged. 'Just a thought, darls. There's always bribery, of course. How much do you reckon it would cost to make him back off?'

Eden sank into a chair beside him. 'Money won't do it. They're loaded. You should see their house, Thwaite Park, for a start. It's going to have to be done properly, legally. Unless—'

'Unless what?'

'Well,' Eden said, somewhat hesitantly, 'Beth seems to think that this is all down to James's mother, rather than James himself. The solicitor who sent the letter is hers, not his, so maybe she's right. Perhaps — perhaps she could be reasoned with? If someone talked to her, explained things.'

'Well have you tried? Why don't you and Eliot go round to Thwaite Park and—'

'No way.' Eden reared away from him. 'Look, the way things are between us and the Fullers, I sincerely doubt that any talking would get done. One look at James and I honestly think Eliot would lose control. The last thing we need is an assault charge on top of a custody battle.'

'What about Beth? Couldn't she have a word? I take it she's on your side?'

'Yes, she is, but that's not an option. She's terrified of Deborah.'

'Bit of a dragon, is she?'

'I've never met her, but Beth really doesn't get on with her. She says she's a cold, unemotional sort of woman, very disapproving. She doesn't like Beth and makes it obvious. Barely cracks a smile from what I've heard.'

'Great. Lovely home they want to take little George into.'

'Exactly! Can you imagine him cocooned down there at Thwaite Park with those awful people, after he's lived here in all this chaos and noise and laughter and — and so much love.' Eden's voice cracked, and she ran a hand through her hair. 'We can't lose him, Cain, we can't. He'd be so frightened. So lonely. And the girls...'

310

'All right, darls, I get the picture.' He patted her hand, then looked up as the door opened and a very grubby, sweaty-looking Eliot and Jed entered the kitchen.

Cain held up his hands as Jed came over to hug him. 'Best not, son. Have you seen the state of yourself? Jesus, I know I told you to help out, but you've really got stuck in, ain't you?'

'He's a good worker,' Eliot said, his tone gruff. He watched Cain through narrowed eyes, and Cain realised he was dying to ask if Cain would be able and willing to help with this custody battle but didn't dare in case the answer was negative.

'Good. That's what I like to hear,' Cain said, nodding at Jed. 'Country life suits you. You're looking a lot better.'

'I feel a lot better.' Jed grinned at him. 'I love it here. I love the rural life. I love — everything.'

'Yeah, steady on, mate,' Cain muttered. 'You'll be singing *All Things Bright and Beautiful* next. Wish some of your happiness would rub off on your sister.'

'Emerald?' Jed looked around. 'Is she not back from the village yet? She was real pleased you were coming up to see us. She went off to get you some beers as a welcome gift.'

Cain felt a bit uncomfortable. She'd been pleased? Christ, he hadn't exactly gone overboard with the greetings, had he? He'd have to seek her out later, apologise.

Eliot went over to the sink and washed his hands and arms while Eden poured two further cups of tea. Jed followed suit and they all sat round the table staring at each other.

Cain decided something was needed to break the ice, so he reached for another ginger cake square and announced, 'Great cake, this.'

'I gave Cain the letter,' Eden told Eliot. 'He's going to get a top solicitor onto it — the best in the region.'

Cain shrugged. 'Probably the second best. Let's face it, Lady Snooty Drawers will have hired the best. Still,' he chewed thoughtfully on his cake, 'if worst comes to worst and they're all clueless, I'll get my London solicitor onto it. It would probably scare the bejesus out of them. Might even be a better plan, come to think of it.' He considered the matter.

311

'It won't be cheap,' Eliot said carefully.

'Course it won't, and I know you're going to say that I can't possibly do that, and you can't take charity and—'

'No,' said Eliot. 'I was going to say thanks.'

There was a silence as everyone digested this unexpected development. Blimey, thought Cain, the poor bloke really was desperate. He must idolise that kid.

'Cain wondered if perhaps Beth could talk to Deborah.'

'That won't happen,' Jed said immediately.

They all looked at him and he cleared his throat. 'I mean, from what we've heard, Deborah's a bit of a bitch, right? Beth certainly doesn't seem too fond of her, and I guess the feeling's mutual. She might be the worst person to speak to her. Probably make things worse, if anything.'

'Hmm. Perhaps you're right. And apparently Fuller territory is off limits to Harlands.' Cain put down his cake and let out a loud and rather satisfying belch. 'I dunno. This is like some western or sumfink. You know, guns at dawn and all that rubbish. Right, well, it seems there's only one solution, and I don't mean sending Emerald over enemy lines.'

He laughed to himself at the very thought, although maybe it wasn't such a crazy idea after all. One look from his venomous daughter and even this snotty bint might turn to stone. 'I'll have to have a word with her myself.'

'You!' Three voices chorused in clear disbelief, leaving Cain mortally offended.

'Do you mind? I can be tactful and diplomatic. Do you think I've survived forty odd years in the music business without knowing when to keep me flaming mouth shut? I could tell you things that would make your hair curl, but I won't.' At least, he thought, not until some publisher somewhere made him a substantial offer for his autobiography. Then all bets were off.

'Are you sure about this, Dad?' Jed sounded doubtful.

Cain tutted. 'Leave it with me. I'll go over to Thwaite Park first thing tomorrow morning and have a reasonable discussion with the snooty bag. I can turn on the charm when I want, and I promise, I'll have her eating out of my hand by the time I leave.'

312

At their stony silence, he threw up his hands in defeat. 'Look, I can but try. The way I see it, we may as well try diplomacy before we go to war. That's what all the great leaders do, innit? If that fails, believe me, I'll be calling in the big guns, but first let's see if we can settle this between us, nice and friendly like.'

'I guess you're right,' Jed admitted. 'It would be better, surely, if this could be sorted without lawyers getting involved.'

Cain nodded, satisfied. 'Exactly.' He glanced at Eden, patting his stomach hopefully. 'Don't suppose you've got any of them nice cheese scones, darls?'

****

Cain whistled to himself as he drove slowly down the driveway of Thwaite Park. He wasn't sure what era the house was from, not being an aficionado of such things, but he suspected it was quite old. Maybe Georgian or something like that. It was a large, square house, with a pleasing symmetry to it. Compared with the farmhouse at Wildflower Farm it was a real showstopper, he couldn't deny it. Glancing to the left then to the right, he saw the sweeping lawns and neat gravel drive, and for the first time he began to worry. These people obviously had money. Real money. Old money, no doubt. Old money always talked. For all he knew, these Fullers were related to all the judges and barristers and solicitors in Yorkshire. This could be tricky.

Pulling up outside the front door, Cain switched off his engine, glad he'd brought his Rolls Royce with him for once. Having a legitimate reason to be in Skimmerdale he'd not bothered with a hire car. There'd have been some awkward questions if he'd turned up at the farm without his beloved Roller. Everyone knew how much he loved it. Now, as he patted the fender lovingly, he realised that it was giving him courage, and he took a deep breath and headed up the steps to the front door, telling himself that he was as good as anyone and better than most, and of course he shouldn't be going round the back like the servants used to. Possibly still did, come to that.

The doorbell was as grand as he'd have expected, with deep

booming chimes that seemed to sound from far within the house. Cain puffed out his cheeks, hoping he looked more confident than he felt. No way was he going to let some jumped up biddy tell him what to do, and no one was going to take George away from Eliot and Eden. He didn't care how much money she had, or how posh she was.

Cain's eyes widened as the heavy door swung open and he beheld, not some ancient imperious old bat, but Constance. Constance! Of all people!

'Jeff! What are you doing here? Are you mad?' She ushered him back down the steps, stopping in surprise when she saw the Rolls Royce. 'Is this yours? Good heavens!'

'Connie! What the hell are you doing here?' Cain only just managed to get his voice back, but it sounded croaky. Shock could do strange things to a body. 'Do you work here?' It didn't seem likely. God forbid she was a friend of the old biddy. 'Oh, Jesus. Don't tell me you know her!'

'Know who?' Connie blinked, clearly confused. 'You have to go, right away. If David sees you... What on earth possessed you to come to my house?'

'*Your* house?' Cain was baffled for a moment, then slowly the fog began to lift. 'You're Deborah Fuller.'

'Well, of course I am. What else would you be doing here?' She frowned. 'You really didn't know, did you? Then what are you doing at Thwaite Park? Don't tell me you're doing business with David?'

Cain swallowed. It felt as if his whole world was collapsing in on him. 'Seriously? You're James Fuller's mother?'

Deborah stiffened. 'What's James got to do with anything?'

'The Deborah Fuller who wants to take a little boy away from the man who's loved him and brought him up since he was a tiny baby?'

Now he had her full attention. Deborah's expression changed. No longer confused or anxious, her eyes hardened, and she fixed him with a furious glare. 'What's any of this got to do with you? Why are you here?'

Cain rubbed his forehead. 'I don't bleeding believe this. How

314

could you do this to me, Connie? How could you do this to Eliot and Eden? To George?'

Deborah glanced behind her at the house. 'You'd better come in,' she said, a coldness in her voice that he'd never heard before. 'If anyone asks, we've never met before today. Understood?'

Cain nodded miserably and followed her inside the house. He didn't know this version of her. She sounded hard, brittle even. Where was the loving, affectionate, passionate woman he'd grown to know and — care about. Was it all a lie? Who was this Deborah Fuller anyway?

He stared around him at the large, formal hall, his eyes widening at the sight of the broad, sweeping staircase that led to a landing where the rays of sunlight, pouring through a huge arched window, shone on the carved mahogany bannister that curved around and upwards to the next floor. The hall was lined with portraits — huge oil paintings in fancy gilt frames that were no doubt of Fuller ancestors. Rich, aristocratic Fuller ancestors.

Cain had never felt so working class and gauche. He looked at Deborah with new eyes. This was where she belonged? This was her world? Despite his own wealth, she seemed suddenly miles out of his reach. A different league. Something inside him withered and died.

She ushered him into a small, snug room, with long, shuttered windows that overlooked a formal garden. Cain sank into a chair at her bidding, feeling dazed and worried. How did he handle this?

'So, I gather you're here about our bid for custody of George. However, I still have no idea what it's got to do with you? Are you a solicitor, Jeff? Are you working for the Harlands? Please explain.'

Cain leaned forward, his voice urgent. 'Never mind all that for a minute, Con — Deborah. What about you? What's with the fake name?'

Deborah folded her arms defensively. 'Is this really the time and place?'

'I can't think of a better time or place,' he assured her, 'and I ain't leaving until I get some answers.'

She seemed to consider for a moment, glancing around her as if making sure no one was hiding behind a chair. Eventually, having apparently decided it was safe, she leaned back and gave a big sigh. 'I suppose I do owe you an explanation. As you've realised, I'm not Constance. I'm Deborah Fuller and I am, indeed, James's mother and George's grandmother.'

Cain simply stared at her, feeling miserable beyond words.

'I didn't tell you my real name when we first met because — well, for obvious reasons,' she said, waving her arms as if indicating the house, her marriage and family in that one gesture. 'Then, later, when we became lovers, it seemed more exciting. It all added to the fun, the thrill of it. I was no longer David Fuller's wife. I was somebody new, with a life of my own, and I loved it.'

Cain nodded. 'But what you told me about him, about your husband, was that true?'

Her eyes widened, and for a moment she looked like his Connie again. 'I never lied to you about anything but my name. Everything I told you was the truth. Unfortunately.'

'But what were you doing at The Paradise Hotel? Don't tell me you'd gone there to pick up a bloke?' Cain couldn't believe it. She seemed so ladylike. But she clearly hadn't been there on business, so whatever she said, that was another lie. How much could he trust her, really?

'I was supposed to be having dinner with David,' she told him. 'I was quite looking forward to it. Not spending time with him, I should add, but with being out of this house, getting away, doing something different.' She sighed. 'You have no idea how much I hate this place. It's a gilded cage.'

'So where was David then?'

'What? Oh, when he didn't arrive, I rang him to find out where he was. He'd been at a meeting in Ripon and was supposed to be meeting me at the hotel, but when I finally got through to him, he admitted he'd forgotten and had gone straight home. I was furious and told him I was at the hotel and was he going to come back for dinner? He told me he'd already eaten and couldn't be bothered to drive all the way to Kirkby Skimmer to meet me, and I should grab something to eat then come home and he'd see me later.'

'Fuck me,' Cain muttered. 'What a catch he is.'

'Exactly,' she agreed. 'I was furious. I told him I was booking a room for the night so not to expect me home, then I ended the call before he could argue. Of course, I knew I'd pay for that with days of silence, and, sure enough, I did. What David fails to realise is that I rather look forward to his epic sulks these days. Oh, it used to tear me apart. The years I spent trying to appease him. Apologising for something I'd done without even knowing what it was. The hours of just sitting there, trying to figure out what I'd said to offend him, begging him to tell me so I could put it right.' She gave a short laugh. 'I used to consider it a punishment, you see. His silence. Nowadays, I think of it as a blessing.' She gave a slight shake of her head. 'I have no idea when that started.'

For a moment she was quiet, as if lost in her thoughts, then she shrugged. 'Anyway, I was sitting at the bar, debating whether or not to get roaring drunk, when I noticed you. I thought—' she gave him an apologetic smile, 'I thought how much fun it would be if David *did* turn up and spotted me sitting with a handsome man, so I asked to buy you a drink and the rest, as they say, is history.'

Cain spluttered. 'Jesus, Debs! What if David had come back? He could have punched my lights out!'

'Yes, I know,' she mused. 'I suppose it *was* rather cruel of me.'

'So, I was just a way to get back at David — to make him jealous?' Cain felt betrayed. 'I thought we were — you know.'

'Oh, Jeff, darling, we were. We are! It was a ruse at first, I'll admit that, but I really did find you terribly attractive. And once I'd got to know you, I totally—'

'You totally what?'

'I like you. A lot.'

Cain felt soothed and rather relieved. 'Yeah, well, I like you a lot an' all. But what was with the name? Why Constance?'

She gave him a sideways look and there was a hint of a smile on her face. *'Lady Chatterley's Lover.* I couldn't resist. It all added to the naughtiness of it, somehow.'

Cain had never read *Lady Chatterley's Lover,* but he knew it was racy. He quite perked up for a moment, then remembered the reason for his visit.

'Looks like we're in a bit of a pickle here, Debs.'

'Quite. If you didn't know who I was, why are you the one who's discussing this with me? What's your connection with the Harlands?'

Cain squirmed inwardly. His turn to 'fess up. 'I'm a friend of Eden's,' he admitted. 'She used to work for me, and she's friends with my daughter. Her and Eliot, well, they're a smashing couple, and they don't deserve this. Have you any idea how devastated they'd be if they lost George?'

'But he's my grandson,' Deborah protested. 'Have you any idea how devastated *I* was to discover that he even existed, and to find that he's been living on that farm with total strangers since his birth?'

'They're not total strangers to him,' Cain pointed out. 'And that's the point, innit, Debs? They're the only family he's ever known.'

'But they're not his real family,' she said. 'They're not Fullers.'

'From what you've told me about your family, I'd say that's a good thing,' Cain said.

Deborah glared at him. 'I thought you, of all people, would understand me. I only discovered I had a grandson a few weeks ago, and yet he's four years old. Do you know how heartbreaking that is? Is it so wrong to want him to be in my life, to get to know him?'

'Course it ain't, Debs,' Cain soothed, 'but getting to know him ain't the same as taking him away from his mum and dad.'

'They're not—'

'Yeah, yeah. I know. But as far as he's concerned, they are. Fact is, from what I can gather, your son didn't want to know the little lad when he was born. George's mum had died, and he could have been left with no one to care for him if Eliot hadn't taken him on as his own. Your son walked away. I reckon he gave up the right to George at that moment.'

'James was grieving!' Deborah snapped. 'Jemima had just been killed. He was heartbroken, in shock.'

'And you think Eliot wasn't?' Cain said quietly. 'And he had two little girls to see to, an' all, who'd lost their mum, as well as a farm to run. He didn't run away though, did he? He stepped up, took George into his heart, and he's loved him like his own ever since.'

Deborah bit her lip, staring hard at the wall. 'Well,' she said eventually, 'the fact remains he's *not* his own. James didn't want to upset his wife. She can't have children, you see. It would have been insensitive to expect her to bring up another woman's child.'

'It was pretty insensitive to have an affair with a married woman,' Cain responded.

'Well, you'd know all about that!' Deborah snapped.

They stared at each other. 'You're not gunna listen to me, are you?' Cain said eventually. His heart felt heavy. Was this really how it was going to end?

'I want my grandson. We can give him a better life here. You can't deny that Thwaite Park is a far better house than Wildflower Farm. We have money. George will have the best of everything.'

'He's already got the best mum and dad and the best sisters he could possibly have,' Cain said, standing up. 'I don't see what you can offer him that could top that, and that's a fact. I thought better of you than that. Thought you understood that money wasn't everything. After the childhoods we had, I thought — oh what does it matter what I thought? I came here hoping to discuss things with you reasonably. I hoped we could do this the civilised way. I can see I was wasting my time. I'm sorry about that, Debs. You'll be hearing from my solicitor.'

'As you wish.' Deborah ushered him to the door, almost pushing him out onto the steps. 'I'm sorry it's ended this way, Jeff. I really am.'

'Actually,' he said, 'it's not Jeff.' He held out his hand in a very formal manner. 'The name's Cain. Cain Carmichael.'

For a moment she simply stared at him in astonishment, then the heavy door was slammed in his face.

Cain took a deep breath and walked slowly down the steps.

Lady Chatterley's lover was dismissed.

Chapter 28

It was with some relief that Beth stumbled upon Jed as she approached the farm. He was leaving the lambing shed, and for a moment, the sight of him as he headed towards the farmhouse left her speechless with pleasure. He was such a big, burly man, and he made her feel safe and loved. She could hardly believe that someone so kind, so loving, could be in love with her. Yet she knew he was. He gave her no reason to doubt it.

'Hey!'

Jed swung round and his face split into a huge grin. 'Hey, yourself!' He strode towards her, glancing around to make sure no one was about, then, clearly satisfied that no one was watching them, he pulled her into his arms.

For a few moments there was nothing and no one else in the world, then reality encroached, and Beth reluctantly pulled away with a sigh.

'What's wrong, baby?'

Beth lay her head on his chest, her fingers stroking the hairs peeping out above the buttons of his shirt. 'I'm here on a mission, and I'm not looking forward to it.'

Jed kissed the top of her head. 'Has this got anything to do with George?'

'It has.' She stepped back and looked at him, wishing she could spend the precious time she had at the farm with him, and him alone. But she'd promised, and this was important. 'I have a message from Deborah.'

'Right.' Jed whistled. 'Then I guess we'd better call a meeting. I think Eden's changing the sheets in the main bunk barn. I'll get her to call Eliot. You go indoors and wait.' He kissed her again, a light kiss, more for luck than anything, and headed out of the yard.

Beth gave a big sigh and headed to the farmhouse, where she found Emerald lying on a sofa, eating chocolate and flicking through a magazine.

'Busy?'

Emerald gave her a haughty stare. 'Actually, I am. I'm studying this bridal magazine for inspiration.'

'Inspiration?' Beth shook her head. 'Surely there's nothing left to do with this wedding? You've been working on it non-stop for weeks. All those meetings you keep having in Leeds and Harrogate — we're expecting something spectacular you know.'

Emerald looked distinctly uncomfortable. 'Oh, half the time things didn't work out when I went to see them in person,' she said vaguely. 'But don't worry. This wedding's going to be very memorable.'

'I hope so,' Beth said. 'They deserve the best.'

'Hmm.' Emerald put down her magazine and swung her legs round, planting her feet firmly back on the floor. 'So, what brings you here, Beth? Like I can't guess.'

Beth frowned as Emerald gave her a wink. 'I have no idea what you mean by that, but I've actually come to see the happy couple. I have a message for them.'

'Really?' Emerald sounded eager. 'From whom?'

'Well, that's for Eliot and Eden to hear,' Beth said, wondering why Emerald was taking such an interest all of a sudden. It was a little nerve wracking, to be honest.

Emerald scowled. 'Fine. I'll be upstairs in my room,' she muttered, snatching up her magazine and chocolate and stalking into the hallway.

Beth shook her head, wondering how Jed had come to have a sister like Emerald, although, from what she knew of her, Honey hadn't been much better. She hoped Jed's twin sister, Scarlett, was a bit more like him. Jed seemed very fond of her, so it would be nice to meet a sister that she got on with.

She tutted inwardly. If she ever got to meet her, that was. How could she say? She had no idea how things were going to pan out with her and Jed. This could be a holiday romance. Jed wouldn't stay here forever and when it was time for him to go, where would that leave them?

She looked up, plastering a smile on her face as Eden entered the room.

'Jed's frightened me to death,' she told Beth. 'He says you have an important message for us. I got hold of Eliot on the walkie talkie, and he's on his way back now. He and Adey were checking and repairing the meadow walls. Don't want any loose stones damaging the mower when they start harvesting, do we?' She stopped gabbling for a moment, then burst out, 'Oh, Beth, please tell me this isn't more bad news.'

'Let's wait until Eliot gets here, shall we?' Beth suggested, wishing for the thousandth time that she wasn't caught in this situation, being piggy-in-the-middle between the Harlands and the Fullers.

Eden sat on the sofa beside her and plucked at the cushion, until they heard the front door shut and the sound of heavy boots striding down the hall. Clearly, Eliot was so upset he'd forgotten to take them off, though judging by Eden's worried face, she wasn't bothered about the fact.

He looked pale with anxiety, his eyes even darker against his skin than usual. 'Go on then,' he said without preamble. 'What's this message?'

'Sit down,' she said, hoping to calm him a little. 'Don't look so worried. It's good news.'

'I'll believe that when I hear it,' he replied, but sat, nevertheless.

'I have a message from Deborah. She said to tell you that, if she is allowed to see George, to meet him properly, she will consider other options. That is, she'll discuss things with James with a view to changing their appeal for custody to regular access.'

There was silence for a moment while the Harlands digested this news. Then Eden turned to Eliot, her voice hopeful. 'Well, that's good news, isn't it?'

'I think it is,' Beth said. 'I don't believe that James wants custody and I know he's only going along with this to please his mother. If we can get Deborah to agree to access only then the battle's won. I can't think what changed her mind, but whatever it was, it's wonderful.'

They both looked at Eliot, who hadn't spoken a word.

'Eliot?' Eden raised her eyebrows.

'You think this is good news?' Eliot shook his head, dark curls bouncing. 'I think it's a bloody cheek! No deal.'

'But — but it's a good offer,' Beth began.

He got to his feet. 'How is that a good offer? The only good offer is if the Fullers bugger off and leave us alone. The sooner they get it into their thick heads that George is a Harland and nothing to do with them, the better.'

Eden sighed. 'Eliot, I understand what you're saying, but—'

'If you understand what I'm saying,' he said furiously, 'then you'll know there's no *but*. No deal. She's not going anywhere near Georgie and that's final.'

Beth glanced at Eden, hoping she'd be able to talk him round, but Eden looked defeated before she'd even tried. Evidently, she'd already recognised that Eliot was having none of it, whatever anyone said. All the same, Beth felt she had to try.

'If you don't agree to this, it will go to court, and they'll demand full custody. You don't want that, do you?'

'Let them try,' Eliot growled.

'Eliot, they have top solicitors. They have Thwaite Park. They have pots of money. And—' she hesitated, but he needed to accept the facts, 'they have a blood connection. George is James's biological son, whether we like it or not.'

'They'll have to prove it first,' Eliot said grimly.

'But they will! Of course they will. You've already had the letter demanding a DNA test. Do you think they'll let that drop? And you falsified a birth certificate.'

'So what?' Eliot snapped. 'Jemima was my wife. Any husband would assume that a child born within a marriage would be his. I'd defy anyone to prove otherwise. Why would I have thought different? I had no idea she'd been unfaithful, did I?'

'We both know that's not true,' Beth said.

'And are you going to tell the court that?' Eliot demanded.

'Of course not! I'm on your side in this.'

'Dun't sound like it.'

'I am! That's why I urge you to accept her offer. Let her meet George, let her spend time with him. I know it will be hard at first, but you'll get used to it. If she gets regular access, I think she'll be happy with that.'

'And then she'll want to tell him who she really is,' he said. 'And how do we explain that? And then it'll be weekend visits, and then holidays. Before I know it, he'll be at Thwaite Park more than he's here. I'll not have it and that's that.'

Beth sighed. 'I can see I'm wasting my time. Is that what you really want me to tell her?'

'Aye, it is.'

Eden reached for his hand. 'Eliot, please think about this.'

He snatched his hand away. 'I don't need to, and if you're really on my side you won't ask me to.'

'How can you say that?' Eden murmured, shaking her head slightly. 'I can't believe you even thought it.'

'Aye, well.' Eliot shrugged. 'If that's all, I'll get back to work. I won't be in for tea tonight,' he added. 'I'm going over to Camacker to help put pens up for't show at weekend. I'll be meeting up with t'others for a few pints and a catch-up. I'll get summat to eat at The Shepherd's Crook.'

As the front door slammed, Beth and Eden looked at each other.

'Stubborn fool,' Beth said, her voice sharp with frustration. 'This could have been settled if he'd only give an inch. Has he made all that up about the show?'

'No, he mentioned it yesterday.' Eden twisted her hands together in her lap. 'It's what they do. The farmers, I mean. Get together to prepare the pens for the first shows of the season and then have a catch-up afterwards. You can't blame them. They're so busy during lambing season that they never go anywhere.'

Even so, Beth thought she sounded rather anxious. 'Is there

something else wrong, Eden? Apart from this stuff with George?'

'No, no.' Eden tutted. 'Just me, being silly. Except...'

'Except what?'

'It's probably nothing. Just that, Eliot seems very drawn to Camacker lately, and I don't know why. Mrs Edwards spotted him there before the barns opened, and he told me it was Adey wanting to try the local ale, but Adey clearly knew nothing about it and was trying to cover for him. And he's gone missing a couple of times, which makes me think he's been in the village then, too. I mean, I don't know for sure but...' She shook her head. 'Ignore me. I'm putting two and two together and making five.'

'But you trust him?' Beth said, shocked at Eden's revelation. 'You don't think he's cheating on you?'

Eden looked genuinely stunned at the idea. 'What! Eliot? No, of course not. He'd never do that. But something's up, Beth, and I don't know what it is.' She shrugged. 'I suppose he'll tell me in his own good time. We've got more important things to worry about anyway.' She twisted her watch on her wrist, clearly agitated. 'What happens now? Do you think Deborah will go all out for custody?'

'I think she will,' Beth admitted. 'She's desperate to see George, and if she thinks Eliot's never going to allow it... It's funny, I'd have expected David to be the one demanding his rights, but he's been strangely quiet on this issue. It's all been Deborah.'

Eden hesitated. 'Beth, do me a favour? When you go back, don't tell Deborah he said no. Give me some time to work on him, please. Tell her — tell her he's thinking it over.'

'Do you think he'll change his mind?' Beth was doubtful. She'd known Eliot for a long time and knew all too well how obstinate he could be.

'I don't know,' Eden confessed, 'but I have to try to get through to him, and I don't want the door shutting before I've given it my best shot. Once she decides to proceed, we're screwed. Even Cain's solicitor thinks it's unlikely that the Fullers will get no access to George at all. Eliot's going to have to accept it, one way or the other. It would be far better for us all if he'd accept it sooner rather than later, and we could do this the pleasant way.'

'If there is a pleasant way,' Beth said with a sigh. 'All right, Eden. I'll try to hold Deborah off as long as I can, but I warn you, it won't be for long. I know her. Please, please try to make him see sense.'

Though, deep down, she knew it was hopeless. Sometimes, Eliot let his heart rule his head, and when it came to his children he was like a lion. She had an awful feeling nothing Eden said would persuade him to back down.

****

The third morning she was sick, Beth finally allowed herself to believe. She'd grown used, over the years, to checking the calendar religiously, and until then she'd never been more than a day or two late with her period.

When it failed to materialise this month, she'd run through a whole range of emotions. At first, she'd tried to dismiss it as a blip. A cruel trick of nature that she must ignore for her own sanity. As the days passed, she felt a prickle of hope that she tried to push away. The hope became a fear, as every day the dread that her hopes would be dashed grew greater. Two weeks after her period should have arrived, Beth felt the first signs of nausea, and for the last few days she'd thrown up within minutes of waking.

As she left the supermarket a few hours later, Beth clutched the pregnancy test to her chest, her heart thudding with a mixture of elation and terror. She'd wanted this for so long, and, apart from the two IVF attempts, she'd never got as far as even needing to buy a test. Now there was a very real chance that she was finally expecting the baby she longed for, but if she was wrong, if it was a false alarm...

She sat in the car for ages, staring at the box and wondering what to do. If she left the test in the car, if she ignored it, she could carry on hoping. If she did it, and it was negative, that would be it. She'd have to face up to the grief, the loss all over again. She didn't know if she was strong enough.

But if she was wrong, wasn't it better to know now? To put the thought of what could be out of her mind before it became an obsession? Beth opened the box and looked at the directions. She'd assumed the test would have to be done first thing in the morning, but no. It said she could do it any time of day, and she did need the loo, after all.

She stared out of the windscreen, watching other people hurrying through the car park, pushing trolleys, dragging reluctant children, checking receipts, struggling with carrier bags. Everything was normal to them — just another day. They had no idea that today was the day that could change everything. Or not.

Beth took a deep breath, then she pushed the test back in its bag and climbed out of the car. She almost ran back into the supermarket and found her way to the toilets, hoping there wasn't a queue. To her relief, it was empty, and she entered the cubicle, slid the lock in place and took the test from the bag, staring at it in terror.

'Just do it,' she muttered. 'You need to know, one way or the other.'

There was no going back now. As she waited for the result, Beth leaned against the cubicle wall, feeling ill. This was it. She might be pregnant. What would Jed say? She felt a sudden clutching of fear. What would James say? Oh, God! It had been so long since she felt anything for James that she'd quite forgotten that strange evening, when he'd come home in a most peculiar mood and practically dragged her to bed. It was the last time they'd had sex. She wouldn't say made love.

Frantically, she tried to remember the exact date it had happened and realised the awful truth. If she was pregnant, the baby could be James's *or* Jed's. She bit her lip. One way or the other, James was going to find out the truth about her and Jed. She wasn't looking forward to that.

She shook her head impatiently. *You're getting ahead of yourself. There isn't a baby. It's a false alarm. Stop being stupid!*

Yet her hand shook as she reached for the little white stick that lay on top of the bag on the cistern, and she closed her eyes for a moment before she dared to look.

For a moment, she stared at the little screen, then she gasped out loud. She was pregnant! There really was a baby in there. Beth pushed her knuckles into her mouth to stop herself from sobbing out loud. It had happened at last.

Life was going to get very complicated indeed, with revelations and recriminations to face. But right now, it didn't matter. No one need know. Not yet. This was her precious secret, and she wanted to enjoy it for a while, just her alone. Gently, she stroked her stomach in wonder. She was going to be a mother.

Chapter 29

'Hello?'

Eden heard the call from where she was working in the kitchen of the small bunk barn. She'd been scrubbing the oven and thinking that, really, some of these hikers were *mucky pups* as the girls would say. Goodness only knows what they'd been cooking in there. It looked as if a casserole had exploded behind that door.

Hearing the rather tentative-sounding shout from the vestibule, she hurried out of the kitchen, pulling off her rubber gloves as she went and pushing back tendrils of hair that had escaped her ponytail.

An elegant and attractive middle-aged brunette stood by the door, clutching an expensive-looking leather bag in her hands.

Eden smiled a welcome, although she couldn't imagine this visitor was interested in booking a bed for the night. Maybe she was lost, looking for directions?

'Eden Robinson?'

Okay, not lost then. 'Yes. Can I help?'

'I do hope you can.' The woman held out her hand. 'Deborah Fuller.'

Eden felt the colour drain from her face. She stared at the enemy in disbelief, making no move to take the proffered hand. What the hell was she doing at Wildflower Farm? 'What do you want?'

The woman withdrew her hand, looking offended. 'Just a little chat, that's all.'

'I thought you did all your talking through third parties,' Eden said coldly. 'You know, a solicitor, or Beth.'

'I'm here to talk, not to argue. Beth is very transparent, and it was easy to decipher that Eliot isn't so keen to reach an agreement with me, regarding access to my grandson. I was hoping we could work something out between us, rather than pursue a legal case.'

Eden didn't know what to think. It would be wonderful if this fiasco could be resolved without solicitors, but she knew the sticking point would be Eliot. He would never agree to anything this woman suggested.

'I'm sorry to disturb you at work,' Deborah murmured. 'I didn't know you had this business, or I would have made it another time.'

'You shouldn't have come to the farm at all,' Eden told her. 'If Eliot sees you...'

'I know that he's having difficulty accepting the situation,' Deborah said. 'And I can understand that, honestly. Nevertheless, you must see that I have rights. James has rights.'

Eden's eyes narrowed. 'I don't see that he has any rights. He gave up all of those when he chose to abandon George when Jemima was killed. What would have happened if Eliot hadn't wanted him either? He'd have gone into care!'

'That would never have happened,' Deborah said quickly. 'James was in shock, and he had Beth to consider. It was all very tricky.'

Eden couldn't believe the damn cheek of her. 'It was a bit more than *tricky* for poor Eliot!' she burst out. 'His wife had just given birth to a child that wasn't his, his marriage was in tatters, thanks to your son, then Jemima was killed, and he was left with two heartbroken little girls and a baby who had no one else in the world to care for him. I'd say that was bloody devastating, never mind tricky!' She gulped back the tears, not wanting to show any weakness to a Fuller, of all people.

Deborah's expression softened. 'Is there somewhere we can talk?'

'I'm too busy, and there's no one to take over.'

Deborah fiddled with the button of her jacket. 'Would you meet me later then? At a more convenient time?'

'I've got the kitchens to clean, then I have to get the tea ready for the kids and Eliot. It's impossible.'

'Please, Eden, I haven't come here for an argument.'

'Then what *have* you come here for?' Eden demanded.

'I want to make an arrangement with you.'

Eden's eyes narrowed. 'What sort of arrangement?'

'I agree with you that seeking custody of George is the wrong path to take.'

'You do?'

'Yes. However, James seems set on it, so I have to tread carefully. Now, if Eliot would agree to access—'

'But he won't.' Eden said in despair. 'He doesn't want James to have anything to do with George.'

'But he will have to realise, eventually, that he'll have no choice. James is George's natural father, and he has rights. Now, this can get as dirty as James and Eliot decide to make it. If this is about their feud, then things could get very ugly indeed. However, if they concentrate on what's best for George, it could be bearable for everyone, including that little boy.'

Eden considered the matter. 'What do you want, Deborah?'

'I know that Eliot won't allow access to George, but would you?'

Eden raised an eyebrow. 'Me?'

Deborah leaned towards her, her voice eager. 'Let me see George, Eden. Eliot need never know, I promise you. I want to see him, that's all. Get to know him a little.'

'And what would that achieve?'

'If you do this for me, I swear to you that I'll work on James. He's already got Beth against him, and so far, I've been his only support. If you let me see my grandson, I'll make sure that he drops all ideas of custody and settles for reasonable access.'

'And you think he'd do that?'

Deborah looked rather ashamed. 'I do, actually, because it was me who persuaded him to pursue this case in the first place.'

'So, it *was* you!'

Deborah reddened. 'James sprang the news on me. I was in shock. When he told me how much he was missing George, how much he longed to have him in his life but that he'd been unable to because of Beth, something snapped. I may have got a little carried away.'

'You think?' Eden said, sarcastically.

'The point is, I was the one who urged him to fight for George, and I was the one who hired the solicitor. James listens to me. Between me and Beth, I think we can get him to drop the idea of full custody.'

'But I'd have to persuade Eliot to accept access.'

'Yes. And I understand that's going to be difficult, but I can give you plenty of time. I can hold James off for months, if necessary, while you bring Eliot round to the idea.'

'As long as you get to see him in the meantime.'

'I just want contact with my grandchild. That's all. I'm not asking for much.'

Eden shook her head. 'You're asking for the world, Mrs Fuller, and I'm sorry, but you're going to be disappointed.'

Deborah sighed. 'I see. So, you won't help me? You won't listen to reason?'

'There's nothing you can say to me unless it's that you'll drop all claims to Georgie.' She rubbed her forehead, feeling exhausted suddenly. 'And you're not going to do that, are you?'

There was a moment's silence, then Deborah said, 'I'm afraid not. I'm sorry to have wasted your time, Eden.'

As she turned and left the barn, Eden slumped in despair. 'Not as sorry as I am,' she murmured.

****

Emerald was in the right mood to tackle James. He'd rung her the evening after Leeds, when she was getting into bed, asking if she'd like to meet up with him. She'd put the phone down on him, too angry to speak.

James hadn't given up. He'd rung her again the next day,

grovelling his apology about his behaviour in Leeds. Emerald wanted to demand if he really thought she was ignoring him because of Leeds? For goodness' sake, she had more about her than that. But if she'd told him so, she'd have had to tell him the real reason she was upset with him, and she couldn't do that. How could she, without revealing that she'd been foolish enough to believe she was special to him, and discovering she was another in a line of women had crushed her? It was impossible, particularly when she'd made it very clear to him that she only wanted friendship. How could someone like James possibly understand such a fragile ego? She barely understood it herself.

Instead, she'd haughtily told him she was too tired to be bothered with that conversation, then switched off her phone and tried to sleep, although it didn't come easily, which was very annoying. When she put her phone back on, there were another two missed calls and a text message from him.

✉ I'm sorry, honestly. Don't let this end our friendship. I miss you, Emerald. Paradise Hotel, tonight, 8pm? I swear I'll be the perfect gentleman. X

She'd ignored the text and hadn't kept the appointment. She had no time for him. He was a liar and a cheat, and he'd played her for a fool. She wanted nothing to do with him.

Then, a few days later, Eden had launched her attack.

She'd been in a funny mood all evening, snappy and irritable. Even the children had ducked out of her way, heading for the living room the minute they'd finished eating. Eliot had sat at the table, turning a slice of bread and butter over and over between his fingers, watching her with a bemused expression on his face, but saying nothing.

Emerald had decided she'd had quite enough of the sour-faced cow and was going upstairs to read her *Wisdom and Spirit* magazine. Jed stood up and began to collect the dishes, but Eden had leapt up and told him to leave them.

'It's no trouble,' he'd assured her, but she'd practically snatched them out of his hands.

'I don't see why you should be doing them,' she said. 'You've been hard at work all day, helping Eliot.'

'And you've been cooking, cleaning, doing the laundry and whatever else,' he pointed out. 'I think you've earned a break.'

'But *she* hasn't been doing anything!'

Emerald jumped, startled, as Eden turned the full blast of her anger upon her.

'Who's rattled your cage?'

'You have!' Eden was quivering with rage. 'Where were you today? I was flat out, and what were you doing? Sat on your fat arse somewhere reading that New Age magazine you love, I suppose?'

Emerald couldn't believe it. 'I was busy,' she spluttered.

'Busy doing nothing as usual. You do remember that your father told you to help us out? Only, you're staying here rent free and doing sod all to earn your keep from what I can see.'

'Well, that's where you're wrong,' Emerald had retorted. 'I've been very busy sorting out something for your wedding.'

'Oh, fuck the wedding!' Eden slammed the dishes back onto the table, causing the whole thing to quiver as if in fear of her temper.

Emerald glanced across at Eliot, who had dropped the bread and was now staring at Eden with evident concern. 'Are you all right, my love?'

'Do I look all right?'

'What is it? What's happened?'

Jed and Emerald exchanged looks as Eliot stood and went to put his arms around Eden.

'Nothing's happened. It's *her*!' Eden jabbed an accusing finger in Emerald's direction. 'I'm sick of her. She just sits around doing nothing, while we all work our fingers to the bone. I've had enough.'

Eliot looked choked. 'It's too much for you, isn't it? I knew it would be.'

'You're not bloody listening,' she snapped. 'This isn't about me. It's about that freeloader, doing nothing and getting away with it. She could have been in the barns today, giving me a hand, but

335

instead — oh, what's the point!'

She pulled away from Eliot's hold and stormed out of the kitchen, slamming the door behind her. Eliot stared at the door for a moment, his face pale, then he looked helplessly at Emerald and Jed.

'She's exhausted, Eliot,' Jed reassured him. 'You know, the barns are nearly fully-booked, and there were quite a few customers wanting cream teas today. I reckon she's tired out.'

'I knew it was going to be too much for her,' Eliot murmured. 'I warned her.'

'Why don't you go and see her?' Jed suggested. 'I think she could use some comforting.'

Eliot nodded and left the room and Jed had turned to Emerald, his face serious. 'You need to start pulling your weight, Emmy.'

Emerald glared at him. 'Don't tell me you're taking her side? After the way she spoke to me!'

'I'm just saying she's got a lot on her plate, and she could use a hand. You're not doing much with your days that I can see.'

'Well, that's where you're wrong,' Emerald said, feeling uncomfortable. 'This wedding takes an awful lot of planning.'

Though, not that much, she had to admit. She'd more-or-less wrapped everything up ages ago. Truthfully, she spent most of her time tripping around New Age shops in Leeds, Ripon or Harrogate. She'd stocked up on crystals and incense, and she'd found a wonderful little shop not far from Harrogate where the lady in charge read tarot cards and had given Emerald a cut-price reading, just because she had such a beautiful aura.

Emerald had been a bit nervous, but it turned out that she was about to get everything she had wished for.

'Love is coming your way, no doubt about it,' the woman told her, turning the cards and beaming at Emerald in delight. 'I see a man you care about very much. There's a veil between you right now, like he's not seeing you properly. But he will. Mark my words, he will. Ooh, you've got some right cracking cards here, love. The future you dream of is within your grasp. Mind you, you've got some obstacles to face first, but you'll do it, never fear, and then — well, a new life. That's what it is. Can't say owt less

336

than that. A whole new life and a load of love. How about that then?'

Emerald had to agree it was wonderful news, and well worth the twenty pounds she'd paid. Thank God for her father's credit card. She knew it was supposed to be for the wedding, but she'd allowed plenty for that, and she wasn't spending much — travel expenses and lunch. She'd never been a big spender, and her father couldn't complain about costs when she was taking her wedding planner duties seriously. Besides, anything was better than hanging around Wildflower Farm all day.

It would have been different if Eliot had let her help him, but he seemed to prefer to work with Jed. He was quite sexist, truth to tell. Gorgeous, but sexist. She'd have to sort him out when they finally got together, which, of course, they would. It was obvious that was what the tarot card reader was talking about. Who else could she mean?

'Emmy, are you listening to me?' Jed's voice brought her back to the kitchen at Wildflower Farm, and all thoughts of her future with Eliot popped like bubbles in the washing up bowl.

'Huh?'

Jed sighed. 'All I'm saying is, maybe make a bit more effort, huh? These guys have taken us in, and it wouldn't hurt you to help out a bit more, especially now the barns are up and running properly.'

Emerald folded her arms, feeling cornered. Jed laughed and hooked his finger under her chin, lifting her face to his. 'Hey, are you sulking?'

'Of course not!'

'Good. I knew someone as kind and mature as you wouldn't sulk.'

'Are you laughing at me?'

'Maybe, a bit. Now, how about I wash, and you dry?'

Reluctantly, Emerald agreed, and picked up a tea towel as Jed began to scrub at the dishes.

'If you're not sure what you're supposed to do with that, I can give you lessons,' he told her, nodding at the tea towel.

Emerald laughed and flicked him with the cloth. 'Cheek of it!'

Jed flicked bubbles at her and she squealed.

'Having fun?' Eliot's gruff voice pulled them both up short and they stared at him. He looked desolate.

'Everything okay, Eliot?' Jed's voice was gentle. 'We thought we'd do the dishes. Help out a bit.'

Eliot nodded, saying nothing. Whatever had been said between him and Eden, it had obviously shaken him. Emerald felt so sorry for him. Poor Eliot.

'Take no notice of her,' she told him. 'It's probably the time of month. I'd ignore her if I were you. Just sit yourself down and I'll make you a cup of tea.'

She'd fixed him with a bright smile, expecting one in return. Instead, he'd positively snarled at her.

'Why would I ignore her? She's right! That lass has worked her fingers to the bone on this farm for two years, and now she's taken on the barns an' all, all to help out with our finances, and you can't even be bothered to wash a pot.'

Emerald was completely taken aback. 'I'm — I'm drying them now.'

'Oh aye, no doubt because Jed made you. Where were you this afternoon, eh? She was cleaning the bunk barn and washing the bedding, and she needed your help. You couldn't even offer to mind the kids or cook the tea. She had to get George to Ravensbridge, bake more scones for tomorrow, and then come back here and cook for us all. It's disgusting. You're lazy, that's the truth of it.'

'Eliot!' Emerald felt wounded to the very soul of her. How could he talk to her like that? What had that evil bitch said? 'I — I was busy.'

'I don't want to hear it,' he told her. 'Things are going to be different around here. You pull your weight, or you can go home, wedding or no. Understand?'

Emerald couldn't answer. She gaped at him, shocked. Eliot had never spoken to her harshly before. She'd thought they were friends. Her heart seemed to plummet to her feet, and she was appalled to feel the unfamiliar sting of tears in her eyes. As they surveyed each other, Emerald wasn't sure what to do or how to

338

respond. It was with huge relief that she heard the ping of her phone.

'I have a message,' she managed to say, quite haughtily. 'If you'll excuse me, this is probably about *your* wedding.'

✉ I'm on my way to the Paradise again. See you there? Please don't let me down this time. I'm sorry. X

She wasn't thrilled to see James's name on the screen yet again, but at least he'd given her the excuse she needed. Pointedly ignoring Eliot, she'd informed Jed that she had to be somewhere, then she'd stormed across the farmyard, ringing for a taxi as she headed towards the gate.

James rose to his feet as she entered The Paradise Hotel's restaurant. 'You look—'

'Oh, save it,' she snapped. 'I don't want to hear any more of your bullshit.'

His mouth fell open. 'Pardon?'

The waiter, who had hurried over to hand them a menu, looked deeply uncomfortable. He muttered something about giving them time to choose and hurried off again.

James leaned forward, a definite scowl on his face. 'What's the matter with you? I told you how sorry I was for that little misunderstanding in Leeds. If you haven't forgiven me, what are you doing here?'

'You're the lesser of two evils right now,' she informed him. 'And, please, let's not pretend that the Leeds fiasco was a misunderstanding. You knew perfectly well what you were doing, and that I'd never given you any cause to believe that I was interested in you so don't try to shift the blame onto me.'

'I never said you had,' he said sulkily. 'We all know you're too smitten with Eliot Harland to even look twice at me.'

It was Emerald's turn to gape. She felt her cheeks start to burn. 'What do you mean? Who said I had any feelings toward Eliot Harland at all?'

'You did, every time you mentioned his bloody name. God!' James threw himself back in his chair and shook his head. 'If I'm not sick and fed up with everything. My life is going to hell in a hand cart and this is all I need. I wanted to get out of the house, have something to eat and a bit of a chat with a person I considered a friend, and I get more grief. As if I haven't got enough going on at home.'

'Well, maybe you shouldn't stir up so much trouble then,' she said, battling with feelings of sympathy for him. He deserved everything he got.

'What do you mean by that?'

'Oh, come off it. Did you really think I wouldn't find out? About you and Jemima Harland, I mean, and about George. You can't send a solicitor's letter to Wildflower Farm when I'm staying there and not realise I was going to find out about it all. Not that you care, obviously.'

James looked baffled. 'Okay, so you know about Jemima. What does that matter to you? It was years ago, and it's not as if you and I are involved. You made that very clear.'

'Maybe I don't like being made to look a fool,' she said.

'How have I made you look a fool?' He sounded genuinely bewildered.

'Because you made me believe I was the only woman you've been attracted to since Beth, and I thought—' She stopped, feeling stupid suddenly. Come to think of it, he'd never said any such thing. It was her stupid pride and gullibility. He'd never told her that she was the first woman he'd fallen for since he got married. She'd assumed because she wanted to. Same as with Eliot.

She slumped, feeling miserable. She'd thought that if only Eden was out of the picture, Eliot would fall into her arms, but she'd been stupid. She could see that now. He'd never look twice at her. They had nothing in common, after all. Could she really see herself living at Wildflower Farm with him, playing mother to his kids and spending her days cooking, cleaning, and up to her knees in mud and sheep shit? Hardly. Whereas Eden seemed to love it.

The truth was, they were meant for each other. Eden was Eliot's world. Emerald would never matter to him. She'd convinced

340

herself that they had something because — because what? Because he'd been *nice* to her. Kind. Paid her attention. Sympathised. Cared.

Was she really that desperate for male attention? Was that all it took? A man only had to be nice to her and she thought they were in love? Emerald felt sickened. What was wrong with her?

'Emerald, are you all right?' James's voice was gentle, and he put his hand on hers.

She shrugged it away. 'I don't need patronising.'

'I wasn't being patronising. I was concerned.'

'It's all right, I get it. I was an idiot. You've had a long string of affairs and I was your latest challenge. And if I'd have said yes, I'd have been another notch on the bedpost. I should have known.'

James was quiet for a moment. Emerald was dimly aware that the waiter was hovering uncertainly at the corner of the room.

'Emerald, there's been no one since Beth apart from Jemima. She needed someone. She and Harland were totally unsuited. Their marriage fell apart immediately, and that's when — when she turned to me. For comfort.'

Emerald's expression was scathing. 'Comfort? Is that what you'd call it?'

'I know how bad this must sound, but you have to understand that Jemima and I were both in a terribly bad place at the time. Our marriages were both dead in the water and—'

'I don't think Eliot and Beth were aware of that.'

James fidgeted, a worm on a hook. 'We'd been struggling for some time. Beth — Beth is unable to have children, you see, and it put an enormous strain on our relationship. Jemima and Harland had realised they weren't suited, but they had two daughters to think about.'

'And then, joy of joys, another baby on the way.'

'Well, quite. Jemima and I had always got on well and — you know how it is.'

'Oh, I do,' she said wryly. 'My father's done an awful lot of *comforting* in his time, too, as you probably read in the papers. In fact, I wouldn't be here right now if he hadn't done a lot of comforting during his first marriage. And he might still be married to my mother if he hadn't felt the need to comfort some cheap waitress from a Steak 'n' Bake pub in Gloucester.'

'Look, I know it sounds bad, but it's hard to explain how unhappy we were back then. We discovered we had a lot in common, and before we knew it, we'd fallen in love. It caused an awful lot of unhappiness, but what can you do when love strikes? Harland never forgave her, of course, and he blamed both Jemima and me entirely without considering for a moment that his behaviour could have had anything to do with it.'

'Eliot's behaviour was impeccable, I'm sure.' Emerald gripped the stem of her glass. 'He's a decent, honourable man. The sort that certain women take advantage of.' *Even if he is a moody, ungrateful, ungracious yob when he puts his mind to it.* She'd certainly seen another side of Eliot Harland tonight.

'You shouldn't put him on a pedestal you know,' James said. 'He's not perfect. He only married Jemima for her money, and to get one over on her family.'

'I don't believe you.'

'It's true! They banned her from seeing him — had a much more suitable chap in mind. Well, he wasn't having that was he? Some jumped up rich people telling him what he could and couldn't do, so he bullied Jemima into marrying him.'

Emerald didn't buy it. 'How can you bully someone into marrying you?'

'Well, perhaps bully is the wrong word,' he admitted. 'Perhaps emotional blackmail better describes it. He made it clear to Jemima that he didn't believe their relationship stood a chance unless she married him. You didn't know Jemima. She was a gentle, caring soul.'

'She was related to Honey,' Emerald said. 'I sincerely doubt it.'

'*You're* related to Honey,' he pointed out. 'Does that make *you* a bad person?'

Emerald hesitated. 'Point taken,' she said at last. 'So, what went wrong between them?'

'It turned out that Eliot and Jemima had nothing in common, but he wouldn't let her go. She was the answer to his prayers, you see. When she arrived at Wildflower Farm it was a rundown farm, and the house was a dilapidated wreck. Jemima used all her own money, improving the house and financing his business. Without her, he'd have gone bankrupt years ago. Do you know, when she died, she had no money to leave? Yet, she'd had a small fortune when they married. He'd drained her entire account.'

Emerald felt a pang of anxiety. 'Are you sure?' It would explain the designer kitchen, the exquisite furniture, the tasteful decoration. She'd never understood how the farmhouse at Wildflower Farm came to be so glamorous. It was all beginning to make sense now.

'Positive. He didn't want her to end the marriage because he needed money and he was hoping her family would step in and finance the farm. Unfortunately for him — and for me, of course — the marriage ended anyway, in the most tragic of circumstances.'

Emerald shifted on her chair. 'Yeah, well, that was pretty awful. I'm sorry she was killed. Must have been horrible for everyone.'

'Yes.' James stared at his empty glass. 'Horrible.'

'But you're still with Beth?'

'We tried to make a go of it, but it's not been the same. It was falling apart long before Jemima. Beth's infertility has taken over her life. Babies are her obsession. She had no room for me or anyone else. Jemima gave me the attention I craved. I know, it sounds pathetic.'

'It doesn't,' Emerald admitted. How could she say it did when her own need for attention had been as strong?

'I tried to put things right with her, to make it up to her.' He gave her a faint smile. 'I even gave up on George, despite longing to claim my son as my own.'

'That must have been hard,' she said, grudgingly. 'Yet now you want him back suddenly?'

'It's not sudden,' he said. 'It seems that way because I've felt unable to tell anyone how I was feeling. I had to pretend that it was okay that Harland was raising my child. Who would I tell? Who would care? I couldn't tell Beth, could I? I'd hurt her enough, and with her inability to get pregnant... I had to be

343

unselfish about her. Then my mother came home, and I found myself wanting to unburden it all to her. She allowed me to express all the pain I've been bottling up for so long. She let me admit that I was grieving, and she gave me the courage to say out loud that I wanted and needed George in my life.'

Emerald bit her lip. She had to admit, she could sympathise with him. He must have gone through an awful lot. This wasn't as clear-cut as she'd supposed. James was so lonely, and he had so few people on his side. It was all right for Eliot. He had Eden and his family and friends around him. He even had her own father working to help him — thanks to her. James had no one except his mother. Not even Beth, though he didn't realise it. She wondered how he'd react when he found out about her and Jed. More pain and grief. He'd said their marriage was struggling, but even so, it would be another blow to him. He'd already been through so much.

Emerald felt terrible. She'd helped the Harlands go against this poor man. She'd got her father involved, got a solicitor onto him. All he wanted was his own son back. Who could blame him for that?

'Emerald,' he pleaded, 'you do know how much you mean to me, don't you? I'm sorry I was so stupid in Leeds. It was unforgivable. I suppose I wanted — hoped—'

'It's all right,' she said cautiously. 'It doesn't matter. You mean a lot to me, too. Maybe we should start all this again?'

He blinked, clearly surprised. 'Really?'

Emerald smiled. 'Shall we order first? Then, let's see how it goes.'

Chapter 30

Eliot sipped his tea, glad of the quiet. The kids were having a rare lie-in and there was no sign of the Carmichaels. Emerald would, no doubt, be in her bedroom, doing her morning yoga routine. It was a daily ritual that she never broke. It was anyone's guess where Jed was. Eliot had fed the dogs and checked the stock and had popped back to the house for a brew, to find Eden alone in the kitchen. It was a rare moment of peace, and he'd hoped to find her in a bit better mood than she'd been in the past few days.

She seemed okay. Not full of the joys of spring, but reasonable. She'd offered to make him some toast and he'd agreed, even though he'd already had breakfast. Worrying, he found, could be hungry work sometimes.

He stifled a groan as Jed rushed into the kitchen, carrying his laptop. 'Morning, Jed.'

Jed didn't return the greeting, which was unusual. Instead, he placed the laptop on the kitchen table and said, 'I don't wanna be the bearer of bad news, but have you seen this?'

He pointed to the review column on the shiny new *Wildflower Farm Bunk Barns* website.

Eden finished buttering rounds of toast, wiped her hands and hurried over to take a look.

'Bloody hell,' Eliot murmured, his hands cupped around his mug of hot tea, his brow furrowed as he stared at the screen in horror, 'which bugger's put this?'

Eden's mouth fell open as she spotted that her precious business now had six reviews, where yesterday there'd been only two. Four new ones, and all of them one-star!

'Dirty, noisy, inadequate facilities...' she shook her head, appalled. 'I don't understand. We've not had a single complaint.'

'Seems like someone's been unhappy, and has used the website rather than approach you,' Jed said.

'But the bunk barns are spotless!' Eden burst out, her eyes glittering with unshed tears. 'And how can they say they're noisy, or have *inadequate facilities*? What does that even mean?'

Eliot clasped her hand, feeling deeply anxious. 'Don't fret, my love. It's all right.'

'How can it be all right?' she demanded. 'This could ruin us before we've even got started.'

Jed and Eliot exchanged uneasy glances. Clearly, Eden was still stressed. She was very much a glass half-full sort of person, usually, and Eliot had never heard her sound so panicky before. He wished Jed had never shown her the reviews, but then, she'd be bound to check them herself at some point, anyway.

'I think someone's got it in for me,' she said, her voice bitter, 'and I can guess who it is.'

'Who?' Eliot pulled her onto his lap, his arms going about her waist. 'No one would have it in for you. How could they?'

'You're blind to her,' Eden muttered. 'You both are. Don't look at me like that,' she snapped, glaring at Jed. 'I know she's your sister, but even so. You're as daft as he is when it comes to Emerald.'

'Emerald would never do this!' Jed sounded astounded that she could even think it. 'Look, I know the other night was heavy—'

'Yeah, and now these appear.' Eden tapped the screen in disgust. 'Amazing, isn't it?'

Eliot sighed. 'Don't take this the wrong way, love, but — well, there's no chance the reviews could be genuine grievances? I mean, happen the farmyard does get a bit noisy sometimes, what with the dogs and the kids and all the comings and goings. Happen the sound carries more than we realised?'

Eden glared at him. 'Right. Thanks for that. And I suppose I don't clean them well enough either? And all those bathrooms and toilets just aren't good enough for our demanding guests? Great to know whose side you're on.'

'Eden,' Eliot said calmly, 'I wasn't saying that. I were just—'

'You were just sticking the blame on me. Anything, rather than accuse your precious Emerald.' She jumped to her feet as a loud knock on the door mercifully interrupted the scene. 'No doubt that's another complaint,' she said, hurrying out of the kitchen.

Jed raised an eyebrow as Eliot looked at him in despair.

'I don't know what's up with her lately,' Eliot confessed. 'Happen I were right. She's overworked, that's what it is.'

They fell silent as the sound of raised voices could be heard in the hallway, then with one accord they headed after Eden to see what on earth was going on now.

'It's a brand-new fridge freezer,' Eden was protesting. 'I don't see how it can possibly have broken down.'

'What's going on?' Eliot demanded, seeing two middle-aged men standing on the doorstep, a bag of clearly defrosted food in their hands, dripping water all over the floor.

'Apparently, the fridge-freezer in the small barn isn't working,' Eden muttered.

'There's no apparently about it,' one of the men assured them. 'I didn't come over here to pull a fast one,' he added, sounding quite indignant. 'I wasn't even demanding compensation. I only came to tell her before we left for the day because I knew she'd need to get it fixed. I certainly didn't expect to be accused of lying.'

'I didn't say you were lying,' Eden said, rubbing her forehead wearily. 'I just asked you if you were sure you hadn't accidentally unplugged it or something?'

'I can assure you we didn't touch the socket at all,' the other man said.

'I'm right sorry about that,' Eliot said. 'We'll refund the cost of all that food, of course.'

'I'll head over and take a look at the fridge-freezer,' Jed offered.

The first man handed Eliot the bag. 'Twelve pounds forty-seven,' he stated. 'I can look for the receipt if you like.'

347

'No need for that,' Eliot assured him. He put the bag on the step and hurried into the kitchen, returning moments later with his wallet. 'Fifteen pounds there,' he said, handing over two notes.

'Of course,' said the man, 'now we'll have to buy breakfast in the village, too. Most inconvenient.'

Eliot risked a glance at Eden. She looked ready to explode. Hastily, he handed over another note. 'For your breakfasts. The King's Head does a full English for a fiver. Enjoy.'

The two men nodded. 'Thank you, that's very decent of you.'

'Isn't it just?' Eden said, her arms folded.

Jed steered her away as Eliot took care of the bag of defrosting food.

'What a bloody con!' she snapped as he returned to the kitchen. 'Twenty-five quid out of our profits! They've practically stayed here for free.'

'Couldn't be helped,' Eliot said, 'and which would you prefer? Paying them off or another nasty review on yon website?'

As Eden glared at him, Jed announced that he would check over the fridge-freezer and made a hasty retreat.

'I told you this would be too much for you,' Eliot began, then shut up as Eden whirled round, looking livid.

'It's not too much for me! What's too much for me is that you're completely oblivious to how devious that little bitch upstairs is. You really think this is a coincidence? Why can't you see what she's really like?'

'Eden, you're not thinking straight. Why would she do summat like this, eh? And I suppose you're gunna tell me next that she sabotaged the electrics or summat?'

'I wouldn't put anything past her,' Eden muttered.

Jed came back into the kitchen. 'All done,' he said. 'I fixed it.'

'What was it?' Eliot said, not daring to look at Eden.

'The fuse had gone. I changed it and it's working fine now.'

'It was a brand-new fuse!' Eden protested. 'It's not possible for it to go so soon.'

Jed shrugged. 'Must've been faulty.'

'Sure it was, on a new appliance.' Her tone was heavy with

348

sarcasm.

Her implication hung in the air. What would someone like Emerald know about fuses, Eliot wondered. Nothing, that's what. Eden was barking up the wrong tree about this. He could understand why she was upset but she was adding two and two and making a million, as far as he could see. It was as he'd said all along — she had too much to do and it was getting to her. Why had he ever believed her when she'd insisted she could cope?

'There's a letter for you,' Jed added, handing Eliot a thick, white envelope.

Eliot recognised that stationery and his stomach lurched in fear. His eyes met Eden's and he saw the same emotion in them that he was feeling. What now?

The kitchen fell silent as he read the letter, the words leaping off the page and attacking him with their venom.

'Well? What do they say?' Eden's voice was shaky, and Eliot gave her a despairing look.

'Want me to get the DNA test organised or they'll be taking steps to enforce it.' He threw the letter across the table. 'They must've decided to pile the pressure on. So much for Cain's intervention.'

'I'm real sorry, guys. What are you gonna do?' Jed dropped into a chair, eyeing Eliot worriedly. 'You do know you're gonna have to comply, right? They'll want absolute proof that George is Fuller's kid and they're gonna make sure they get it. There's no getting out of this.'

No getting out of it at all, Eliot acknowledged to himself. No escape. The net was closing. But, by God, he'd go down fighting.

****

Eden's stomach churned as she bundled George into her car and fastened him into his car seat. She'd never felt guiltier in her life — well, not since the last time she'd lied to and betrayed Eliot because of a Fuller. God, she was a horrible person. If he found out, he would be furious.

349

I've got no choice, she persuaded herself. The truth was Deborah was clearly prepared to sink to despicably low levels and Eliot was far too honest and decent to compete. He would be torn apart by the Fullers. Reading the letter from the solicitor that Monday morning, she'd realised that Deborah had acted quickly to assure her that, if she didn't agree to her plan, things would get very bad for them indeed.

It had then occurred to her that maybe Deborah was responsible for the horrible reviews, rather than Emerald. She wouldn't put anything past her. How much worse could things get? The truth was, with that family she suspected they could get a *lot* worse, and she had finally reached the conclusion that it was up to her to try to appease them by agreeing to Deborah's terms.

She'd called Thwaite Park, her hands trembling as she waited for someone to answer the phone. Her tremors were as much born of anger as nerves. She hated the fact that she'd been reduced to this, but it would have to be her that tried to reach a compromise. Eliot never would.

Frankly, she couldn't imagine the day that Eliot would ever agree to James having access to George, but he would soon have no choice. If she agreed to Deborah seeing her grandson, it might halt legal proceedings and the battle for sole custody. At the very least, it would buy the Harlands some time.

Deborah had agreed to meet her at the bunk barn again, and Eden had waited for her, giving her a curt nod upon her arrival and ushering her into the dining room.

She could see Deborah looking around her, clearly impressed by the oak flooring, and the cream painted walls, broken up with the odd patch of bare stone that revealed the age and character of the building. Overhead, thick oak beams criss-crossed the room, another reminder that this barn had stood for centuries, despite its contemporary furnishings. French doors opened out onto a small garden, with the car park and fields beyond.

Deborah *should* be impressed. A lot of thought and money had gone into making the barns a viable business, while retaining their character. She would show the Fullers that there was far more to her family than they dreamed of.

Eden indicated a table. Deborah sat, and Eden pulled out a chair and sat opposite her.

'We got your solicitor's letter.' Her voice was accusing, but she couldn't help it.

'Eden.' Deborah leaned forward and fixed her with a sympathetic look. 'I do understand how difficult this has all been, really I do. It's come as a real shock to me. I had no idea I had a grandchild until a few weeks ago. You can imagine how I felt.'

'I suppose so,' Eden admitted. 'But that's no reason to set the lawyers on us.'

'No,' Deborah conceded. 'In hindsight, I should have approached you both first in person. It was foolish of me to get the solicitors involved straightaway. I see now that it turned Eliot against me from the start.'

'To be honest,' Eden said, 'I doubt he'd have listened if you'd come here in person, but you could have done it anyway. Given him a chance, some warning.' She swallowed, blinking away tears. 'I don't think you realise what this is doing to him. How much he loves George. How much we all love him. Eliot has two daughters, and they have no idea about any of this. How do you think they'll feel if we have to explain that their mother had an affair with your son? That George has a different dad?'

'I know that,' Deborah said. 'I understand.'

'And have you thought about George in all this?' Eden's voice had risen. The more she tried to explain to Deborah the more her own panic increased. 'Can you imagine what it would be like for him? Eliot's the only dad he's ever known. Wildflower Farm is his home. How can you even think of taking him away from us? From his home, his parents, his sisters? To live with strangers!'

Deborah flinched. 'We're hardly strangers. We're blood relatives.'

'You're strangers to him! The only Fuller he knows is Beth. And what about Beth, while we're at it? Have you asked her how she'd feel about taking George on? Because I'll tell you now, she won't do it. She'd never do that to Eliot, or to George.'

'And what her husband wants doesn't count?'

'Did *she* count when he was having sex with Eliot's wife?'

Deborah took a deep breath. 'Touché. Look, you said you wanted to see me. Surely, it's not just to rehash this argument?'

Eden massaged her temples. 'Eliot will never forgive me if I do this. If I let you see George without telling him, I mean. He'll be furious if he finds out.'

'So, you're going to let me see him?' Deborah's face lit up. 'It's for Eliot's own good, Eden. We'll just make sure he doesn't find out. Like I said, we can do this the easy way or the hard way. It's in your hands now.'

'Great.' Eden shook her head. 'I've been in this position before. I can see who your son takes after.'

Deborah looked wounded, as if it were an insult, which it was. Clearly, she didn't take kindly to being compared with James, which was pretty revealing in itself. Not that it helped her now.

'I suppose I have no choice then,' Eden said heavily.

'You'll let me meet him? When? Today? Tomorrow?'

Eden stood up. 'I'm supposed to be dropping him off at the childminder's tomorrow morning at nine. If you meet me in Ravensbridge at the playground, around nine o'clock, I'll let you see him for an hour, and I'll tell the childminder we'll be there at ten. Hang on,' she added, as Deborah began to gush her thanks. 'There are two conditions. One, you don't tell anyone about this, and I mean anyone, even Beth. Two, you don't tell George you're his grandmother. In fact, as far as he's concerned, you're a lady who happens to be at the park and strikes up a conversation with us. That's vital. George would tell Eliot immediately, and so you can't give the meeting any more significance than a casual encounter in the playground. Right?'

Deborah nodded eagerly. Eden had a feeling she would have agreed to anything. 'Right.'

Eden stood and led Deborah to the door. 'Then we're done,' she said. 'Now, if you'll excuse me, I have tea to cook for my family.'

She'd practically pushed Deborah out of the barn, feeling sick to her stomach, and she hadn't been able to look at Eliot last night. She felt like a traitor, and only the hope that she was doing the right thing for them all had given her the strength to resist picking up the phone and telling Mrs Fuller that she could stick it.

She almost died of fright as she backed out of the car and collided with Eliot. What the hell was he doing here?

'Thought I'd come and see how you were doing this morning, since you were that quiet last night,' he said, waving at George, who was sitting placidly in the back seat. 'Where's Ophelia?'

'Here.' Ophelia came running up to the car, her school bag over her shoulder. She attended the primary school in Ravensbridge, and every morning Eden dropped her off before taking George to the childminder. After lunch, Mrs Thompson would take George to nursery, then Eden would collect him, along with Ophelia, at the end of the school day. Libby, meanwhile, had progressed to secondary school in Kirkby Skimmer, and caught the school bus every morning. It picked her up from the end of the farm track and dropped her off every afternoon, saving Eden a long trek.

'Have a good day at school, love.' Eliot dropped a kiss on his daughter's cheek, and she pulled a face.

'It's not likely, is it? Still, only five weeks to the summer holidays.'

Eliot laughed. 'You've only just gone back after half term!'

Ophelia grinned and climbed into the front seat beside Eden, who was fumbling with her seat belt.

Eliot leaned into the car, his brow puckered. 'Are you all right?'

She gulped, sure her face was burning. 'Why shouldn't I be?'

'Well, you've been a bit off lately. Not yourself like. You're not sickening for owt?'

Eden cast a desperate look around the farmyard, unwilling to lie to his face. 'I told you, I'm just worried about the business.'

'Obviously.' He shrugged. 'But you know, don't you, that Emerald didn't do them things? The fuse was just faulty, and happen we were unlucky with some guests, that's all.'

Eden bit her lip and choked down a response. Whether it was Emerald or Deborah who was responsible, she loathed them both. She nodded.

Eliot hesitated then said, 'Okay, well if you're sure you're okay, I'll leave you to it.'

He leaned into the car, blowing a kiss at his son. 'See you later, Georgie. Have a nice day at Mrs Thompson's.'

George waved, and Eden started the car, without even telling Ophelia to fasten her seat belt, such was her haste to get away. She felt disgusted by her behaviour. She would have to talk to Deborah Fuller. Try to make her see that this wasn't fair, and there had to be another solution. She couldn't be expected to lie to Eliot like this. It was breaking her heart.

'Ophelia, seat belt, love! Don't I even get a goodbye kiss, Eden?' Eliot's tone was challenging as she put the car into gear.

'What? Oh, yeah. Yes of course.' Eden tilted her face towards him, her eyes fixed on the windscreen. If he saw her expression of misery and guilt, he would rumble her at once.

Eliot hesitated, then planted a quick kiss on her cheek. 'I'll see you when you get back,' he said.

'Okey dokey,' she replied, with as much cheerfulness as she could muster. 'See you then.'

She shut the window as he stepped away, and without another glance at him, she headed out of the farmyard.

The journey to Ravensbridge seemed to take forever. Eden kept glancing at the clock on the dashboard, half hoping that she would be late, and Deborah would leave, half terrified that she would miss her and cause an acceleration in the Fullers' determination to proceed with a legal claim. Ophelia and George chattered on and on, but Eden had no idea what they were talking about.

Approaching Camacker, she cast a teary glance at St Mary's, her mind dwelling on the vows that she and Eliot were about to make to each other and wondering exactly how she could reconcile them with her current deceitful behaviour.

I'll have to tell him, she thought in anguish. *I can't keep this from him. It's too big!*

As she reached Ravensbridge, Eden was almost convinced. Whatever happened today with Deborah Fuller, she would have to confess all to Eliot. It was crazy to go behind his back. Yes,

354

he would no doubt have a fit that she'd done it, and there would be hell to pay, and he'd probably be even more determined to keep the Fullers away from George, but really, did it matter? The main thing was, George was Eliot's son, and if he didn't want the boy to have contact, then that was his business. She should support him. Whatever the decisions made, they were supposed to be a team, and they should work together and face the consequences together.

She dropped Ophelia outside the school gates, wishing her a good day, then drove off, her mind whirling. Pulling into the car park at the playground, Eden made up her mind. There was no way Deborah Fuller was meeting George. She would have to tell her so and hope to goodness she didn't cause a scene.

Turning off her engine, she sat for a few moments, scanning the playground for a sign of the woman. She couldn't see her and checking the clock she realised it was ten-past nine. Deborah was late, which surprised her. Unless — unless she'd already been and gone. But surely, if she was so desperate to see George, she would have given her longer than that?

'Can I go on the swings?' George asked, clearly wondering why he was sitting in the back of a car when there was a whole playground full of adventures just outside.

'Not today, Georgie. We're going to see Mrs Thompson in a minute.' Eden thought fast. If she could tell Deborah the deal was off, leaving George in the car, she could then take him to the childminder's early. She was sure she wouldn't mind. And she would have to make sure that Deborah didn't follow her and find out where Mrs Thompson lived. That's if she turned up at all, of course. It was looking increasingly unlikely. Eden sighed and scanned the playground again. Still nothing. She glanced in her rear-view mirror, wondering if Deborah was approaching from the car park. Her heart almost leapt out of her mouth as she saw, instead, a furious-looking Eliot slam his Land Rover door shut and stride towards her.

'Oh, God.' There was no time to formulate an excuse, as he banged on the window. Trembling, she unlocked the door and he wrenched it open and glared at her.

'Go on then.'

She swallowed. 'Go on, what?'

'Don't give me that, Eden. Don't lie to me, for God's sake. Not you.'

'Can I go on the swings now?' George whined, kicking at his car seat in boredom.

'Not now, Georgie,' Eliot said, his eyes fixed on Eden. 'Wait there a minute, there's a good lad. Me and your mum need to talk.'

Realising there was no escape, Eden unclipped her seat belt and climbed out of the car. Eliot grasped her arm and pulled her to the Land Rover.

'You're hurting,' she protested.

He dropped her arm immediately. 'Sorry. I didn't mean to. I'm just that wound up, Eden. Please tell me this isn't what I think it is.'

His gaze pierced her soul as he silently pleaded with her to put his mind at rest. Eden couldn't bear it.

'What do you think it is?' she murmured.

'I'm thinking this is you, bringing my lad to meet Fuller,' he said. 'Please, please tell me I'm wrong.'

It was a fragile straw, but Eden grabbed it with both hands. 'Of course you're wrong,' she said, feeling guilty as relief lightened his face. 'I wouldn't do that. Not ever.'

He visibly slumped. 'Thank God. I'm sorry, my love. You've bin acting right weird these past few days, and I could see you weren't right, and then this morning, the way you rushed off... I feel bad now, but it reminded me, you see, of that time you took the bairns to Thwaite Park, and I suppose I panicked — put two and two together and made a thousand.' He took her hands in his. 'Forgive me?'

Eden realised she couldn't see him properly, as tears of remorse were blurring her eyes. 'Eliot, you need to know. It's me who should be sorry, and I am, really, I am. It wasn't James Fuller I brought George to meet. It was his mother.'

For a moment, Eliot stared at her without saying a word. She saw the pain in his eyes and steeled herself for what was to come.

If he'd shouted, raged, she would have understood, could have borne it. Instead, he dropped her hands and pushed past her, heading for her car.

Eden watched, shaking, as he unbuckled George's car seat and carried it, George still fastened in, to the Land Rover. 'What are you doing?'

'Taking my son home.' He didn't look at her, intent on fixing the car seat in place.

'Eliot, I need to explain — it's not what you think. I wasn't going to go through with it. I'd changed my mind. I was sitting here, waiting for her, so I could tell her the deal was off.'

He straightened, slammed the back door of the Land Rover shut and headed to the driver's side.

'Eliot, are you listening?'

'Aye, I'm listening. You made a deal with Deborah Fuller, so she could see George behind my back. Says it all, dun't it?'

'I thought I had no choice,' Eden said, tears spilling down her cheeks. 'She said if I let her see George, she would speak to James about dropping the custody battle.'

He gave her a scornful look. 'And you believed her.'

It sounded so pathetic now when she came to think of it. She'd been played by Deborah Fuller. Why should she do as she said she would? Eliot was right. It was probably a trick. For all she knew, James would have turned up, too. She'd been an idiot.

'I'm so sorry,' she murmured, but he didn't seem interested. He climbed into the front seat, clipped his seat belt and slammed the door shut. Without so much as a glance at her, he reversed out of the car park, and headed out on the road back to Wildflower Farm, leaving her standing there, feeling sick to her stomach and so, so afraid. Where did this leave them now? Would Eliot ever be able to forgive her?

Chapter 31

'Well,' David said, pushing his empty plate across the table towards Deborah, as some sort of signal that she could take it away from him, 'that was a decent breakfast, at least. Better than bloody dinner last night, at any rate.' He drained his cup of tea and reached for his paper. 'No sign of *her* yet, I see.'

James bristled with indignation, knowing his father was referring to Beth. He couldn't blame her for not making an appearance, after David's disgusting verbal attack on her the previous evening.

'No. Funny that,' his mother said, sounding sarcastic. She hadn't been too impressed with his father's behaviour either. In fact, he had to admit with some shame, that she'd been more defensive of Beth than he had. But his father was a hard man to go against, and he had James over a barrel. And didn't he know it!

He watched, curious, as Deborah glanced at the clock on the kitchen wall and sighed. James followed her gaze. Half past nine. 'Somewhere you need to be, Mother?'

Deborah pushed away her empty cup. 'Not at all. That is, I was considering going somewhere this morning, but I changed my mind.'

'Oh?' James was glad of a conversation to break the uncomfortable silence that had hung over them all during breakfast. 'Where were you going?'

'Just for a drive,' she said vaguely. 'After last night's performance, I didn't feel like going, after all.'

'Huh!' came from behind the newspaper.

'Let's just say I had an epiphany,' she continued, smiling sweetly at him.

James eyed her suspiciously. What the hell was she talking about? Last night had been a nightmare, but he couldn't see what sort of epiphany it would give her. He wished it had given him one. He wished he could figure out a way to get his dratted father off his case. Things were going from bad to worse.

It was his father who'd started it, of course. He was being his usual obnoxious self, moaning about dinner and threatening to sack Mrs Ketley and hire a new cook.

'I thought dinner was delicious,' his mother had retorted.

'So did I. Mrs Ketley makes a wonderful quiche.'

James's eyes widened in surprise. Was that Beth, being brave enough to contradict David? Wonders would never cease. He considered Beth for a moment, noting the sparkling eyes, and soft glow to her skin. She looked well, he thought. Better than she'd looked in ages.

His father, on the other hand, looked furious. 'Rubbish,' he snapped. 'She can't cook to save her life.' He smirked. 'Maybe she bought it cheap from Wildflower Farm. Damaged stock.'

James shifted uncomfortably as his mother frowned. 'What do you mean, damaged stock?'

'Didn't you hear?' David's eyes positively gleamed with malice. 'There was an *incident* at their so-called bunk barns the other day. One of the new fridge-freezers stopped working. Had to throw away a whole load of food that had defrosted.' He grinned at them, and James's lip curled in disgust. Why did his father always have to push it? 'The guests weren't happy since it was *their* food. Lots of refunds and red faces all round, I should imagine.'

'How did you know about that?' Beth's voice was sharp, and James cringed.

'Word travels fast around Beckthwaite,' he said hastily. 'How did *you* know, for instance?'

'I — spoke to Eden on the phone.'

David shrugged. 'You know what villages are like.'

'But no one from the village knew,' Beth persisted.

'Oh, for goodness' sake, Beth, one of the guests must have been complaining about it. What does it matter? So, there was a mishap at the farm. Who cares? It's not the end of the world, is it?' James tutted, anxious to change the subject.

'Actually, it was a pretty major deal for them,' Beth snapped. 'When every penny counts it's a real blow.'

David settled back comfortably in his chair. 'What a shame.'

Beth glared at him. 'Yes, it was. They've worked bloody hard on those bunk barns, and they deserve for them to work.' She turned an appealing gaze on Deborah. 'They're good people — the best. They've been through so much, and they've earned some good luck. The last thing they need are any setbacks, of any kind.'

'Should be more careful with the electrics then,' James pointed out, stung by her defence of the Harlands.

'Exactly,' David agreed. 'If they can't even manage to run a bloody fridge-freezer, how are they going to look after my grandson properly?'

There was a shocked silence. Trust David to mention the unmentionable, James thought. He didn't care. He looked over to Beth, expecting to see her in tears. He was surprised — and rather uneasy — to see her eyeing David with pure loathing.

'No one could look after George better than those two,' she said, with a sudden and most unexpected courage. 'And no one should get the chance to try.'

To his amazement, he saw his mother's lips twitch with amusement as his father's face lost its smug look and he spluttered with indignant rage.

'That boy belongs here at Thwaite Park with his real family. He deserves the chance to grow up in a good home, with everything he could possibly need or want — never mind living in that dump, scratting around for a few pennies. And we deserve to have our own flesh and blood under our roof. You wouldn't understand that, obviously, and you never will, but you shouldn't try to deprive James of his son, because you have no child of your own.'

'David!' His mother sounded shocked.

'Steady on, Father,' James muttered.

David turned to his son, one bushy grey eyebrow raised. 'Oh, you think I'm being harsh?'

'No need for all that,' James said, beginning to perspire.

'I'm sorry. Do you think I was being mean to Beth? Goodness, we wouldn't want that, would we? After all, poor Beth has been through quite enough already, hasn't she? It must be terrible trying for a baby for all those years. All those disappointments. Month after month of—'

'David! That's quite enough!' His mother rose and hurried over to Beth, who clearly flinched as she put her arm around her, which wasn't surprising, he supposed. After all, she'd never made any attempt at affection towards her daughter-in-law before. 'I don't know what you think you're achieving by this.'

'Achieving?' His father put his hand to his heart, feigning hurt. 'I'm not hoping to achieve anything. I'm merely pointing out that it's a shame for Beth, not being able to conceive. It must be hard to realise you'll never have a baby. That's why I'm so glad that James managed to have a son with his mistress. I know it's difficult all round, but at least we have a grandchild, and James hasn't missed out on being a father.' He beamed at his son. 'You wouldn't have wanted that, now would you, James?'

'Father, can we please drop it?' James squirmed in his seat, and Deborah looked from father to son, clearly puzzled. He wished his father would just shut his big fat mouth.

'If you'll excuse me, I think I'll go to my room.'

Deborah had released her daughter-in-law, and Beth stood and headed to the door. He watched, rather awestruck, as she stalked out of the room, head held high. There were no tears, no trembling lip. Where the hell had this new courage come from?

James couldn't deny he was relieved she'd gone, and he felt even better when David picked up the evening paper with a contented sigh.

Now, as he saw his mother staring at his father's morning newspaper, he felt distinctly uneasy. What epiphany had she had? There was no disguising the look of disgust on her face and he squirmed as she turned to face him with the same expression.

Realising he was watching her, she picked up her cup of tea and took a sip, lowering her eyes. It was a fleeting glimpse of her emotions, and then they were shut down as usual. But it was enough for James to realise that Deborah had no great opinion of either him or his father, and it unnerved him. He would have to watch it. He needed her onside or his father would bring everything out into the open, and then his life wouldn't be worth living.

****

'You're being ridiculous!' Eden stared wide-eyed in anguish as Eliot shrugged on his jacket and grabbed his car keys. 'Where are you going anyway?'

'Out. Funnily enough, I don't want to be here tonight. Not with you.'

Jed and Emerald exchanged incredulous glances. Emerald thought how often she'd longed to hear Eliot say something similar to Eden, but now that he had it sounded all wrong. They were meant to get along, not row like this. What the hell had Eden done?

'Look, guys, I don't know what's going on, but—'

'No, you don't.' Eliot interrupted Jed, his jaw pulsing with tension. 'And you don't need to know. All I ask is that you do as you promised. Make sure that George doesn't leave this house until I get back, and if *she* says different, ignore her.'

Eden's face was scarlet and streaked with tears. 'If you'd just listen!'

'To what?' Eliot turned to face her at last, and his voice was so quiet that Emerald had to strain to hear it. 'I don't see what you can say that would justify what you did today. Of all the people in the world, I trusted *you*. Believed in *you*. Even after the last time when you put the Fullers first.' He shook his head. 'It's always them bloody Fullers.'

'Eliot, please.'

He swallowed hard, as if noticing for the first time the distress in her face. For a moment, Emerald saw a fleeting softening of his expression, and his whole body seemed to lean towards Eden like a flower reaching for the sunlight.

'I can't do this tonight,' he murmured. 'There's nowt you can say, and I can't listen. It's best I go, give us both some time.' Straightening, he turned and strode out of the kitchen. They heard the front door shut, and Eden visibly slumped.

Jed shot over to her and led her to a chair, then he glanced over at Emerald. 'I think, maybe, tea?'

Emerald nodded. 'With lots of sugar for shock.' Although, she wasn't quite sure who was in the deepest shock — herself or Eden. She had never imagined these two would behave like this. It was an uncomfortable revelation to her that she hadn't enjoyed the scene half as much as she thought she would have.

When Eden had arrived home that morning, she'd been frantic with worry, and desperate to know where Eliot and George were. Neither Emerald nor Jed had a clue, and Eden had struggled all day to hold it together, while continuing to work.

She'd gone to pick up Ophelia from the school in Ravensbridge, and Emerald could see that she'd hoped Eliot would be home by the time she got in, but there was still no sign of him. Libby, upon her return home, sensed immediately that something was wrong, and Emerald had to admire the way Eden kept a reassuring smile on her face, promising both girls that everything was fine, and George was with his father, having a nice afternoon out.

When he'd finally got home it was gone seven, and George was beaming from ear to ear. Apparently, Eden had been correct, and he and his father *had* been having a nice afternoon out. They'd been all the way to Whitby — a journey of more than two hours. They'd spent the day on the beach, paddling in the sea, eating fish and chips and ice creams, and had spent a small fortune in the amusement arcade, too. George was clutching a bucket and spade, a Paddington Bear, and a bag of sweets, and couldn't have sounded more excited if he'd tried.

Needless to say, Libby and Ophelia had been most put out that their dad had spent the day at the seaside without taking them, and the sticks of rock and sparkly t-shirts that Eliot had brought them back did not appease them. In fact, Ophelia wouldn't shut up moaning about it, cranking the tension in an already crackling atmosphere up to explosion point.

Eden could obviously see it building, as she got the children to bed early, much to their disgust, and only bribery persuaded them to shut up and stay in their rooms for once.

'Now we have to take the girls to Whitby as soon as school breaks up,' she announced, trying to sound normal as she re-entered the living room.

Emerald hadn't missed the look of disgust that Eliot gave her, and when he'd got up from the sofa and headed into the kitchen, she couldn't resist following him.

'Is everything all right?' Stupid question, as quite plainly it was far from all right.

'Nope,' he'd grunted, opening the drawer then slamming it shut in frustration.

'What are you looking for?' Eden had crept in, followed by Jed who, evidently, had only come to entice Emerald back to the living room, judging by his frantic hand gestures and the way he kept nodding his head towards the door. Emerald studiously ignored her brother, as Eliot ignored Eden.

'Eliot,' Eden repeated, 'What are you looking for?'

Eliot turned to Emerald as if Eden didn't exist. 'Where did I put me car keys?'

Emerald's mouth opened and closed without speaking.

'They're on the dresser,' Eden managed. 'But what do you need the keys for? You're not going out?'

'I am,' he said, finally acknowledging her. 'But before I do — Jed, Emerald, George is to stay in this house, right?'

'Sorry?'

'You heard me. George isn't to leave this house, no matter what.'

'Eliot, will you listen to me!' Eden was openly crying now. 'I was trying to help, that's all! I'd changed my mind by the time you got to the park, I swear it. I was waiting for Deborah to arrive, so I could tell her the deal was off and she would have to go through her solicitor as planned. I would have already told her, except that she was late. Please!' She ran her hand through her hair. 'Where are you going?'

'I've got nowt to say to you,' Eliot announced. He'd rummaged around on the dresser, finally spotted his keys and that was that.

As Emerald handed her the tea, she hoped that Jed would be able to worm out of Eden exactly what she'd done to cause this cataclysmic scene in the life of the Harlands.

Sure enough, bit by bit, her brother's calm, soothing voice and genuine concern for Eden coaxed the whole story out of her. Emerald couldn't believe it.

'No wonder he's angry! What the hell possessed you?'

Jed glared at her. 'We all make mistakes when we're stressed, Emerald. It's quite clear that Eden only did what she thought was right. She was trying to help. And she didn't go through with it, did she?'

Huh! Only because Eliot turned up and stopped her, thought Emerald, annoyed that Jed had called her by her full name. She was always Emmy to him. What was he so mad at her for? Typical.

Eden sipped her tea and Jed sat with her, talking to her for what seemed like ages. Emerald got quite bored and headed back into the living room to watch television. At least she'd got control of the remote for once.

Her mind kept wandering away from her favourite reality show to Eliot's whereabouts. Where would he go, and did he intend to come back at all tonight? She couldn't imagine him staying out too late. She grinned to herself. He was hardly the type to head to the city and drown his sorrows in gin while watching a lap dance in some seedy club. That was more her father's style.

After a couple of hours, Jed came through and sat down on the sofa with a heavy sigh.

'You haven't left her all alone in the kitchen!' Emerald clasped a hand to her chest in mock horror.

Jed frowned. 'Don't be so mean, Emmy. She's had a shock.'

'And Eliot hasn't? I don't get why you're on her side, after what she did.'

'If you listened to her, you'd know that it's not what he thought. Yeah, she made a mistake, but she was putting it right, and she only did what she thought would help him. She was scared for him. They're in an impossible situation, Em, you must see that? They're both under massive pressure, and they're petrified of losing that kid. Eliot's not thinking straight. If he was, he wouldn't have flown off the handle like that. I mean, that was a massive overreaction, right?'

Emerald shrugged. 'Not really.'

'Oh, come on!' Jed sighed. 'Anyway, Eden's worn herself out worrying and crying, so she's gone to bed.' He glanced at his watch. 'I don't think Eliot will be back tonight, do you?'

'But where would he go?'

He pulled a face. 'Who knows? Probably sleeping in his car to prove a point. Hopefully tomorrow he'll have come to his senses and he'll come home and apologise.'

'I don't see why he should.'

'Oh, Emerald.' Jed sounded so disappointed in her that she felt quite miserable. 'Look, I've had a long day. I'm going to bed, too. Night, Emmy.'

'Night, Jed.'

Emerald curled up in the armchair with Bella on her knee and turned her attentions back to the television. Two heavily made-up walking mannequins with nails like talons were screeching abuse at each other, hurling accusations of infidelity and betrayal, while a rather gormless looking young man watched, visibly puffing up with pride as the two harpies fought for him. Emerald turned the television off, wondering why she'd ever thought the programme interesting. It was all so shallow and pointless.

For no accountable reason, she found herself wondering how little Tiggy was getting on, now she was out in the lower fields. The ewes who'd had healthy, single lambs were up on the moors with their offspring, but Eliot said he liked to keep the lambs who'd had problems, or who were one of twins or triplets, closer to the house with their mothers, so he could keep an eye on them. As she idly stroked Bella's sleeping form, she wondered when she'd retained all that information. It wasn't as if it was important was it?

She must have dozed off, because when the telephone rang, she jolted, not quite sure where she was for a moment. Remembering that Eliot was missing, she carefully placed Bella on the armchair and rushed into the hallway and grabbed the phone before it could wake up anyone else in the house.

'Is that Eden?' An anxious-sounding voice came through the receiver. Emerald could picture its owner — middle-aged, female, Yorkshire born and bred judging by the broad accent.

'No, it's Emerald. Eden's in bed. Who is this?'

'Oh, dear. It's Liz Thompson here, love.'

'Who?'

'I look after George for Eden and Eliot.'

'Oh, the childminder in Ravensbridge.' Emerald's mind cleared, and she nodded. Then she realised the time and frowned. 'What do you want at this time of night?'

'I really wanted to speak to Eden. It's about Eliot. I'm right worried about him.'

'Worried?' Emerald's heart sped up. 'What's wrong with him?'

'Oh, nothing bad, love. At least, not yet. I've been out with my husband for a few drinks to celebrate our wedding anniversary. Thirty-five years, can you believe it?'

If she was waiting for Emerald to congratulate her, she would be disappointed. Emerald tapped the receiver impatiently. 'And?'

'Well, Eliot were there. In the pub. Now, I'm not saying this to gossip because I never do, as anyone who knows me will tell you, but he was on the whisky, and it looked to me like he was already the worse for wear when we left. Not like Eliot at all. He doesn't really drink, does he? Anyway, I can't settle, thinking about it. Bob — that's my husband — thinks it's none of our business, but I noticed Eliot's Land Rover parked in the pub car park, and I wouldn't want him driving home in that state. Not that I think he would, of course,' she added hastily, 'but you never know, do you? Not when drink's involved.'

Emerald shuddered at the thought. 'Where is he? Which pub?'

'It's The Green Dragon in Ravensbridge,' Mrs Thompson told her. 'So, will you tell Eden? I think maybe he needs her.'

'Yes, yes I'll tell her. Thanks for letting us know.'

'No problem, love, and you will make sure he knows I only told you for his own good? I wouldn't want him to think I was interfering.'

'I'll tell him,' Emerald assured her.

She replaced the receiver and glanced up the stairs, wondering if anyone had heard, but all was quiet. She guessed Eden was worn out with crying. Emerald had cried herself to sleep enough times in the past to know how exhausting it could be. There was no deeper sleep than that of the heartbroken.

Emerald grabbed her jacket and shoes from the boot room and crept into the kitchen. Rummaging in the drawer, she found Eden's car keys and let herself out the back way, crossing the farmyard to where Eden's little Nissan was parked.

Ravensbridge was nearly ten miles from the farm and, unfortunately, it was the location of the nearest police station. It wouldn't do Eliot any good if he risked driving home. She couldn't imagine he would be stupid or selfish enough, but then, alcohol could do strange things to people. She hoped, if he tried, someone in the pub would take his keys from him if she didn't get there in time.

Eden's satnav was in her glove compartment, or Emerald would probably never have found the way to the village, but eventually she passed the sign that announced she was entering Ravensbridge and began to look out for The Green Dragon.

It wasn't difficult to find. It was one of the buildings which clustered around the village green, and Emerald parked up in the car park round the back, relieved to see Eliot's Land Rover was still there.

When she entered the pub, she couldn't see him at first. It was quite dark inside. The Green Dragon was old, with dark wooden beams and a slate floor, and lots of cosy little nooks and crannies. It was almost closing time, the pub was half-empty, and for a moment, she wondered if he'd been daft enough to try to walk home, or if he'd maybe called a taxi. Then she spotted him, tucked away in a corner, head down, staring into a half-empty glass of whisky.

'Eliot! What on earth do you think you're playing at?' She plonked herself down on the seat opposite his and, rather daringly, placed her hand over his. He didn't shake it off but looked up at her rather dazedly. For a moment or two he seemed to have trouble focusing, then his face cleared, and he gave her a beaming smile that made her heart leap.

'Emmy! What are you doing here?'

Emmy! She felt ridiculously excited to hear him call her that. Only Jed had ever called her it before, but it took on a whole new meaning when Eliot said it. 'I've come to take you home,' she said. 'I was worried you'd try to drive.'

He frowned at her. 'Why would I drive? That's bad. Bad things can happen. Do you know, my wife died in a car crash?'

Emerald nodded soothingly. 'Yes, I know. It was all very tragic.'

'It was, it was.' He rubbed his forehead. 'I'd never drive after — after drinking this stuff,' he added, jabbing a finger at the whisky. He leaned towards her. 'I've booked a room,' he whispered, putting a finger to his lips as if to signify that it was a huge secret.

Emerald thought that was a rather wonderful piece of news.

'Have you? Where?'

He leaned back again, surveying her in bewilderment. 'Where do you think? Here!' He nodded towards the ceiling. 'Up there. Can't go home, can I? What is there to go home to?'

'Eden? Your children? Your farm?' Even as she said it, Emerald wondered why she hadn't agreed with him outright. It would have been to her advantage, she was sure, but he looked so bloody miserable.

Eliot downed the rest of the whisky. 'Not going home,' he said. 'Can't go home.'

'Why can't you go home?'

'I was — I said — I did it again.'

'Did what again?'

'Hurt her. Let me temper get the better of me. Like before. Stubborn bugger I am. Don't deserve her.'

He blinked furiously, and Emerald wasn't sure if it was because he was trying to clear his thoughts or if he was blinking back tears. She hoped it was the first. The thought of Eliot crying made her depressed beyond words. She shuffled out of her seat and went to the bar to order a glass of wine.

'Just in time,' the landlord said. 'I'm about to call last orders.'

'Good-oh,' she said, taking the glass and hurrying back to the table, where Eliot was slumped dejectedly.

'Cheers,' she said, raising her glass, not in the slightest bit surprised when he didn't respond.

They sat there for another ten minutes or so, making stilted and mostly one-sided conversation until Emerald finished her wine. 'We have to leave the bar,' she told him at last. 'Do you think you can manage the stairs?'

She heard several customers bid the landlord goodnight, and the door opened and closed a couple of times.

'Eliot,' she said, when he still didn't answer her, 'shall I take you up to your room?'

'I can manage,' he slurred, standing up and swaying alarmingly, almost knocking over the table in the process.

The landlord hurried over to the table. 'Now then, sir, I'm about to close the bar, so I need you to get upstairs to your room.'

'I'm going, I'm going,' Eliot assured him. He looked helplessly at Emerald. 'Where am I going?'

'To your room,' Emerald stated. 'I'll take you.'

The landlord looked her up and down. 'Are you staying with him, miss? Just that, he's only paid for one person.'

Emerald fumbled in her jacket pocket and handed him the credit card Cain had given her. 'There. I'll pay. Now, do you mind if I get him upstairs, only, as you can see, he's rather the worse for wear.'

'Right. You take him up and get him settled, then come down and we'll sort this payment out. I'll be locking up in the meantime.' The landlord gave her a beaming smile. Evidently, he had no interest in whether she should be spending the night in the same room as Eliot. Good job he hadn't booked into the pub in Beckthwaite. There'd have been no chance that Emerald could have shared a room with him there, since everyone knew he was half of a couple, and Eden was the other half.

Between herself and the landlord, they managed to get Eliot to the foot of the stairs, then Emerald helped him up to the first floor while the landlord went off to get rid of the last of his customers.

The room they'd been assigned was basic but clean and comfortable. Eliot had to bend his head to avoid banging it on the beams, but other than that it was fine. Besides, Emerald didn't think he'd be standing up for long. Sure enough, as soon as he spotted the double bed, he practically fell onto it, and when she spoke to him there was no response whatsoever. Checking that he was breathing, she pushed him onto his side, just in case, then hurried downstairs to settle the bill.

'Will you be requiring breakfast in the morning?' The landlord handed her the card and receipt with a smile.

'Has Eliot ordered a breakfast?' she enquired.

He shook his head. 'Said he would be out first thing, so no.'

'Then no thank you,' she said, although she did think it would do Eliot good to have a lie in and something to eat. He was going to feel like shit in the morning. 'On second thoughts,' she said suddenly, 'put us both down for a breakfast. I've got a feeling he's going to need it.'

The landlord laughed. 'Aye, I were thinking that an' all. Early start, my eye. I'll cook you two full English breakfasts and bring 'em up to your room. Shall we say seven-thirty?'

Emerald considered the matter. 'Best make it eight.'

He nodded. 'Fair enough. Goodnight then, Miss.'

Emerald bid him goodnight and galloped up the stairs to the room, hoping Eliot hadn't recovered, and decided to call a taxi home after all. Thankfully he was still fast asleep.

Now that she was here, Emerald was no longer so sure of her actions. Maybe she should have called Eden, after all? But she'd wanted to be the one to help. She couldn't deny that she'd hoped he would turn to her in his hour of need. Despite the recent downturn in their relationship, she wanted him. Knowing it would never happen hadn't changed that, whatever she'd said to James.

She thought about the way she'd behaved recently, taking the fuse out of the plug in the fridge-freezer, writing those awful reviews. She'd thought it was for the best. She was helping a man get back the child he craved. He had no one else. Like her, James was alone in a family that didn't care about him or understand him. She'd wanted to put things right for him, but it hurt her more than she wanted to admit that she had to hurt Eliot to do so. If it hadn't been for her loathing of Eden, maybe she'd never have had the nerve to do it at all, James or no James. He'd assured her that the best chance he had of getting his son back was if the Harlands seemed unstable, not only financially but emotionally, too. It was weird that, just as Eliot and Eden seemed about to self-destruct, Emerald was having the most enormous attack of doubt and guilt. Was she doing the right thing, after all?

She hesitated a moment, then took out her phone and called James, needing reassurance.

'Hello?'

'Emerald? Why are you whispering?'

'Because Eliot's asleep,' she told him, eyeing the sleeping form on the bed nervously, and hoping this conversation wouldn't rouse him from his slumber.

'Eliot? What are you talking about?'

Briefly, Emerald filled him in on the events at the farm, and where she currently was, not to mention who with. James whooped with delight, so loudly that Emerald winced and pulled the phone away from her ear.

'But this is marvellous. Don't you see? You've got the perfect chance to finish them off for good!'

'I have? How?' Emerald couldn't see it herself. All right, they'd had an almighty bust-up earlier, but speaking to Eliot in the bar earlier, she'd been left in no doubt that he was ashamed of his actions, and more than ready to apologise for them. She thought — she hoped — they would sort it out tomorrow. Nothing felt right any more.

'Don't you see?' James sounded quite impatient. 'You're spending the night with Harland! What do you think Eden's going to make of that?'

'Nothing's going to happen,' Emerald said, almost wistfully. 'He's fast asleep and totally blotto on whisky. And of course,' she added 'I wouldn't do that sort of thing.'

'Oh, of course.' James didn't sound too convinced. 'That's

hardly the point, though, is it? It doesn't matter whether you have sex with him or not. It only matters that Eden thinks you did, and that shouldn't be too difficult, should it? He's spending the night with a beautiful blonde in his bed, for God's sake. Would *you* believe it was innocent?'

Emerald felt a thrill of delight. Beautiful blonde? Was that how James saw her?

'Eliot will tell her the truth and she'll believe him,' she said flatly. 'They trust each other.'

'But they've been rowing. People do stupid things when they're rowing. What were they rowing about, anyway?'

Emerald thought it best not to mention his mother. If James didn't know, she wasn't going to tell him. 'I don't know. Farm stuff, work pressure, money. Who knows?'

'Well, whatever.' He was quiet for a moment, then he said, 'You know, if you can convince Harland that something happened, it would be even better. He's so damn honourable he'd confess all to her, and that would be the end of that.'

'How do I convince him of that?' Emerald whispered.

'Oh, come on, girl. Use your imagination.' She heard him chuckle and felt a prickling of indignation. 'Look, Emerald, darling, this is our one big chance to get this sorted once and for all. Don't let me down.' She heard a door slam and he said hurriedly, 'Got to go. Remember what I said. Please, this is for George. Do it for him, if not for me.'

The phone went dead, and Emerald put the device on the bedside table, taking a deep breath as her eyes strayed to the sleeping Eliot, her mind in turmoil.

She stood looking at him for a moment, admiring the raven curls and strong jaw with that sexy stubble. His breathing was deep and even, and she sighed as she watched his chest rising and falling. She longed to take off his shirt and stroke the dark hair beneath, but she couldn't bring herself to do it. It felt all wrong. Imagine if it had been the other way around and he'd done that to her! Not that she had a hairy chest, of course, but that was hardly the point.

To be fair, she wouldn't have minded much, having Eliot's

hands on her skin, but even so, it was the principle of the thing.

Whatever James said, she couldn't be that sort of person. It felt all wrong, and she knew she'd never forgive herself if she stooped so low.

She could do one thing with a clear conscience, though. Emerald gently pulled off his boots and stuck them by the door, then she carefully eased him out of his jacket, releasing one arm and then gently turning him over onto his other side so she could release the other. He would be boiling hot if she didn't take it off. It was a warm night, after all.

Now that she'd solved that problem, Emerald realised she was worn out. She took off her coat and shoes, removed all her outer clothes, then climbed into bed beside him, covering herself with the duvet so there was a clear barrier between them. She could feel his breath on the back of her neck, and she thought how lovely it was to go to sleep with someone beside you for once, instead of alone as she usually did.

Then she didn't think anything more, because exhaustion overwhelmed her, and sleep came quickly.

Chapter 32

Someone was banging on the door. 'Breakfast!'

The pain hit Eliot as he tried to open his eyes. Rays of sunlight filtered through a gap in the curtains and pierced his lids like arrows shot through a balistraria. He winced, wondering what was happening, as their sharp points penetrated his skull. He reached out a hand, groping towards Eden for comfort. His fingers touched something hard, and he forced open his eyes, flinching at the effort. He was staring, not at Eden's sleeping face, but at a whitewashed wall. Where the hell was he?

He tried to turn his head, but the effort was too much. He lay still for a moment, struggling to make sense of where he was and what was going on. With a huge effort, he managed to drag some jumbled memories from his throbbing brain. An argument, the pub, drowning his sorrows. Too much damn beer! Then that whisky. Oh, he should have steered well clear of the whisky. It had an awful effect on him. He should have remembered that when Emerald — Emerald!

'Are you up? I've got your breakfasts here,' came the voice from the other side of the door.

Eliot groaned as it began to come back to him. Slowly, he turned his head to confirm what he already feared he was about to see. Emerald! She was fast asleep, curled up against his back, golden hair spread out over the pillow. No wonder he was so close to the wall. They were in a double bed, but she'd taken up more than half of it, leaving him with barely any room to move.

Bloody hell!

He was in bed with Emerald. How was this going to look to Eden? She'd never believe that nothing had happened, and he couldn't say he'd blame her. She was going to take a lot of convincing that this was an entirely innocent situation.

Making an enormous effort, he managed to shift himself over onto his other side and tried to remember how Emerald had ended up staying with him.

'Look, if you don't open this door now, I'll leave the breakfast tray outside. Don't blame me if it gets cold. You ordered it, so there'll be a charge whether you eat it or not.'

There was a loud muttering and then the sound of a tray being set down outside the door.

Eliot closed his eyes again, wondering what he was going to tell Eden. What if his kids found out? Of course they'd find out! How could they not once Eden had thrown him out? Because she *would* throw him out. Who could deny that she had every right, and not just because of this little performance. It was all coming back to him now, the way he'd spoken to her, the cruelty he'd shown. He ran a shaking hand through his hair. He felt disgusted with himself, and quite nauseated. No, *really* nauseated.

The realisation that he was about to be sick had him bolting upright, despite the stabbing pain in his head, all his previous attempts not to disturb the sleeping Emerald forgotten, as he scrambled over her and rushed to the en-suite bathroom.

Afterwards, he swilled his mouth out with water and stared at his reflection in the mirror, hating the man he saw there. He couldn't believe it. How had he come to this, for God's sake? Anger, he realised bitterly. His temper, his lack of understanding, and his usual trick of running away from an argument. He deserved everything he had coming.

He jumped nervously as Emerald appeared at the door, her hair tangled, her eyes sleepy as she yawned and said, 'Bloody hell. What a night!'

He closed his eyes to her reflection, realising she was wearing only her underwear. When she didn't move, he turned to face her, heart thudding.

'Emerald, I'm so sorry.'

She looked surprised. 'Sorry? For what?'

'Last night. You know—'

'Oh.' She blinked. 'Would you like a coffee? I can ask the landlord. I could murder one myself.'

'No thanks.' Was she serious? Who could think about coffee at a time like this? Any road, he always started the day with tea. Good strong tea. Eden made a cracking brew, just the way he liked it. What time was it anyway? He looked around for a clock, wishing he had his watch on. Eden had bought him a beautiful one for Christmas, but he only ever wore it for best.

'We need to talk.'

It seemed to have finally dawned on Emerald what she was wearing. She belatedly folded her arms across her chest. 'I guess we do. I'll get dressed. Won't be a minute.'

He waited in the bathroom, pacing up and down until she called him out into the bedroom again. Seeing the clock on the wall, he could hardly believe it. Twenty-past eight! He'd never slept in that late in his life! He had to get out of here. 'I know this sounds stupid,' he began, hardly able to stand the sound of his own treacherous voice, 'but, what exactly happened last night?'

Emerald was wearing jeans and a t-shirt. She surveyed him in silence for a moment, then she sighed and folded her arms. 'Don't look so worried, Eliot. Nothing happened. We talked for a while and then I helped you up to your room, that's all.'

'I know that,' he assured her. 'I don't care how drunk I were, I wouldn't have done owt with you.'

'Oh, thanks,' she said, sounding bitter.

'I mean, I'd never take advantage of you, that's all. And I'd never cheat on Eden. What sort of man do you think I am?'

'Then why ask?'

'I mean, how did you end up staying here? I can barely remember talking to you, to be honest.' A faint memory stirred. Emerald's face, full of sympathy as he whined about not being able to go home. Bloody hell, he was an idiot. 'How did you end up in my bed, is what I'm asking.'

Emerald went crimson. 'Er, we talked a lot and I'm afraid I had

377

a few drinks, too. I couldn't drive home and, as I had to get you upstairs anyway, it seemed easiest to crash out next to you.'

'I'm so sorry, lass.'

'Sorry?' Her voice sounded choked. 'What have you got to be sorry about?'

'For dragging you out at that time of night and putting you in this position.'

She laughed. 'You haven't put me in any position. Stop worrying.'

'I need to get home.'

Emerald tutted. 'I ordered breakfast for us both. He's late.'

'The landlord? He left it outside the door. That's what woke me up.'

Emerald's eyes lit up. 'Then let's eat!'

She opened the door and lifted the tray, carrying it into the room. 'Looks okay. Tea might be a bit cold but it's better than nothing.'

'I haven't got time,' Eliot began.

'You may as well be hung for a sheep as a lamb,' Emerald pointed out, quite appropriately he supposed. 'You're late anyway. Might as well eat. Besides, you need something to mop up that alcohol.'

He realised she was right and sat down at the tiny foldaway table in the corner.

They ate in silence. Eliot wasn't hungry, but Emerald seemed to be starving. She even finished his leftovers. They both swilled the whole thing down with lukewarm tea and he thought about the cups of tea Eden made, and longed for home.

'How am I going to face her?'

Emerald eyed him over her mug. 'Eden?'

'Who else?'

'Just tell her the truth. I'm sure she'll believe you. She should know you well enough by now. You're so bloody honest that there'll be no doubt in her mind.'

Eliot wasn't so sure. Maybe any other time he'd agree, but after the way he'd spoken to her last night, why should she think well of him? Why should she trust him? He'd let her down again.

'Would you, after the things I said to her?' He shook his head, wincing as the pain shot through his eyes. He was never drinking whisky again. Ever. 'I was a cruel sod, and that's the truth of it.'

'I think you're being too hard on yourself.' Having finished her full English, Emerald was now buttering a slice of toast. 'She went behind your back, after all. She was going to take George to see Deborah Fuller when you'd expressly forbidden any contact with that family.'

'But she was only doing it for the best,' he said. He could see it all so clearly now. Eden would never do anything to hurt him, or to risk losing George. She loved his children as if they were her own. If she'd succumbed to Deborah Fuller's blackmail it was only because she'd thought she had no choice. And, anyway, she'd said she'd changed her mind. Why hadn't he believed her? She wasn't a liar.

Yet here he was, expecting her to believe that he'd spent the night with Emerald in a double bed and nothing had happened. He had no right to ask her to trust him. Not any more. Where the hell could they go from here?

'She's going to hate me,' he groaned.

Emerald chewed her toast, considering. 'I'll explain the situation,' she said at last. 'Tell her what happened. Look, Eliot, I'm no fan of Eden's as she's no fan of mine, but I do know that she loves you, and she'll trust you. I'm sure of it.'

'But will she forgive me? For everything I said? For the way I behaved yesterday?'

Emerald sighed. 'I'm pretty sure she will. Stop worrying.'

He glanced at his watch, appalled to see the time. 'I have to go,' he said. 'She'll be frantic, and there's jobs to be done an' all.' He stood up, and Emerald dropped her toast and pushed her plate away.

'You can't drive,' she told him. 'You'll still have alcohol in your blood. I'll drive you home.'

'But you were drinking an' all,' he pointed out.

Emerald shrugged. 'Only a couple of glasses of wine. They'll be out of my system by now. You, on the other hand, are lucky not to have alcohol poisoning, so there's no way I'm letting you risk your licence.'

'Fair enough. You're right. I'd be sunk if I couldn't drive,' he admitted. 'Can we get off, though? I need to get this sorted, one way or t'other.'

Emerald was already handing him his jacket. Eliot tugged on his boots and waited while she collected the rest of her things, then they left the room and headed downstairs. His heart thudded with guilt, as if he'd had a torrid night of passion with her or something. How could he ever convince Eden that he hadn't betrayed her — and with Emerald of all people?

****

Any hopes Eliot had harboured that he could make a quiet return to the farm and seek out Eden alone were dashed as they drove into the farmyard, to see her walking towards the house, carrying a couple of bulging black bags.

'She's collected the sheets and towels from t'bunk barn,' he murmured, feeling guilty all over again. Like she didn't have enough on her plate already, and here he was about to burden her with yet more worry.

Emerald pulled over and turned off the engine, and Eliot flinched as Eden swung round and stared at them. As she dropped the black bags on the ground, he climbed out of the car and stood, waiting for her to reach them.

'Where the hell have you been?' she demanded, 'and what were *you* doing driving my car?' she added, jabbing a finger in Emerald's direction. 'I was going to call the police to report a stolen car until I realised the keys had been taken and Jed said you weren't in your room. You do realise I had to get a taxi to take Ophelia to school?'

Eliot hadn't even thought about that. He should have realised Ophelia would be stranded with both cars stuck at Ravensbridge, since Jed didn't have a car either, using Eden's when he needed it. Some father he was.

'Where's George?' he asked, realising she hadn't mentioned taking him to Mrs Thompson's.

'You said he wasn't to leave the house, so he hasn't. He's inside with Jed. I rang her and then I rang the nursery and told them both he wouldn't be in today.' There was a challenge in her eyes. 'So? Where were you? And why did *she* bring you home?'

He gave Emerald an apologetic look. It wasn't her fault — any of it. He didn't want her getting any blame. 'I were at The Green Dragon getting hammered,' he admitted, shamefaced.

To his surprise, Eden tutted impatiently. 'I know that. Mrs Thompson informed me that she rang here last night and spoke to Emerald to warn her that you were getting drunk on whisky and she was worried you might drive home.'

'Ah.' Eliot's heart sank. 'Right.'

'So, what I want to know,' Eden continued, 'is firstly, where did you go after the pub shut? Secondly, why didn't Emerald wake me up to tell me where you were? And thirdly, why did she wait until this morning to collect you, and what took you so long?'

Emerald raised an eyebrow at him, and he felt his spirits sinking into his boots, along with his stomach. 'Eden, about last night—'

'Yes?' She eyed him coldly, no trace of the apologetic, weeping Eden she'd been last night. He knew he should be glad. He'd hated to see her so upset and loathed himself for making her cry. Even so, this new stony-faced Eden was scary. He couldn't imagine her being willing to accept his apology or believe his story.

'First off, I'm right sorry for the way I behaved,' he began. 'I was out of order, and—'

'I'll leave you to it, shall I?' Emerald offered, slamming the car door shut and handing Eden the keys.

Eden grabbed her arm. 'Oh, no you don't. I want to know why you didn't wake me up when Mrs Thompson rang last night.'

'You were exhausted,' Emerald protested. 'Jed said you'd been crying nonstop for two hours. I thought you needed your sleep.'

'Bloody hell, Eden, I'm that sorry,' Eliot murmured. 'I was a right pig to you.'

Eden stared at him for a moment, then she sighed, her whole posture relaxing. 'Yes, you were. But I should never have taken

George to meet Deborah Fuller. You had every right to be angry with me.'

'Not like that! I were totally over the top, and I can't tell you how sorry I am.'

Eden swallowed. 'I'm sorry, too. Really I am.'

'Aw, that's lovely. All sorted,' Emerald said brightly. 'So, if that's everything, I'll just—'

'It's not everything.' Eden and Eliot spoke at the same time, then looked at each other.

'It's not everything,' Eliot repeated, hanging his head. 'There's summat else you should know.'

'What should I know?' Eden looked from him to Emerald and back again. 'What's going on?'

'Look, I know I were out of order last night and I'm that sorry, but I swear to you, nowt happened.'

'What do you mean, nothing happened?' She turned to Emerald. 'What's he talking about?'

Emerald shot Eliot an impatient look. 'You could have explained that a bit better,' she said. 'Eliot got drunk last night, as you know. Mrs Thompson tipped me off, so I thought, rather than wake you, I'd go and pick him up from The Green Dragon.'

Eden waited, then she turned slowly to Eliot. 'But that was last night.'

'Aye,' he said heavily. 'It were.'

'What — what are you saying?' she said faintly.

'When I got there, Eliot had booked a room. We were in the bar, and I had a few drinks, too. We were talking, going over things — you know. Anyway, I helped him up to his room and — well, I ended up spending the night there, too.'

Eden's eyes were like saucers. 'In his room? With him?'

Eliot stepped forward, putting his hands on her shoulders.

'Eden, love, I'm asking you to believe me when I tell you, nowt happened. I fell asleep straight away and slept right through. Only woke up at eight when landlord knocked on't door with breakfast. We had summat to eat and then we came straight back here.'

'I drove him because I was afraid he was still over the limit,'

Emerald chimed in. 'His Land Rover will need collecting later.'

Eden said nothing for a moment, her eyes searching Eliot's until he felt as if he were having laser surgery.

'I know I've got no right to ask you to believe me,' he said desperately. 'Especially not after the way I refused to believe *you* yesterday. But I swear to you, Eden, I never did owt, and I don't know what else to say to convince you. I'll do anything — anything you want to prove it to you. '

He shut up as she reached out a hand and held it to his cheek.

'I don't need proof,' she said calmly. 'Do you think I don't know you by now, Eliot Harland? Of course nothing happened. I trust you one hundred per cent.'

Relief and gratitude washed over him. 'I really don't deserve you,' he murmured, staring at her in amazement.

'Look, I was stupid yesterday,' Eden said, 'and so were you. Let's forget it, shall we? Let's learn from it and put it behind us.'

'Gladly,' he said. 'I'm so sorry.' He put his arms around her and held her to him. 'Thank you,' he whispered against her ear, and she squeezed him tightly.

'Well, er, I'll just—'

Emerald's voice broke the spell, and Eden pulled away, fixing her nemesis with a cold stare. 'Don't think I haven't sussed you out,' she said. 'I know perfectly well what you were up to, and I could have told you from the off it wouldn't work.'

Eliot blinked, confused. What was she on about?

Emerald tossed her hair defiantly. 'I have no idea what you mean. I was doing you both a favour, and here I am again getting the blame.'

'Eden, it wasn't Emerald's fault,' Eliot said. 'She tried to help, that's all.'

'You're a good man,' Eden told him, 'but you can be a bit dim sometimes. I know full well who Emerald was trying to help — herself. To you.'

'Don't be daft!' Eliot was mortified. As if Emerald was interested in the likes of him! Eden was looking at him through rose-tinted glasses, which was nice in a way but quite humiliating in another.

Eden ignored him. 'Back off, Emerald. I've been patient with you, because I knew nothing would come of it, but I'm not blind and I'm not a saint. I think you know perfectly well what I'm talking about.'

Eliot watched as Emerald's face suffused with colour. She looked across at him, her eyes revealing her embarrassment.

As she turned back to Eden, however, he saw Emerald's expression change. She put her hands on her hips and a coldness gleamed in her eyes suddenly.

'Oh, I know what you're talking about, all right,' she said. 'You're judging me by your standards. That's what.'

Eden gasped. 'And what the hell do you mean by that?'

'I mean,' Emerald snapped, 'just because you happily had an affair with a married man, doesn't mean I was hoping to do the same. We don't all have the morals of alley cats.'

There was a stunned silence as Eliot registered what had been said, and its implications. Slowly, Eden turned to look at him, and he winced as he saw the devastation in her face.

'You told her!' she whispered.

'What? No, no of course I never,' he protested. As if he'd ever do that! He'd promised Eden her secret was safe with him and he'd never break that promise.

But then, how would Emerald know? There was only him and Eden in on it. He reeled, remembering the previous night, when he and Emerald had sat together in The Green Dragon. He remembered the seemingly endless glasses of beer and whisky he'd consumed before she'd even got to the pub. He remembered that they'd sat together — and talked. What exactly had they talked about?

'I'm sorry, Eliot,' Emerald said, her eyes fixed on the tarmac. 'I never meant to — I'm so sorry.'

'I can't believe this,' Eden said. She backed away from them both, holding up her hands to halt Eliot in his tracks as he moved towards her. 'Leave me alone! Just leave me alone!'

She ran to her car and jumped in, refusing to stop despite his shouts to her to please listen to him. He watched as the car pulled out of the farmyard, feeling sick to his stomach.

384

'I'm so sorry,' Emerald pleaded.

'It wasn't your fault,' Eliot said. 'This is down to me. This whole bloody mess is down to me.'

Chapter 33

Cain whistled cheerfully as he squirted himself with a liberal dose of *Savage—the aftershave for manly men*. He surveyed himself in the bathroom mirror, pleased with the result of his efforts during the last half hour to look clean, fresh and devastatingly handsome for Connie. *Deborah*, he reminded himself. *She's Deborah, not Connie*. Yet she'd signed her texts C not D. Evidently, she was trying to tell him something, and he hoped it was that she was still up for it.

He'd Googled *Lady Chatterley's Lover* on his return to Upper Bourbury and had been a bit miffed to discover that Constance's lover was a lowly gamekeeper. After all, Cain was a toff these days, mixing with the cream of society. He was the one shooting and fishing with the posh gits in their tweeds, and he had the photos to prove it. He weren't no bleeding servant!

Then, as he'd thought about it and read a few steamy passages from the novel, he'd changed his mind. This Mellors bloke had really worked his magic on the lady of the manor, and he knew his stuff all right. If Cain was being compared to a geezer who made a posh woman melt into a puddle of desire, then bring it on. He was happy with that.

He'd been over the moon when he'd received her text last night:

✉ You were right, and I was wrong. I understand now. I want a fair outcome to this — not just for me but for the Harlands. Can we please meet up and talk next time you're in Skimmerdale?

I miss you. C.

He supposed he should have played hard to get, but sod it, he wasn't getting any younger. He'd pinged off a reply the second he finished reading:

✉ I'll set off first thing in morning. See you around lunch time at The Paradise. Missed you too. J. xx

After arriving at the hotel, he'd texted Connie as soon as he knew his room number, and she'd replied with a smiley face and a kiss. That had to be a good thing, right? If she wanted to talk, they could have met in the hotel restaurant. It wasn't like they would be doing anything improper, and they had the perfect excuse if, by some miracle, they were spotted. They were discussing the George problem.

The George problem. Cain slumped suddenly, feeling fed up. That was a fly in the ointment all right. He prayed Connie had thought twice about court action, because he couldn't go against Eden and Eliot on this. He understood Connie's desperation for a grandson, but this wasn't the answer. It was the only reason he hadn't contacted her before now. He couldn't see a way to be with her if she persisted in hurting the people he loved. When he'd received her text message, hope had flared that maybe there was a solution to this mess, and he and Connie could pick up where they left off. He hoped so 'cos, frankly, he was gagging for it.

Cain refused to acknowledge, even to himself, that there was any other reason for his longing to see her again. It was just sex, he reminded himself. Nothing else to it. His exes had destroyed his libido between them, and this classy bird had rebuilt it — reawakened a desire that he'd thought had long since left him. It was as simple as that.

Even so, he felt a peculiar fluttering in his stomach as he heard a knock on the door, and it was the thought of Connie's smile, her warmth and her kind heart that made his heart leap.

He opened the door and there she was, looking as nervous and unsure as he felt. As they stared at each other, Cain felt as if all the stuff that had gone on between them recently didn't matter in the slightest. He smiled at her and held out his arms, and suddenly she was within them and he held her close, forgetting all about the sexual side of their relationship, and revelling in the scent of her and the feel of her so close to him.

'I'm so sorry, Je — Cain.' She pulled away from him, staring up at him with those dark, doe eyes that he simply couldn't resist. 'I know I've behaved terribly, and I have tried to put it right, really I have. There's something you should know.'

'Never mind all that, Connie,' he soothed. 'It can wait. Come in. Let me make you a nice cup of tea and we'll have a chat, eh?'

She nodded, and he ushered her inside, closing the door behind her.

'Could I ask one favour?' she said. 'Could you please not call me Connie. I feel that, if we're to continue seeing each other from this point on, there should be no more games. Would you mind?'

'Course not, Debs. I only called you Connie because you signed yourself C on your texts.'

She looked embarrassed. 'I know. I wanted you to associate the text with the person you knew and — cared about. Not the cold, heartless woman you met at Thwaite Park that day. But now that we're together again, here in this room, I want us to be completely honest with each other. Do you understand?'

'Yeah. Yeah, I do, and that's fine by me.'

He made her a cup of tea as she hung her jacket in the tiny wardrobe and settled herself on the small and not particularly comfortable sofa. Cain studiously avoided looking at the bed as he handed her a drink, even though it was the dominant feature in the room, and practically screamed at them to remember what their relationship had started as.

'Now then,' Cain said, settling himself next to her. 'What's this something that I should know?'

Between sips of tea and apologetic glances, Deborah revealed her visit to Eden, her attempt to force a meeting with George, and her moment of revelation the other night as she'd sat with her vile husband and son. Cain listened, not speaking, nodding now and then.

'It came to me, as clear as day, that I was behaving as badly as they do, and I couldn't bear it. I'm not like them, really I'm not. They disgust me. I didn't go to meet George. I hope Eden will realise that I've changed my mind about this.'

'I'd tell her, Debs, but she don't know about us so it could be a bit awkward.'

'I know. I understand that. But you do see, don't you, that I have tried to put it right? I really, really hope you can forgive me.'

"Course I forgive you, Debs.' There was no question of it. She'd been courageous and unselfish in his book, trying to make amends for the things she'd done. He'd known she was a good 'un deep down. 'What's your son got to say about all this though?'

She put her cup on the bedside table. 'I haven't told him,' she confessed, folding her arms defensively. 'The truth is, I didn't even tell him about visiting Eden, or about our little arrangement. It had nothing to do with James. It was about me, and my selfish desire to see my grandson.'

As Cain considered this, a thought occurred to him, and he wondered if he dared put it into words, or if it would frighten her off.

'Debs,' he said at last, 'do you believe James? I mean, do you believe he wants his kid, after all this time?'

To his relief, she didn't rear away from him, protesting in defence of her son. Instead, she remained quiet, clearly phrasing her response in her mind.

'There's something odd about it all,' she said at last. 'I can't quite put my finger on it. I suppose, firstly, it's surprising that James put Beth's feelings ahead of his own all these years — most unlike him. But even more peculiar is David's silence on the subject. I'd have thought he'd have been throwing his weight around, making all sorts of threats and taking over, but he's sat back, seeming quite content to let James and I do all the pushing. That's not David. He never trusts anyone else to do something that matters to him, and even if he didn't particularly care about George, he'd pursue this on principle. He can't bear the thought of someone else having something he perceives is his.'

It must have dawned on her what she'd said, as she gave Cain a rueful smile. 'Don't worry. I won't let him hit you.'

'He can bleeding try,' Cain said, hoping he sounded convincing. He wondered if he should get his private dentist on standby, in case.

'I'm not his,' Deborah said, sounding defiant. 'He doesn't own me, and he can't stop me from doing what I want.'

'I'm sure he'll have a damn good go at it, though, Debs,' Cain muttered. 'Still,' he added, his finger tracing the outline of her lips, 'you're worth it.'

His libido was taking over his common sense again. He knew it but was powerless to resist. As Deborah kissed him, all thoughts of David flew out of the window, and before he knew it, he was half-naked on the hotel bed, with a lusty-gazed Deborah straddling him. Now how, he wondered, had that happened? It was a complete mystery. Then again, he thought, as she leaned over him, her neat little breasts brushing his chest, what did it matter? What did anything matter? Jesus, she was good!

As they lay together afterwards, Cain thought he maybe ought to get a medical, just in case. His old ticker was going like the clappers, and he should make sure he was okay to be doing this sort of thing at his age. He'd never expected it, and although he thought vaguely that he'd read somewhere that sex in later life kept you young, maybe it was best to check. After all, he didn't want to keel over and die, did he? Not now when he finally had something to look forward to.

He couldn't wait to tell Debs about the project he had in mind. It had taken seed after their day at Skimmerdale Abbey, when they'd talked about their childhoods and reminisced about life in a two-up-two-down with not a blade of grass in sight. It had quite got his creative juices flowing in a way that even music hadn't for a long time. He hoped Debs would be as enthusiastic as he was about it. He was sure she would be.

Before he could speak, however, Deborah turned to him, her fingers playing gently with his grey chest hair. 'I've got something to tell you. I've quite made my mind up on this. I'm leaving David.'

Cain's mouth fell open. 'Leaving him? But...' His mind raced. He could see it now: Deborah arriving with her luggage in tow on his doorstep in Upper Bourbury; newspaper headlines screaming the news that Cain Carmichael was up to his old tricks again; the years he'd spent building a reputation as a respectable, reformed character wasted, ruined; and worse, being landed with yet another woman who would, no doubt, bleed him dry with her financial demands.

He was no fool. Deborah Fuller had married a very wealthy man. She'd got used to posh homes like Thwaite Park. No doubt she'd always had a healthy allowance, and she would expect to be kept in much the same manner by him. Cain had plenty of money, but frankly, he was sick of doling it out to wives, girlfriends, kids and exes. What if things didn't work out between him and Debs. Would she take him to the cleaners, too?

He remembered the bitter battles he'd fought with Lowri, Cassandra, Sandy and Freya. There'd been various payoffs to his old paramour Lucinda Farquhar, to his most recent live-in bird Roxy, and her sister Suki, not to mention the substantial financial gifts he'd bunged various casual flings over the years.

He'd been a mug, he held his hands up. Couldn't keep it in his trousers, that was his problem. Nothing illegal or dodgy, but he'd kidded himself it was love far too many times. He'd sworn off women altogether after Roxy and Suki and had made a promise to himself that he'd never be caught out like that again, but now look what had happened. How could he trust Deborah?

But if she was leaving David for him, what could he do?

'Are you sure that's what you want, Debs?' he asked, trying not to sound appalled.

'Quite sure,' she said. 'I've had enough. Of course, it's going to get terribly messy, and the solicitors will have a field day sorting out a financial settlement, but it will be worth it in the end.'

Cain sighed inwardly. As he'd suspected. Debs was already thinking about how much money she could get out of her old man, and even though he despised David Fuller and was quite glad for her sake that she was finally planning to leave, he couldn't help but feel a sense of dread and disappointment.

Deborah glanced at her watch. 'I have to go, I'm afraid. They'll be wondering where I am and with things the way they are at home it's probably best I don't draw any attention to myself—at least, until I've seen a solicitor.'

Cain gulped. 'Yeah, yeah. Fair enough, Debs. I'll come down with you to the lobby.'

'You don't have to,' she said, smiling. 'If you want to stay here and get your breath back it's fine.'

Cain felt indignant. 'Get me breath back? I could do that all over again, don't you worry.'

She laughed. 'I'm sure you could, but right now isn't the time to prove it.' She climbed out of bed and proceeded to get dressed, and Cain — after taking a few deep breaths — followed suit.

Peering through the glass door, Deborah ascertained that the lobby seemed quiet and, after glancing around to make sure there was no one there she knew, she pushed open the door and strolled in, Cain by her side.

It was Cain who spotted Jed and Beth first, and he almost threw Deborah against the wall, urging her to stay back as his son and his companion lingered by the entrance door.

'What on earth?'

'Shh, Debs. Look who's over there!'

Deborah followed his gaze and her eyes widened in shock as Jed put his arms around Beth and kissed her.

Cain glared at his son. What the bleeding hell did he think he was doing, kissing Debs' daughter-in-law, of all people! Christ, this would go down well with her — not. All hell was about to break loose at Thwaite Park, what with Beth's behaviour and Debs about to leave David. The Carmichael name would be mud.

He saw Jed stroke Beth's hair, and watched as they stood murmuring to each other. He wondered what they were talking about, deceitful, treacherous little gits.

'I'm ever so sorry, Debs,' he muttered. 'I'll kill Jed. I had no idea this was going on, honest I didn't.'

He looked down at her, expecting to see a thunderous expression on her face, and was amazed to see her smiling.

'Look at the way he's looking at her,' she whispered. 'Look at their faces, Cain. *Look at them!*'

Cain looked and, as he did so, his anger slowly ebbed away. There was no mistaking the feeling between Beth and Jed. It made him feel quite humble to see it — all that love radiating from them. Beth might be a married woman, and Jed might be a sneaky git, but there was something weirdly beautiful about the two of them — a purity that quite took his breath away.

'How lovely,' Deborah breathed, and Cain wondered if she'd forgotten that Beth was married to her own son.

They waited until Beth left the hotel and Jed headed into the bar, no doubt to have a quick drink before heading for the farm, after giving his lover a head start. Cain wondered how long it had been going on, and what the hell was going to happen now.

'Well,' Deborah said eventually, 'that's quite made my day. Now, I'd better get back to Thwaite Park and organise dinner.' She giggled. 'I suspect both Beth and I will have quite an appetite this evening.'

'But ain't you bothered? Ain't you mad at them?'

'Mad at them?' Deborah shook her head. 'Cain, if you lived at Thwaite Park, you'd feel the same way I do about this. Absolutely thrilled to pieces for them. She did it. She finally did it.'

She kissed him lightly on the cheek, then headed towards the door. Cain watched her, blinking in confusion. He would never understand women. Best to lie back and enjoy it while they quietly ran the world.

****

James was in the garden, going over financial papers from the estate agency with his father. Documents were spread all over the patio table, and David picked them up in turn, droning instructions to James about how he should be running his own business. His father never believed that anyone could do anything better than he could. He had no faith in James at all. It was a relief when his mother joined them. Anything to shut his father up.

'Ah, Mother.' James shuffled the papers around and put them inside his briefcase. 'We were just finishing up. Would you care to join us for a glass of whisky or wine?'

'No thank you.' Maybe Deborah was as aware of her husband's angry expression as he was. No doubt his father resented having *the little woman* interrupt their business chat. He wasn't the most enlightened of men.

'I want to talk to you, James.' She sat down beside him, and he steadied himself. *Lord, what now?* 'It's about George.'

He felt, rather than saw, David's bristling, and gave him a nervous glance, praying he'd keep his trap shut for once.

'I've been giving the matter a lot of thought and I've concluded that we've — I've — been going about this all wrong.'

'Oh?' James shuffled in his seat, as David got up and headed into the sitting room, where the clink of glass through the open French doors revealed he'd made straight for the drinks cabinet.

'I charged in without thinking through all the consequences,' Deborah admitted. 'I should have taken stock, assessed the situation before I called in my solicitor. The fact is George is very happily settled with the Harlands. He's one of the family.' She glanced up as David approached, carrying two glasses. Ignoring him, she continued her appeal to James. 'To send Eliot Harland a letter demanding a DNA test and threatening to fight for custody was crass and, I hate to admit it, rather cruel.'

James accepted a glass of whisky from his father and gulped it down in one go.

'I do understand that you want your child back, James, but have you really thought about the effect it would have on him? Being wrenched away from his family would break his heart and have a traumatic effect on him. That's even supposing we won the case, and I'm not entirely sure we would. After all, you can't deny that George sees Eliot as his father and—'

'So, what are you saying, Mother?' James interrupted. 'That you're no longer interested in George?'

Deborah sighed. 'I suppose I'm saying it's too late for custody. Maybe, in time, we could gently push for access? But it would have to be handled carefully, as George isn't aware that Eliot isn't his father, and I think he's too young to deal with all that yet. It would have to be a conversation that Eliot could have with him when he feels he's ready to hear it.'

James couldn't agree with her more. 'So, you think it's best to back off for now? Not have anything to do with George at all?' he asked, hopefully.

'N-ooo.' Deborah thought about it. 'I think we should get our solicitor to write a conciliatory letter to the Harlands, detailing our intention to ease off, and requesting occasional contact with George in a non-threatening manner. The child doesn't have to know we're related to him, after all. Not yet. By the time Eliot judges that he's ready to hear the truth, he'll already be familiar with us. Surely, that's a kinder way to approach this?'

James nodded. 'I can see that.' Couldn't he just. But how to persuade his father of that?

'The thing is, it will take a lot longer,' she said, 'but it will be beneficial in the long run, for everyone. Give us all time to get used to this. George, after all, is the most important person in this mess, and we have to allow him plenty of time to adjust.'

'Bollocks!'

James flinched as David slammed down his glass. 'I've never heard such bullshit in my life. George is our grandson, James's son, for fuck's sake! Are you seriously telling me, boy, that you're happy for a child of yours to be raised at that dump of a farm, when by rights, all this should be his one day? You're okay with an uneducated, common brute like Harland to have sole responsibility for bringing up your son? Are you?'

James glanced across at a stunned-looking Deborah. Defeated, he shook his head and whined, 'Of course not. I want George here with me, full time.'

'There you go then,' David boomed, giving Deborah one of his best withering stares. 'There's your answer. Never mind asking the solicitor to backtrack, get him to push harder. I want this sorted pronto, and so does James. For God's sake, get a grip, woman.'

James opened and closed his mouth but found himself unable to utter a single word.

Deborah stood and smoothed down her skirt.

'I'll leave you to it,' she said. 'I can see you've made up your minds.'

'Yes, we have,' David said. 'And if you were any sort of a grandmother, it wouldn't even have occurred to you to back down. I'm telling you now, get your solicitor to push Harland hard. He's not keeping our grandson a minute longer than he has to.'

Deborah left the room, head held high. James had to admire her spirit. He wished he had the strength to defy his father, but there was no way out for him. The fact was, David had him exactly where he wanted him, and didn't he just know it.

Chapter 34

Deborah was waiting outside the bathroom door when Beth emerged, feeling pretty wrung-out and wretched. She jumped, startled to see her mother-in-law standing there, her arms folded.

'Sorry. I didn't know you were waiting.' Her voice trailed off. Why *was* Deborah waiting? There was hardly any shortage of bathrooms in Thwaite Park.

Her confusion increased as Deborah put her hand on Beth's arm and murmured, 'I want to talk to you. Come with me, Beth.'

Deborah wrapped her arm around Beth's waist and guided her along the landing towards her bedroom.

Stunned, Beth sank onto the plush, dove grey sofa by the window, as Deborah sat beside her and took hold of her hand. 'Beth, I need to ask you something. Are you, by any chance, pregnant?'

Beth took a deep breath. So that was it! Now she was in for it. But hadn't she known it was coming? This huge showdown was inevitable. She might have known it would be her mother-in-law she had to face first, rather than James. Nothing got past Deborah. Well, she wasn't going to cower or grovel any longer.

She held her head high. 'Yes, I am.'

Deborah beamed. 'That's wonderful news, Beth. I know how long you've wanted this and I'm so happy for you.'

The last thing she'd expected to hear in response was that. Nothing could have surprised her more.

'Now, the only question I have to ask is, do you know who the father is?'

Okay, so maybe *that* surprised her more. Beth's mouth dropped open and she felt the blood drain from her face. 'What do you mean?'

Deborah sighed. 'I know there's someone else. It's all right, Beth,' she added as Beth pulled her hand away, 'I don't blame you. Frankly, when I found out what you were up to, I silently cheered. I expect that's the last thing you expected to hear me say.'

'I don't understand.' *Understatement of the year.*

'I shouldn't think you do. It's not surprising. We don't exactly talk much, do we? My fault entirely. I've been an absolute cow to you, and none of it's your fault.' She stood and began to pace the room, her hands running through her hair.

If Beth hadn't known better, she would have sworn Deborah was nervous.

'I don't know how much you know about my own marriage,' she said eventually. 'I'm sure James has filled you in on some of his father's past behaviour, but I don't think even he knows the full extent of David's infidelity. I know how it feels, you see. What you went through with James and Jemima, I get it. All too well. Luckily for me, I didn't have to contend with a child as evidence of an affair, but I did have to contend with repeated humiliation and rejection. I know what that does to you. I know how it breaks you down, wears you out, until in the end you just disappear. I should have been kinder towards you, but the truth is, Beth, you reminded me far too much of my own mistakes, and I couldn't bear to watch.'

Beth was bewildered. 'I'm not sure I understand.'

Deborah sat down again, her hands twisting in her lap. 'You don't need to know the details, my dear, and I don't want to remember them. Suffice it to say, I wish I'd left David Fuller years ago.'

'Then why didn't you?' Beth was sympathetic, but she'd never understood how anyone could live with David Fuller if there was a choice.

'I'm really not sure,' Deborah admitted. 'I've asked myself that question so often and I come up with different responses every time. I'd fallen out with my family over him, insisted they'd got him all wrong. I suppose I didn't want them to know they'd been right. Then I had James, and I didn't want him to be raised without his father. I think I knew, even then, that if we weren't together our child would hardly ever see David. I just wish I'd realised that would have been for the best.'

She gave a sigh that sounded full of regret. 'Perhaps there was some fear; of the future, of being alone, of never being loved by another man. I thought I wasn't good enough for anyone else. He'd done a great job of shattering my self-esteem. When all you hear, day in and day out, is the constant drip-drip of criticism, you end up believing it. I was very insecure and convinced myself David was all I would ever have. And then, I suppose, the biggest lie of all. I told myself that I still loved him. I actually believed it, too.'

'But you didn't love him?'

'No.' Deborah rolled her eyes. 'I don't think I ever did, if I'm honest. He was something different and challenging. I was attracted to him. Our sex life was amazing at first. And he was the only man I'd ever — you know.' She paused. 'I'm sorry. I didn't mean to embarrass you.'

'You haven't,' Beth said hurriedly. 'It's — well, to be honest, I can't believe you're speaking to me like this. You never talk to me. About anything.'

'I'm so sorry, Beth. The thing is, I grew to accept the situation. I told myself I didn't care any more. That was the way things were and I had to accept it. I realised that if I didn't protect myself from the pain I would be broken. So, I built a wall around myself, locked my feelings away, forgot how to let anyone in. But you — I could see you going through the same issues with James. I could see how broken you were. I was so angry with you. I couldn't help it. I wanted to scream at you to wake up, to take control, to kick him out. In short, I wanted you to do what I never had the courage to do. When you didn't... I know it sounds stupid and so unfair, but I felt you were letting us both down.

Betraying us. I needed you to break free for *me*, as well as for yourself.'

Beth let out a long breath. 'I thought you didn't think I was good enough for James.'

Deborah gave a bitter laugh. 'On the contrary, I thought you were far too good for him. Oh, don't get me wrong. He's my son and I would do anything for him. But he's also his father's son, and, quite honestly, I don't like him very much. He's not good husband material. He's not good father material either. I was wrong to threaten Eliot and Eden the way I did. Eliot's been a better father to George than James could ever be. George is much better off at Wildflower Farm. Cain was quite right about that.'

There was something wistful in her tone. Beth watched her curiously.

Deborah gave a little shake of her head. 'So,' she continued, 'the baby. Is it James's? Or is it Jed's?'

Beth gasped. 'You know about Jed?'

'You were spotted together. I wanted to applaud you when I found out.'

'I thought you'd be furious!'

'I can hardly condemn you when I'm doing much the same thing myself with his father.'

Beth's mouth fell open. 'Cain! You and Cain?'

'I know. It's terrible, isn't it? We're absolutely shameless, aren't we?'

They stared at each other for a moment, then they laughed and hugged each other.

'I don't know who the baby's father is,' Beth admitted. 'I'm almost sure it must be Jed's because James and I — well, let's just say the chances are remote. Even so, there *is* a chance.' She sighed. 'I suppose I'll have to wait until the baby's born to find out.'

'And what will you do?'

Beth shrugged. 'I don't know. I feel so bad, Deborah. I know James did wrong, but he's tried so hard to make it up to me ever since Jemima, and if it's his baby how can I let another man bring it up?'

'But if it's Jed's?'

There was silence as Beth struggled with her answer. Deborah patted her hand. 'Beth, deep down, who are you hoping is the father?'

There was no hesitation in Beth's mind. 'Jed,' she confessed.

'Then you should be with Jed, whatever the outcome,' Deborah told her. 'You only get one life. Don't waste it on someone who doesn't deserve you. You've been a different woman these last few weeks. Jed clearly makes you happy. This is your chance to make a real life for yourself with a man who loves you. Don't throw that away.'

'But James has already given up one child because of me,' Beth murmured. 'How can I do it to him again?'

There was quiet for a moment, then Deborah said, 'Beth, may I ask you something?'

'Of course.'

'Do you really believe James wants George back?'

As Beth raised an eyebrow, Deborah ploughed on. 'What I mean is, did he ever, in all these years, give you any indication that he wanted to be George's father?'

Beth shook her head vehemently. 'Never. Just the opposite. He was always adamant that he didn't want anything to do with George. He told me George was a huge mistake that he'd rather forget. That's why I was so shocked when I discovered the truth. I felt terrible. He'd lied all those years to protect me.'

Deborah seemed to be considering her next words. Eventually, she said, 'Does he really strike you as the sort of man who'd act so unselfishly all those years?'

Beth was puzzled. 'What do you mean?'

'I'm not sure,' she admitted. 'I just think this is a very sudden change of heart, and maybe someone else is behind it.'

Beth stared at her. 'Someone else? Well, it did occur to me, but I thought it was you, to be honest. Are you saying — you mean David?'

'Exactly.' Deborah folded her arms grimly. 'Something's wrong, I can feel it. I talked it over with Cain and he convinced me

George belongs at Wildflower Farm. When I said as much to James yesterday, he seemed to agree, at first. He seemed relieved. Then David opened his big trap and James seemed to crumble.'

'He always does where his father's concerned,' Beth said with a sigh. 'He can't bear being shouted at by him. David has a way of making him feel very small and insignificant.'

'Yes, it's a real talent,' Deborah said. 'But that's even more reason to keep George away from here. Who'd want any child to be raised by a man like David? And he would be involved, make no mistake about it. The biggest regret of my life is saddling James with a father like that. I have no doubt it's led to him becoming the man he is today — one I'm rather ashamed of, much as I love him.'

'He's not all bad,' Beth insisted. 'I should have been forgiving. Everyone's entitled to one mistake. I just couldn't seem to get past it.'

'Hmm,' was all Deborah seemed to have to say to that.

'So, what are you going to do?' Beth asked. 'About George I mean.'

'I'm going to do what I intended to do. I'm heading to Richmond today to discuss the matter with my solicitor, and the Harlands will be getting a letter that should put their minds at ease. The problem I have is that David won't let it drop there, and James will do whatever David wants. I wish I could work out what's really going on here.' She smiled and patted Beth's knee. 'And what about you? What are you going to do about the baby?'

'I guess the next thing is to tell Jed,' Beth admitted.

'You mean, he doesn't know? Why not?'

'I wanted to have it all to myself for a little while, without worrying about who the father was, or thinking about all the mess this is going to cause. I've waited so long for this, Deborah. I wanted to cherish it, while I still could.'

Deborah smiled and put her arms around her daughter-in-law. 'I don't blame you for that. Well, know this, I'm on your side, I really am. And I don't believe I said it earlier, so, congratulations.'

Beth was hugged tightly and wondered dazedly if the day could get any stranger.

'Now,' Deborah said, pulling away eventually, 'I have another child who needs my help, and it's time I got started.'

****

'Face like a wet weekend.'

Eliot knew Adey was talking about him, but he had no energy to respond. He leaned against the stone wall, clutching the plastic cup from his flask in his hand, and stared unseeingly at the dale below him.

'Happen that tea's stone cold by now.' Adey tutted. 'Oy,' he yelled, 'are you going to eat summat or what? Nearly time to get back to work and you've had nowt.'

Eliot blinked. 'Not hungry.'

'Leave the lad alone,' Mickey growled. He chewed his ham sandwich and surveyed Eliot through rheumy old eyes. 'Tha needs to eat, though. He's reight about that.'

Eliot glanced down at the sandwich that Mickey held out to him and his stomach turned. He shook his head and tipped the last of the cold tea onto the grass. 'Best get back to work.'

'Not 'til you've had summat to eat and that's flat,' Mickey announced. He watched Eliot for a moment, then sighed. 'Look, lad, I know it looks bad, but things'll come reight. They allus do.'

'You reckon?' Eliot gave a half laugh. 'Wish I had your faith.'

'Eden'll come round,' said Adey. 'People row all the time. You and her are made for each other, anyone can see that. Just give her a chance to get over it and then it'll be back to normal in no time.'

'Normal?' Eliot gaped at his friend in amazement. 'How the hell can things ever be normal again?'

'Whatever you've done, she'll forgive you, lad,' Mickey began, but Eliot cut in.

'Why should she? I let her down!' His voice cracked, and he punched the wall. 'You have no idea what a bloody fool I am.'

'Oh, have I not? A bloody fool for punching stone walls, for a start. Does tha want broken knuckles?' Mickey tutted. 'And whatever it is that tha's done, tha's a bloody fool for telling her, an' all,' he added. 'Tha should have kept tha gob shut.'

'Weren't me that opened it,' Eliot muttered. 'Leastways, not to Eden. But the blame's all mine, no doubt about it.'

Mickey pulled a face. 'I'm thinking yon lass is to blame.'

Eliot frowned. 'Eden?'

Adey laughed. 'Nah. Baby Spice up at t'house. We've seen her, batting her lashes at you, staring at you with them big blue eyes.'

'Aye, and I said, did I not, Adey, that one's trouble. But you, you wouldn't see it. *She's vulnerable*, you said. *She needs understanding*, you said. Very kind of you, I'm sure.'

Adey nudged Eliot. 'You didn't, did ya?'

'Didn't what?'

'Well, come on. What's Baby Spice opened her gob about to Eden? Dun't take much working out, especially after you used me as your alibi that day. You could've warned me! And couldn't you have come up with owt better than that, any road?'

'It wasn't like that!'

'Glad to hear it, you daft bugger. Well, whatever's gone on, all hell's broke loose now and you're going to have to do some major grovelling to put it reight.' Mickey's eyes softened. 'Mind you, happen it'll be worth it. Adey's reight. You and Eden are made for each other. You'll sort it.'

Eliot's mouth set. 'If I were her, I wouldn't forgive me.'

'Aye, well.' Mickey sighed. 'Mebbe so. No use mithering on about it either way. Eat your dinner, lad. What will be, will be.'

'I'm only messing with ya,' Adey said kindly. 'Eden'll come around, you'll see.'

Eliot didn't answer. He felt a clutch of fear as he watched a figure heading towards them up the side of the hill. Eden. What had she come to tell him? Whatever it was, it was no more than he deserved. He knew that the next few moments were going to decide the course of his future, and he'd never been more scared in his life.

****

Eliot's face was stricken as Eden approached. She stood still, some distance from him, and watched as Mickey and Adey gathered up the dinner things. There was some mumbling going on, then Eliot moved towards her as the others walked away, and she waited, her heart thumping in her chest.

She folded her arms, almost as if protecting herself from him, which was ridiculous. She swallowed, her mouth feeling dry, as he approached her, and she saw from the look on his face that he was as terrified as she was. He came to a halt in front of her, not trying to touch her, not speaking. His eyes were crying out to her, and she had a desperate longing to pull him to her. What was stopping her?

'This thing with Emerald,' she heard herself say, then stopped.

He closed his eyes briefly, then met her gaze, his mouth a straight line. She saw the tension in his face and a part of her ached for him. 'Aye?'

She could hear the reluctance in his voice. He didn't want to talk about it, but she had to be sure of one thing.

'What's really going on with her?'

His head shot up and he stared at her incredulously. 'Nowt. Nowt's going on. I thought you believed me!'

'So did I, 'til I realised you'd told her the one thing I begged you never to tell anyone. Now I don't know what to think.'

'You don't mean that. You can't.'

'Why can't I?' she said, wanting to hurt him and hating herself for doing so at the same time. 'You spent the night with her, got drunk with her, spilled my secrets. For all I know, you had sex with her, too.'

'I did not! I would never do that.'

'You can't remember telling her about me and Ryan?'

'I swear, I can't.'

'Then how do you know you've not forgotten you had sex with Emerald?'

He looked incredulous. 'How would you forget that?'

'Oh! So, it would be memorable, would it?'

'That's not what I meant! You're twisting my words. You know I'd never betray you like that.'

405

'You just did!'

They stared at each other, dumb with misery.

Eventually, Eden spoke, her voice hoarse with grief. 'You've been weird about Emerald from the start. Blind to her. She's a devious little cow and you can't see it. Always on her side, always defending her. I know she's pretty, but even so. I thought you were more sensible than that.'

'Eden, please believe me. It's nowt to do with how she looks. I feel sorry for the lass, that's all. The way Cain's bin with her and being left out of everything. You didn't see her at the wedding. She was so upset and hurt, and I ... I just felt for her, that's all.'

'So, she can behave how she likes because *you're* sorry for her.' Eden bit her lip, trying to control her temper. 'I wonder how sorry you'd feel for her if she looked like a yow's backside.'

Eliot slumped, seeming defeated. He dropped to the ground and tugged violently at the grass. 'Are we going to go round and round with this all day?' He looked up at her. 'Two days it's bin, and you've not said a word to me. The kids are worrying.'

Eden blinked away tears. 'I know that, but I can't help it,' she murmured. 'I could never understand your attitude towards Emerald, and then the way you kicked off at me about taking George — where was the understanding and forgiveness for *me*? You're quick enough to forgive *her*! You were horrible to me, Eliot. I know I shouldn't have done what I did, but you didn't give me the chance to explain, wouldn't listen. Instead, you went off to get drunk, spent the night with that — that bitch, and told her my deepest secret. The one thing I begged you never to tell anyone!'

'I know. I know that! God, Eden, you think I don't know?' His voice rose, a hint of panic in his tone, and he clamped his mouth shut, staring at the grass. She saw him take a deep breath. 'Are you going to leave me?'

Eden's stomach plummeted. The despair in his voice broke her. 'For God's sake, Eliot, why the hell would I do that?'

He raised his eyes to hers. "Cos of what I did, the way things are.' He sounded bewildered, totally out of his depth. Did he really think that was how relationships worked?

'We've had a row. A big one,' she conceded, 'but still just a row. Do you really think I'd leave you because of that?'

His face was full of confusion. She thought, not for the first time, how much damage his relationship with Jemima had inflicted upon him.

Sighing, she stuck her hands in her pockets and gazed down at him. 'We're a couple, Eliot. Whatever's gone on, we handle it together. We work it out together. You don't run away — at least, I don't. You, on the other hand, seem incapable of facing up to an argument. You've got to learn not to run from our problems. You promised you'd work on that.'

'Aye,' he admitted shamefaced. 'I did.'

His misery tugged at her heart. 'You've been doing so well,' she said grudgingly. 'Let's count this as one setback and go forward.'

'You mean it?'

She shrugged. 'We're not out of the woods yet. I don't know where we go from here, and I'm not sure what we can do to fix it.'

He scrambled to his feet. 'We'll do whatever we can,' he said. 'Whatever it takes. But you know, don't you, that I didn't sleep with Emerald? That I would never do that to you?'

She hesitated, then nodded. 'I know. Even so,' she added quickly, 'Emerald has to go. Not because I have any doubts, but because I've simply had enough of her behaviour and her attitude. She can go to The Paradise or back to Cain's, or to Timbuktu for all I care.'

'Aye.' Eliot rubbed his forehead, clearly torn, but he seemed to accept he had no choice. It wasn't up for discussion. 'I understand that.'

'And if you and I are having problems, you don't storm off and confide in other people. You stay. You talk to me.'

He nodded. 'I promise.'

They stared at each other, and she saw the pain, relief and fear in his eyes.

'Is there anything else you'd like to tell me, Eliot?' She had to ask, although she suspected she was on a hiding to nothing.

The struggle he was clearly having was painful to watch.

'Nowt,' he said eventually, his voice sounding shaky.

Eden let it go, knowing that he would have to come to her in his own good time. Right now, there was something she had to make clear. Something he really needed to know, with absolute certainty.

'One more thing,' she said, her voice thick with emotion.

'Anything, Eden,' he said.

She choked back a sob. 'I love you.'

She saw the look of amazement on his face, then he held out his arms and she was safe within them once again, where she belonged, and he held her tightly and kissed her fiercely, and told her he loved her, too, and how sorry he was, over and over again.

Chapter 35

Jed pushed open the door and ushered Beth inside the hotel room. He wondered what the reception staff at The Paradise Hotel made of them. They were becoming such frequent visitors they'd be invited to the staff Christmas party at this rate. But the fact was, choices were limited. Wildflower Farm was out of the question, and he could hardly visit Beth at Thwaite Park. At least Kirkby Skimmer was far enough away from Beckthwaite to be reasonably safe, and once they were inside their room, they felt secure at last.

He was glad she'd called him. He'd missed her, and things had been tense at the farm this past couple of days. He didn't know for sure what had gone on, but clearly Emerald had done something to stir things up between Eden and Eliot. There was a big row going on in the kitchen when he left. Emerald had been yelling at Eden and Eden had been yelling back.

Maybe Jed should have stayed, tried to mediate as he usually did, but he wasn't in the mood. Besides, he'd been too eager to get to The Paradise and meet up with Beth. Her text had come out of the blue, and he wasn't going to miss any opportunity to be with her, however much Emerald might need him. They would sort it out. They always did.

Beth looked beautiful, he thought, as she sat on the sofa, her hands on her lap. So classy and graceful. Although, he considered, she also looked strained. She was watching him with those large, dark eyes, and he could see a trace of nerves in them.

He swallowed, wondering if this was the day he'd feared. Was Beth going to tell him they were over?

'Sit down, Jed.' That voice, usually so gentle and loving, was brittle and crackled with tension.

Jed sat, his mouth feeling dry. He tried to work out how he could persuade her to give him another chance, to not end their affair. She couldn't go back to the life she had before, surely?

'Beth,' he said, taking her hand, 'I'm trying to be cool with this, honest I am, but I can't do it.'

Her eyes widened. 'I'm sorry?'

'You can't throw this away,' he said, squeezing her fingers. 'What we have is special. Surely you feel it, too? I can't stand the thought of you living the rest of your life with that jerk. Don't do it, Beth, please.'

He held his breath as she stared at him for a moment, then slowly let it out as she reached out and stroked the side of his face, a smile on her lips.

'Oh, my poor darling Jed,' she whispered. 'Don't you understand how much I love you?'

He cupped her face gently. 'I thought — you looked as if you had something big to tell me.'

'And I do,' she confessed. 'There's no easy way to say this, and I have no idea how you're going to react, so I'll come out with it. Jed, I'm pregnant.'

The words echoed back through time. JoJo, standing before him, her tiny frame shivering as she stared up at him through tear-filled eyes.

'Jed, I'm pregnant,' she'd told him, and he'd let out a whoop of delight and squeezed her tightly, telling her how wonderful and clever and beautiful she was, and how she'd made him the happiest man in the world.

Beth was watching him, and there were no tears in *her* eyes. Just a trace of anxiety.

'Jed?'

He blinked as a delight so intense that it was painful battled with the fear. He fought to stay in control of his emotions.

'Are you pleased?' he asked her.

He saw the trace of disappointment in her face and felt like a heel. It wasn't what he wanted to say. What he wanted to say was how wonderful it was, and how happy he felt. He wanted to swoop her up in his arms and smother her with kisses. But he'd been here before, and it was terrifying.

'I'm more than pleased,' she said. 'I'm over the moon. Whatever happens, I want this baby more than anything.'

Now there really were tears in her eyes, and he remembered how long she'd waited for this moment, and suddenly JoJo vanished from his mind and he threw his arms around her, reassuring her that he couldn't be happier, and admitting how much he wanted this baby, too.

'You haven't asked me,' she said, when he finally gave her room to breathe, and she pushed him away laughing.

'Asked you what?'

The laughter in her face died, and she stared at him in anguish. 'You haven't asked me if it's yours.'

Jed reeled back. 'Are you saying...?'

He'd never asked, but he'd assumed that, once their relationship moved to an intimate level, she'd stopped sleeping with her husband. Had he been wrong?

'No,' she assured him when he voiced his fears. 'I swear to you, Jed, there's been nothing between James and me since you and I first made love.' She took a deep breath. 'But just before — after we first kissed.' She frowned. 'I already knew I didn't want him any longer, but I — I let him, because...' She shrugged self-consciously. 'It was stupid, I know, but I felt guilty. I'd kissed you, and I knew what my heart was telling me, and I felt ashamed. I'd withdrawn from James because of his affair, and here I was, desperate to begin one with you. I know it sounds crazy, but I felt like I owed him, so I let it happen. But it was the last time, I promise.'

'You didn't owe him anything,' Jed said, aghast. 'Least of all sex.'

'I know! I know that now,' she said. 'But you have to remember the state I was in at the time. I was so low, so full of self-loathing. I wasn't the person I am now. You've given me my self-confidence back. You've made me stronger. It would never

411

happen again.'

'But in the meantime, you don't know who the baby's father is.'

'No,' she admitted. 'I don't. Not for sure. I mean, the chances are it's yours. It would be a massive coincidence if James had got me pregnant now. But—'

'But we can't rule out the possibility.' Jed took her hands again. 'Whatever happens, Beth, I wanna be with you. I want to bring this baby up with you. I guess this is it. Crunch time. James is gonna have to know about us. Who do you want to be with?'

Beth's eyes gleamed with tears. 'You don't even have to ask me that, do you? I want to be with you, Jed. I love you. I don't feel anything for James at all, and I want us to be together.' She smiled. 'The three of us.'

Jed hugged her tightly. 'Then it's settled.'

'No,' she said, pushing him gently away. 'It's not. Much as I would love it to be. How can I do this to him? I've already caused him to lose one child. If this baby turns out to be his, how can I deprive him of a second child?'

Jed's stomach turned over in dread. He felt icy cold. 'So, what are you saying?'

'I can't make any decision until I know whose baby this is. I just can't. And how can I expect you to bring up another man's child? Do you even want children? I've never asked you.'

Jed stood and wandered over to the bed. He didn't know why, but suddenly it felt like he needed some distance between him and Beth.

'Jed?' Beth watched him nervously. 'What is it?'

'I never told you why I came back to Britain,' he said at last. 'I never really explained why I left the band.'

'You said you realised it wasn't what you wanted,' she said, puzzled.

'That's true enough. But it was what made me realise that counts. That's the stuff I never told you. About me and JoJo.'

'JoJo?' Beth frowned. 'Isn't she the singer in the band? I Googled Raven's Wing and there was a lot of stuff about her.' She sat up straight, her face suddenly closed off. 'She's very pretty. Very petite.'

'Yeah. Just five feet tall and a real powerhouse. The voice of her generation, according to *Rolling Stone*.'

'And you and JoJo were together?'

'For two years,' he confessed. 'We lived together, worked together, wrote songs together, performed together.'

'And you didn't think to mention it before?' Her voice was barely a whisper.

Jed heard her pain and tried to ignore his own. It felt like Groundhog Day. He'd been here before. He couldn't bear it all over again.

'We broke up, a couple of months before I came back to Britain,' he told her.

'And that's why you quit the band? Because you couldn't bear to work with her and not be part of a couple?'

He shook his head. 'No, Beth. I quit the band because I realised it wasn't what I wanted from my life. What I wanted was something I could never have, the whole time I was in Raven's Wing.'

She looked puzzled. 'So, what did you want?'

'A real life,' he said. 'For years, I thought I wanted a life like Dad's, but when I got it, I realised it was everything I hated. His own life was a car wreck. Why would I want to recreate that? I thought I could make it work, make it as normal as it's possible to be, when I was with JoJo. I thought we could have a life outside the band, but I was so wrong.'

'What happened?' she asked. 'Why did you break up?'

'JoJo got pregnant,' he told her. He saw her flinch and understood her reaction. 'I'm sorry, Beth. I should have told you sooner, but it was too raw at first, and then I didn't want to think about it when I was with you. I was so happy for the first time in ages, and I wanted to concentrate on that feeling. There'd been so much darkness beforehand.'

'But — but the baby?'

His fists clenched as he forced himself to remember. 'We didn't plan it, but I was over the moon. JoJo was apprehensive. She loved her career. She had big plans. She didn't want a baby to get in the way. But I told her we could make it work, and gradually she seemed to come around to the idea. We started buying baby clothes, thinking about names. We had a sonogram, and I saw its little heart beating.' He broke off, shaking his head as the memories overwhelmed him.

Beth moved over to the bed. Sitting beside him, she put her arm around him, and he leaned into her, grateful for her support.

'She wouldn't let us tell anyone, but I kind of understood, because lots of moms wait until after the sonogram, right? But even after that, she was telling me to keep it quiet. She was worried the record company would freak, that the band members would want her out. I told her she was far too valuable for that to ever happen.'

'Jed,' Beth said softly. 'What happened to the baby?'

He gulped. 'Gone.'

'Gone?' She put her head on his shoulder. 'She lost it? I'm so sorry, Jed.'

'She didn't lose it,' he said, his voice hard. 'She got rid of it.'

Beth sat up. He could feel her eyes boring into the side of his face, but he couldn't look at her.

'Got rid of it?'

'Yeah. She went to a clinic without even telling me. Turns out, our baby was an inconvenience to her, and her career was far more important.'

'Oh, Jed.'

'I don't want you to think I'm not supportive of a woman's right to choose,' he said, finally turning to her. 'I'm not that guy, Beth, honest I'm not. But she let me believe — she let me buy clothes for it, discuss names. We saw its heartbeat on the sonogram, for God's sake! How could she take that away from me?'

'How could she bear to do it?' Beth wondered aloud. She took his hand, squeezing it tightly. 'It was cruel, Jed. If she didn't want the baby, she should have told you so from the start.'

'I think she thought she'd fit it in,' he said. 'Then the guys started discussing a European tour. She got all excited about it. But it would have clashed with the pregnancy. She'd have been too close to her due date to do it.'

'Surely they'd have postponed the tour?'

'They'd have had no choice. JoJo was a big part of the band. But clearly, the tour was more exciting to her than our child. She made her choice. And that's when I made mine. I wanted no part of that world any more. I wanted to walk away, to find some peace, a different way of life. I never really expected to find all this happiness, all this love. You.'

Beth was quiet for a moment, absorbing all the new information. 'You wanted a baby so much,' she said finally, 'yet, as far as you knew, I could never give you one. Why did you stay with me?'

He gasped. How could she even ask that question? 'Because I fell in love with you! With or without children, I wanted my life to be with you. And there are always options. I figured we could adopt or even foster. There are so many kids needing love, right?'

Beth was openly sobbing. 'I can't believe the difference between you and James. I love you so much, you know that? I'm so sorry it's such a mess.'

'It doesn't have to be,' he said, cupping her face. 'Beth, you and I have waited for the chance to be parents for so long. We can't throw it away now. We love each other, right? We can make a great life together.'

'But if the baby's James's?'

'Then — then obviously he has access. We wouldn't stop the guy from seeing his kid, would we? But that's no reason to give up our relationship. Wouldn't it be better for a child to be with two people who love each other, even if one of them isn't his or her real dad?'

'I suppose so.' Beth shook her head. 'What am I saying? Of course it is. It's just that James has already lost one child, and I feel so responsible for that. To take away another child... But then, the baby may be yours, and if I stay with James until we can find out for sure, you're going to miss out on all the exciting pregnancy stuff that you missed out on before.'

Jed was quiet for a moment, thinking it through. He saw the anxiety in her face and knew the only honourable thing to do was to put his own feelings to one side.

'Look, Beth, you have enough pressure on you. Forget me.

415

Forget James. You have to do what's right for you, and for the baby now. Whatever it takes. You need calm and peace, and no pressure. Do what you have to do. If that means things stay as they are until the baby's born, then we'll do it. Just please, don't shut me out, okay?'

'I'll never shut you out, Jed,' she promised. 'I don't know what's going to happen yet but thank you for saying that. It seems I have a lot of thinking to do.'

'Just know I love you, no matter what,' he murmured.

'I know that,' she said, smiling. 'Believe me. I know.'

****

Emerald flung her suitcase on the bed and began to stuff her belongings into it. She was raging inside, after having a violent argument with Eden. That cow had accused her of all sorts, saying she'd manipulated Eliot from the start, and that she was a liar and a cheat, and a spoilt little brat. Spoilt! How the hell did she work that one out? Eden had no idea what her life had been like. None at all. She had some weird illusion that Emerald had been a rich little princess like Honey. As if!

She sank onto the bed, her anger ebbing away to be replaced with an overwhelming sorrow. She'd been far from a princess. Cain may have sent her an allowance every month, but she'd never been able to spend any of it. It had gone on paying rent and buying food. Keeping a roof over her head, and her mother's head.

If Honey hadn't reluctantly invited her to the wedding, if Cassandra hadn't insisted that she attend, and if she hadn't been so desperate to see her father again, she might still be with Cassandra now. Instead, events had conspired to lead her into Eliot Harland's path, and to Wildflower Farm, where she'd begun to see how a real family operated. She had continued to send every penny of her allowance to her mother, however, so the allegation that Eden had hurled at her infuriated her.

Where did she go now? Taking out her phone, she stared at it for a moment, then pressed James Fuller's number. If anyone could help her, it had to be him.

'This is a pleasant surprise,' he said, his voice soothing her frazzled nerves. 'How are things on the farm? Still World War Three, I hope?'

Emerald sniffed. 'It's awful. Eliot and Eden have made up and I'm getting all the blame and they said I've got to go. Dad will be furious with me and I have nowhere to stay and—'

'The Harlands have made up?' James sounded disgusted. 'For God's sake! What does it take to destroy their sodding world? You *did* tell Harland that you and he slept together?'

Emerald clutched the phone. He was obsessed with Eliot and Eden. Hadn't he heard what she'd just said?

'Don't you understand?' she said. 'I'm homeless and all my family will hate me. What do I do?'

As the tears fell, she tried desperately to keep her voice steady. The last thing she wanted was to come across all needy and clinging. The trouble was, without James what did she have? She *was* needy. He was her last hope.

He seemed to sense it, too, because his tone changed. 'Oh, darling Emerald, I'm so sorry,' he said. 'I never thought. Forgive me?'

'I don't know what to do,' she whimpered, feeling totally out of her depth and hoping he could wave a magic wand and make everything all right again somehow.

He seemed to hesitate a moment, then he said, 'I have several properties, you know. I could put you up in one?'

Emerald wiped her eyes. 'Really? But how much would you charge?' She thought about her father's allowance. It was needed by her mother. She would have to get a job. Could she get some sort of help from the state to cover her rent and food until she found one? Where would she get a job? Who would take on someone as useless as she was? 'I can't afford much,' she admitted.

'I'm sure we could come to some sort of arrangement,' he assured her. 'You know.'

No, she didn't know, and she wanted to be clear. She didn't want to move into a flat somewhere and then find out she couldn't afford the rent, did she?

'What do you mean?' she said. 'If you could just give me a figure…'

'Darling, there's no need to pay at all,' he said, his voice as thick and sweet as treacle. 'If I were to spend a few nights each week with you, I could hardly charge you rent, could I?'

Emerald felt nauseated. 'Spend a few nights a week with me? What do you mean?'

'It could be our little secret,' he told her. 'You get to live rent-free and I get to spend time with you. I'd never be so unappreciative of your beauty, you know. You wouldn't catch me sleeping beside you and not paying the slightest bit of attention to you. Believe me, Emerald, I'll show you how a real man treats a woman. I'm not Eliot Harland.'

Emerald stared at the phone in her hand, her mind whirling in horror. How had she been so stupid?

'Emerald?'

'No,' she said faintly, 'you're not Eliot Harland. And you never will be.'

She threw the phone on the bed, making Bella jump. Emerald reached for the cat immediately, disgusted with herself and with James Fuller. How had she got it so wrong?

She thought about Eliot, who had shown her nothing but kindness, apart from that one night when he'd snapped at her, and how that one little argument had wiped out all the good things he'd done for her and sent her scuttling off to James Fuller. She'd convinced herself that James was the good one, the innocent one, and she'd worked with him to hurt the Harlands any way she could. How childish and petty it seemed. And for what?

Tears rolled down Emerald's cheeks, dropping into Bella's fur, as she contemplated the future. Now Eden had made it clear she had to leave, wedding or no wedding, she would *have* to go back to Cassandra. Back to her mother's tantrums, her tears, her days of reproachful silence. Back to never knowing what mood she would be in when Emerald walked through the door. Back to that tight knot of anxiety in her chest when she woke each morning, wondering what the day would bring. How would she bear it?

Yet, what choice did she have? She couldn't afford to stay at The Paradise, and her father wouldn't want her. In fact, when he found out about her behaviour from Eden, he would probably never speak to her again. All the hopes she'd had of making him proud of her, of finally showing him she was worth paying attention to, worth loving, had come to nothing.

Bella nudged her softly and Emerald gazed into the cat's blue eyes, her own so blurry she could barely see. She would even have to leave this beautiful creature behind — probably her best friend in the world. At least Bella never judged her. She let out a strangled sob of despair, then jumped at a knock on the bedroom door.

As the door pushed open, she wiped her tears away with the back of her hand.

Jed looked down at her, his face full of concern.

'Hey, honey.' He rushed over to her and put his arm around her. 'I heard what happened. Are you okay?'

The fact that her big brother cared enough to enquire after her, despite Eden's undoubted efforts to make her sound like evil personified, just about finished Emerald off.

'Oh, Jed,' she sobbed. 'I've been so stupid.'

Bella made a leap for freedom as Jed held Emerald tightly while she cried noisily into his chest. It was a relief to stop pretending, to admit openly that things were dire, that her life was a train crash and she felt totally out of control. Jed listened patiently as she poured it all out, stroking her hair as she revealed the truth about her sense of woeful inadequacy, her appalling behaviour, and the shame she was now feeling.

'What can I do? I don't want to go home to Mother, and Dad's not going to want to know,' she finished, her throat sore and her eyes stinging from the unfamiliar outpouring of emotion.

'Wow, you really have got yourself into a mess,' he said. 'Why the hell didn't you tell me all this sooner? I could have helped you.'

She shook her head, wiping her nose before she dripped snot

419

onto his shirt. 'You wouldn't want to help me if you knew what I'd done.'

'Why not tell me and let me be the judge of that,' he said kindly. 'I'm sure it's not as bad as you think.'

'You don't know,' she said. 'And I don't want to lose you. Not you. I couldn't bear it.'

He gave a gentle laugh and smoothed her hair away from her tear-soaked face. 'Emmy, trust me. I'm going nowhere. You're my kid sister, and I won't leave you, no matter what you've done.'

She sniffed. 'Promise?'

'Promise.'

Emerald seemed to consider for a moment. 'Not even if I tell you, it was me who wrote those awful reviews and put a dud fuse in the freezer and ruined the guests' food?'

Jed narrowed his eyes. 'You're kidding?'

'Not so fond of me now, are you?'

'I told you. I love you no matter what.'

Emerald took a deep breath. 'Okay. I deliberately didn't tell Eden that Mrs Thompson had rung, because I wanted to go find Eliot myself.'

'But why?'

She eyed him nervously. 'Because I really like him, and I was kind of hoping he liked me too.'

'Oh, Emmy!' Jed sighed. 'He loves Eden. Besotted with her. You can't play games with people like that.'

'I know,' Emerald protested, 'but James said she broke him and Daisy up, and she went behind his back before, and—'

'James?' Jed's voice was sharp. 'James Fuller?'

'Yes.' Emerald looked down at her lap, ashamed.

'How do you know him? When have you spoken to him?'

'I've spoken to him loads. I've — I've been meeting up with him. He — oh, Jed, I thought he was my friend, but it's all gone so wrong!'

Jed studied her face for a moment, his expression grim. 'Okay, Emmy. I think you'd better start at the beginning. And no more lies, right? You want me to help you sort this mess out, you need to be honest with me. What the hell's been going on?'

Emerald hesitated, but only for a minute. She needed Jed to be on her side. She had no one else left. Besides, it would be a relief to tell him the truth — about James's attentions, about his obvious desire for her, about his hatred of the Harlands and their plot to ruin things for them so they would lose George. It needed to be shared. It was all too much for her.

'All right, Jed,' she said heavily. 'I'll tell you. But I warn you, it's not going to be pretty.'

Chapter 36

James threw down his briefcase and headed straight to the drinks cabinet to pour himself a whisky. He'd had a pig of a day at the office. He hated going in, and seldom did these days, but even work had seemed a better place to be than at home with his father. The bloody menace never seemed to shut up, going on and on about George and this damned custody case.

How, he wondered, did he get out of this? He didn't want the bloody kid hanging round his neck all day, every day. He didn't want trouble or inconvenience. He liked his life the way it was — well, mostly.

He thought about Emerald and Beth. Beth was his wife and, if he had his way, she would stay that way for good. He was quite fond of her, and there was no doubt that she was an extremely attractive woman to have at his side. But Emerald was driving him crazy. She was curvy and pretty and downright sexy, without seeming to have the faintest idea of how attractive to him she was.

She was so naïve and innocent it was unbelievable. He found it a huge turn-on and wondered how long she would continue to play hard-to-get before she finally succumbed, and he could take her to bed at last. It was getting ridiculous. The girl needed somewhere to stay, and he could provide it, if only she'd stop messing around and admit she wanted him, too.

It was driving him mad — the waiting, the longing. It had been bad enough that first night at the restaurant, when he'd wanted her so badly that he'd had to go home and have sex with Beth to get the lust out of his system. Now, even Beth wouldn't do. It had to be Emerald. He couldn't wait much longer. He couldn't believe she'd rebuffed him yet again. She was playing games, she had to be.

He could do without all this custody rubbish to distract him from his purpose. At least Emerald seemed to have accepted that nothing was going to happen with Harland.

He tutted in disgust. Harland! What an idiot. He had Emerald all to himself in a hotel room for a whole night, and he hadn't so much as touched her. But at least it had made Emerald realise he never would. Maybe she needed a little time to come to terms with that. Maybe he'd made his move too soon. Still, he could remedy that. She had no one else, after all. She needed him, and he would take full advantage of that when the time was right.

James decided he needed to clear the decks of the custody business and then he could concentrate fully on winning her round. There was just the little matter of his father to deal with.

At the sound of the front door slamming, James winced. No doubt that was his father now. No one else banged doors the way he did. Great. Another lecture. He gulped down the whisky and poured himself another.

'Would you like a drink?' he enquired, forcing himself to sound civil as the door of the sitting room was thrown open. He turned around, the fake smile dropping to be replaced by a look of stunned amazement as he came face to face with a tall, bearded, fair-haired man, whose piercing blue eyes only added to the impression that he had Viking blood in him somewhere. Jesus, was he a burglar? He would never be able to fight him off. Well, he could take whatever he wanted. No way was James going into battle with Thor. 'Who the hell are you?'

'You bastard!' It was little more than a growl, but James backed up hard against the drinks cabinet, suddenly very afraid.

'I said, who are you?' Then it occurred to him that the man had spoken with an American accent. A vague recollection came to him of Emerald speaking about her American brother, Jed, who was staying at the farm with her. 'Jed Carmichael?'

'Yeah, that's me.'

The man moved slowly towards him, his fists clenched, and James swallowed as he saw the muscle twitching in the man's jaw. What the hell was he so mad about?

'Emerald's brother. You know, Emerald? The innocent kid you've drawn into your web of lies? I should flatten you, right here, right now.'

'I beg your pardon?' James tried to sound cool and unconcerned but was very much afraid he'd failed dismally. 'I don't know what she's told you—'

'Everything. She's told me everything. I could kill you. How dare you drag her into your stupid vendetta against the Harlands? How dare you use my kid sister like that, you snake?'

'Now, hang on!'

He flinched as a hand shot out and grabbed the front of his shirt. He was slammed up against the wall and found himself staring into eyes that were like chips of blue ice.

'Give me one good reason why I shouldn't punch you, right here, right now.'

'Because if you do I will call the police immediately and you'll be jailed, you hooligan.'

James had never expected to feel gratitude towards his father but hearing his voice he almost wept with joy.

Jed, however, didn't even bother to look round. 'Totally worth it,' he drawled, keeping his eyes on James and not moving an inch.

James peered over the American's shoulder, frantically signalling to his father with his eyes to phone the police anyway. He could have shouted with frustration when David sauntered over to the cabinet and poured himself a drink instead. Charming.

'May I ask why you're manhandling my son?' he enquired.

'You may ask,' Jed replied. 'But maybe I should leave it to James to explain.'

James spluttered. 'Let me go,' he protested. 'I don't know what you're talking about.'

'Sure you do,' Jed said encouragingly. 'Go ahead. Tell your dad all about it.'

James thought he was about to lose consciousness. He could feel his head expanding by the second, and his heart was pounding so hard he could barely hear Jed's voice any more.

'Jed! What on earth are you doing?'

Fresh hope seared through James at the sound of his mother's voice, but then he felt a terrible shame as she called, 'Beth, Beth! You'd better come here, quickly.'

James wondered why on earth his mother was calling Beth. The last thing he needed was for his wife to witness his shame. This was embarrassing enough. He realised suddenly that the Viking had loosened his grip on his shirt and seemed distracted. James took his chance and kneed Jed in a most delicate place.

Jed leapt back. 'Son of a bitch!'

James ran for his life but had only just reached his father when Beth entered the room. She took one brief look at him, then her gaze fell on Jed.

'Oh my God!'

He watched, dumbfounded, as she ran over to the Viking and put her arm around him.

'What's he done to you?'

'Jed, what on earth are you *doing* here?'

His mother sounded quite urgent. James and his father exchanged bewildered looks. How did she even know this man?

'Can someone please tell me what's going on?' David demanded of his wife. 'How the hell do you and Beth know this brute?'

As Jed straightened, Beth looked up at him, her face full of misery.

'I don't understand. I thought we'd agreed—'

'It's about Emerald,' he said quickly.

'Emerald?' Deborah sounded puzzled.

'My sister.'

'What's happened to her?' Beth asked.

'*He* happened to her!' Jed jabbed his finger in James's direction. 'Go on, you gutless bastard. Tell them.'

'Tell us what?' Deborah said.

'I have no idea what he's talking about,' James whined,

425

wondering if he could get past his mother and escape.

'Jed, please, what's this about?' Beth said, and James frowned. What the hell was going on here? It was like Beth really knew this brute. She must have met him when she visited the farm, but there was no excuse for this easy familiarity.

'Okay, I'll tell you. That snake there, he's been using my kid sister. He's spent weeks flattering her, smarming his way around her, getting her to do his dirty work for her, all so he could get custody of George from the Harlands.'

Beth and Deborah stared at James, who felt his face burn with humiliation.

'Is this true?' Deborah demanded.

'Of course not. His sister is clearly delusional,' James snapped.

'You're a liar,' Jed yelled. 'You took her for dinner. You tried to persuade her to stay overnight in a hotel room with you. You'd already booked the room, but she said no. She got a taxi all the way back from Leeds because she didn't want to sleep with you. Then, when you knew she had nowhere else to go, when you realised how vulnerable she was, you offered to set her up in an apartment, rent-free in exchange for sex!'

'What?' The gasp came from his mother. Beth simply stared at him, her expression showing nothing but disgust.

'You got her to sabotage the Harlands' business,' Jed continued. 'She damaged the freezer because you said the more stress they were under, the more chance they'd break up, and if they failed financially there was a better chance they'd lose custody.'

Beth shook her head. 'You did that?'

'Not only that,' Jed added, 'but he and Emmy were the ones who wrote those reviews. Oh, my, I bet you had fun with that, didn't you? And then, when Eliot got drunk at the pub the other night, Emmy phoned you, and you tried to persuade her to convince the Harlands something had happened between them. You wanted everyone to think he was cheating, no doubt so the judge would look more favourably on you.'

'James!' Deborah's voice was loaded with shame. 'I always knew you were your father's son, but this is despicable, even by *his* standards.'

426

Beth had gone very pale. 'I should have known. It all seemed so unlikely. You put all that strain on Eliot and Eden. You're a disgrace.'

James could see the tide had turned, and not in his favour.

'It wasn't all my fault,' he pleaded. 'Father wanted George. He insisted we go for custody because of Owen and his three brats. He didn't want them to inherit Thwaite Park. What could I do? I didn't want George any more than Harland wanted to give him up, but we have to have an heir.'

'Seriously?' Deborah reached for the back of the armchair, seeming to need support. 'You're honestly telling me that all this was about this house? You never cared for that boy at all?'

'I knew it.' Beth seemed to slump, and James watched, annoyed, as Jed put his arm around her and held her to him. They were terribly familiar, weren't they?

A suspicion took hold in him that he tried to dismiss. Not Beth. She wouldn't have the nerve, surely?

'You never showed the slightest sign of wanting George, all these years. How could you lie to me? Pretend that you'd missed him, wanted him all this time?' She let out a sob. 'You told me it was my fault. That you'd sacrificed a life with your son for *my* sake. You made me feel like dirt.'

'It's not what you think,' James pleaded. 'I wasn't interested, honestly, Beth. I didn't care about the house, or any of the properties. Owen's brats could have the lot for all I cared. But Father said—'

Deborah turned a furious gaze on her husband. 'Oh, I might have guessed you'd be behind all this,' she said. 'I should have known. I thought it was strange that you kept out of the whole custody thing. Well, you both played me for a fool, didn't you? You wound me up like a clockwork mouse, then watched me scuttle off to my solicitors, making all those threats, making life for the Harlands miserable, and for what? So your precious Thwaite Park would be safe, just because you hate Kathryn and her family so much! Well, congratulations. I hope you're very proud of yourselves.'

'You make me sick,' Beth told James.

'But it wasn't my idea,' James pleaded. 'It was all Father.'

David had turned puce. 'Oh, really? Well, it may have been my idea, but why don't you tell your precious wife the reason you went along with it? Go on, boy, don't be shy.'

James felt the colour drain from his face as Beth stared at him, a challenge in her eyes.

'What's he on about?' she demanded.

'I'd rather like to know that myself,' Deborah said.

'Yeah, and me.' Jed tightened his grip on Beth, and James thought he would like to punch the bloody yob, if only he didn't have more pressing concerns.

'Father, I think we've all said quite enough for one day,' he said, hoping against hope that there was one scrap of decency left in David, but knowing in his heart that it had long gone.

'Oh, but James, your poor wife. Hasn't she suffered enough? Shouldn't you put her out of her misery?'

'Father. Please.'

'The reason James went along with my plan was because I told him that if he didn't, I would tell you the truth about him. The truth he's kept hidden for five years.'

'If this is about all the affairs he's had, save your breath,' Deborah snarled. 'He's your son, and we all know it. I doubt Beth cares any more how many women he's slept with.'

'There's been more than Jemima?' Beth whispered.

'Never mind the women,' David snapped. 'All those hospital tests, two rounds of IVF treatment, years of disappointment and heartbreak. James must've known how much having a baby meant to you. And yet, do you want to know something extraordinary about your precious husband, Beth?'

James watched in anguish, as Beth reared back from David's gloating face.

'When Jemima announced she was pregnant, James was so appalled, he went off and had a vasectomy.'

As everyone in the room gaped at him, David let out a shout of laughter. 'That's right! Five years he's been telling you to be patient, to wait a while longer, and in all that time he failed to reveal he was firing blanks. And the best part of it is, because of

George, you assumed it was your fault. And he let you! And you never wondered why he avoided any more treatment or tests during all that time. Oh, Beth, you *have* been a fool.'

There was a sudden movement, and David was pinned against the wall, as James had been moments before.

'If you weren't an old man, I would teach you to gloat at Beth,' Jed snarled. 'You pathetic, spiteful, evil old bastard.' He cast a sideways glance at James. 'As for you, words fail me. You don't deserve a wife like Beth. You never did. But you're gonna get what's coming to you, and I don't need to hit you to wipe the smile off your face.'

'What do you mean by that?'

James's words died in his throat as Beth walked over to him.

'All those years,' she said, sounding hoarse. 'All those months and months of despair. All your promises and reassurances and excuses. All that pain and heartbreak, and all the time, you knew. You *knew*!'

'Beth please.' James could see his world crashing down around his ears, but he had to try. 'I'm sorry. We can talk about it. Maybe we could adopt after all? You wanted to adopt, didn't you? I'd be up for that.'

'You must be joking.' Beth shook her head, and James watched incredulously as she took hold of one of Jed's hands, forcing him to release David, who slid down the wall and then struggled to look composed and in control. 'I'm leaving you, James. Thanks for making this easy for me.'

'Leaving me?' James looked from her to the Viking. 'For him?'

'Yes, for Jed,' she confirmed. 'I love him. And, for your information, we're having a baby together.' She looked at Jed and smiled suddenly. '*Our* baby.'

Jed's face lit up as if the truth had only just dawned on him. 'Our baby,' he murmured, and hugged her tightly.

'I'm going to make your life hell,' David growled. 'You won't—'

'Shut up, David.'

James gasped as his mother stepped in front of his father, her lip curled in disdain. 'You'll do nothing to Beth or to Jed. Nor,' she added, 'will you do anything to try to take George away from the Harlands.'

David laughed. 'Oh, will I not? You watch me!'

'If you do,' Deborah said coldly, 'I shall make your life hell. And you know I can. I won't just ruin you financially, I'll hit you where it really hurts. I'll make sure everyone who has ever met you knows the real reason we left Barnes behind.'

James watched, fascinated, as David seemed to shrink before his eyes.

'You wouldn't.'

'Oh, but I would. And I'm quite sure the lady in question would be more than happy to back me up. You do remember how freely she liked to gossip?' She turned to Beth. 'Go and get your things, Beth. We're leaving.'

'What do you mean, *we're* leaving. You're not going anywhere!' David spluttered.

'Wrong again. I'm leaving you, David, and not a moment too soon. I should have left you years ago — probably from the moment you started having affairs, which would have meant our marriage survived less than a year. Certainly, I should have walked away from you the minute you stopped being a real husband to me in any physical sense.' She shrugged. 'I think I've been far too lenient with you. Impotency is one thing. Refusing to do anything about it for a whole decade is quite another.'

'You're a lying bitch,' snarled David.

James couldn't take it in. 'Impotent? But— but he came back here because he'd had another affair!'

His mouth fell open as his mother let out a peal of laughter.

'Is that what he told you? Oh no, James. Bless him, he tried his best. He couldn't resist trying it on with a so-called friend of mine, and she was up for it, make no mistake. But it just wasn't happening, was it, David? And, unlike his previous failed conquests, she didn't keep her mouth shut. She wasn't married. She had nothing to lose. She entertained our entire social circle with all the sordid details. That's why we came back here. It was far too humiliating for either of us to stay. You know,' she said, shaking her head, 'I thought having to leave Barnes was the worst thing that could happen to me. Who'd have thought it would be the best?'

Stunned, James turned to his father. David's burning face was all the proof he needed that his mother was telling the truth. All that bluster and innuendo and showing off! And it was all lies. James sneered. So much for the big man. Well, he was never going to order him around again, that was for sure.

'You two deserve each other,' his mother finished. 'You're so alike it's painful to see. How did I ever think a sweet little boy like George could thrive in this environment? This family is poison, and I won't allow him to be contaminated. He stays with the Harlands. Do I make myself clear?'

David's eyes were full of hatred. 'Guess I have no choice.'

'No, you don't. Not if you want to see out the rest of your days in relative comfort.' She turned to James. 'You'll leave Beth and George alone, got it?'

He nodded sullenly. 'Bit much when your own mother takes sides with your cheating wife.'

'Yes, it is,' she agreed. 'And it breaks my heart because it just shows how low you've sunk. Well, I hope you'll be very happy, living here with your father in this luxury prison. I can only hope — and I do hope, James — that in time, you'll come to realise that there's no credit in being a chip off the old block. Not when this particular block is a lump of cold, unfeeling granite. You're still young, perhaps it's not too late for you to start again, be a better man.'

She glanced back at David. 'You, on the other hand, will never change. You'll be hearing from my solicitor in due course,' she said, then walked out of the room, followed by Beth and Jed.

There was a moment of shocked silence as James fought to take in the enormity of everything that had just happened.

'Well, congratulations, boy,' David growled, finally. 'You've really gone and done it now, haven't you? You always were a stupid waste of space.'

'Oh, fuck off, Father,' said James.

Chapter 37

Emerald hovered nervously by the farmyard gatepost as she waited for the sound of a taxi. She daren't step out into the lane in case she was spotted through the window of the bunk barn. Somehow, she didn't think Eden would appreciate another glimpse of her.

She sighed and looked down at her suitcase, wondering how it had come to this. What was she going to do?

Jed had called her around half an hour previously and told her he had booked a room for her at The Paradise Hotel, and that he would pick her up and take her there and she wasn't to worry. Easier said than done. The fact that she had been thrown out of Wildflower Farm would not escape her father's notice, and he was going to be furious.

She hitched up the large carrier bag she had tucked under her arm. It contained her Filofax and a folder with information and plans and receipts, all for Eden's and Eliot's wedding. The wedding which would leave them uncomfortable and unhappy. She'd been so wrapped up in revenge and playing games that she'd not given a thought to how they would feel at their own wedding. Eden was right. She was a selfish cow.

She glanced across the fields, spread out before her like a glorious watercolour painting. A great wash in various shades of green, with daubs of red, white, yellow and purple paint adding to the beauty of the scene. The masterpiece of wildflowers in Eliot's hay meadows.

Soon, they would be gone, and harvesting would begin. She realised how much she would miss these views, this farm. The Yorkshire Dales were the last place she'd wanted to be when she arrived in Skimmerdale all those months ago, but they had won her over. It was a shame that she had taken so long to realise it.

Hearing a car's approach, she quickly picked up her suitcase and stepped forward. It wasn't a taxi. It was Beth's car, and as Jed waved out of the window, she saw that it was Beth who was driving. Like this wasn't humiliating enough!

'Sorry I took so long,' Jed said, climbing out of the car and taking her suitcase from her. 'Packing took longer than expected.' He smiled at Beth and Emerald turned to him in surprise.

'Packing? She's left James?'

'I have,' Beth said calmly.

'Not because of me!' Emerald was horrified. 'Nothing happened, Beth, I swear it.'

'Not because of you, Emerald. It wasn't your fault. Please don't feel bad. This has been coming for a long time, and I'm just glad I finally had the courage to leave for good. It's the best thing that could have happened.'

'Come on, Emmy. Get in,' Jed said softly, as she stood taking a last look back at the farmhouse. She'd spent a good ten minutes saying goodbye to Bella and had shed a great many tears into the cat's fur.

There was no sign of Eliot, and she knew he wasn't likely to come over to say goodbye. Eden had made it very clear that they were in total agreement that she had to leave, and that was before they found out about the freezer and the reviews. She shivered, dreading the moment when that little revelation reached their ears.

The drive to Kirkby Skimmer was a quiet one. Now and then, Jed and Beth had a murmured conversation, but Emerald couldn't hear what they were saying, and she didn't much care. She could only think how she hadn't even had the chance to say goodbye to Libby, Ophelia and George. They were at school, enjoying the last couple of weeks of term before the long summer holidays. She hadn't realised how fond of them she'd grown. She would miss them, she thought with some surprise.

Jed, it turned out, had booked a room for himself and Beth, too. 'Just 'til we figure out what we're doing and where we're going,' he reassured her, as he helped Beth out of the car. 'It's a real family affair. Deborah Fuller's checked in, too.'

'Deborah Fuller?' Emerald's voice rose. 'What's she doing here?'

'Long story,' Jed said grimly. 'I'm gonna get Beth settled in our room, then I'll come over to your room and tell you all about it, okay?'

The receptionist gave them a welcoming smile. 'Mr Carmichael. Lovely to see you again. And I can see you're staying with us for longer this time,' she added, staring meaningfully at the luggage. 'I'll get someone to take your bags up to your room.'

Beth put her hand on Jed's arm. 'I can unpack. You go with your sister.'

Jed raised an eyebrow. 'You sure, honey?'

She nodded. 'I think Emerald needs you right now.'

Emerald flushed as Jed nodded and planted a light kiss on Beth's cheek. 'I'll be with you soon,' he promised, then grabbed Emerald's case. 'I can carry this,' he told the receptionist. 'If you can take my partner's cases upstairs, I'd be very grateful.'

'Straight away, sir,' she assured him.

Jed led Emerald to the lift and then along the second-floor corridor until they found her room.

'Back to where it all started,' Emerald said, trying to sound cheerful as Jed put her case on the carpet and bounced onto the bed.

'It could be worse,' he said cheerfully. 'At least the beds are nice and springy, and it's clean here. Food's not bad, either. Chin up, Emmy. You've got your big bro and your future sister-in-law living here with you, too. What's not to love?'

'Future sister-in-law?' Emerald smiled, despite her sadness. 'Wow. That's really serious.'

His eyes softened. 'Couldn't be more serious, Em. We're having a baby.'

Emerald gasped. 'Really?'

'Yeah. And before you ask, it's mine. No question.'

434

'I wasn't going to ask,' she said. 'It's just, Fuller said Beth couldn't have children. I don't understand. Was that another lie?'

'Not exactly. She'd never have children while she was with him. It's a long story.'

'Well, whatever, I'm so happy for you, Jed. You're going to be a great father.'

'Thanks, Emmy. That means a lot. So,' he continued, holding out his hand to her, 'now we have to sort your life out.'

Emerald pulled a face. 'I'm beyond redemption.'

As she plonked down on the bed beside him, Jed put his arm around her shoulders. 'No one's beyond redemption, sweetie. Well,' he added as an afterthought, 'almost no one. I might have to make an exception for James Fuller and his father.'

'What's his father got to do with it?'

'Everything. Turns out, he was the one pulling the strings.' Gently, Jed told her about the conversation that had taken place at Thwaite Park. 'So, you see,' he finished, 'they were manipulating everyone. It wasn't just you who got taken in. They fooled Beth and Deborah, too.'

Emerald's eyes shone with tears. 'It was all a lie!' She shook her head, appalled. 'He never wanted George. Not at all.'

'No. He wanted to appease his father, so that David would keep his secret.' He shook his head. 'Can you imagine anyone so cruel? All those years he let Beth hope that, one day, she would get pregnant, and all the time he knew it was impossible. My God, what I'd like to do to him.'

Emerald let out a strangled sob. 'But Eliot could have lost George,' she cried. 'I was helping James to destroy the Harlands, because I believed he loved his son and wanted him back. All the time, it was to protect their inheritance. George could have ended up living with a father who had no interest in him, all because of me.'

'Not because of you,' Jed said firmly. 'You made a mistake. An error of judgement. You weren't the only one taken in by the Fullers.'

'But poor George.' Emerald shook her head. 'What if he'd succeeded? What if Fuller had got custody? That poor little boy would have spent the rest of his life trying to get love from a father who didn't even want him.'

Jed reached over and wiped away her tears with his hand. 'I guess this is a bit close to home for you, right?'

Emerald swallowed. 'What do you mean?'

Jed sighed. 'I know how you feel about Dad, Emmy. I get it. You've tried so hard to get his attention, his love. It's not your fault that he doesn't respond the way you want. You know that, right?'

'But what is it about me?' she burst out. 'Why doesn't he love me? Why does he prefer Honey to me? Why does he prefer *Eden* to me when she's not even related to him!'

'Is this what it's all been about?' he asked. 'Your hatred for Eden — is it because Dad seems to care about her?'

'There's no *seems to* about it. He *does* care for her. He didn't even mention me in that wedding speech, but he sang her praises to everyone. Can you imagine how that felt?'

'No,' Jed admitted. 'I guess I've never experienced anything like that. But that doesn't mean I haven't been hurt, Emmy. It doesn't mean I haven't been through pain, had my heart broken in a different way. You asked me once what I was running away from. I'll tell you. I was running from my feelings. I was devastated. Someone had really screwed me over, acted like I wasn't important, like what mattered to me was of no consequence. She ripped my heart out. Destroyed me. That's what I ran from. I knew I had to find a way to forgive her, make peace with her and with myself, or what future did I have?

'You know, I could have stayed put. I could have made life very difficult for her. I could have told the world what she did, made things awkward and uncomfortable, turned people against her. What good would that have done any of us?'

Emerald sniffed. 'You're a better person than I am.'

'No. Just a bit older, that's all. And maybe I'm luckier than you, because I know who I am. I know my worth. When shit happens — and it happens to everyone — you gotta stay true to yourself. You gotta know what you stand for. Because, if you don't, when the storms hit, they're gonna blow you first one way, then the

436

other, 'til you don't even know where you are, or which way is up any more.'

He hooked his finger under her chin and lifted her face, so she couldn't avoid his gaze any longer. 'I think that's been your problem, Emmy. You don't know who you are, so when people let you down or bad stuff happens, you shift constantly.

'First, you're on one side, then the other. You agreed to organising this wedding because you wanted to win Dad's approval and get funding for the business. But Dad was cruel to you and Eden was your perceived enemy, so you decided to make the wedding a mess — everything Eden would hate.

'But then Eliot was so good to you, so kind. You wanted to help him, so you got Dad to hire a solicitor for him and went against Fuller, even though you were friends with the guy.

'Then Eliot turned on you, and what did you do? Instead of thinking, well, everyone has bad days, and maybe I should have helped more, you went running to Fuller and decided that he was the good guy after all, and you were gonna make the Harlands suffer.' He shook his head. 'If you knew who you were and what you stood for, you'd have made a choice and stuck to it a long time ago. And that's the question, Emerald. Who do you want to be? What sort of a person are you?'

Emerald's vision had gone blurry again. 'I don't know,' she whispered. 'A lost one.'

'The good thing is,' Jed reassured her, 'it's never too late to make the decision. Every moment of every day, you can change. You can get a fresh start. You can say to yourself, right now, this is the person I am, and this is how I want to be, and you can make the right choices. Then, no matter how hard the wind blows, you don't get knocked over. You stand strong and true. Emmy, the simple thing is, it doesn't matter who loves you or who hates you, who is kind to you or who is cruel. The only person who needs to love you and be kind to you, is you.'

'But I'm a horrible person,' she whimpered.

'No, you're not. You need to stop telling yourself that. Come on, Em. All that New Age therapy stuff you've learned! Surely, the first thing they teach you is to love yourself? It all starts there.'

'I don't know how,' she admitted sadly. 'All I see is the bad stuff I've done.'

'But it's past and gone,' he told her firmly. 'Right now, here,' he clicked his fingers, 'new start. Decide to love yourself. Decide to be good to yourself. Decide to do the right thing and listen to your heart, not all the chattering that comes from other people. Trust yourself.'

Emerald rubbed her eyes. 'I'll try,' she promised. 'What are you going to do now? Are you going home to Dad, or to America, or...?'

'Not America,' he said firmly. 'I'm back in the UK for good. I don't know where we'll end up,' he admitted. 'We have a lot to discuss. I'm lucky. I have money and I can afford to go anywhere, but I need to figure out what I'm going to do with my life, and I need to talk to Beth about where she sees us raising our child. Don't worry,' he added quickly, 'I'm not going to abandon you. For now, I'm gonna carry on working at Wildflower Farm. The shearing starts in a day or two, and in a couple of weeks they'll start harvesting. It's gonna be busy.'

'And there's the wedding,' Emerald murmured. 'That's next week don't forget.'

'How can I forget?' Jed surveyed her. 'Is everything done? Nothing left to organise?'

She shook her head, feeling sick. 'Everything's in place,' she said faintly, not wanting to think about the formal wedding she had organised out of sheer spite. Eden and Eliot were going to loathe every moment of it.

Jed was right. She couldn't go on like this. She didn't want to hate herself any longer. She was sick of guilt. She needed a fresh start, and it was all up to her, her choice. She had to be true to who she really was, and for the first time, Emerald realised what that meant.

It was time to act from the heart. It was time to be Emerald.

Chapter 38

Ophelia twirled around, her arms outstretched like a prima ballerina. 'What do you think, then, Dad? Do I pass muster or what?'

'You look daft.' George giggled, earning himself a disgusted look from his sister.

Eliot's eyes twinkled as he glanced across at an amused Eden. 'Well, I don't know. What do you reckon, love? Does she fit the bill, or should we give the job to another little lass?'

Ophelia stopped twirling and glared at her father indignantly. 'Like who?'

Libby nudged her. 'He's having you on, you daft ha'porth.'

He laughed. 'Of course I am! You look proper grand, both of you.'

Eden walked around the two girls, as they stood in the centre of the living room in their new bridesmaid dresses. 'And do they feel comfortable? Not too tight when you put your arms up?'

It was Libby's turn to look indignant. 'What do you mean? Do they *look* too tight, or summat?'

'Oh, you girls.' Eden shook her head. 'Honestly, I'm trying to have a decent conversation with you. I want you to be comfortable, that's all. I'm not accusing you of getting fat.'

'Hmm. If you say so.' Ophelia smirked. 'Although Libby *is* looking a bit porky. Happen it's best she gives up riding. Flora'll collapse soon under her weight.'

She staggered backwards, laughing, as Libby poked her in the ribs.

Eliot shook his head, smoothing George's hair as his son leaned against his knees, watching his sisters in bemusement. 'I dunno. You two are daft as brushes. I don't know why your mum puts up with you.'

He gazed across at Eden, who quickly looked away, feeling uncomfortable. She wondered if things would ever feel totally right between them again and found herself asking the same old question that had plagued her for days. Were they really ready to get married? Everything had changed, and it was no use pretending it hadn't. She felt as if they were going through the motions and it hurt her more than she could express.

Pushing the doubts away, she gathered the girls to her and squeezed them both. 'Because they're adorable, and I love them. You both look beautiful. We'll have to think about headdresses.'

'Headdresses!' Ophelia looked horrified. 'You're kidding, right?'

'Don't you want a headdress?' Eden queried, winking at George who was giggling to himself.

'What do you reckon?' Ophelia plonked herself down on the sofa, smoothing down the pretty Duchess satin print dress. 'Bad enough we have to wear a frock, but a headdress!' She squealed as George bounced onto the sofa and wrapped his arms around her neck. 'Don't mucky my dress up, George! Mum'll have our guts for garters.'

'I'm joking,' Eden assured her, ruffling her dark curls affectionately. Goodness knows, she'd been only too aware that Ophelia and Libby weren't the long, chiffon dress types, and had bought simple knee-length dresses with a pretty, summery, floral print. She'd bought them matching shoes, but other than that, she wasn't going to push her luck. She wondered what they'd say if she asked them to carry a posy of flowers each. Libby might be up for it, but Ophelia...

'There *was* one thing I were wondering,' Ophelia said suddenly.

Libby sat beside her sister on the sofa, giving Ophelia a slight shake of the head. Ophelia's eyes widened, as she gave Libby a meaningful look and turned back to Eden. 'We were wondering, would it be all right if we wore our lockets?'

'Lockets?'

'You know.' Ophelia glanced over at her father, and Eden did the same, noting that he'd gone very still suddenly. 'The ones you bought us that Christmas, Dad, with Mummy's photo in.' She shrugged. 'I thought — well, it's a special day, and it would be grand if Mummy could be a part of it.' She looked from one to the other, as Libby sat with her head down. 'Libby says I shouldn't ask, it's not the right time, but I reckon Mummy would want to be part of the day, don't you? She'd always want Dad to be happy and—'

Libby kicked her hard on the shin, as Eliot stood and headed out of the room.

'Ow! What was that for?' Ophelia glared at her sister, then looked up at Eden, an appeal in her eyes. 'Have I said summat wrong? It's not bad to want Mummy at the wedding, is it?'

Tears blurred Eden's eyes. 'No, sweetheart. Of course it isn't. Look, why don't you two go and hang those dresses up for me and keep an eye on George. I'm going to check on your dad. Okay?'

'Is he all right?' Libby sounded doubtful, which didn't surprise Eden in the slightest. The girls — and Libby especially — had become attuned to Eliot's moods since the death of his wife and were keen to protect his feelings at all costs.

'I'm sure he's fine,' Eden reassured her, though privately she was wondering exactly how he'd taken Ophelia's request. 'I'll go and talk to him now, okay?'

The girls nodded and went upstairs, Libby holding George's hand. Eden took a deep breath. She'd known this conversation was coming, and the truth was, it was desperately needed. Time to clear the air at last. They'd both been so shocked and scared after their recent crisis that it seemed to her they were now afraid to express any deeper truths to each other, for fear of driving an even bigger wedge between them, but Eden knew things weren't right, and she couldn't go on pretending. This wasn't the basis for a happy marriage.

Eliot wasn't in the house, and Eden wandered through the yard, glancing across at the bunk barn as she went. They had four guests currently, but another eight booked in for the weekend. By August, their bookings had risen sharply, and every bed was taken for the first four weeks of the summer holidays. At least the appalling reviews hadn't put people off. She'd been surprised that morning to discover that three of the negative reviews had disappeared, and that she had a handful of new reviews, all very positive. She had no idea what was going on, but she wasn't going to question it. It was a huge relief, after all.

She found Eliot leaning on a gate at the lower hay meadow, gazing out over the last of the wildflowers. In a couple of weeks mowing would start, providing the good weather held. It was a busy time of year, but a satisfying one, and the children loved it.

First though, they had to get through the shearing. They'd already gathered the sheep on the moors and brought them to the lower fields near the house.

If the weather stayed fine the shearing would be over inside a week, and she smiled to herself, remembering how the children had joined in last year, helping to round up the sheep and herd them into the shearing shed, with even George bouncing up and down on the wool sheets to pack the wool down tightly. Mickey was wonderful at shearing, despite his age, and even Eliot bowed to his superior skills, leaving most of the clipping to him. The farmyard was always chaos at that time of year, but it was enjoyable work.

Then there would be a short lull before harvesting, which was why she'd booked in the wedding before the next round of really hard work started. The wedding was only days away, really. If it went ahead.

Eliot turned to look at her as she approached, and she swallowed hard as she realised his eyes were wet.

'Sorry,' he said as she came to stand by his side. 'I know I said I wouldn't walk out again if we had words, but this was different. I wasn't storming off. I just needed some space.'

'It's okay. I understand.' Eden slipped her arm through his, and she felt him relax against her, as if he'd been tensed up waiting for an argument, and her acceptance had given him permission to breathe again. 'But I do think we need to talk,' she said. 'Things aren't right, are they?'

He studied her face, his eyes showing anxiety. 'Is this about Emerald again?'

She smiled. 'No, it's not. All the stuff with Emerald — well, she's gone now. It's done. But there's something else going on, isn't there? There's something between us and I don't know what it is, but I feel like there's a barrier, and it's breaking my heart.'

'It's my fault,' he said, sounding choked. 'It's all my fault.'

'It takes two,' she pointed out. 'It can't be all your fault.'

'But it is.' He leaned heavily on the gate. 'There's summat I haven't told you. Summat I haven't been really honest about.' He massaged the bridge of his nose with his thumb and finger. 'Truth is, I don't know how to start.'

Eden stayed silent for a moment, but when she saw his grim expression and realised he was making no move to begin, she let out a little sigh and said, 'How about I start for you?'

He looked down at her, startled, as she whispered, 'This is about Jemima, isn't it?'

'How — what do you mean?' His voice was thick with emotion, and her heart went out to him.

'It's okay, Eliot. It's all right to admit you're grieving for her.'

'What's to grieve?' he said harshly. 'She didn't love me anyway.'

Eden pulled him round to face her and wrapped her arms around his waist, resting her head on his chest.

'Yes, she did,' she said. 'She loved you deeply, and you loved her, and that's absolutely fine. Nothing and nobody can take those early years away from you. You have two beautiful daughters to prove it.'

She felt him shudder against her skin and held him tighter. 'What happened later has no bearing on the fact that you loved her enough to marry her, and she loved you enough to marry you. To move to Wildflower Farm. To give you two children. What came later doesn't erase what happened first. Those memories are yours to cherish.' She lifted her head, her gaze soft with compassion as she saw the battle he was clearly fighting to stay in control of his emotions. 'The problem with you, Eliot, is that you've told yourself she never loved you, so you have no

443

right to grieve for her. You've let what happened at the end colour your reaction to her death, and it's crippling you.'

She could feel him trembling, but he still said nothing. She persisted, determined to reach him. 'You kept disappearing, and I wondered where you were going and why you never said, but then Mrs Edwards mentioned seeing you in Camacker and you came up with that daft story about Adey and the beer, and gradually it dawned on me that you were going to visit Jemima's grave. I'm right, aren't I?'

Eliot gripped her tightly. 'It dun't mean I don't love you, Eden. It takes nowt from what we have.'

Relieved that he was finally talking, Eden moved to reassure him. 'I know that! Is that what you were worried about? That I'd see Jemima as some sort of threat? Eliot, she was a huge part of your life. I'd be amazed if you didn't want to visit her grave at times. I'm glad you went to visit her. I'm just surprised and a bit hurt that you didn't feel you could tell me.'

'How could I tell you?' He gazed at her in anguish. 'I've spent over two year telling you me and Jemima meant nowt to each other. How could I tell you I—' He broke off, shaking his head.

'Go on,' she urged. 'Tell me now.'

He slumped against her. 'I don't understand it meself, love,' he confessed. 'I thought I were past all this, but it keeps getting stronger and stronger and — truth is, I don't know how to handle it.'

'Handle what?'

He closed his eyes. 'I miss her sometimes,' he murmured. His eyes flew open and he added fiercely, 'But that dun't affect how much I love you. You have to believe me about that.'

A stab of jealousy pierced her heart, but she ignored it. This was more important than her own stupid insecurities. Eliot needed her to understand, and she did, deep down.

'I do believe you,' she said truthfully, knowing that only her faith in his love was giving her the strength for this conversation. 'Go on. Tell me how you feel about Jemima now. Don't be afraid. Trust me.'

'I — I thought I was over it, but I keep remembering stuff. Stuff

444

from when we were first wed.' He tutted. 'Stuff I'd forgotten, buried along with her. But it wasn't always bad. Truth is, you're right. Whatever I've said in the past, I loved her.' He drew a great, shuddering breath. 'I loved her so much, and then it all went wrong, and she — she *died*, Eden.'

Suddenly, Eden found herself crying, as great, wracking sobs shook his body and vibrated through hers. 'I know,' she soothed through her tears, 'I know. It's okay. It's all right.'

'I don't know why,' he kept repeating, clearly bewildered by his own emotions.

'I think, maybe this wedding has brought it all back. Stirred it up.' Eden stroked his hair. 'You've not been yourself ever since we booked it, let's face it. I thought it was because of the stress of this fancy wedding you've set your heart on, but clearly there's been more to it than that.'

'I'm worried about Georgie — whether I'm doing what Jemima wants. She loved Fuller. Mebbe she'd want him to have the lad?'

'You can't really think that?'

'I don't know! That's the trouble. She was taking him away from me. She wanted Fuller's name on the birth certificate. What if she can't rest, knowing I'm bringing their son up?'

'Eliot, this is ridiculous. The one thing I know about Jemima is that she loved her children. Really loved them. The last thing she'd want is for George to be brought up by someone who couldn't be bothered with him when he was a helpless baby. And she'd want her children to be together, I'm sure of that. Whatever happened between you, you're a good father, and Jemima knew that. I'll bet she'd be so grateful to you for all you've done for the children. Really.'

'I keep trying to tell meself that. Truth is, I feel guilty that I can move on,' he confessed. 'Here I am, with you at my side. You've made me so happy, and I love you so much. But Jemima's in the ground. No second chances for her are there? She was so young, and so beautiful. It isn't fair. Whatever she did, however she behaved, that's not fair is it?'

'No,' Eden agreed softly. 'It isn't. Life isn't fair sometimes, and we can't change that. All we can do is try to make the best of the good times while we can.' She paused. 'But if you feel so guilty about Jemima, why were you insistent that we had a big, formal wedding?'

Eliot wiped his eyes. 'I know it sounds daft, but I kept remembering my first wedding. Just the two of us, there were, and a couple of people she knew as witnesses. I wouldn't call them friends, since they never bothered to visit afterwards. We nipped into registry office and had a quick drink in the pub, then it were back to farm. That were it.' He gave a mirthless laugh. 'We thought it was romantic at the time. Whole world seemed against us, but we had each other. Well, look how that turned out.

'I thought — I thought it had to be different this time. Maybe, if we could have a beginning that was completely the opposite, we'd have an ending that were different an' all. I wanted us to be happy ever after, Eden, and I thought, maybe having the works would give us that. I wanted a church wedding, with God's blessing on us.' He shrugged. 'Not even sure I believe in God, but if He is up there, I want Him on our side from the off. And a church full of all the people we know and love, wishing us well. And no quick nipping in to get wed then going home. I wanted us to have it all — a right big party with all the stuff me and Jemima should have had but didn't. Mebbe—' he tutted, 'and I know how daft it sounds, but mebbe if we'd had all that stuff, things might have worked out different.'

Eden narrowed her eyes. 'You really believe that?'

He hesitated for a moment. 'I suppose not, not when I think about it logically. But I didn't want to challenge fate, so to speak. Do you understand?'

'I think I do, yes.'

'Jemima gave up everything to be with me,' he murmured, looking out across the meadows. 'She didn't realise it, of course. She thought her family would come round, that her dad would cave in and come and visit her, but he never did.' His tone hardened. 'How could he cut her off like that? Broke her heart. She did some bad things, made some big mistakes, but at heart, she just wanted her dad, truth be told.'

Eden stepped back and stared up at him, aghast. 'Like Emerald!'

She saw the sheepish expression on his face and gasped. 'That's it, isn't it? That's why you kept taking Emerald's side, gave her chance after chance, felt so sorry for her! To you, she's another Jemima.'

'I thought I could help her in a way I couldn't help Jemima,' he confessed. 'Jemima had no one to turn to, no one on her side. I let her down badly. I didn't realise how much it got to her, how much she gave up for me, for us. Emerald loves Cain, and all she wants is for him to love her back. I wanted her to know that, whatever her dad did or didn't do, she had friends. People who cared about her no matter what. Jemima didn't.' He tutted. 'Except for Fuller, who sensed her vulnerability and moved in on her.'

Hesitantly, he placed his hand on Eden's shoulder. 'Do you understand what I'm saying, my love? Have I made things between us even worse?'

'Of course you haven't. I understand completely.' Eden felt a bubbling surge of relief and joy. 'I knew there was something between us, I just couldn't figure out what. Then I started to put two and two together, but I knew you had to work it out for yourself first. I'm so glad Ophelia mentioned the lockets, because it finally made you crack. I was beginning to think you never would.'

Eliot sighed and pulled her to him, and they stood for a few moments, worn out and battered, but united at last.

'This wedding,' Eden said eventually, 'it's not what you want at all, is it?'

'I want what you want,' he said. 'Truth is, you deserve the best, like Cain says.'

'But what if what I want isn't what you think?' she said. 'I told you, months ago, that I'd be happy with a registry office wedding and straight home again. All that matters to me is that we're married.'

'But you said you were looking forward to a big do,' he protested. 'You let Cain put Emerald in charge and everything.'

'Because I thought it was what you wanted, and I can see now that we've been at cross purposes.'

Eliot frowned. 'What did you really think to Emerald's mood board?'

Eden burst out laughing. 'Appalling! Everything I don't want! How about you?'

'Same,' he admitted. 'I were gutted, but I thought you liked it.'

'I thought *you* liked it.'

They pressed their foreheads together, wide grins on their faces.

'We've proper messed this up,' Eliot said.

'It's not too late, though,' Eden said slowly. 'I don't want this wedding, you don't want this wedding.'

'What are you saying, my love?'

'Eliot, I think we should scrap the whole bloody thing.' She reached up and planted a kiss on his lips. 'Shall we visit Mr Edwards?'

He paused for a moment, then nodded. 'Aye, we will. But first, there's summat I've got to do, and now I know you'll understand why.'

As his gaze fell on the last of the wildflowers, Eden smiled.

'I think that's a lovely idea,' she said softly. 'Let's go and say goodbye to Jemima properly.'

****

Eden opened the oven door and peered in, nodding in satisfaction at the sight of the well-risen, golden scones. 'They'll do,' she pronounced, reaching for her oven gloves and carefully lifting the baking trays out. It would be all she needed if she dropped them after all that effort!

With great attention, she placed them all on wire racks to cool, then shoved the baking trays on the draining board, yawning as she did so. She'd tackle the washing up in a minute, she thought.

Outside, she heard the protesting bleats from the sheep, as Lug and Jake herded them through the farmyard where Eliot and Jed shut them into pens, ready for Mickey to begin the shearing. Eliot would be clipping them, too, but he readily admitted he wasn't as fast as Mickey and, frankly, he hated the job. Maybe, she thought, it would have appealed more if he made any money from the fleeces. Those days seemed to be long gone, though.

She knew the men would be hot and bothered by now. The sheep hated being penned in, and they struggled ferociously when they were handled. They seemed unable to grasp that it was for their own good. They needed rid of those thick fleeces now that summer was well and truly here.

She filled the kettle with water, knowing all too well that the men would be desperate for a cup of tea.

There was a knock on the door, and she hurried through to the hallway, scooping down to collect a bundle of letters from the floor before opening the door.

'Sorry to bother you.' A middle-aged couple with rucksacks on their backs smiled at her uncertainly. 'There's a sign by the gate saying cream teas, and that chap over there,' the man added, nodding over at Jed, who was currently struggling with a rather lively and thoroughly stubborn gimmer, 'said to knock here. Is that all right?'

She smiled. 'Yes, of course. Scone, jam and cream and a cup of tea?'

'Lovely,' they said, enthusiastically.

'If you go and sit at one of the picnic tables by the beck, I'll bring it out to you,' she promised.

She hurried back into the kitchen, flicking through the letters as she did so. Her heart stopped as she saw the lettering on the back of a particularly thick, expensive looking envelope. *Hebblewhite and Wilson, Solicitors, Richmond.* Eden's stomach churned in dread. What did they want now?

She pushed the letters to one side and concentrated on the job in hand. She made tea for everyone, using cups for the hikers and mugs for the workers, then she reached into the cupboard and brought out the large cake tin which contained an earlier batch of scones.

Quickly, she placed two of them on plates, added dishes of clotted cream and jam and put them all on a tray, along with the cups of tea and cutlery.

She carried the tray over to the picnic table, where the hikers

449

greeted her with great eagerness and much appreciation, along with their payment.

Assuring them that they were welcome, she headed back to the farmhouse, deep in thought. She would have to tell Eliot, of course, but was it best to wait until the evening, when the kids were in bed and shearing was over for the day? Would he be able to concentrate if the letter was yet more bad news?

In the event, she had no need to decide. As she re-entered the kitchen, Eliot was leaning back against the sink, his brows knitted together in a frown as he perused the letter in question.

He looked up as she approached and waved the piece of paper at her. 'You have to see this!'

Nervously she stretched out a hand. 'Bad news?'

He looked dazed. 'I dunno what to make of it. It dun't make no sense, my love. What do you think?'

Eden quickly read through it, her eyes widening the further down she got. 'But — but — why?'

'I have no idea.' He sounded bewildered, as well he might. Deborah Fuller's solicitor was more-or-less apologising for his previous letters and had assured them there would be no further action taken, regarding seeking custody of George Harland, nor even in seeking to finally determine his true parentage. In other words, case closed.

'All I can think,' Eliot murmured, 'is that Beth leaving Fuller's had summat do with it.'

'Maybe Jed would know,' she suggested, still reeling from the recent revelation that Beth and Jed were a couple.

When Jed had told them that morning, she'd been so excited for them. Jed had eyed Eliot doubtfully, aware that he and Beth went back a long way. It must have come as a big relief to him when Eliot clasped his hand and told him he couldn't be happier for them. Personally, Eden hadn't expected any other reaction.

'Happen. I'll ask him.' He shook his head. 'I dunno, I only came in to see if there were any chance of a brew, and what do I find? Mugs of tea all ready and waiting for us, and this! What a day.'

'We must find out if he knows anything,' Eden said, a part of her afraid that this was some trick. She couldn't believe the nightmare could be over so easily. 'I'll carry mine and Mickey's mugs over, you take Jed's.'

Jed was watching Mickey in awe.

'This guy's incredible,' he said, nodding his thanks as Eliot handed him his tea. 'Ninety seconds! Ninety seconds to shear a whole sheep. How is that even possible?'

'No idea,' Eliot admitted. 'Takes me that bloody long to switch yon clippers on.'

'Jed, we've had a letter,' Eden said, failing to keep the anxiety from her voice. 'We wonder if you had any idea what brought it on? It's from Deborah Fuller's solicitor.'

Mickey pushed the sheared gimmer out from between his legs and switched off the clippers. Wiping the sweat from his eyes, he reached for the mug of tea in Eden's hand and sipped gratefully, his eyes shrewd as Jed scoured the letter.

'I was expecting this,' Jed admitted at last. 'I didn't think it would be this quick. I guess Deborah's a woman of her word.'

'You knew?' Eliot said.

'Yeah, but I didn't want to get your hopes up, just in case. Thing is, Deborah kind of threatened her husband and son. She had some interesting information about David Fuller that he wouldn't want made public, and since it seems it was him pulling the strings, not James, when he backed off, the whole thing crumbled.'

'Threatened them with what?' Eden said, curious.

Jed shook his head. 'Not my business,' he said. 'What I can tell you is, James never wanted George at all. He was doing what his father ordered. And the truth is, for David Fuller, it was all about money and spite. James's grandfather tied up Thwaite Park and some other properties, so that they had to remain in the possession of direct family. If James dies without an heir, it all passes to his cousin and his kids, and apparently, David loathes them. He was adamant that James needed a child, and when he found out about George — well, it kinda solved the problem. Except, he didn't want George to grow up a sheep farmer who had no clue about business or money. They planned to bring him up a Fuller through and through, so he'd inherit Thwaite Park

451

and be worthy of it — in their eyes, at least.'

Eliot slumped against the wall.

'They never really wanted him,' he muttered, as if he couldn't believe it. 'They never wanted Georgie at all. He was just part of their business plan.'

Eden rubbed his arm sympathetically. 'It's over now,' she told him. 'They lost, remember? And George is ours, for good.'

'Eden's right,' Jed said earnestly. 'You don't have to worry about losing him ever again. This is great news all round, right?'

Eliot nodded. 'Aye. You're right.'

'And it means you can enjoy the wedding, without even worrying about all of this. No dark clouds hanging over you. It's gonna be a great day.'

Eliot and Eden looked at each other.

Eden cleared her throat. 'Ah yes, Jed. The wedding. About that ...'

Chapter 39

Cain felt as if his head were about to explode. 'This is a bleeding catastrophe,' he yelled. 'Disaster! I should have known. Fancy leaving you two alone here. I must need me head read.'

'Calm down, Dad,' Jed soothed. 'Things are never as bad as they seem.'

'Never as bad as they seem!' Cain's face was purple. 'I've got me son shacked up with someone else's missus, and now he tells me there's a sprog on the way, me daughter's bin playing fast and loose with Eden's fiancé, spending the sodding night with him no less, and now this! All that money! All that time! All that planning! And now the wedding's off. Well!' He waved a handful of papers in Emerald's face. 'I hope you're happy with yourself, 'cos this wedding-that-is-no-more has cost me a small fortune, and that money's coming off the cash I was gunna lend you for your business. So, see how you like that!'

Emerald hung her head, as well she might. Little git. Cain couldn't believe how badly things had deteriorated since his last visit. He should never have trusted his children. Jed was Lowri's son, after all, and everyone knew what a conniving, scheming bitch *she* was. As for Emerald. Well. Cassandra. 'Nuff said.

'I wouldn't be so quick to fling accusations around,' Jed said quietly. 'And I'll thank you not to refer to my unborn child as a sprog.'

'Let's hope it is *your* unborn child,' Cain snapped. 'You might spend the next twenty years raising another bloke's kid. See how you like that.'

He stepped back, suddenly alarmed at the expression on Jed's face.

'The baby is mine, no question,' Jed blasted. 'And maybe you ought to stop with the insults, considering you've been having an affair with Beth's mother-in-law.'

Cain felt the blood drain from his face. 'Who told you that?'

'Beth and I have no secrets, and Deborah seemed happy to tell Beth all about it. She knows Beth won't spread it around. I might not be so courteous if you don't stop hurling insults at me and my family.'

'Yeah, well, fair point.' Cain had to concede Jed was right. People in glass houses and all that. He glanced over at Emerald. 'You're very quiet. Not gunna have a pop at me?'

When she merely shook her head, he frowned. Well, what was up with her? He'd been expecting a mouthful of abuse, especially when she found out about him and Debs, but there was nothing. She looked shrunken, defeated. He felt a sudden alarm. 'You ain't ill, are you?'

She shook her head, listless. Cain dropped onto the bed beside her, feeling worried. 'So, the wedding's definitely off? No going back?'

She didn't respond, so he cast an appealing look at Jed.

'Seems like it,' his son confirmed. 'Eden told me yesterday when I went over to help with the shearing. Said they'd been to see the vicar and had cancelled the service, and could I ask Emerald to cancel everything else.'

Cain sighed. 'I need to go see them, straighten all this out. They can't throw away a good relationship because Eliot spent the night with Emerald. Unless—' He glared at his daughter suspiciously, 'you *are* telling me the truth, ain't you? Nuffink happened, right?'

'Nothing happened,' she mumbled. 'He was a perfect gentleman.'

'Then I don't get it,' Cain said. 'I thought those two were rock solid.'

'It's all my fault,' Emerald said.

Cain watched, aghast, as a tear rolled down her cheek.

'Yeah, well.' He shifted uncomfortably, not sure how to handle this contrite version of his daughter. 'I don't doubt it. Point is, what do we do about it?'

'Eden never said they'd split,' Jed said. 'Just that the wedding was off.'

'A week to go,' Cain sighed. 'If they'd given me a bit more notice I'd have got me deposits back.'

'Is that really all you care about?' Jed asked.

Cain tutted. 'Nah. Course not. It's nothing much, really. I can't believe it. Can't get me head around it. No rhyme or reason. You said you were at the farm today? How did they seem to you?'

Jed shrugged. 'Business as usual. Eden was busy making cream teas, and Eliot was flat out, bringing the sheep to the shed for clipping. But they were happy when I told them about me and Beth, and then, ' he smiled at the memory, 'later on, they'd gotten Deborah's solicitor's letter, and they were floating on air. Took a whole weight off their minds.'

'Yeah, well,' Cain muttered, feeling a sharp pang at the mention of Deborah. He couldn't think about her now or he'd be lost. 'This better be a mutual decision. That git better not have broken Eden's heart, that's all.'

Emerald sniffed, and he rummaged in his pocket and handed her a crumpled tissue.

'It's clean,' he assured her, as she looked at it doubtfully. He gave a big sigh. 'Well, I suppose I'd better start writing some cheques. Seems not only have I left it too late to get me deposits back, but some of these firms want the full whack due to late cancellation. Got to say, Emerald, you really went to town on this wedding, didn't you? Must've bought half the florist's. And a stretch limo! What was the point of that, eh?'

'I was thinking they could all travel in it together on the way to the reception — the children, too. I thought they'd like it.'

'I think they'd have loved it,' Jed reassured her.

'And this menu! Fuck me! Look at the price of it. Thank Christ we didn't hire Ashington Hall, that's all I can say. I mean, a

455

toastmaster! What were you thinking? Can you see them two wanting one of those, eh?'

'I'm sorry,' Emerald said, wiping her nose. 'I feel bad about this, really I do. You said you wanted a grand wedding for them, and so that's what I went for. I got it wrong. I can see that now.'

'You're all heart,' Cain said, feeling distinctly uncomfortable. This new, humble Emerald was freaking him out. Why wasn't she ranting and raving at him, blaming everyone but herself for this debacle? Maybe the Yorkshire air had frazzled her brain.

'Well, I suppose you did what I asked — more than what I asked. Let's be grateful they refused a honeymoon. Thank God they insisted they couldn't spare the time, else I'd be forking out another couple of grand, no doubt.' He sighed. 'I'm guessing you won't be coming with me to Wildflower Farm?'

She shook her head and he frowned, looking up at Jed for some sort of reassurance or explanation.

Jed looked back, his eyes full of sadness. 'Tell you what, Emmy,' he said, 'how about I go with Dad and you keep Beth company? She'll be heading down to dinner soon and I don't want her alone. Would you mind staying with her until I get back?'

Emerald shrugged. 'If you like, though I'm not very hungry.'

'Thanks.' Jed turned to his father, who was sitting with his mouth wide open at the news that Emerald wasn't hungry. 'Dad, you ready to go? The sooner we head off the sooner we get back.'

'What? Oh yeah, yeah.' Cain hoped Eden had some grub on the go. Broken hearted or not, people had to eat, after all, and he was starving.

He needed to keep his energy up, anyway, 'cos he intended to visit Debs tonight in her room. Not to get his leg over. No, he wasn't in the mood for that. When Jed had informed him that she'd done it, that she'd actually left her husband, he'd had a real panic. This was real. He'd broken up a marriage, and now Debs was his responsibility. He didn't want to think about it too much. Not until he had to. But he supposed he'd better go to see her later to discuss their future. Maybe.

He'd been quite right in his earlier pronouncement, he decided. It was all a bleeding catastrophe. He didn't have the faintest idea how it was all going to pan out.

****

Eden opened the door and Jed was relieved to see she looked quite cheerful, if a little flushed. 'Oh! I didn't expect to see you,' she said, casting a hurried glance over her shoulder. 'Er, come in. Everyone! Cain and Jed are here!'

Cain gave Jed a meaningful look as she hurried back along the hallway, leaving them to close the door behind them.

'She's all flustered,' he muttered. 'Bet you a pound to a penny they've bin rowing.'

Jed followed his father along the hallway and into the kitchen, where Eliot was bundling some papers into a folder and the girls were sitting at the table, watching Cain with wide eyes. Jed frowned. They were definitely behaving oddly. Maybe his dad was right. Maybe they had walked in on a row.

Eliot handed the folder to Eden, and she stuffed it in a cupboard.

'Cain,' he said pleasantly. 'Nice to see you.'

'Is it?' Cain sounded less than certain. 'Well, wish I could say the same to you, mate, but I ain't happy and that's a fact.'

Eden began to chivvy the girls away from the table. 'Why don't you go and see Flora?' she suggested. 'It's a lovely evening out there. Go and get some fresh air before bedtime.'

The girls needed no further encouragement, shooting out of the room without a glance at Jed or his father. It wasn't like them. They were usually so friendly and talkative.

'Where's George?' he enquired.

'In bed,' Eliot said briefly. 'No Beth?'

'She's at the hotel with Emerald,' Jed said. He saw Eliot tense at the mention of his sister, but Eden forced a smile.

'How is Beth?' she enquired.

Jed and Cain exchanged glances. Jed could barely wipe the smile from his face.

'Pregnant and blooming,' he announced.

Eliot and Eden stood stock still, their faces showing profound

457

astonishment. They glanced at each other, then there was a loud whoop and they gathered around him, patting him on the back and offering their heartiest congratulations.

'I can't believe it,' Eden said, her eyes shining. 'After all this time. It's fantastic.'

'Tell her I'm right glad for her,' Eliot said. 'It's brilliant news. The best.'

'That's all very well,' Cain said grumpily, 'but what about your news, eh? That ain't exactly brilliant, is it?'

Jed pulled out a chair and sat down as Eden and Eliot turned away. Eliot leaned against the worktop, while Eden put the kettle on.

'Cup of tea and a piece of ginger cake, Cain?' she offered, at an outrageous attempt at bribery.

'Don't change the subject,' Cain said crossly. He hesitated a moment then added, 'But yeah. In fact, make it two. All the stress has made me hungry.'

Jed noted the sly grins Eliot and Eden exchanged, as she reached for the cake tin. He smiled to himself. Whatever was going on, they were evidently still very much a couple, which cheered him up enormously. He knew it would be a huge relief to Beth, too.

As the sound of mewing reached his ears, he bent down and stroked Bella. 'Hey, kitty,' he murmured. 'I know someone who's really missing you.' The cat looked at him hopefully, then seemed to sigh in defeat and stalked out of the kitchen.

'She's not herself,' Eden admitted. 'I think she's pining for Emerald.'

Cain looked astounded at that information. 'You're telling me she bonded with the cat? Bleeding hell, who'd have thought it?'

Jed grinned. 'She adores that cat. Not so fond of old Tuppence,' he admitted, nodding over at the elderly sheepdog who was lying in her basket. 'Emerald has issues with her health problems.'

Cain frowned. 'Health problems?'

Eden smirked. 'Tuppence does suffer from wind, sometimes. We're all used to it, but Emerald struggled quite badly.'

She sounded quite pleased about the fact, and Jed supposed he couldn't blame her. He felt a pang of sadness for his sister, all the same.

As Cain sipped tea and ate cake, Eden tried to explain to him why they had called off the wedding.

'It didn't feel right,' she said. 'We've had a rough time of it lately, and there were things that gave us cause to believe that this wasn't the time to be getting married. We have a lot to sort out first. I'm sorry for the inconvenience.'

'And the money,' Cain muttered through a mouthful of ginger cake.

Eliot's eyebrows knitted together. 'I'll pay you back,' he said. 'Every penny.'

Cain waved an arm in the air. 'Bugger off, daft bleeder. It ain't about the money. Not really.' He pushed away his empty plate and sighed. 'Anyway, let's face it, this is my fault, not yours.'

'How on earth is it your fault?' Eden said.

'I put Emerald in charge of your wedding. Should have known it was a mistake. Doomed to failure, weren't it? Bet she'd have made a right pig's ear of it anyway. Probably best you called it off, eh? Maybe, in a few months, you can organise your own wedding, the way you want it.'

Jed didn't miss the flicker of Eliot's eyes as he shot a sideways glance at Eden who, in turn, moved hastily towards the sink and dropped her cup in the bowl, but not before Jed noticed the faint flush of pink on her cheeks. He folded his arms, suddenly curious. What were they up to?

'Mebbe, one day,' Eliot said gruffly. 'No rush is there?'

Jed narrowed his eyes. After living and working with this man all these months, the one thing he knew for sure was that, for Eliot, his marriage to Eden couldn't come soon enough. And frankly, neither he nor his intended were very good liars. They looked guilty as hell, and he had a shrewd idea why. He also thought he'd sussed why Libby and Ophelia couldn't wait to get away from the kitchen. He glanced at the cupboard where Eden had hastily shoved the folder that Eliot had handed her, and his lips twitched with sudden amusement. So that was their game!

'You know what? While you guys discuss this, I think I'm gonna head outside to see the girls and pay my respects to that little pony of theirs.' He had to stop himself from grinning as he saw their anxious looks.

'Wouldn't you like some cake, Jed?' Eden said. 'Or another cup of tea, perhaps.'

'No thanks,' he said pleasantly. 'Fresh air will do me good.'

Cain waved his hand in the air. 'Oh, let him go if he wants to,' he said. 'Now, about this wedding...'

Jed left them to it and headed out of the house into the yard. As he strode towards the paddock, he spotted Libby and Ophelia standing on the bottom bar of the gate, patting Flora and fussing over her.

'She sure is a pretty little pony,' he announced, as he drew near.

'We know,' Ophelia said proudly. 'The prettiest in Skimmerdale.'

'In Yorkshire,' he contradicted her. 'Maybe even in the whole of Britain.'

Libby laughed. 'You haven't even seen all the ponies in Britain.'

'Don't need to,' he assured her. 'What pony could possibly be better looking than this little beauty, huh?'

He leaned on the gate and rubbed Flora's nose. It wasn't a lie. He genuinely thought that the little Welsh Mountain pony was stunning, but he did have other motives for flattering the girls.

'So,' he said carefully, 'how do you guys feel about the wedding being cancelled?'

Libby and Ophelia looked at each other and he saw an immediate rush of colour to Libby's face. She was always the more transparent one, he thought. She would give any secret away with an expression. But she was also fiercely loyal. Ophelia was the one most likely to spill family secrets deliberately. Tricky.

'It's a bit sad,' Ophelia said with a shrug, 'but happen they'll get wed one day.'

'It is sad,' he agreed solemnly. 'Your mom and dad are perfect for each other, and they've been through such a lot that they deserve a wedding. I feel real bad that it won't be happening.'

Libby looked distinctly uneasy. 'It will happen,' she said at last. 'Just not yet.'

'But everything was going so well,' he persisted. 'Everything was organised — all the flowers, and the car, the cake, and the photographer, the church. It's such a shame.'

'But it wasn't really what Mum and Dad wanted,' Ophelia explained, clearly ignoring the warning look that Libby shot her. 'It were all posh and stuffy and they didn't want that. Emerald spoilt the wedding, and it should be how they want it, not how she wanted it, shouldn't it?'

'Definitely,' he agreed. 'But, you know, they only had to say what they wanted, and Emerald would have done it that way for them. Maybe, if we go and have a talk to them, we can persuade them to go ahead with it after all?'

'They don't want Emerald to do it,' Libby said quickly.

'They can do it best themselves,' Ophelia insisted.

Jed smiled at them. 'And is that what they're doing?'

At their horrified faces, he said, 'Don't worry. I won't tell on you. It was your dad and Eden who gave themselves away. They're terrible liars.'

'You can't say anything,' Ophelia said. 'It will spoil it all if you do.'

'So, what's the plan?' Jed enquired. 'Emerald's cancelled everything she arranged, so what next?'

'Emerald didn't arrange everything,' Ophelia said.

'Shush, Ophelia,' Libby said urgently. 'We can't say.'

'It's only Jed, though,' Ophelia said, obviously relieved to be able to blurt it all out. 'He's our friend, aren't you, Jed?'

'I sure hope so,' he agreed. 'I certainly think of you and your parents as my friends.'

'See?' Ophelia looked around, as if checking for approaching parents, then leaned towards him, her eyes wide and serious. 'They didn't cancel the church service. They went to see Mr Edwards, and he agreed to move it back to half past two in the afternoon, so no one would know about it. They're gunna carry on as normal during the morning, so everyone will believe it's off, then after dinner, we're all getting changed and rushing off to Camacker.'

Jed nodded. 'Sounds like a great plan,' he said. 'Who's all?'

'Me, Libby, Dad, Mum, Georgie, Mickey, Adey, and Mum's mam and dad.'

'No one else?'

Libby shook her head. 'Nope. They're getting wed, then they're coming straight home. Mum says we're going to have a little tea party, though. She's making some sandwiches and a little cake, and they're having a bottle of wine and she says we can have a little bit mixed with lemonade. Not Georgie, though, 'cos he's a kid.'

'Obviously. Well, that sounds a bit sad, though. Just a little tea party? What about photographs? Flowers? A car?'

'They're going in Dad's Land Rover.' Ophelia shrugged. 'He says he'll wash it first. And Eden's dad takes photos. He's got a posh camera cos he's retired, and Eden's mam says he's got nowt better to do these days. We spoke to her on the phone t'other night. She's ever so funny.'

'And Mum's having flowers,' Libby continued. 'Same as ours but a big bigger. Ours match our frocks.'

'Mum said she wanted a natural look,' Ophelia added. 'Our frocks aren't too fancy, you see. Even hers. Dad hasn't seen her dress yet, but he's going to love it. She looks right bonny, doesn't she, Libby? We went to the fitting with her, and she looked gorgeous. Dad's going to be proper happy. Mum said she felt a bit overdressed, what with their being no party afterwards or owt, but Dad said it were still a church wedding, and she were still his princess.'

Jed nodded. 'It all sounds amazing. I'm real happy for you guys.'

'And you promise you won't say owt? Mum and Dad might call it off properly if they know anyone's found out,' Libby said anxiously.

'I swear I won't tell your Mom and Dad that you breathed a word,' Jed promised.

'Thanks, Jed,' Ophelia said happily. 'I knew you were our friend.'

They turned back to Flora and the conversation changed to the forthcoming Skimmerdale Show, and their plans for gymkhana victory. Jed joined in enthusiastically, but a part of him was thinking sadly about a little tea party, and an almost empty church.

****

Beth passed the jam to Emerald, who nodded her thanks. She was evidently too deep in thought to immediately dive on her teacake, which they all knew was a bad sign. Emerald loved her food, but the fact was, she'd barely eaten a thing since they'd been staying at the hotel. Seeing her picking at her grub worried Cain.

'I know they're not quite up to Eden's standards, but even so—'

Emerald sighed. 'I'm not hungry, to be honest.'

Cain gave Jed an anxious look.

'Come on, Emmy,' Jed said gently. 'You didn't eat dinner last night, and you barely touched your breakfast.'

'Ain't like you, Ems,' Cain said, giving her an affectionate nudge. 'You usually can't wait to stuff the grub down yer neck.'

Beth rolled her eyes and Jed grinned. 'Really got a way with words, haven't you, Dad? Explains all those beautiful love songs you wrote back in the day.' He winked at Beth. 'I won't repeat the titles. You're far too much of a lady.'

'Yeah, well, I had a reputation to think of,' Cain pointed out. 'Can you imagine the metal heads crooning some of the soppy stuff you write about?' He felt a sudden glow of satisfaction as he recalled the conversation he'd had that morning with his manager, Derek. Industry insiders were raving about the track he'd recorded with Sun King, and the record company had decided it would be the first single release from the album.

Let Quentin, Kent and the rest of them jumped up public schoolboys stick that up their arses. He wished he'd been around to see their faces when they'd been given that little gem of information.

'Speaking of which, have you done any song writing lately, or is that sumfink else you've given up on?'

Jed spread butter on his teacake and shook his head. 'Not at all.

Song writing's always gonna be something I do. I don't see any reason to stop.'

'Good boy,' Cain said approvingly. 'That's where the real money is, ya know. I made enough from singing and recording and stuff, but the real dosh is from the songs I wrote. You wanna try selling some. Even if you don't want to perform any more, you could still make a packet writing for other artists. Maybe even carry on writing for Raven's Wing.'

Jed and Beth exchanged glances and Cain wondered what the story was.

'I think I've moved on from Raven's Wing,' Jed said lightly. 'But you're right about selling my songs. I'm gonna need an income, after all, now I'm gonna be a dad.'

'You ain't skint?' Cain was appalled. All he needed was another kid with no dosh. 'Tell me you ain't wasted all your royalties.'

'Of course not.' Jed shrugged. 'I'm okay for money for a good while, but that's not the point, is it? Truth is, I need something to occupy my time. Something to do with my life.'

'More than song writing?'

'I love writing songs, but I want—' Jed tutted in frustration. 'To be honest, I don't know what I want, but I know I don't want what I had before. I wanna do something that means something, you know? I feel real lucky. I've been so blessed. I wanna give something back. Do something that matters to someone.'

'Hmm, careful. You're beginning to sound like Rex bleeding Scotman,' Cain warned. 'Well, we need to start making some plans, 'cos there's no reason to hang around Skimmerdale any longer, is there? And I might have the thing to interest you, Jed, now that you come to mention it. I've got a few things to sort out first, but then I'll let you in on it. I think — I hope — I may have a job for you, after all. And you, Beth.'

Beth looked up, startled. 'Me?'

'Dad, Beth's not looking for a job,' Jed said.

'Who says I'm not?' Beth sounded quite eager. 'I've spent the last few years of my life feeling bored witless. If you've got something to challenge me, Cain, I'd love it.'

'What about the baby?' Jed reminded her.

Beth put her hand over his and smiled reassuringly. 'The baby will always be our first priority, won't it? But it doesn't mean we can't do other things. Does it?'

He hesitated for a moment, then seemed to relax as he nodded. 'Of course it doesn't. I'm curious, though, Dad. What job could you possibly have that would suit me *and* Beth?'

Cain stuffed half a teacake in his mouth. 'Wait and see,' he said mysteriously.

'So, I guess we need to start thinking about where we're heading,' Jed said. 'Is it okay for me and Beth to go back to Upper Bourbury with you for now?'

'I insist upon it,' Cain said. 'I suppose we may as well start packing. You an' all, kid,' he added, tapping Emerald on the arm.

She looked at him, clearly surprised. 'Me? You want me to go back to your house with you?'

'Well, where else are you gunna go?' he demanded. 'Back to the batty Cassandra in her latest hovel? I don't think so. No kid of mine's gunna shit in a bucket ever again.'

'I didn't think you'd want me,' Emerald murmured.

'Well, you know what thought did,' Cain said comfortably. He looked gloomy suddenly. 'Ain't nuffink to keep us here, is there?'

Beth sipped her tea thoughtfully. 'What about Deborah? Is it over between you?'

Cain felt thoroughly fed up. 'Looks that way. Can't believe she checked out of here without even telling me. Or at least telling you, Beth! Where would she go? And why didn't she wait for me? I thought we had sumfink, but clearly, I was wrong. She ain't even answered the phone or picked up me texts.'

'Maybe she needed to think things through,' Beth suggested. 'She's been with David for such a long time, it must be very strange for her to cut loose from him.'

'If she *has* cut loose,' Cain remarked. 'For all we know, she's gone back to him.'

'What? I can't believe that!' Beth shook her head, denying all possibility of such a monstrous event.

Cain admired her optimism, but he wasn't so sure. He knew Debs was struggling with leaving James in such a bad way.

Whatever he'd done, he was still her kid, after all, and she felt she'd failed him. He knew she was desperate for him to break away from his father and grow into the man she'd always hoped he would be. Maybe she'd decided that going back to him was the only way to help him?

He sighed inwardly. Maybe the truth was less palatable. Fact was, Debs had grown used to being the wife of a multi-millionaire. Maybe in the cold light of day she'd realised that she'd be stupid to throw away that sort of lifestyle. Cain could probably have kept her in as much luxury, but then, he hadn't made any offers towards her. Maybe she'd expected him to. Maybe she'd hoped she could swap one rich husband for another? But Cain was too scared to jump into another marriage. He couldn't offer Debs that kind of security. Maybe she'd sussed him out and decided to stick with the devil she knew. He supposed he couldn't blame her really.

It's for the best, mate, he told himself. *You can't get saddled with another potential gold digger. Let her go and move on.*

He blinked, pushing all thoughts of the lovely Deborah from his mind. 'So, I guess that's us done. It didn't exactly turn out as we planned, but hey ho. At least we've got a new family member,' he said, nodding graciously at Beth, 'and a new grandkid on the way. Time for us to go home and start looking to the future.'

Emerald pushed her plate away. 'I can't go,' she announced.

Cain blinked. 'Eh? What do you mean you can't go?' He narrowed his eyes, suddenly suspicious. 'Please tell me you ain't still hoping you and Eliot are gunna get it together. Trust me, it ain't gunna happen.'

'Of course not,' she snapped. 'I'm not stupid!' She looked around at them all, her face expressing a mixture of hope, sadness and desperation. 'I can't leave it at that, though, can I?'

'What you on about, Emerald?' Cain rolled his eyes. He might have known it would be too good to be true. She had to make things difficult, right to the end.

'I'm talking about Eliot and Eden,' she said. She looked pleadingly at Beth. 'You know what I mean, surely? All this time, they've waited for their dream wedding day. Now they're going to run off and get married on the quiet. Does that seem fair?'

'But they don't want a dream wedding day,' Cain reminded her. 'They rejected everything you had planned!'

'Because that wasn't their dream wedding,' she said. 'It was more *your* dream wedding — or the wedding you thought they ought to have. Eliot and Eden aren't those people, and I should never have organised such a formal event for them.' She folded her arms. 'I was an idiot. A selfish idiot. I can't let this happen.'

Beth's eyes were shining. 'What do you plan to do?'

Emerald pursed her lips, thinking. 'Give them the wedding they wanted all along!' she burst out suddenly.

Cain let out a snort of laughter. 'You do know the wedding's in five days! How the hell would you organise that?'

Emerald looked hopefully at Beth. 'No one around here really knows me,' she said, 'but you must know lots of people. Would they help? Would they be up for it?'

Beth clapped her hands. 'Everyone loves Eliot, and Eden's part of the village now. I'm sure people would do all they could to help.'

'And you?'

Beth nodded. 'Of course, Emerald. I'd be happy to.'

Emerald looked at Jed and Cain. Jed raised his eyebrows and shrugged. 'I'm in,' he said.

Cain gave a big sigh. 'Gawd almighty, talk about last minute. This is gunna cost me more money, ain't it?'

'If you help me out,' Emerald promised, 'I won't ask you ever again for any money for the retreat.'

Cain's eyes widened. 'You'd give up your retreat for this wedding?'

'It's the least I can do,' she mumbled. 'I have to try to put this right somehow, don't I? You understand, don't you?'

Cain thought his kids never ceased to amaze him. For the first time in his life, he felt a real sense of pride in his middle daughter. She had a sense of responsibility, a streak of compassion and a kind heart under that brittle exterior, just like her old dad. Maybe she was more his kid than Cassandra's after all.

'Right,' he said, pushing his own plate away at last. 'Guess we'd better not check out of here yet. Seems like we're gunna be very busy.'

Chapter 40

Eden gazed up at Eliot as she placed the ring on his finger. His eyes met hers and they smiled at each other. They'd done it!

'I now pronounce you man and wife. That which God has joined together, let no man put asunder.' Mr Edwards beamed at them, as the tiny congregation clapped and cheered.

'Well,' the vicar added, nodding at Eliot, 'aren't you going to kiss the bride?'

Eliot shuffled uncomfortably, sneaking a quick glance at the people sitting in the pews behind them. They all smiled back at him.

After a short pause, Mickey rolled his eyes and said, 'Bloody 'ell, lad, get on wi' it or I'll step in an' do it meself.'

Eliot could hardly consign Eden to that fate so, pushing aside his embarrassment, he drew his new wife to him and kissed her gently and lovingly, much to the delight of their wedding guests. It was hardly a chore. She had never looked more beautiful, and that was saying something. There was something quite radiant about her, he thought, realising he'd never felt happier, and the joy bubbled up inside him like Wildflower Farm Beck after summer rain.

Eden laughed and cupped his face. 'Well done,' she told him. She knew how awkward he felt, demonstrating affection in front of people, but she never minded. He kissed her hand, proud to be the husband of such a wonderful woman.

'Steady on, Eliot,' called Adey. 'Tha'll be telling us you're gunna carry her over't threshold next!'

'Happen that's what I plan to do,' Eliot informed him, laughing.

'Well, before you do that, shall we sign the register?' Mr Edwards pushed his spectacles further up his nose and beamed at them both. 'We don't want you rushing off before we make this legal, do we?'

No, they bloody didn't, Eliot thought. This was going to be official, all right. No one was ever going to break him and Eden up and that was a fact. He glanced around at the almost empty church, wondering if she really minded that it had turned into such a small wedding, after all. At least her parents had turned up, which was more than Jemima's had.

'It was perfect,' Eden whispered to him. 'Stop worrying.'

How did she always know? He squeezed her arm. 'You look grand,' he told her. 'Never seen owt so beautiful in all me life.'

'Why, thank you, you smooth-talker,' she said. Her eyes softened, and she murmured in his ear, 'And I've never seen you look more handsome. I love you, Mr Harland.'

'And I love you, Mrs Harland,' he murmured back. 'Come on, let's go and get this thing made official, then we can go home.'

As they finally left the church, blinking in the sunlight, they were startled as a car blasted its horn.

Eliot scowled. 'What the heck were that about?'

'Cain! Good grief, I don't believe it!'

Everyone turned at Eden's cry, and Eliot realised that the sound of the horn had come from a vintage Rolls Royce. Standing beside it, almost unrecognisable, was Cain, smartly attired in a dark suit, white shirt and navy-blue tie, topped off with a chauffeur's hat.

'Thought you were gunna sneak off and get married without any fuss?' He shook his head. 'Oh no. I'm your chauffeur for the day, and you're to get in me Roller right now.'

Eliot and Eden exchanged nervous glances. 'What about the Land Rover?' Eliot pointed out. 'Can't leave it here.'

Adey stepped forward. 'I'm driving it back,' he said, 'and I'll take the kids with me, so don't worry.'

'You knew about this?' Eden gasped as Mickey, Adey, and even her parents nodded and smiled. 'You *all* knew?'

Mrs Edwards patted her on the shoulder. 'I'd go with it, if I were you, my dear. I'll see you at the reception.'

'Reception?' Eliot frowned. 'What bloody reception?'

'In the car,' Cain ordered. 'No arguments.'

'Go on,' Ophelia urged. 'We're starving.'

Eliot and Eden reluctantly clambered into the Rolls Royce. Cain gave a cheery wave to the wedding guests, then jumped in the front seat. Slowly, the beautiful car pulled away.

'I think we've bin had,' Eliot whispered. 'They all bloody knew about this. Who do you think told Cain?'

'I'm not so much worried about that,' Eden admitted, 'as what's in store for us next. A wedding reception, Cain said. Oh, Eliot, you don't think Emerald didn't cancel everything, do you?'

Eliot closed his eyes for a moment, remembering her mood board, her bulging Filofax, and the fancy menus she'd shown them. It would have taken a while and cost a lot to cancel the wedding. Maybe she and Cain had decided not to bother. He opened his eyes again and his gaze fell upon Eden, sitting beside him, looking so beautiful she made his heart ache. Her fair hair was adorned with flowers, and she was wearing a simple white gown that made her look like an angel. He felt a lump in his throat, and suddenly none of it mattered.

'Let them do what they want,' he told her softly. 'Who cares? We're wed now, Eden. Me and you are man and wife. Nowt can spoil this day. Nothing. It's the happiest day of my life, and that's a fact.'

Her face brightened. 'Really?'

'Really.' He pulled her to him, and his mouth covered hers. With no congregation to worry about, he could really show her how much he loved her.

'Oy, do you mind? I'm too young for that kind of thing,' Cain piped up from the front.

'Don't bloody look then,' Eliot grumbled.

'By hell, you don't get any more charming. Marriage ain't softened you, has it?'

471

Eden laughed. 'Sorry, Cain, but we're a bit taken aback,' she said. 'How did you find out about the wedding, anyway? We were so careful.'

'Not careful enough,' he said, 'but no matter. You deserve a decent wedding and you're gunna get it, whether you like it or not.'

****

Eden gazed out of the window, then nudged him gently. 'We're not heading towards Kirkby Skimmer,' she said, relieved. 'We can't be going to The Paradise Hotel, after all.'

Eliot looked hopeful. 'Mebbe they've booked The King's Head, like we said,' he murmured.

Eden couldn't imagine it. It was very short notice, and it was high summer, after all. Maybe they'd got lucky...

As the car left Beckthwaite behind, though, they could only look at each other in bewilderment.

'Maybe he's picking someone else up? Or perhaps they've forgotten something?' Eden leaned forward and tapped Cain on the shoulder. 'Where are we going?'

Cain grinned. 'That's for me to know and you to find out. Why don't you relax and get back to your snogging? Leave the driving to me.'

Eliot raised an eyebrow. 'Fine by me,' he said, amazing Eden as he pulled her to him, seeming to no longer care that he had an audience.

'Wow,' she breathed, as he finally released her, 'is this what married life's going to be like?'

'It's going to get better and better,' he promised her, his eyes shining. Eden smiled to herself. She had a feeling he was quite right.

As the car headed down the track towards Wildflower Farm, Eliot shrugged.

'No idea,' he said to her unspoken question. Glancing out of the back window he added, 'looks like Adey and your mam and dad are right behind us, though, so mebbe we've reached our final destination.'

'Could we be that lucky?' Eden queried.

Eliot nudged her, his eyes wide. 'Look!'

She followed his gaze, her mouth opening in surprise as she saw the strings of bunting draped across the front of the largest bunk barn. Balloons were tied to the drainpipes, and there was a large 'Congratulations' banner over the door.

Cain swept his Rolls Royce over the packhorse bridge, then turned — not into the farmyard — but into the new road that ran between the beck and the barns, following it round to the rear of the farmyard, where Eden realised that the field behind the small, new car park had been transformed. The picnic tables had all been moved there, as had several of the dining room tables and chairs. Bunting was draped around the fencing and the tables wore crisp white cloths.

The happy couple exchanged incredulous glances as the Rolls Royce drew to a halt, and what seemed like half the village — plus several of the overnight guests from the bunk barn — tumbled out of the barn, through the French doors, to greet them with much laughter, countless hugs, and loud shouts of congratulations.

Within a few minutes, the children, along with Adey, Mickey, and Eden's parents had joined them, having evidently parked up in the farmyard.

'What on earth?' Eden could only gasp, and she saw Eliot looking as amazed as she was.

Beth and Jed rushed over to them, laughing.

'Congratulations!' they called, and Beth kissed them both, while Jed hugged Eden and shook Eliot's hand, then clapped him heartily on the back.

Eden shook her head. 'What — I mean, how did you—?'

'Doesn't matter how we found out,' Jed said firmly. 'What matters is that none of us — the whole village, too — thought you should be allowed to sneak off without including us. We wanted you to have the wedding of your dreams. We hope this is it.'

'It's — it's—' Eden looked around, noticing for the first time

473

the mismatched vintage bowls, cups, jugs and teapots adorning every table, each filled with pretty sweet peas in whites, pinks, lilacs and purples. Looking down at her own bouquet of pink and lilac sweet peas, mixed in with white roses, dahlias, chamomile, clematis and stocks in various pastel shades, she realised that they matched perfectly.

Laughing, she and Eliot pointed to two pairs of green wellies, standing at either side of the French doors, each filled to the brim with larkspur in shades of blue, violet, pink and white.

Eliot steered her round, and they followed the crowds, who were now swarming into the field. She saw that everyone was heading towards a long trestle table, draped in a white cloth and shaded by a stripy sun canopy. As she drew near, she noticed it bore plate after plate of sandwiches, quiches, cakes, and scones, bowls of clotted cream and jam, pots of tea, and large jugs full of pink lemonade. Taking pride of place was a beautiful wedding cake, exquisite in its simplicity — a single round creation with white icing, adorned with pink and white roses. Eden gulped down the tears as she turned to look at Eliot and saw the delight she felt reflected in his eyes.

'It's grand,' he said, shaking his head.

'You said you wanted a tea party,' Beth said, smiling. 'So that's what you've got. A proper, vintage tea party, bunting, china and all.'

'Thank you so much, Beth,' Eden breathed. 'I don't know what to say.'

Beth held up her hands. 'Don't thank me,' she insisted. 'I helped a bit, but so many people contributed.' She nodded over at a group of women who were standing, smiling at them. 'Mrs Long, Mrs Malory and Mrs Harvey made the sandwiches,' she said. 'Jill and Dave from The King's Head donated the tablecloths and the trestle table. Mr and Mrs Tucker from the shop gave us the lemonade. Mrs Edwards,' she said, smiling over at the vicar's wife, 'made the cake.'

Eden gasped. 'Really? It's amazing.'

Mrs Edwards shook her head. 'Just a plain vanilla sponge, my dear, but I filled it with my homemade raspberry jam and a raspberry ripple buttercream. I hope you enjoy it. I got the ladies of the WI to make the scones, and there's more of the jam to go with them.'

'And bowls of raspberries from my garden,' added Mr Edwards, who was sitting at one of the tables, drinking tea. He raised his cup to them. 'Cheers, my dears, and long life and much happiness to you both.'

'I don't know what to say,' Eliot murmured.

'We all wanted you to know how happy we were for you, Eliot,' said Mrs Malory. 'You deserve this, love. You both do.'

Eliot swallowed, clearly overwhelmed. Eden squeezed his hand.

'Even Granny Allen chipped in,' Mrs Harvey called.

As Eden and Eliot cast a nervous look at the food, she laughed and added, 'Don't worry. She didn't cook owt. Chipped in for the flowers, though, bless her.'

'She did?'

'Aye. She couldn't come, 'cos of her arthritis playing her up, but she said to tell you she wished you both all the luck in the world, and she'd be thinking of you.'

'I'll take her some food round,' Eliot said glancing down at Eden for her approval. 'Least she deserves.'

'Er, I think you'll be a bit busy later on.' Mrs Long rolled her eyes at the folly of men. 'We'll take her a plateful round, never fear.'

Eliot wrapped his arms around Eden and turned to face them all. 'I can't thank you all enough,' he said. 'This is—' He shrugged, clearly unable to find the words.

'Perfect?' suggested Ophelia, who was already munching on a sandwich.

Eliot grinned. 'Aye, love, happen that's the word. Perfect. It's all perfect, and this is the happiest day of my life. Thank you. Thank you all for doing this. I don't rightly know how to tell you how much it means to us.' He cleared his throat, embarrassed. 'All I will say is, since it's our wedding, there'll be no standing on ceremony. Nowt formal we said, and we meant it. So, come on everyone, tuck in.'

As the villagers laughed and surged towards the trestle table,

Eden hugged him tightly, then looked up as Beth said, 'You know who organised it all, though?'

'You, no doubt,' she said smiling, but Beth shook her head.

'Not me, Eden. It was Emerald. She did it all. It was her idea, and she was determined to give you the best wedding possible.'

Eden stared at her. 'Emerald?'

Jed nodded. 'She wanted to make it up to you,' he explained. 'She's spent all morning getting this place decorated, rushing round collecting the flowers and getting them in place. She ordered the flowers, she bought the bunting, she co-ordinated the whole thing. She's spent the last couple of days trawling through local markets and antique shops to get the china for the tables. It was her idea to go with the vintage tea party theme. She thought it was more the sort of thing you'd want.'

'She were right,' Eliot said. He glanced down at Eden. 'Weren't she?'

'Yes, she was,' Eden said, feeling uncomfortable suddenly. 'Isn't she here?'

'She shot inside the bunk barn as soon as she saw Dad's car pull up,' Jed said. 'She didn't think you'd want to see her. I persuaded her to stick around, at least have something to eat. She's in the dining room. That was going to be Plan B if it rained, by the way.'

'She's done her best, Eden,' Cain said gently. 'I know she did some stupid things, but she's sorry and she's really tried to make it up to you.'

Eliot draped his arm over Eden's shoulders. 'It's all in the past now, my love,' he said. 'Nothing can hurt us. She was daft, but happen we've all bin a bit daft at times, eh?'

Eden frowned, but nodded. He was right, she supposed, although she didn't think she'd ever totally trust Emerald. Even so, it was a beautiful day. The sun was shining, her family, her parents, her friends and half the village were here to celebrate with her, and she was married to the best man in the world. She had every reason to be happy. More reason than even Eliot knew. She could spare Emerald some kindness.

'Go and tell her she's welcome to join us,' she said. 'I want to thank her personally, anyway.'

Jed's face lit up as he hurried inside, and Eden took a deep breath, as two of her bunk barn guests hurried towards her, each carrying a plate of food.

'Thanks so much for inviting us,' one of them said.

The other nudged him. 'They didn't. It was a surprise, remember?'

'Even so.' The two of them beamed at Eden and Eliot. 'Never had this at any of the other places we've stayed, did they? We're not likely to forget Wildflower Farm in a hurry. You'll be getting a cracking review from us.'

They each planted a kiss on Eden's cheek, then Eliot shook their proffered hands.

'Congratulations to you both!' they called, wandering towards an empty table.

'Mum, these sandwiches are scrummy,' Libby informed her. 'Have one?'

'Maybe in a minute,' she said.

'You all right, my love? Did I do the right thing, saying that about Emerald?' Eliot looked at her anxiously, and she smiled.

'Yes, of course. You were quite right.' She laughed suddenly, nodding over to where Mrs Long, Mrs Malory, Mrs Harvey and Mrs Edwards were posing proudly, as her father snapped them with his posh new camera.

'Goodness knows what your wedding album's going to look like,' her mother said, coming to stand beside her. 'I think he's taken pictures of everything and everyone. He's trying out all sorts of crazy angles. You've probably got sixteen photos of those wellies.'

'Dun't matter,' Eliot said. 'All adds to the fun.'

Eden's heart melted as her mother put her arms around Eliot and hugged him. 'We're so happy Eden found you, Eliot. Welcome to our family.'

Eliot looked thoroughly sheepish, but the sparkle in his eyes revealed his pleasure as she kissed him warmly on the cheek.

As she moved away to warn Eden's father that he'd better start taking some decent photographs, like normal people, Eden turned, and her smile dropped as she saw Emerald hovering by the French doors, hands behind her back, head down. Jed shot Eden an appealing look, and Eliot squeezed her arm.

Eden took a deep breath and walked over to the barn to face Emerald, her hand clasped firmly in Eliot's.

'I wanted to say thank you for organising this,' she said, waving her arm to encompass the scene. 'It's really kind of you. I appreciate how much hard work must have gone into this, considering the short notice you had, so — well, thanks.'

Emerald nodded. 'It's okay. If I'd done my job properly in the first place, there wouldn't have been all this mad rush, would there?'

Eden shrugged. 'No, probably not,' she said.

Emerald looked deeply wounded but Eden didn't add to her comment. She wanted to walk away, get back to her own wedding reception. It wasn't too much to ask, was it?

'I need to talk to you about something.' Emerald's voice was urgent, and Eden groaned inwardly.

She caught Eliot's eye and he put his arm firmly around her shoulders and smiled pleasantly at Emerald.

'You've done a grand job here today,' he told her. 'Me and my wife thank you for it. No need to say owt else, is there?'

Eden bit her lip, determined not to smile. Eliot couldn't have been more obvious if he tried, bless him.

Emerald, however, didn't seem to notice. She looked extremely agitated, and Eden realised she was trembling.

'There's something I have to talk to you about,' she repeated. 'Both of you.'

'I think you should hear her out,' Jed said quietly.

'Does it have to be today?' Eden said, her hackles rising. 'This is our wedding day, Emerald. Does even *this* have to be about you?'

'It's not about me, not really.' There was a note of desperation in Emerald's voice, and Eden could tell by the way Eliot straightened beside her that he sensed it, too. She rolled her eyes, knowing she was beaten.

'All right. What do you want to talk about?'

Emerald glanced around. 'Can we go inside?'

Eden tutted impatiently. 'It's our wedding reception!'

'I know,' Emerald said, 'but trust me, Eden. You're going to want to hear this.'

Chapter 41

The bunk barn dining room was, unsurprisingly, completely empty of people. Emerald was comforted by the presence of Jed, who had led her inside, making it clear that, however the Harlands·reacted, he was there for her. She really didn't deserve him, she thought, feeling wretched as Eliot and Eden sat down opposite her, arms folded, faces pensive.

'I wanted you to know the truth,' Emerald began. Her voice cracked, and she swallowed desperately.

'Take your time, Emmy,' Jed said, his hand squeezing her shoulder reassuringly.

Emerald gave a weak smile. 'Thanks, Jed, but I think these two are itching to get back to their wedding, and who can blame them? I need to be quick. Believe it or not,' she added, her eyes pleading as she surveyed the Harlands, 'I want you to enjoy yourselves today, with nothing hanging over you.'

'There's nothing hanging over us,' Eden assured her. 'We're perfectly fine.'

'Good. I'm glad. Even so, I can't let you go on thinking—' Emerald shook her head, feeling sick with dread. Time to confess all. 'It was me who sabotaged the freezer,' she said, her face burning.

'I knew it!' Eden's voice rose, and she turned to Eliot, her eyes wide. 'Didn't I say so!'

Eliot looked sickened. 'But why? Why would you do that, Emerald?'

Emerald couldn't bear the disappointment in his face. 'And I wrote those bad reviews,' she added, the words tumbling out in a torrent of shame.

Eliot shook his head, evidently lost for words. Eden glared at her. 'And you're confessing this now because—?'

'Hang on, Eden,' Jed interjected. 'She hasn't finished yet.'

'There's more? Bloody hell.' Eden leaned back, her arms folded, her eyes shooting laser beams at Emerald.

There was a moment's silence as Emerald tried to gather her courage. 'That day Eliot and I got back from The Green Dragon, and I blurted out—' she cast a wary eye at Jed, who knew nothing of the finer details, Emerald having decided the least she owed Eden was to keep quiet about her affair, '—what I blurted out.'

Eden shifted uncomfortably on her chair and Eliot studied the floor.

'It wasn't Eliot who told me!' There, she'd said it.

The Harlands moved as one, their heads shooting up as they stared at her open-mouthed.

'It wasn't?' they chorused.

'I didn't?' Eliot slumped, clearly overwhelmed with relief.

Eden shook her head, dazed. 'But no one else knew!'

'I knew ages before,' Emerald confessed. 'It was one evening, when Jed had taken the kids to town for their tea, remember? You and Eliot — er, you were in the bedroom. Talking. I'd got home early and headed straight upstairs, thinking you were in the living room. I heard what you were saying.'

Eliot and Eden exchanged incredulous glances, then she saw them both colour up as they evidently remembered what else they'd been doing that evening, apart from talking.

'I didn't want you to think I'd heard,' she continued desperately, 'so I sneaked back downstairs, slammed the front door shut and shouted up to you, pretending I'd just got in. I'm so sorry.'

'Then why let us think *I'd* told you?' Eliot sounded so wounded that Emerald couldn't bear it. Her eyes filled with tears and she shook her head.

'Because I'm a bitch,' she whispered. 'I wanted to hurt Eden, and I knew that was a great way to do it.'

Eliot looked across at Eden, who was white with rage.

'Have you any idea what you've done?' she said through gritted teeth. 'The damage you did, the trouble you caused? All that heartache for what? Some sort of petty revenge? What did I ever do to you?'

Emerald blinked away the tears. 'You had my dad,' she said eventually. 'You had Eliot. Even Jed thought the world of you. Everyone I loved seemed to prefer you to me.'

'Everyone you—' Eliot's voice trailed off and there was an uncomfortable silence.

'I'm so sorry!' Emerald couldn't bear it any longer. She jumped up and ran out of the room, unable to face their scorn and anger. She knew Cain was still angry with her, and he'd probably push her away, or make a sarcastic comment, but right then she didn't care. She needed her father.

****

For a moment, no one moved, and the silence hung over them, heavy and oppressive. Then Jed said, 'I'm sorry, guys. This must have come as such a shock to you.'

Eliot was stunned. 'I can't get me head around all this,' he said eventually. 'It dun't make sense.'

'It makes perfect sense,' Eden said. 'I've known for ages that she had a crush on you, but even I didn't think she'd go that far.'

Jed sighed. 'Neither did I. I was kinda shocked when she told me. I don't know what Eliot's supposed to have told her, by the way, but I can see it's something important.' He held up his hands. 'None of my business, and Emmy wouldn't tell me, which I think shows she's not all bad, right?'

Eliot couldn't take it all in. Emerald had a crush on him? And Eden had realised it. No wonder she was suspicious of them. No wonder she'd questioned his attitude towards her. How had he not spotted it earlier? But then, he wasn't good at picking up signals. Look how long it had taken him to realise that Eden had feelings for him!

'Look, guys, there's something else you should know,' Jed

admitted, and Eden groaned.

'Bloody hell, what else has she done?'

'It's not what she's done. It's who she was seeing that might interest you.'

'What do you mean?' Eden leaned forward, her voice sharp. 'Seeing?'

Jed took a deep breath. 'She met James Fuller some time ago,' he said, 'and they struck up a friendship. Emerald thought it was a genuine friendship, but it turns out he was using her to get at you two.'

Every muscle in Eliot's body seemed to tense. 'Get at us, how?'

'The reviews, the fridge, even the night at The Green Dragon. He wanted you two to suffer financially, and even more, he wanted your relationship to struggle, all so it would make him getting custody of George more likely.'

'You're kidding!' Eden turned to Eliot and held out her hand to him. He grasped it tightly.

'Nowt surprises me about Fuller,' he said, his throat tight. 'And he got his clutches into Emerald?'

'When he found out she was your wedding planner, and staying at the farm, it was the perfect set-up. I know it looks bad, guys, really I do, but she was lost, lonely, and she trusted him.'

'Match made in heaven,' Eden muttered.

'No,' Jed said firmly. 'She wised up to him. She didn't do what he wanted her to do.'

'What *did* he want her to do?' Eliot said harshly. He knew what *he* wanted to do. Paste the walls with James bloody Fuller, that's what. He'd taken advantage of Emerald's vulnerability, just as he'd taken advantage of Jemima's.

He noticed the muscle in Jed's jaw pulsing and recognised the same anger in him. He forgot about his own fury as it occurred to him that, after all, Emerald was Jed's little sister, and she'd been used by that man. Jed must be in turmoil about this.

'Tried to seduce her, for a start,' Jed growled. 'Several times. Luckily, Emmy was having none of it. Thanks mainly,' he said, rather apologetically, 'to her feelings for you, Eliot. Fuller couldn't compete, and boy, I'll bet that pleased him no end!'

Eden stood up suddenly and wrapped her arms around herself. 'That night at the pub,' she said, 'with you and Emerald.'

'Nowt happened,' Eliot repeated urgently. 'I told you—'

'But don't you see?' she said, her brow wrinkling in obvious confusion. 'She had the perfect opportunity. She could have told us something *did* happen. You said you had no memory of that night. She could have lied to break us up, but she denied outright that anything had gone on between you.'

'Aye,' Eliot said, remembering Emerald's immediate confirmation to him that nothing had happened that night. 'She did.' She could have told him anything, he thought, and he'd felt that bad about himself he might well have believed it. She could have strung it out, made him suffer, made Eden suffer. But she'd been honest from the start. Why?

'Fuller wanted her to do that — lie to you. Lie to you both. She couldn't bring herself to do it. You see, guys, I know she's done bad things, and she's been swayed by a very devious man, but at heart she's not a bad person. Just kinda lost. And wanting some love.'

Eliot raised an eyebrow as he met Eden's gaze. He knew how furious she was with Emerald, but couldn't she see Jed was right? The lass had been daft, but she'd been used an' all. Another victim of James Fuller. Eden, of all people, should know how easy it was to be manipulated by him. Hadn't she fallen into the same trap, that summer she first arrived at Wildflower Farm? He sent her a silent plea to understand, to forgive.

'It's you she damaged most of all,' Eden murmured, recognising what he was silently asking. 'She made you believe you'd betrayed my trust. Yes, it hurt me, but for you, that must have been agony.'

She knew him so well.

He smiled at her. 'It was, but it's past and done. I *didn't* betray you, that's the main thing. And, Eden, I don't want to start our married life with this cloud hanging over us. All this bitterness — it's got to end, or Fuller's won, and I won't let him win. He's taking nowt from us. Not George, not our happiness, not our trust.' He shook his head. 'Not even Emerald. Do you see? We've already won, my love, because look what we've got, and look what he's got. An empty house and no one to love. You know what?' he breathed, feeling a sudden, unexpected lightness as the realisation hit him. 'I pity him. I really do.'

He watched, feeling a surge of relief as Eden's mouth slowly curved into a smile.

'Go and find her, Eliot,' she said gently. 'Go and find Emerald, and tell her from both of us, everything's going to be all right.'

****

Cain was trying hard to be the life and soul of the party but found, to his despair, that it was proving harder than he'd expected. He was happy for Eden and Eliot — over the moon, in fact. They were a smashing couple who deserved every happiness, no doubt about it. Even so, as he glanced around the field, watching the wedding guests laughing, eating, and chatting to each other so freely, he felt a sudden crashing gloom that he couldn't dispel.

He wondered where Debs was and how she was doing. No one had heard a word from her except for the letter that had arrived at Wildflower Farm from her solicitor, assuring the Harlands that all claims to George had been dropped and would not be pursued again. He grinned to himself. Yeah, that had gone down a treat. Good old Debs. She'd promised she'd put things right and she had. One in the eye for David bleeding Fuller at any rate. He'd bet a pound to a penny that the geezer was steeling himself for a solicitor's letter of his own, any day, demanding half his fortune. Couldn't happen to a nicer fella.

He sighed, remembering how many times he'd been in Fuller's position. His wallet was still stinging from the various attacks. His solicitor had a fancy new office, thanks to him. He should get a knighthood just for his services to London law firms.

Truth was, he had no intention of being legal fodder ever again. Fuller deserved all that he had coming, but Cain had been down that road too many times. Him and women — it never worked. It was best to keep a safe distance.

Besides, he thought, a flicker of excitement sparking within him at last, he had other things to think about. A new project that had got him through the last couple of weeks, given him something to hope for, something to believe in again. Cain realised that this was what he'd been waiting for. He'd found a new passion, and funnily enough, that was down to Debs, too.

He slumped, wondering if everything in his life was going to come back to her. Where was she? Why hadn't she been in touch? He couldn't, wouldn't offer her anything, but even so, it would be nice to know she was okay. Why had she left The Paradise without so much as a by-your-leave?

He wandered out of the field, strolling unthinkingly to the farmyard, and headed for the paddock at the far end, where the girls' little pony grazed.

Leaning on the gate, he watched the pretty grey tugging at the grass, and thought about his forthcoming project. Debs would be excited about it, too, he thought. She'd approve, he knew she would. If only he could tell her.

When his phone rang, Cain didn't bother to answer it at first, he was so lost in his own thoughts. Whoever was ringing was persistent, though, and eventually he pulled the mobile from his pocket and frowned at the screen, acknowledging to himself that, maybe, it was time to admit defeat and buy some glasses.

'Debs!' He almost dropped his phone in his eagerness to accept her call, and when he heard her voice saying his name in reply, his heart swelled with affection. 'You okay, love? I've been worried sick. Why did you go off like that? Why did you walk away? Why didn't you at least say goodbye? Where are you? What's happening?'

'Good heavens, Cain,' she said, laughing, 'let me get a word in edgeways, will you?'

'Sorry, darls,' he said, feeling stupid. 'I've bin that worried.'

'I'm sorry,' she said. 'I should have told you, but it all got a bit overwhelming. I needed space. It suddenly hit me that I'd finally done it, that I'd ended my marriage. I really couldn't believe it was real. I had to have some time alone, to think things through.'

'I understand that,' he said. 'Kind of like, when you get out of jail and you have to adjust to life on the outside.'

She giggled. 'Well, I wouldn't know about that, but I should imagine something similar, yes.'

'So, where are you?'

'I'm at Ashington Hall,' she told him. 'It's about thirty miles away.'

Ashington Hall! He pulled a face. That would be costing a fortune. 'You bin there all this time?'

'Yes. It's a bit more comfortable than The Paradise, and more private.'

And a hell of a lot more expensive! He rolled his eyes. No doubt about it, Debs was used to the finer things in life. David Fuller would be hung out to dry.

'And how are you, my darling?' Debs' diamond-cut tones sliced through his thoughts and he shivered, reminded suddenly of Freya. He'd really fallen for Honey's mother when he first met her. Proper posh bird she was, complete with stately home and family title. Voice very much like Debs. He'd loved her to bits, and she'd loved him. At first. Didn't take long for it to go sour, though. Fact is, they had nothing in common, and before he knew it, they were speaking only through their respective solicitors, and she was gunning for every penny she could get, even though he'd practically restored her dad's stately pile for him and never had a bleeding word of thanks. Ungrateful gits.

'Me? I'm all right,' he said. 'I'm at the wedding, actually. You could've come if we'd known where you were.'

'The Harlands' wedding? How lovely. Did they get the letter from my solicitor?'

Cain's expression softened at the memory. 'They did. Over the moon they were, Debs. Couldn't believe it. You made their day — their lives!'

'I'm so glad.' She sounded wistful. 'Is George a page boy?'

Cain felt for her, he really did. No denying it. 'Yeah. He looks really cute. Eden's dad's bin taking loads of photos, though, and I'm sure they'll give you some copies.' He hesitated, then added, 'I reckon, now you're not part of the Fuller clan any more, they'll be open to you having contact with George, you know. They know what you did for them, love, and they appreciate it.'

She sighed and murmured, 'Maybe one day.'

'Are you sure you're all right, love?' Cain was fighting a battle. Common sense was telling him to let her go, to back away while he still could, but his wretched heart was pushing him towards her, telling him to grab hold of her and hold on tight. He'd never met anyone like Debs before. Yeah, she was posh like Freya, but she had a kind heart. And they'd had similar childhoods, and she shared his concern for the children of inner cities who'd never so much as seen a real sheep in their lives. There was a basis there for a real relationship. It didn't always have to end in court, did it? Maybe he and Debs could be different, make it work, live happily ever after?

'I'm fine. Just making sense of this strange new world I find myself in. Well,' she added, 'I must go. Enjoy the wedding and do please give my congratulations to the happy couple. Tell Beth I'll be in touch with her in a day or two. I don't want to lose contact with her.'

'I will, promise.' In his head, Cain was shouting at her, *Don't go! Come to Wildflower Farm, join in the fun. Then I'll come back to Ashington Hall with you and we'll make plans together. There's a whole world out there, Debs, and you and me, we could see it together. I've got so much I want to show you.* Out loud he said, 'Take care, Debs.'

'You, too, Cain. Goodbye.'

The phone went dead, and Cain shoved it back in his pocket, staring at the little grey pony who was still grazing unconcernedly before him. *You did the right thing*, he told himself. *There's no future with any woman. You can't trust them. Anyway, you've got more important things to be getting on with. You don't need romance and all that guff. Them days are well behind you.*

So why, he thought desperately, did he feel as if his heart were about to break?

****

Emerald shivered as she spotted Eliot approaching, his face grim. Involuntarily, she looked around in another desperate bid to find her father, but he was nowhere in sight. Where had he gone? Just when she needed him most, too. Typical.

Eliot folded his long legs under the picnic table and sat opposite her, his chin propped on one hand as he surveyed her steadily. 'Well,' he said.

Emerald's face was burning. 'I said I'm sorry,' she pleaded. 'I really don't know what else you want me to say.'

'You don't have to say owt else,' he assured her. 'I wanted to check you were okay, and to pass on a message from Eden.'

Emerald steeled herself. 'Go on.'

'She said to tell you,' he said kindly, 'that everything's going to be reight.'

Emerald's eyes narrowed with suspicion. 'Really?' It didn't sound like something Eden would say.

He smiled. 'Aye. Really.' He gave a big sigh and shook his head slightly. 'I dunno, Emerald, what a palaver this has bin. I had no idea. I'm so sorry.'

'What are you sorry for?' She couldn't see that he, of all people, had any reason to apologise.

'I should have realised. I'm not good at picking up on body language, as anyone who knows me will tell you.'

'Yes, well...' Emerald felt stupid. 'It wasn't your fault. I suppose you were so kind to me at Honey's wedding that it sparked something in my mind. Made me read more into it than there was. I'm an idiot.'

'No, you're not an idiot,' he said firmly. 'Happen you were looking for someone to care for, and I was there.' He rubbed his forehead, looking embarrassed. 'You know, I'm no catch. Reckon Eden's drawn the short straw.' He gave an abrupt laugh. 'Can you honestly see yourself mucking out sheep pens, checking hens for mites, or even washing strangers' bedding every morning?'

Emerald shuddered. 'Not really,' she admitted. 'I suppose I pushed all that side of things out of my mind.'

'Aye, well, life on a sheep farm doesn't suit everyone,' he told her. 'Takes a certain kind of person. I was lucky to find Eden.'

'She was lucky to find you, too,' Emerald told him, meaning it. 'Fact is, you two were made for each other, and I'm sorry I got in the way for a while.'

Eliot looked around, taking in the happy scene around him. 'This has made up for it,' he told her. 'Just the sort of do we wanted — all the people we care about and no fuss or formal stuff to wade through. Thanks Emerald.'

She nodded, swallowing down the lump in her throat. 'Least I could do.'

'You know,' he said carefully, 'I get it, I really do. It's hard, when you've bin hurt, to let people in. To trust them. If you'd bin kinder to Eden from the off, she'd have bin your best friend. Trust me on that. She's the kindest person you could meet, and she's loyal an' all. But you attacked her from the off, gave her no chance to like you. And I understand that because I was the same.'

'You were?' Emerald raised an eyebrow, unable to imagine it.

'When Eden arrived at Wildflower Farm, I was still wounded from losing Jemima, from her affair, from the whole sorry mess. I didn't let anyone in, except the kids. Didn't discuss how I were feeling, didn't trust anyone.' He shook his head, his gaze faraway as he remembered. 'She chipped away at me,' he said softly. 'Took down my defences, brick by brick, and before I knew what was happening, I'd let her in.'

'Sounds to me like your fourth chakra was out of balance,' Emerald informed him. 'The Anahata chakra that is.'

Eliot blinked. 'Eh?'

'Never mind. Anyway, you let her in and got your happy ever after,' Emerald said.

'Not at first. Not by a long chalk. I didn't make it easy for her. I were scared stiff when I realised what she meant to me. It's terrifying, loving someone. You're at their mercy. They have all this power, and they could choose to hurt you. I gave her a rough time, kept pushing her away.'

'But she didn't give up?'

'I think she did, for a little while. She went away — I pushed her away, made her go. And I think, for a few weeks, she thought it was over, as did I.'

'What happened?'

'I thought to meself, who am I hurting here? And why? Eden had done something that scared me, and I didn't trust her any more. But the truth was, I was suffering without her. I realised that, whatever she'd done, there was no need for me to be so cruel to her. I didn't like who I was, or how I'd behaved. So, I swallowed me pride and I went to find her and bring her home.'

Emerald nodded. 'I'm glad you were brave enough.'

'It's not just about bravery,' he said, considering. 'It was admitting that I'd behaved in a way I were ashamed of. Was that how I wanted her to think of me? Could I live with meself knowing what I'd done? Truth is, that man weren't me. I'd acted out of fear instead of love. I was scared and that made me angry and that pushed her away.' He frowned. 'Is this making any sense to you at all?'

'I think so,' she said slowly. 'Kind of like what Jed told me the other day. How I shouldn't let other people's actions change the person I am.'

'Aye, that's it,' Eliot said. 'See, I had all these voices pulling me in one direction then another — Jemima's, Fuller's, Beth's, Mickey's, even your dad's. But I needed to ignore all that and figure out what I wanted — who I wanted to be. Once I'd done that, rest came easy. You've got to learn to trust again, Emerald. I don't just mean other people. I mean, you've got to trust yourself.'

'It's not easy,' she murmured, 'when everyone seems to see you as worthless.'

'You're not worthless,' he said fiercely. 'I know what Fuller did to you. Jed's told us. You didn't give in. You could have done summat daft and gone to bed with him or told me and Eden that I'd gone to bed with you. You didn't. You have good in you. Trust that, build on it. We all make mistakes, lass, me more than most, but we can put them right if we want to.' He reached over and took her hands in his. 'Give your dad the chance to put it right,' he said with alarming perception.

She frowned. 'My dad?'

'He's hurt you. He's been daft, no doubt about it. You don't trust him — fair enough, I can see why. But you've pushed him away instead of telling him what you really want to tell him. I'm right, aren't I?'

Emerald nodded hesitantly. 'I'm scared. He doesn't really see me, Eliot. He sees Honey, and Jed, and even Eden. But it's like I'm invisible. And it hurts so much. And then I—'

'Get narky and have a load off to him which makes him back away from you even more,' Eliot said with a sigh. 'I know. So where does it end? Are you going to keep attacking, so he keeps backing off, and you end up so far apart there's no going back? Or are you going take a chance?'

'But what if he rejects me?' she whispered. 'What if there's no repairing this?'

Eliot squeezed her hands. 'Then at least you've been true to yourself and acted out of love, not fear. You can make peace with yourself, even if not with your dad.' He smiled at her. 'I'm a dad meself, love, and I'm telling you, I reckon he'll be glad to meet you halfway. Maybe he's scared, too. What do you think?'

She smiled back at him, tears glistening in her eyes. 'Thanks, Eliot.'

'Aye aye, what's going on here then?'

Eliot dropped Emerald's hands, as she rolled her eyes at him upon hearing Cain's booming voice.

She glanced up as her father strode over to them and seated himself next to Eliot.

'Interrupting something, am I?' he said, sounding deeply suspicious.

'You're interrupting nowt,' Eliot assured him, clambering off the bench with some difficulty. 'I was delivering a message from Eden, and I've done that now, so if you'll excuse me, I'll be heading back to my wife.'

He gave her a warm smile, which she returned, then headed off to the trestle table, where Eden and George were sampling the scones.

Cain watched him leave for a moment, then turned to Emerald, who was waiting for the interrogation.

'I hope, for all your sakes, that nuffink's going on with you two.'

A biting remark was on the tip of her tongue. Why did he always suspect the worst of her? And, anyway, he could talk! Hadn't he spent the last couple of months shagging Beth's mother-in-law behind her husband's back?

Fighting for control, she was silent for a moment, then she reached over and took his hand. 'Nothing at all, Dad. He's a friend, that's all, and he was giving me some good advice.'

She forced herself to smile as he gave her a nervous look. 'How are you? Are you missing Deborah?'

Cain opened his mouth, then closed it again as he surveyed her warily. 'Well, er, yeah. She's rung me, as it happens. She's all right, thank God.'

'And are you two going to make a go of it?'

Cain slumped, suddenly off-guard. 'Don't think so. Too much has gone on before. Anyway,' he said, straightening again, 'never mind all that. Have you made your peace with Eden?'

She gave him a genuine smile of relief. 'I think I have, yes.'

'Well, that's good. She's a nice woman, you know. I don't know why you're so horrible to her.'

Emerald hesitated, her heart thumping. Dare she take the plunge? Her fingers wrapped around his, and she squeezed tightly, hanging on for dear life. 'I was jealous, simple as that.'

Cain tutted. 'Yeah, I get that. But Eliot was hers long before you came on the scene. Weren't her fault that—'

'Not of Eliot,' she said quickly, before she could change her mind. 'Of you.'

Cain looked baffled. 'Eh? What do you mean, of me?'

Her mouth felt dry. She'd kill for a glass of something alcoholic. 'At Honey's wedding, you were all over her — Eden, I mean. And — and you missed me out of the speech, but you were singing her praises in it. You have no idea how much that hurt.'

Cain's mouth fell open. 'Emerald! I — I'm sorry.' He shifted nervously, his eyes darting around the field as if he couldn't look her in the face. 'I didn't realise about the speech until afterwards, when Jed and Scarlet had a proper go at me. But you never said, so I thought you hadn't noticed, or didn't care. I had no idea it was bothering you. I'm proper ashamed of meself, Emmy. Honest I am.'

Emerald didn't know what to say. As her father's eyes finally settled on hers, she crumbled inside, all her defences shattering.

'Emmy,' he said, leaning towards her, his face deathly serious, 'I never meant to leave you out. I never meant to hurt you. Jesus, I've bin such a crap dad to you, and I don't know what I can say to put that right. I mean, when you told me you'd lived like that with your mother! Shitting in a bucket for gawd's sake! It ain't right! Jed told me about you hardly going to school, and about where your allowance has bin going. I wanted to say sumfink to you ages ago, but I thought it was too late. Thought you hated me and there was nuffink I could do to put it right. I was gutless, that's the truth. I'm proper sorry, chick.'

He let out an exclamation of despair as the tears rolled down her cheeks. 'Aw, don't. Don't. Look, we can start again, can't we? You and me? Can you forgive me?'

She couldn't speak. She could only watch as her father extricated himself from the picnic table and came around to sit beside her. Then his arms were around her, and Emerald sobbed on his chest, knowing that, finally, she was exactly where she belonged.

Chapter 42

Beth cupped Jed's hand in hers and leaned contentedly against him as they sat together, watching Eden and Eliot cut the wedding cake.

Much laughter ensued as Eden's father insisted they pose for what felt like forever while he experimented with his new camera. Beth burst out laughing as she noticed Eliot's smile was becoming more and more strained with every passing second.

'Okay, Dad, that's quite enough,' Eden called and, to prove her point, she pushed the knife down through the stiff white icing, plunging it into the vanilla and raspberry ripple concoction beneath.

Eliot, looking highly relieved, finally let go of his wife and ran a hand through his hair, clearly dazed by the whole experience.

'He's doing well, isn't he?' she said to Jed, nodding over at the stoic groom. 'Although, we've tried to make it as painless as possible for him. He can't complain. He hasn't even had to make a speech.'

'I know,' Jed said. 'I asked him if he intended to and he looked at me like I was crazy. I said, don't you wanna tell Eden how much she means to you, and thank her for marrying you?'

Beth's mouth twitched with amusement. 'And what did he say to that?'

'He said—' Jed puffed himself up, knitted his eyebrows together and put on a gruff Yorkshire accent, '*Eden knows all that, and I don't see why I need to tell other folk about it. Surely, they know*

495

already, else why would we be getting wed?'

Beth collapsed in giggles as he grinned at her. 'That was quite a passable accent,' she said. 'We'll make a Yorkshireman of you yet.'

'You two look like you're having fun.'

Beth pulled herself together and smiled up at Cain and Emerald as they approached. She glanced at Jed and realised he was as surprised as she was to see that Cain had his arm firmly around his daughter's shoulders. Well, well. As Jed's eyes twinkled, Beth knew this would make his day. She gave a little sigh, knowing that she'd never felt so happy. Everything was perfect. She was a lucky woman.

Cain and Emerald slipped into the seats opposite them, and Cain reached over and pinched a sandwich from Jed's plate.

Jed winked at his sister. 'You okay, honey?'

She beamed back at him. 'I am, Jed, thank you.'

Beth sipped some of her pink lemonade. 'We were just laughing at Eliot's attempts to pose for photographs,' she said. 'Not the most patient man in the world, is he?'

'No,' Cain admitted, 'but give him his due. He's a good bloke. Looks after his family well, works hard.' He gave Emerald a little squeeze. 'His kids know how much he loves them and that's the main thing. Reckon we could all learn a lot from him.'

'I guess we'll be heading back to the Cotswolds now?' Jed said with a contented sigh. He dropped his napkin on his now empty plate and leaned back in his chair, his hand still firmly in Beth's. 'Time to face reality.'

'You ain't forgotten what I said, about that job?' Cain said.

'*Jobs,*' Beth reminded him, and he nodded.

'Yeah, *jobs.*'

'I'm real curious, Dad,' Jed admitted. 'What exactly have you got planned?'

Cain rested his elbows on the table and looked from his son to his future daughter-in-law. 'Right, here's the thing. Me and Debs were having a conversation one day about city kids — about how they never get to see a real-life farm animal or visit the countryside. Do you know, some of the poor little bleeders don't even realise bacon comes from cows?'

Beth bit her lip, as Emerald bent her head and Jed let out a hearty laugh.

'Bacon doesn't come from cows, Dad,' he explained. 'It comes from pigs.'

'Eh?' Cain shook his head impatiently. 'Yeah, I meant pigs. Just got mixed up. What?' He looked round at them all indignantly. 'I knew that! Course I did! Anyway, do you want to hear this or not?'

'Sure we do,' Jed promised him. 'Carry on.'

'Hmm. Well.' Cain looked a bit indignant, but he evidently decided to put his embarrassment behind him. 'Thing is, things are tough for some kids out there. Not everyone's got the dosh to take their kids on holiday. Me and Debs, we were remembering how important getting away was for us when we were young. I remember, you know, the first time I ever went to the seaside, and the first time I ever went to the country. It was like another planet! Breaks my heart that some kids will never get to experience that, especially when I look at *them*,' he added, nodding over to where Ophelia and George were laughing and shoving each other over on the grass, while Libby lay propped up against a tree, drinking pink lemonade and watching her siblings with the detached amusement of a girl who was nearly a teenager.

'Them kiddies, they've got a pony and hens and sheep. They know about lambing. They paddle in that there stream, and they run around with the dogs and collect eggs and have all that freedom and fresh air. Imagine them cooped up in a block of flats with no garden. They'd be different people.'

Beth nodded, feeling sad. 'So true,' she murmured. 'It's such a shame.'

Jed circled his glass with his finger, considering. 'So, what are you saying, Dad?'

'I'm saying, it's time I did sumfink about it,' Cain said. 'I'm gunna set up a new charity.'

Jed looked at him cautiously. 'More charity work?'

'I can see you're cynical,' Cain said, 'and I can see why. I know

497

I've been a bit half-hearted about it in the past. I didn't really get involved at all. To be honest, it was all about the bleeding knighthood. I hated Rex Scotman, but when I think about it, I was judging him by my standards. I thought he was a phoney, but I think now that he was genuine about this African charity he runs. He couldn't possibly have sustained all this effort all these years if he wasn't. I didn't get it, see? But when I thought about this cause, I got all excited about it. I can see meself dedicating the rest of me life to it, 'cos it matters. It really does.'

Beth glanced across at Emerald, who was smiling widely. She looked like a different person, she thought suddenly. That uncertain, guarded look had gone from her eyes, and her smile was genuine. She'd always been pretty, but now she looked beautiful.

Emerald evidently sensed that Beth was looking at her and met her gaze openly. The two of them shared a moment of pure happiness — no hostility, no hidden agenda. Beth thought that, one day, she and Emerald could be very good friends indeed.

'So, what's this charity aiming to achieve?' Jed asked. 'Are you talking about city farms?'

Cain sounded very eager as he nodded. 'Absolutely, city farms. I think they're a great idea. Get kids to muck in and help with the animals, grow their own veg, take it home with them. Can you think of anything better?'

'No. It's a great idea,' Jed said, 'but I still don't see where Beth and I fit in?'

'I was thinking,' Cain said, 'about buying a proper farm, out in the countryside. You know, stocking it properly with different animals and growing crops an' all. My thought was, we could get parties of kids to come and stay for the week. Kids who've never had a holiday could get away from the city estates and spend a week in the fresh air, learning all about country life.'

Jed nodded enthusiastically. 'I love that idea,' he said.

'Good,' Cain said. 'Cos I want you and Beth to manage the farm for me.'

'You want—' Jed's voice trailed off as he looked from his father to Beth then back again. 'Are you serious?'

'Look, what I know about farming can be written on the back of a postage stamp,' Cain admitted. 'You, on the other hand, spent years on your stepdad's ranch, and you've bin helping Eliot out all summer and doing a grand job from what he tells me. I mean, I wouldn't expect you to do it all alone. We could hire farmhands who know what they're doing.'

'And what about me?' Beth said. 'I know even less than you about farming.'

'You'd be in charge of the kiddies,' Cain said. 'I reckon they're gunna need someone around who actually cares about their welfare and wants to make sure they get a holiday to remember. Can't think of anyone better than you, Beth.'

Beth could hardly believe it. 'I'd love to!' She turned to Jed, but there was no need to ask him how he felt about it. The smile on his face said it all.

'Where were you thinking of buying this farm?'

Cain rubbed his chin. 'Well,' he said, suddenly nervous, 'I was kind of hoping you'd be okay if it was in the Cotswolds. After all, you're about to give me my third grandkid, and I'd love to have you all close by. That's if you can stand it.'

Beth looked at Jed, and the sparkle in his eyes gave her the permission she sought. She reached over and gave Cain a kiss on the cheek. 'We can't think of anything we'd like more,' she said. 'Our baby needs his grandpa around.' As Cain beamed at her, she turned to Emerald and added, 'and his Auntie Emerald, too.'

Auntie Emerald looked flustered.

Cain ruffled her hair. 'Don't worry, darls, I ain't forgotten about your retreat.' He held up his hands as she started to protest. 'I know you said you'd forgo the retreat if I'd pay for this wedding but really, it didn't end up costing me nuffink, did it? Everyone round here wanted to chip in, so...'

'There was the money you lost on the original wedding,' she reminded him.

'Totally worth it in the end,' he said. 'Whatever this has cost me, it got me me daughter back. Reckon it was worth it.'

Emerald put her arms around his neck and hugged him. 'Thank you, Dad,' she said softly.

'Then it's settled,' he said gruffly.

She shook her head. 'No. It's not. The fact is, I'm not ready to run a retreat — or any business. I don't know enough about anything. I was so determined to make you pay for not being around that I didn't really think it through.'

Jed frowned. 'Are you saying you don't want a retreat, Emmy?'

'No,' she said thoughtfully. 'One day I'd like to run one, but I know that I'm not capable of it yet. There's so much more involved than reading auras, after all. I've never had a proper job. Maybe I need to think smaller to start with.'

Cain snapped his mouth shut and blinked, clearly taken aback. 'Strewth, never thought I'd hear you say that,' he said. 'Well, okay darls, we'll have a think about it all later. For now, are you coming back to Upper Bourbury with us?'

'If that's okay,' she said.

'More than okay, chick,' he told her, dropping a kiss on her forehead. 'Much more than okay.'

****

Eliot kicked the door closed and leaned against it, heaving a sigh of relief.

Eden wheeled the suitcase to the side of the bed and dropped down onto the duvet, letting out a whoop. 'We did it! We got married!'

'We did, my love. We really did.' Eliot's face broke into a huge smile and he hurried round to join her on the bed.

'Did you mind?' she asked him, as his arm curled around her and she snuggled into his chest. 'About them finding out and taking over the wedding, I mean?'

Eliot considered. 'I was a bit narked at first,' he admitted, "cos it felt like, we'd taken back control, and then they'd snatched it away again.'

'I thought you might feel like that,' she said.

'Aye, but it didn't last long. How could it? That wedding — well, it was as perfect as it gets.' He shook his head in wonder. 'It were everything we'd hoped for from start to finish. Better. I'd never

500

have imagined in a million years that folks round here would chip in to pay for everything.'

'It's because they love you,' she told him. 'They know what you've been through, and they're happy to see you've come through the other side at last.'

'Aye.' Eliot thought about it for a moment. 'Happen you're right.'

'Wow!' Eden nudged him delightedly. 'I never thought I'd see the day!'

'When I admitted you were right?' He laughed mischievously. 'Make the most of it, it may never happen again.'

'No, you daft ha'porth,' she said gently. 'I mean, I never thought I'd see the day that you accepted people's sympathy and good wishes, without protesting that you didn't deserve them. That, my darling, is real progress.'

He tilted his head to rest against hers. 'I suppose so. It's like you said, my love, I did love Jemima once, and I lost her, in more ways than one. Whatever happened in the end, I was allowed to feel that sadness, that grief. I don't know why I didn't realise that earlier. I guess I'm a stubborn bugger, when all's said and done.'

'You are,' she assured him, 'but I wouldn't have you any other way.'

'Does it make a difference?' he asked her softly. 'What Emerald told us? That I didn't tell her your secret.'

Eden let out a long sigh. Her hand found his, and their fingers entwined. 'Not to me,' she admitted eventually. 'I'd already forgiven you for it, anyway. I knew that if you *had* told her, it wouldn't have been deliberate. But I'm glad it wasn't you, for your sake. I suspect forgiving yourself would be a much harder task.'

'I don't think I'd ever have done it,' he confessed. 'I hated meself when I thought I'd let you down.'

'You're only human,' she reminded him. 'We all make mistakes. The point is, Eliot, we got through it. With or without Emerald's confession, we fixed it between us, because we love each other.'

She shifted onto her side and looked at him, her expression serious. 'You have to know that this marriage is going to be all

501

about that. Whatever life throws at us, we're in it together. Don't be afraid that it will get too much for me, that I'll walk away. I never will. I'm yours, Eliot Harland, and that's the way it's going to stay. You're stuck with me, for better or worse.'

'And you with me,' he promised, his eyes glittering with love. He rolled over onto his side and his finger traced the line of her cheekbone, his gaze lingering on her lips. 'It were good of Cain to pay for this night away,' he murmured.

'And good of Beth and Jed to stay with the children for the night,' she added. 'Imagine! No getting up at five o'clock tomorrow morning. Breakfast in bed. Luxury.'

'You missed out the most important part,' he said.

'Oh? And what's that?' she teased.

'A whole night in bed,' he said, pulling her to him. 'And I intend to spend every minute of it making sure this marriage is well and truly consummated.'

****

Cain realised he'd made a mistake, placing a rose between his teeth, as soon as he opened his mouth to speak and the dratted thing dropped onto the carpet. He cursed and stooped to pick it up, wincing and rubbing his back.

'Bleeding hell, this isn't how it was supposed to be.'

Warily, he looked up, his eyes narrowing in suspicion. He was pretty sure Deborah was doing her absolute best not to laugh.

To her credit, she managed to keep it together as she said, 'Well, this is a surprise. I was stunned when reception rang to say you were here. Funnily enough, they never mentioned this charming adornment.'

She stepped aside as Cain hobbled into the room, accepting the rose he offered her with great solemnity.

'Thank you. I'm touched by your thoughtfulness.'

He wondered if she was being facetious but decided to give her the benefit of the doubt.

'I wanted to show you — that is, I wanted to prove to you how much you mean to me.'

Deborah smiled and planted a kiss on his lips. 'I already know how much I mean to you.'

'But do you? See, I don't think you do, Debs, cos the truth is, *I* wasn't even sure how much you meant to me.' His eyes bored into hers, willing her to believe him. 'I need to explain.'

'Why don't you sit down, and I'll make us both a coffee?' She indicated the sofa and Cain limped over to it, still rubbing his back. Deborah switched on the kettle and emptied coffee sachets into two mugs.

'Now, Cain, why don't you tell me why you're here,' she said eventually, as she handed him his drink. She settled herself on the edge of her bed and cupped her coffee, waiting.

Cain blew on the steaming liquid but made no attempt to drink it. 'Thing is, Debs, I've been doing a heck of a lot of thinking lately. About you and me.'

'That's good,' she said. 'So have I.'

'Have you? Yeah, I kind of thought you would be,' he said.

Deborah raised an eyebrow. 'Cain, whatever it is you have to say, you can say it, you know. I'd rather you were honest with me. That's all I ask. The one thing I don't want is any more lies. I've had a lifetime of them.'

'I know, Debs. And you and me — well, we're different, aren't we?'

'I hope so,' she agreed.

'I mean, you and David, it was seven kinds of shite, wannit?'

He noticed that her lips twitched in amusement. 'That's one way of putting it.'

'And the thing is, me and my exes — well, it weren't much better, truth to tell. Now, I hold me hands up and I've always told you straight, ain't I, that it was at least as much my fault as theirs. I mean, probably seventy-five per cent of the time if I'm honest. I was daft. I was touring the world with a bunch of lads, with groupies chucking themselves at us in hotel rooms and no one to tell us to get a grip and behave. We were off our heads a lot of the time. And when you're in a rock band — well your head's the size of a planet. People are so keen to tell you how fantastic you are, and you end up believing them. I was a stupid git, no denying it.' He sighed and rubbed the back of his head. 'I ain't selling meself to you, am I?'

'It's nothing I didn't already know,' she assured him.

'Fing is, I've cheated on nearly all my exes,' he admitted. 'But I weren't the only one. Most of them cheated on me an' all, one way or the other. Lowri had loads of flings when the kids were little, and I was away touring. Boredom, she said. Reckoned she needed to prove she was still sexy and desirable to men. Charming. And Freya — gawd, don't get me started on Freya. Sauce for the goose, she said. Couldn't really argue with her about that, but by hell I paid for it. Cost me thousands, that one. Millions.' He sighed. 'They all did, really. Every time I broke up with a bird, I ended up forking out. Wonder I've got any cash left. Made me wary, you know.'

'I know.' She smiled. 'Cain, what are you trying to tell me?'

He took a gulp of coffee and then set his mug down on the bedside table. 'I suppose, what I'm trying to explain is, after all my exes — the ones I married, the ones I lived with, even the ones I just shagged when there was nothing else to do — well, I got wary. I knew a lot of them only wanted me for my money, and fair enough. I mean, I only really wanted them for their looks. It was a massive ego boost, having some glam blonde on my arm at an awards do or whatever. But I grew out of it, Debs. I felt lonely. I wanted more. I stopped having relationships. I kept away from women. I decided to devote meself to me kids and the charity work.' He played nervously with the sovereign ring on his little finger. 'Then you came along.'

'Yes, I suppose it did all get a bit out of hand,' she mused. 'I certainly never expected to find myself in bed with any man — let alone Cain Carmichael.'

'And it was a big surprise for me,' he said immediately. 'I didn't plan it. It seemed natural, and — well, it was bleeding good, weren't it?'

'It was,' she confirmed. 'Bleeding great, in fact.'

He grinned at her, finding it most amusing to hear her swear with her posh accent. 'Well, yeah. But sex is one thing. Love and commitment's another.'

'Cain, I've never—'

He held up his hand. 'Let me finish, please, Debs. This is taking some courage so don't stop me now. I didn't want to get involved with anyone again. I swore I'd never be fleeced by any other woman. It was supposed to be casual. A fling. But you can't switch off your emotions, no matter how you try. You got to me, Debs.' He patted his jacket lapel dramatically, flattening the white rose he was wearing as a buttonhole. 'In here. In me heart. I've bin trying to tell meself it's just an affair and it will pass, but the truth is, I don't think it will. I think — I know — I love you, Debs. You're the woman I've bin looking for all me life. So, what I want to say is, it's okay that you've left David, and you don't have to be scared, 'cos I'll look after you. You can come and live with me, and we'll be happy, and when your divorce comes through, I'll make an honest woman of you, and you'll never have to worry about anything again.'

He stopped, then took a deep breath as he waited for her response. Deborah took a sip of her coffee as she evidently considered his words. She put her mug on the bedside table beside his, then went to sit next to him on the sofa. Her arms went around him, and then they kissed — a gentle tender kiss.

'So, that's a yes then?' he said eventually, smiling at her.

Deborah looked at him fondly. 'That's a no.'

'Eh?' Cain felt crushed. 'But — but why?'

'At least,' she corrected herself, 'it's a no for now.'

'But, but Debs—'

'Cain, darling, I know how much it cost you to say all those things to me, and I so appreciate them. And yes, you're quite right. We are a good team, and I know you've changed. I trust you completely. You've been an absolute darling to me, and I do love you, so very much.'

'Then?'

'I've been with David since I was eighteen,' Deborah explained. 'All my adult life has revolved around the wants and needs of a man — a rather selfish, self-obsessed man at that. Now I've finally had the courage to break free, the last thing I want is to be tied to yet another man — however sweet and caring and terribly sexy he may be.'

'So, what are you gunna do?' Cain was dazed. It had barely registered when she'd called him sexy.

'I'm going to travel the world for a while. Take a year or so to do all the things I want to do. Have some fun. Please myself. Live life. I can't wait.'

'But, sweetheart, how are you gunna do that? It could take ages before your divorce is finalised, and David ain't gunna fund you while you're waiting.'

Deborah's eyes narrowed. 'Pardon?'

Cain took a deep breath. 'Okay, love. I get ya. This is something you need to do. So, here's what I'll do. I'll fund you for the year — or for however long you need to get yourself sorted. Go and do what you have to do. Travel first class. Take a world cruise — whatever you like. I'll pay. Just promise me, when you're done, you'll come back to me.'

Deborah's eyes filled with tears. 'You'd really do that? You'd really pay for me? You'd support me for a whole year or more?'

'Absolutely.' Cain rubbed his eyes wearily. 'You know what, Debs, that wasn't fair of me. I shouldn't have asked for a promise from you. It's like buying you. You don't have to promise me anything. No strings attached. I'll fund you anyway, and if, at the end of that year, you don't feel we've got a future together, well then, that's okay. You owe me nothing. But if you still want me — well, I'll be waiting.'

A tear rolled down Deborah's cheek. 'That's quite possibly the loveliest thing anyone's ever done for me,' she murmured, wrapping her arms around him and nuzzling against him. 'I love you, Cain.'

'Then what more can I ask for?' His heart was heavy with grief, but he held her to him, and inhaled the scent of her, realising that it might be the last time he was this close to her.

Gently, she pulled away from him and stroked his cheek with clear affection. 'You're a wonderful man, but there's absolutely no need for you to fund me. I don't want your money, Cain.'

'But I want you to have it,' he said, shocked. 'I want you to have a perfect year. I want you to travel in luxury, no skimping or worrying.'

'Oh, don't worry, I'll be going first class,' she assured him. 'Darling, you really don't know, do you?'

'Know what?' He was baffled. What was she on about now?

'The money. The entire fortune — it's not David's. It's mine. Even Thwaite Park is mine. Why do you think my family disapproved of him so much? They were convinced he was a gold-digger from the off, and they were probably right.'

Cain looked staggered. 'But — but you said your grandad lived in a two-up, two-down, with a tin bath!'

'So he did,' she admitted. 'That is, my grandad on my father's side. My maternal grandfather, on the other hand, lived at Thwaite Park. He was Alfred Bach of *Bach's Biscuits*? His family were already terribly wealthy, but then he built up his company and added even more to the family fortune before he died and passed it all to my mother. She, God love her, sold the company for a huge profit then left the lot to me — including the house. Grandad Bunting, I'm afraid, was as poor as a church mouse, but he was a proud man. He wouldn't take any handouts from my parents, and said he was quite happy where he was, thank you very much — tin bath or no tin bath. He was so lovely, and my parents were quite happy for me to spend my holidays with him — kept me grounded, in their opinion. They didn't want me to be a spoilt little rich girl, and I'm very glad they were so wise.

'Pity I didn't inherit their wisdom. David's father, you see, was my father's land agent, and David grew up at Thwaite Park. He was there more than I was, and he considered it his home. I suppose, one way or the other, he was determined to get it. I rather think that's why he set his cap at me. My sister, Kathryn, didn't trust him an inch, and she told my parents he was only after the money and properties. She also told me that he'd tried it on with her and she'd sent him packing. Of course, David denied it, and I believed him at the time, but it was probably true in hindsight, and my parents were certainly convinced. He's always hated my sister since. The thought that she or her son would inherit his beloved Thwaite Park was too much for him to bear.'

'I can't believe this.' Cain sank back onto the sofa. *'Bach's Biscuits!* I've wolfed enough of them in me time. You're richer than I am, and there was I, offering to help you out financially. You must think I'm a proper clown.'

'Not at all,' she said firmly. 'I think you're an absolute gentleman, and I can never thank you enough for offering. I can't tell you how much it means to me.'

'But David,' Cain said, 'he'll not let you walk out of that marriage without giving him half.'

She smiled. 'My solicitors are already working on it,' she assured him. 'Luckily for me, my parents insisted on a pre-nuptial agreement, which may or may not be worth something, but if David wants to cause trouble about that I have plenty of evidence of his affairs, not to mention a certain lady in Barnes who would be only too happy to give evidence that he desperately tried to have an affair with her but failed dismally. David could never stand that. The humiliation would kill him.' She shrugged. 'I'll give him a fair settlement. I would never leave him penniless. But he's not getting more than that. He's had quite enough from me already, thank you very much.'

'You're one hell of a woman,' Cain said admiringly.

'Thank you, Cain. And you're one hell of a man.'

'So, when are you starting your adventure?'

'Tomorrow. I have the tickets booked. I'm flying to Miami to board the ship. A nice little Caribbean cruise to start things off, then we'll see.'

'Tomorrow? So soon?' His face fell. 'Gawd. I'll miss you so much, sweetheart.'

'And I'll miss you.' She held out a hand. 'But we still have the rest of the evening, and we have a lovely little hotel room, and this bed is terribly comfortable. Let's make it a long goodbye, shall we?'

Cain nodded as she began to loosen his tie. He knew she couldn't make any promises — to him, or to herself. Even so, as he pressed his lips to hers, he held within him the hope that, one day, she would seek him out again. When she was ready.

Chapter 43

'So, I guess this is it,' Beth said, her eyes filling with tears as she faced Eden and Eliot for what felt like the last time. 'This is goodbye.'

'We'll see you again, Beth,' Eden promised.

'Course you will,' Cain assured them. 'We'll pop back and visit sometimes, and you're always welcome at Upper Bourbury. We're going to be needing expert advice on our new farm, after all.'

Eliot met Beth's anguished gaze with a surprising rush of emotion. 'I'll miss you,' he told her. They had, after all, been through the worst of times together, supported each other and come through the other side. He was happy that they were both having the best of times at last, but he would be sad to see her leave, no question.

'I'll miss you, too,' she whispered, then tutted as he hovered uncertainly. 'Oh, sod it. Give me a hug!'

They held each other tightly and Eliot murmured, 'Be happy, Beth.'

'I will be,' she whispered back. 'As will you. And God knows, Eliot, we both deserve it.'

He nodded, feeling too choked to reply, and released her.

'Where's Jed?' Eden said, sounding rather tearful herself.

'Just gone to get your wedding present,' Emerald said, smiling. 'He'll be here in a minute.'

'Wedding present! There was no need for that,' Eliot assured

509

her. 'I reckon you've all done more than enough for us already.'

'Oh, but this is special,' she told him, a light of mischief in her eyes.

Eliot eyed her doubtfully, his suspicions aroused, but still pleased to see her looking so happy. She'd been even more thrilled when he and Eden had presented her with a goodbye present earlier that day. Bella was now safely stowed in a carrier in Cain's car, and would be living with Emerald in future. Bella had never really bonded with Eliot or his children, or Eden for that matter, having been Jemima's cat, so her obvious affection for Emerald had made it an easy decision, and Emerald had been delighted to accept her — though how pleased Cain was about it was anyone's guess.

'Have you told them about your own venture, Emerald?' Beth said, slipping her arm through that of her future sister-in-law.

'What's this?' Eliot said, interested. 'Thought the retreat was out of the picture for now?'

'It is,' Emerald confirmed. She shot a look of gratitude at her father, who beamed back at her. 'But Dad's been looking at college courses in Lowminster, and there's a business studies course starting in September. I'm going to enrol. Start at the bottom and work my way up.'

'Good idea,' Eden said approvingly. 'You'll be ready to run the retreat one day, Emerald. Good luck with it all.'

'Thanks, Eden,' Emerald said, 'and in the meantime, I'm going to be living with Dad at his house, and we're going to find Jed and Beth the perfect farm, as well as look into the city farm idea. We're all going to be very busy, especially with a new baby in the family to look forward to as well.'

'Oh, aye,' Eliot agreed. 'Nowt takes up more time than a new baby, trust me. Your lives are never going to be the same again.'

'But you wouldn't have it any other way, would you?' Eden said, nudging him.

'Never.' He glanced down at his children who were all standing solemnly beside him, having shed a few tears as Auntie Beth said goodbye to them all. 'There's nothing in this world brings more happiness than your kids. Nothing. They make life worth living.'

The children's heads spun round as they heard an unmistakable sound of hooves in the distance.

'I meant to say,' Eden murmured to him, 'this is such a wonderful area for riding, maybe we ought to offer stabling for pony trekkers, too? Those stables are going to waste and it's another money-making opportunity, after all.'

Eliot nodded. 'You might be right. We'll have a think and—' he broke off as Jed entered the farmyard, leading a rather handsome bay pony, who was having a good look around as he walked — or rather danced — towards them. 'What's this?'

'A pony!' Ophelia and Libby squealed in excitement. 'You've got a pony, Jed?'

Jed brought the attractive animal to a halt and smiled down at them. 'Not me, no.' He looked appealingly at Eliot and Eden. 'Don't take this the wrong way, okay? I know you said they had to wait, and they're your kids an' all, but I figured, what better way to say thank you for everything you've done for us than to give these great kids a gift? Is that okay?'

Everyone looked at Eliot, and he saw the plea in his daughters' eyes and smiled. 'It's right kind of you, Jed. I see no reason to refuse, providing he's a safe pony, of course.'

Jed beamed at him. 'I've been riding for most of my life, and I know a lot about horseflesh,' he said. 'Trust me, I was real thorough. I wouldn't risk your kids on a bad pony. This one's a real gent. Eight years old.' He winked at Libby and Ophelia. 'Won a whole load of rosettes, too, and a cup.'

'I knew it!' Libby squealed. 'That's Beau!'

'No way,' Ophelia gasped. 'Blimey, it is, too!'

'You know him?' Eden asked, surprised.

Ophelia and Libby were practically hopping up and down in excitement. 'He belonged to Peter Robbins. They won all sorts at the shows round here. Everyone knows Beau.'

'That's right,' Jed confirmed. 'Peter's going to university after summer, so they needed a new home for this guy. Peter's dad's bringing the paperwork over this afternoon, but I wanted to see the girls' faces before I left. I reckon he'll fit Libby nicely.'

'We can go riding together!' Ophelia squealed. 'It's going to be great!'

'Thanks ever so much, Uncle Jed,' Libby said, giving him a hug.

'Aye.' Eliot held out his hand and Jed shook it. 'Thank you. For everything.'

The two men exchanged understanding smiles.

'I'll take care of Beth,' Jed promised. 'And when the baby arrives, you'll be the first to know.'

'We'd better be,' Eden said.

'Time to go,' Cain told them, looking suspiciously damp-eyed himself. He hooked an arm over Emerald's shoulders and began to steer her towards the car, but she broke free suddenly and ran over to the Harlands. Throwing her arms around them both she whispered, 'Thank you. Thank you so much.'

Without waiting for a reply, she rushed to the Rolls Royce and clambered into the back seat. Cain winked at Eden and Eliot. 'Reckon my life's changed for good now, you know.'

'Happen it has,' Eliot agreed.

'But I think,' Eden added, 'that it's all going to be for the best.'

****

'Reckon we'll be getting on with the mowing early this year,' Eliot said, nodding at the hay meadows as he and Eden leaned against the fence.

The evening sun daubed rays of faded gold upon the landscape, and a light breeze gently stroked the leaves on the trees and hedgerows. In the lower fields, they heard the distant bleating of ewes and lambs, safe and secure on Wildflower Farm land like so many had been before them.

Eden heaved a sigh. 'It will be all hands on deck again before we know it,' she said. 'It never stops, does it?'

'Never.' Eliot shook his head then turned to her with a smile. 'But that's all right, isn't it? It's what we want, after all.'

'It is,' she told him, glad that he'd finally accepted that this was the life she had chosen.

He took her hand in his and she rested her head on his shoulder, worn out after the events of the last couple of days.

512

'It's been a funny old few months, hasn't it?' she murmured.

Eliot laughed. 'Aye, you could say that. I feel like we've run a marathon, what with all the building work and them barns opening, and the house full of Carmichaels, and — and Georgie.' He shook his head. 'Can't believe it's over, Eden. We beat him. We beat Fuller.'

'Thanks to Deborah. Who'd have thought she'd have turned out to be so nice?'

'Cain obviously saw that side of her before we did,' he said, his voice mischievous.

'I know! What a dark horse.'

'I'd love to have been a fly on the wall when James bloody Fuller and his dad got what was coming to them,' Eliot admitted. 'Thank God for Jed.'

'Thank God for Emerald,' Eden pointed out. 'She had the guts to stand her ground and tell the truth after all. She's a better person than I ever imagined. You were right, Eliot. I should have given her the benefit of the doubt like you did.'

'She made it a lot easier for me than she did for you,' he told her. 'Any road, it's over and done with now. Life can go back to normal. Although—'

'Although what?'

He looked troubled for a moment. 'Although, we're going to have to tell the truth to the kids one day, aren't we? George is going to have to know that I'm not his real father. The girls are going to find out about their mother.'

'That's all for the future,' she replied. 'No need to worry about it now, and when the time comes, we'll tell them together. You're not alone in this now, Eliot. You're never going to be alone in anything.'

He squeezed her hand. 'You're right. Time enough for worrying when it happens. Right now, life's grand, and I'm grateful for it.'

'I think the kids will sleep well tonight,' she said, stifling a yawn. 'They've had a busy few days after all.'

'Fancy Jed getting them that pony,' Eliot said.

'You didn't really mind?'

'Nah. Not at all. Let's face it, they deserve it, and it was kind of him to do it. Mind, as wedding presents go, it's not exactly what I were expecting. Better than that bloody awful painting from Honey and Teddy, though.'

'You don't like impressionist art?' she teased. 'It's probably worth a fortune.'

'I can think of better ways to spend the money,' he said. 'Wonder how Honey'll take to having Emerald living under her dad's roof?'

Eden whistled. 'Going to be fireworks there, I think. But, you know, I really believe she'll have to learn to live with it. Cain's not going to give up on Emerald now, after everything they've been through.'

'You watch,' he said darkly, 'it'll be bloody Scarlet's turn next. She'll turn up on Cain's doorstep in some crisis or other and, pound to a penny, they'll all end up at Wildflower Farm.'

Eden laughed, then slowly turned to face him. 'Thank you for my wedding present,' she told him, her fingers curling around the necklace that he'd presented to her on the morning of the big day and which she'd proudly worn ever since. 'It's absolutely beautiful. You're a real romantic these days, Mr Harland.'

'You've made me soppy, Mrs Harland,' he said. 'I'll never be able to face Mickey and Adey again. They're gunna rag me nonstop for buying you that.'

'I never got to give you my present,' she said. 'I meant to do it at the hotel, but we got a bit, er, busy doing other things.'

'We did,' he remembered, a gleam in his eye. 'But you didn't have to give me a present. I've got everything I ever wanted.'

'Not quite everything.' Eden rummaged in the pocket of her jeans and brought out an object that she handed to him.

He stared down at it, hardly believing what he was seeing, then he gazed at her, his eyes brimming with tears. 'When — when did you find out?'

'A few weeks ago,' she admitted. 'I was going to tell you then, but things got so messed up and I wanted to wait until the right moment. I think this is it. Funnily enough,' she added, 'I think our baby's due around the same time as Beth's.'

He dropped the pregnancy test on the ground and flung his

arms around her, twirling her round in the air until she felt quite dizzy.

'I can't believe it! Oh, my love, this is grand. The best news ever.' He shook his head, looking quite dazed. 'But how? I mean, we weren't trying. After the wedding we said.'

'My fault,' she admitted. 'With everything that's been going on, I got careless. I shall definitely have to be more careful in the future.'

He laughed and pulled her gently to his side, and they gazed out together over Wildflower Farm land which stretched, green and golden, as far as they could see. For a while, neither spoke, as they contemplated a rosy future — one filled with haymaking, sheep shearing, lambing and dipping, harsh winters, glorious summers, Christmas mornings, children's laughter, and the sound of a new baby's cry.

Eliot broke the silence at last.

'Well, my love,' he said, his voice full of wonder, 'now the adventure really begins.'

The End

To find out more about Sharon Booth and her books
visit her website

www.sharonboothwriter.com

where you can also sign up for her newsletter and get a free and
exclusive novella!

Acknowledgements

Summer Wedding at Wildflower Farm was a real labour of love for me, in the sense that I adored being back in my fictional world of Skimmerdale with my much-loved characters, Eliot, Eden, Cain and the others. That's not to say, however, that it was an easy book to write. Far from it. With so many points of view and intertwining storylines it had me tearing my hair out with frustration on many occasions!

At such times, I relied on several people to keep me focused and make sure I didn't lose faith in this project, and it's those people I'd like to say my first big thank you to: Steve, Jemma, Julie and Alex – thanks for the pep talks and the reassurance, and for everything you said and did to make me keep going with this huge beast of a book!

I owe my beta-readers a debt of gratitude, as not only did they spot typos, but they also came up with some amazing suggestions and insights which really helped me to tighten this story up. Jessica, Jo, Liz and Pat – thank you so much.

Huge thanks to Alys West for her "book whispering" services, to the talented Berni Stevens, who designed the wonderful cover which I absolutely adore, and to Trisha Sherwood for the copy edits and proofreading.

Thank you to Steve, who drove me to the Yorkshire Dales on several occasions, so I could immerse myself in the "Skimmerdale vibe". And special thanks for all the cups of Yorkshire Tea that you made for me while I got on with the writing. There's no way I could have finished this book without that special fuel, and I didn't even have to ask!

Finally, thank you to every single one of you for reading this book. I really can't explain how much it means to me, nor adequately express how much you are all appreciated. Thank you!
Sharon xx

Also in the Skimmerdale series

Summer Secrets at Wildflower Farm (Skimmerdale 1)

Welcome to the beautiful Yorkshire Dales.

Eden Robinson was living a quiet, if dull, sort of life, until the fateful day her world collided with that of Honey Carmichael, spoilt daughter of seventies' rock god Cain Carmichael. Working for the Carmichaels in their Cotswolds home is surprisingly uneventful, until the day that Eden makes a big mistake and Honey takes full advantage of the fact.

Packed off to the Yorkshire Dales to care for the three motherless children of sheep farmer, Eliot Harland, Eden is plunged into a world she knows nothing about. Her summer in Skimmerdale is far from easy, as she confronts her fear of horses, learns the pecking order in the cake tent at the local show, and discovers that two-year-olds can be surprisingly devious – all while dealing with a double identity, a jealous family friend, and a charming blackmailer.

But as summer draws to a close Eden faces her toughest challenge yet. She's about to say goodbye to a family she now feels part of, and worse, the man she loves has no idea who she really is, and it seems she's left it far too late to tell him. Can she escape the Honey trap in time, or will this sheep farmer discover he's had the wool pulled over his eyes?

www.ingramcontent.com/pod-product-compliance
Lightning Source LLC
Chambersburg PA
CBHW020227110726
47898CB00004B/1174